CROWN OF BLOOD AND RUIN

By: LJ Andrews

Copyright © 2022 by LJ Andrews

All rights reserved.

No portion of this book may be reproduced in any form without written permission from the publisher or author, except as permitted by U.S. copyright law.

Editing by Jennifer Murgia and Sara Sorensen

Developmental Edits by Jasmine Mckie @faye_reads

Cover and Formatting Design by Clara Stone at Authortree.co & Merry Book Round Designs

Artwork by @artworkbyzoeholland, Eric Bunnell, and Linnea Childs

For rights inquiries please contact Katie Shea Boutillier at ksboutillier@maassagency.com

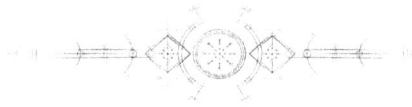

Dedicated, not to the villains who'd burn the world for her, but to the queens who'd do the same for him… only better.

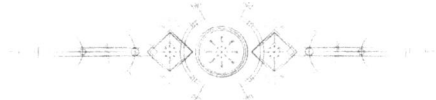

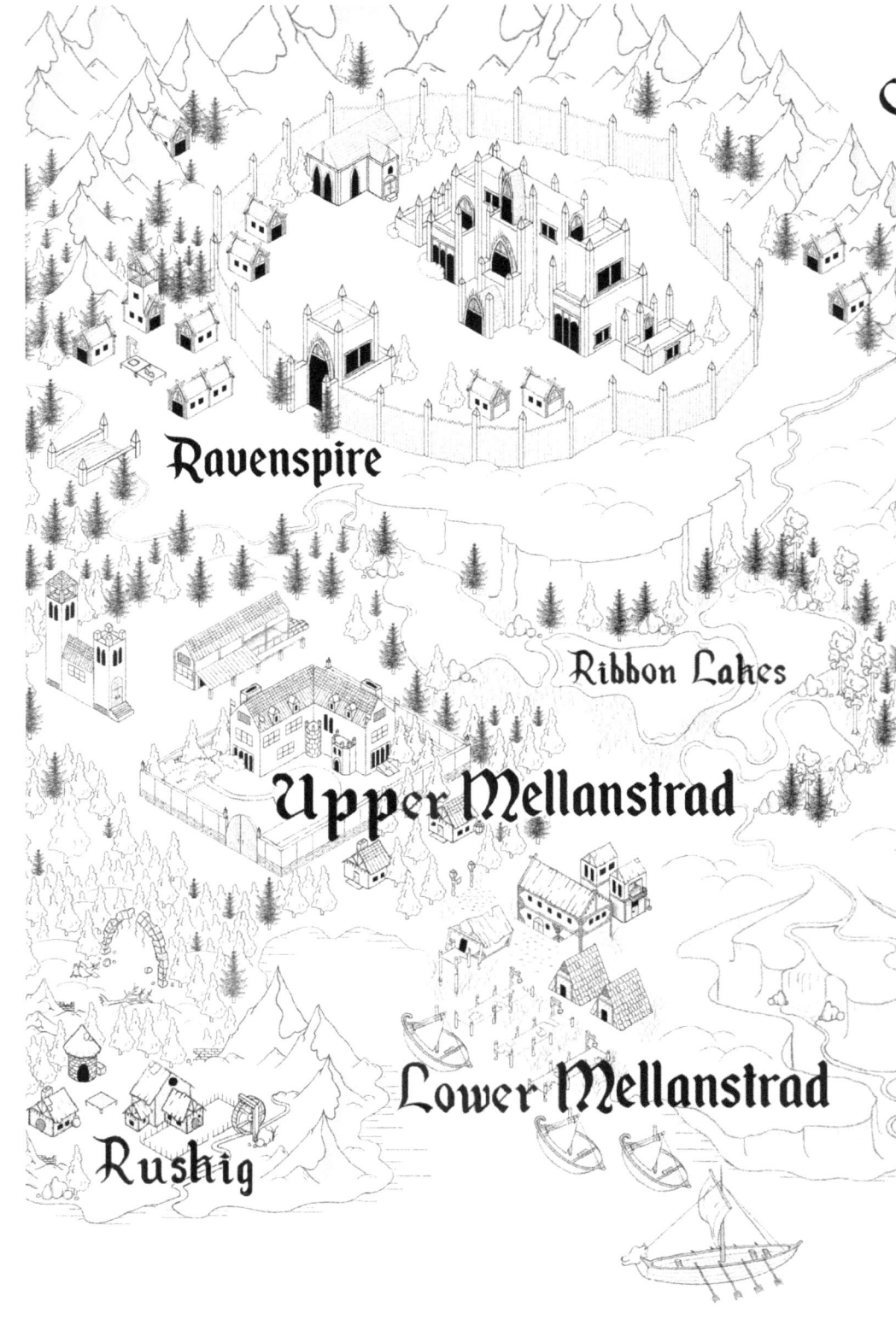

AUTHOR NOTE

Hello wicked darlings, for audiobook listeners who also read along, take note there have been slight changes to some passages since the recording. It in no way changes the meaning, but it might not align perfectly with the audiobook. Should be a steamy, wild ride either way.

CHAPTER ONE
NIGHT PRINCE

The wood laths reeked of vomit.

The burn of it coated the back of my throat with each breath. No one at the table seemed to mind. The man across from me kept dropping bits of his smoked herring, then eating them as if they weren't coated in someone else's rank insides.

With a smack of his lips, he slouched back in his chair, eyes on me. "It's *Herr* Legion Grey, yes?"

One half of my mouth curled. "Has been all day."

He snorted, then wiped what came out of his nose away with the back of his hand. "Tell me why I should sell to you? Your king offered me a fine price. And he's the bleeding king."

The trader glanced out the foggy window where three dozen serfs were chained like hogs going to slaughter. He tapped his left hand, then reached for his drinking horn. Left-handed. The short blade on his waist would meet me on my weaker side. Easily adjusted.

I took a drink of hard ale.

His blade wasn't made poorly, but neither was it expertly

crafted. Slightly unbalanced in the steel. Bulky. Heavy. Strikes would be swift and hard, but with less control.

"Well?" he asked. "Why d'you want them?"

I lifted my gaze. "I'm ambitious, *Herr*, and these are uncertain times in Timoran. You are not from these shores, but I have deep coffers. I'm offering for no other reason than I could do with a few bulky serfs guarding my gates."

He lifted a brow. The trader kept stretching his right leg. Sore perhaps? Old injury? I'd test it if he earned the chance to stand.

"From the looks of it, *Herr* Grey, you've already got plenty of good meat to watch your back." His eyes drifted over the formidable wall of men at my back. Tor, Ari, and Brant stood with arms folded, blades on their belts, scowls in place.

I fought the urge to roll my eyes.

Fools. I was here as Legion Grey, arrogant, feckless trader of New Timoran. They were meant to be my partners, my companions. Once, we were known to play our hands at game tables, were known as reckless, young, wealthy men with an eye for a good deal.

Not warriors to a king.

Ari was the only one who had reason to look as if he were in pain. Doubtless, he was. Skilled in illusion fury, Ari was the sole reason my fae features were hidden, but fury had a way of draining the body when exerted too much.

And this bastard of a trader wouldn't stop talking.

"They are sour we have not invited them to drink," I said with meaning and a sharp glare at Tor. He rarely smiled before, but since we last left Castle Ravenspire, only one person could bring out any emotion from my old friend.

Elise wasn't here, so the least he could do was play his part as carefree, ambitious trade partner to Legion Grey.

Like Mattis.

The carpenter knew how to slip into a role without giving away how skilled he was with the sword on his waist. Mattis laughed and smacked a tabletop in the corner, tossing back a horn of red spice with another man who remained hidden beneath a hood.

Frey wouldn't show his face. Not yet. Here, he'd be recognized too easily.

My smelly drinking companion tipped his horn back, eyes on me. "Apologies, Herr. But I'm not going to be stepping back from a deal with a king to feed your ambition. Take your business to Ravenspire's open market. And a bit of advice—don't go making it a habit of undercutting your own royal court."

"I think you're making a mistake."

This conversation was about to change. As the trader blustered and paraded his importance like an arrogant cock, hidden under the table, the ax grew heavy on my lap.

A smug grin cut across his wind burned face. "I did not get to the point of trading with kings by making mistakes, boy."

"Boy?" I said with a laugh. "Bold of you, *Herr*."

"Don't think the reputation of the wild Legion Grey, trader who beds merchant daughters while robbing their father's blind has escaped me. To me, you're only a wandering boy with a thick purse."

I lifted a brow. "Do they say all that about me?"

He grinned, showing off the gold tooth in front. "They do. Good thing I don't have no daughter, *Herr* Grey. I'm not trading with you. A friendly relationship with a king is more intriguing than a deal with a boy like you."

My lips curled as I lifted my drinking horn. "I couldn't agree more. Of course, I'd like to offer you one final chance to give over the trade on your own volition."

"Now I'm to simply give them up?" He chuckled. "You're

mighty strange. How you've made it this long in a trade world, I'll never know."

"I take it you're refusing?"

The trader glanced at me like I'd lost my wits. "Yes, *Herr* Grey. I refuse to give you my serf trade."

"Understood." My grip tightened around the handle of my battle ax. A comfort lived there, in the leather, the wood, the steel. Something familiar and deadly. "Unfortunately, this night is not going to go well for you. The king has no interest in friendly trade with the likes of you. He was simply offering a fair shot."

His grin faded. "What are you—"

Before the trader finished, the curved edge of my ax sliced through the fingers he'd rested on the tabletop. A guttural, sick scream broke the peace of the alehouse. My men from Ruskig rose against his men before they even realized what was happening.

Mattis's sword cut through the spine of a trader. Frey pulled back his hood and threw a dagger at the aleman, the point piercing the man's throat. I didn't question, doubtless the Ettan guard had his reasons to kill him.

Patrons in the alehouse screamed. Some reached for weapons. They didn't live long. A few gaped at Frey, even smiled with a touch of victory. As I rose from my seat, Tor, Mattis, and Brant handled the rest of the trade crew, shoving them onto their knees, knives at their throats.

Ari let out a breath of relief when he released the illusion over my features.

I adjusted the cuffs of my jacket and went to the trader's side. His brow was limned in sweat, his skin pallid. Blood blossomed over the table, mingling with spilled ale.

He winced at the darkness in my eyes, the points of my ears. I stroked a finger down the edge of the battle ax, and lowered into a crouch, hand on the back of his neck.

"I should apologize. You see, I haven't been entirely truthful about our meet." I dropped the weight of my hand on the handle of the ax cutting into his knuckles. The trader groaned and closed his eyes. "First, though, I feel I should clear up some of the more atrocious rumors about me. I don't bed daughters. I'm wholly satisfied with one daughter of Timoran. You would understand if you saw her, *Herr*, I assure you. Truly beautiful and frightening all at once—"

"Perhaps we could move this along. These sods think they can break free, and it's rather irritating," Ari said, grinning. The traders in my men's grip struggled and tried to reach for weapons sheathed on belts.

"Forgive me," I said with a blithe look at my trader. "When I start to speak about Elise, I tend to go on and on."

"Who are you?" he choked out.

"You came to trade with the king, did you not? As I said, he—*I* —do not wish to trade with you. But I will be taking your haul."

Perhaps the loss of blood and fingers drew out a bit of madness in the trader. He laughed, and spittle tangled in his wiry beard. "You're mad. Your k-king will slaughter you f-for this."

I turned a bemused look to Tor. "He keeps saying my king. Oh, I think I understand." My eyes narrowed. "You must be talking about the false king. So like Calder to keep up with his game of pretend."

"F-false king?"

I stood and leaned my lips close to his ear. "You came to my land with the intent to trade magic, to trade my people. To me, you have practically declared war." I nodded at Tor. "Kill them."

It happened swiftly. Knives and daggers cut into the trade crew; the lead trader jolted at each thud against the pungent floorboards. With less care than I could've given, I ripped the ax

5

off his slaughtered hand. The trader cried out, curling over the table. He trembled.

"I let you live today," I said. "You're welcome. When the Ravenspire guards come—and they will—to bring you before the false king, I do hope you give him my best wishes. Tell him King Valen Ferus is coming. And again, I do so appreciate taking his trade. His caravans have been incredibly useful to the true people of the land."

The trader stared at me with heady fear. There was a bit of satisfaction that came from such a look. One I reveled in each time we did this. For months we'd attacked Calder's trade, cutting him at the knees, weakening him.

With a quick gesture, I signaled at my men to leave. Brant dropped a linen cloth near the trader, clapped him on the shoulder, and left him with the mangy bandage. The ravens would come for the man, they'd take him to Calder. Either the boy king would kill him, or . . . no, odds were Calder's temper would demand the trader be killed.

Outside, Frey and Mattis worked on freeing the serfs. I stripped the damn waistcoat from my shoulders.

Never would I understand why Timorans found comfort in these clothes.

Mattis tossed me my second battle ax, grinning. "Well done, My King."

Laughter rang into the night. Some folk were clearly not from Timoran and their blood from bruised and battered bodies held a pungent scent of cloying rot. Alvers. Magic folk from a distant kingdom. I grinned, imagining Junius, our Alver friend, would be pleased to know we'd found her people and snatched them back from Ravenspire.

"Frey? Frey!" A deep, throaty voice called over the others.

Frey dropped his sword, a broken smile carved over his lips.

He sprinted through the messy crowd and collided with another man dressed in rags. More eyes fell to my guard; they whispered his name. Then again, this was Frey's township. His home. A place where Ravenspire had destroyed and robbed its people. Killed its women, its children, enslaved its men.

"King Valen," he'd said weeks ago. "I have a request of a personal nature."

"Personal as in?"

"Call it revenge."

The call to vengeance was all too familiar to me. I'd nodded. "What is it?"

"I want to liberate my folk, my brother. Then, I want to slaughter those who have kept him prisoner for two turns."

He'd given a few details. Explained how the Ettans in the southern townships fought for Old Etta, for my family. They were killed and traded for their rebellion. They would be yet another caravan we could take from Calder. But more, Frey had tracked this particular trader with this particular haul.

When his brother, who shared nearly identical features, pulled back from his embrace, clasping Frey's face between his palms, an ache pierced my chest. Strange how the joy of brothers reunited soured my stomach.

Frey had saved his brother; I abandoned mine.

"You've been freed by King Valen Ferus," Tor shouted over the laughter. Voices hushed at once; only a few mutters with my name carried on the wind. "We stand with magic folk. All magic. We stand to take back this land."

No mistake, these serfs had been abused and beaten for gods knew how long. Still, as Tor spoke, more smiles brightened the night, more hope gleamed in dark eyes.

"Stand with us!" Frey called. "Many of you are my people, you are Axel's people." He gripped his brother's thin shoulder.

7

Axel turned his gaze to me and held my stare for half a breath before he lowered to one knee, fist over his heart. "I stand with the true king."

Others kneeled, some hesitated.

Brant stepped forward and sliced his palm. His blood held the stink of sweet, like many of the serfs in the trade. "We fight for all magic."

More smiles curled over lips. Those with smelly blood chuckled and slammed fists over their chests.

Brant hardly understood his own magic, having only discovered he was one of the Alver folk half a turn before. His magic blood proved useful, though. Brant's gift of premonitions and warnings of danger had saved our necks more than once.

Since I'd revealed my true name, more Ettan folk and Night Folk had traveled to Ruskig for refuge and to join their people. Calder was being forced to trade outside our borders, and he'd brought strange fury—or mesmer as Junie called their magic—and with Brant's help, we'd taken that from the false king, too.

Mattis came to my side, arms folded over his chest. "Another success, I'd say. Calder grows weaker. He fears you."

"Us," I said. "He fears us."

True enough. Castle Ravenspire had increased its defenses tenfold. They feared the growing threat of fury, but it also meant Calder was desperate. One thing I knew about powerful men hells-bent on keeping their control—they were unpredictable. Dangerous. We needed to rise carefully.

Some still resisted and demanded all Timorans be slaughtered. I thought of Elise. Hated to think it, but there were new faces in Ruskig who eyed her like she ought to join those at Ravenspire when they burned.

It wouldn't happen.

She would help heal the scars between people in this land.

Elise Lysander was the choice of my heart, and these people would need to grow accustomed to their temporary king loving a Timoran royal.

"Calder will bite back," Tor muttered as Frey and Brant arranged the serfs into travel units.

"Let him," I said. "He is slipping. We're close, and he knows it. He will start to bring him out, and when he does, Sol is ours."

Tor closed his eyes. "Valen, I will not be able to kill him."

Sol was Calder's one weapon against me. I'd believed the Sun Prince to be dead, but all this time Castle Ravenspire had my brother—a dark fae—and used his fury to create wicked poisons; they used Sol as their own kind of beast.

In my mind, if Sol were a threat to our people, he'd want me to kill him. But much like Tor, I didn't know if I'd be able to follow through if the time came.

"I have no plans to kill my brother. But when they bring him back into the light, I have grand plans to take him back. To bring him home to you." I rested a hand on Tor's shoulder, then turned away to lead the new caravan back to Ruskig.

Yes, Calder would bite back. But we'd be ready.

Crippled by our attacks, the boy king could hardly feed his own people, and I doubted he cared. He was too focused on taking my head to have time for actual strategy.

Soon enough his head would be mine.

CHAPTER TWO
ROGUE PRINCESS

"Again! This time actually block. That is what we're doing, is it not? I'm not going to be the one scraping your innards off a battlefield because you fools forget how to lift a damn blade," Halvar barked at us.

At the head of the grassy field, he gripped two battered short blades, one in each hand. The emblem of his tunic was an ax crossed with a dagger wrapped in thorns. The Ferus seal. He looked every bit the first knight that he was.

Still, playful as the man could be, Halvar was rather frightening with his weapons, and terribly demanding. For good reason, I supposed. And he had a point—no one wanted the innards of our neighbors on the battlefield.

I lifted my seax. The hilt was thick, and the leather binding had come loose, so a bit of sharp metal dug into my palm.

A kiss pressed to my cheek before I struck. Startled, I reeled back only to meet Halvar's sly grin.

"Of course, you are no fool," he said. "I exclude you from all my vulgarities." He looked to Kari, my sparring partner. "And you as well, my beautiful warrior."

Kari narrowed her eyes. "*Halvar.*"

He looked to me. "She gets so timid when I whisper my sweet sentiments in public. I don't understand it." He turned back to Kari. "I would put my lips upon you in the most indecent places, my love, no matter who saw. You need only let me!"

A few chuckles rippled through the line of sparring partners. Kari's face turned pink, and her eyes flashed in a warning. No doubt Halvar would pay later, and no doubt he'd enjoy every moment of it.

I grinned and adjusted my grip on the blade. "Step aside and let us spar."

"So long as we have an understanding. You, my two lovelies, do not take me at my cruel words."

"Hardly seems fair," I said. "I am under your tutelage the same as everyone else."

"Ah." His voice softened, so only I heard. "But they are not my future queen."

A rush of heat twisted my stomach. "I've yet to be asked by a king to be more than a consort."

"Pretend it is not fated to happen all you wish, dear Elise."

I jabbed Halvar's ribs with my elbow. Others were staring. "Even still, treat me as you treat anyone. I need to learn the blade like a knight."

"As you say. Blade up. Wider stance." Halvar swatted my middle with the back of his hand, forcing a breathy grunt from my throat. "Core tight."

After a final wink at Kari, Halvar returned to the front of the lines and raised one of his swords. When he cut the blade down, we attacked.

Twenty steps later I coughed when Kari tossed me onto my back once again.

Dust fluttered over my cheeks, sticking to the sweat on my skin. She leaned over her knees, catching her breath, then reached her hand out to help me up.

"All right, Elise?" Kari wiped her light hair out of her eyes. Timoran like me, but also a former raven. I found some kinship with her from our past lives, but also because Kari had captivated the heart of a fae the same as me. Halvar never stuttered, never even blinked over her life in Timoran. I wished others would do the same.

"I'm fine." I staggered to my feet, scanning the others still fighting with a touch of envy. My friend, Siv, struck with such fluid strength as she sparred with two opponents, and already had one woman in a headlock.

"You've improved," Kari said, wiping her brow with the back of her hand. Shy as she was about Halvar's public declarations, she kept him in her sights as he stalked the lines, correcting stances and grips.

"I've improved, yet still end up on the ground. At this rate, I might as well serve as the bait while you all sack Ravenspire."

Kari snickered and shook her head. "Like Hal said, as consort, you will likely have no need to lift a blade."

She said it to brighten my spirits, but it didn't.

I needed to know how to fight. I planned to stand at Valen's side until he won back the throne that was rightfully his. No part of me intended to be an ornament who watched from a padded seat above the battlefield.

"All right," Halvar shouted when the last pair called a draw. "Be gone with you all. Rest, eat, drink, bed each other, I care little. All but you, my lovely raven."

He pointed at Kari, dark eyes smoldering in desire. She

pretended to ignore him, but the moment his lips whispered against her ear, her irises flashed with similar need.

Siv sheathed her daggers, then hurried to my side, linking her arm with mine. "They return tonight."

I let out a sigh of relief. "Yes. I hope before nightfall. Calder places too many ravens near the gates of Ruskig after dark."

Siv nodded, a twitch in the corner of her mouth. "Do you ever stop to think of how much has changed? I picture Mattis at the Night Prince's side, fighting, at last, for Etta. It still astounds me. And you—once a *Kvinna*, now consort to the King of Etta."

"I cannot think on it too long or my head hurts," I said with a laugh. I cared little whether Valen called me consort or queen, so long as he called me his.

When he had posed as Legion Grey, I did not expect to love him. Certainly not as a king of fury.

My body trembled the more I thought of him. Too long he'd been away, gathering more of his people from slavers and traders. His absence was felt by everyone, but I liked to think I felt it the most.

Siv left me once we reached the shanty she shared with Mattis.

Moments alone gave me time to reflect. Like Siv said, a great many things had happened in less than a turn. But more was to come before we could claim victory. The heaviest weight on my heart was Sol Ferus.

Valen rarely spoke of his brother. But I could see the pain behind his eyes. Sol was used for the benefit of Ravenspire, and more than anything I wanted to rescue him. For Valen, for Sol, for Tor.

To know he lived but was tortured and manipulated daily was almost too much for his consort to bear.

Tor spoke little to others, but to me he shared some burdens.

Perhaps it was because I also knew the risks of being a Ferus consort.

Perhaps it was because we were friends.

Sol needed to go free. I felt it in my bones he would be needed to restore Etta as much as Valen. With the Sun Prince's dark fury against us, he was also the greatest obstacle.

Some called for his death, calling it mercy. A way to free him from his torture. But I'd already promised myself to do anything within my power to bring Sol here alive. Valen had lost so many.

He'd already mourned his brother before; he would not do it again.

I kicked at some brambles on the path to the royal longhouse. Ruskig was fading into winter, but still the buds of moonvane, nettles, and rowan were vibrant against the dark mossy trees.

Shanties kept popping up, and now the Night Folk refuge looked like a small town. In the center was a worship chantry, a square for announcements, and a small marketplace. We didn't use shim coin in Ruskig, but trade was growing with our numbers.

A narrow canyon path led to a private beach where we caught salmon and herring. Calder blocked most trade routes, hoping to starve us out, no doubt. The thing about earth fury, though, was there was often enough magic to grow plumper berries, heartier vegetables, and it helped when Stieg and Casper used their air and water fury to pull the tides over our fishing nets.

For now, we had enough to fill our bellies.

Over the treetops, the sun faded. Lanterns speckled windows of shanties, and by the time I reached the longhouse, I didn't notice the huddle of men guarding the door.

I groaned. Klok was an elder of Ruskig, and kind enough. But the others were new or from Crispin's refugees. I'd been among the party to bring the refugees from the damp sea caves into Ruskig.

Crispin, their leader, didn't give me much thought. He'd wrinkle his nose at the sight of me sometimes, but never said a word. I wish I could say the same for some of his men.

The more they prattled on about Timorans, the more newcomers looked at me with the same reservation, the same disdain.

At the door of the longhouse, Klok bid the men farewell. He noticed me and tipped his head in a greeting. I returned his smile, wishing he'd stay until I was inside. With Valen gone, some of the folk were a bit bolder in their words toward me.

Of course, I'd never mentioned it to the king. Valen had enough to fret over than a few harsh words aimed at me.

Holding my breath, I did my best to duck my head and slip through the doorway without drawing any notice. But the Norns of fate were fickle, and certainly held no love for me.

A thick, muscled arm shot out in front of me, blocking my way. "Where are you going, *de hän*?"

"Stave." I lifted my chin. "Let me pass."

"Into my king's chambers? A Timoran? You must think me mad." Stave was one of Crispin's men. He stood two heads taller than me. His beard was rough and braided. A tapered point to his ears gave away his proclivity to magic. Basic earth fury, but he knew how to handle a blade. Brutally so.

I didn't doubt his loyalty to Valen. But I didn't doubt his hatred of all things Timoran either.

"I grow weary of this," I said, voice harsh. "You would not dare speak this way to his consort if the king were here. Now move aside."

"I'm tasked with protecting the king," Stave whispered. "And I plan to, Timoran.

"Stave?"

Relief filled my chest. From around the corner, Casper appeared, a plate of nuts and berries in his hands. The water fae had severe points to his ears, and his eyes reminded me of a stormy sea rather than a starlit night. Most believed him to be part nyk, a type of sea fae, not only Night Folk.

He popped two nuts onto his tongue, eyes flicking between us. "What's going on?"

The entire Guild of Shade, with the addition of Ari, Kari, Brant, Siv, and Mattis, served Valen as his inner council.

As a show of respect for Casper's position, Stave dipped his chin and pulled back his arm from my path. "Nothing. Simply wishing *de hän* Elise a good night."

Casper narrowed his eyes. "Lady Elise, is what I think you meant."

Stave's face twitched, but he nodded. "Of course."

Casper pushed the thick door open. "Elise, allow me."

"Thank you, Casper." I didn't look at Stave as I passed, but when Casper closed the door shut at my back, I slumped against the wall.

The reluctance to accept me was getting worse. As Timorans, Kari and Brant dealt with their own prejudice, but since Brant held strange foreign magic in his blood, the fae of Etta seemed to accept the former ravens more readily.

Stave did not touch me, but this was the first time anyone had been so bold as to say they did not want me near Valen.

I shook away the disquiet and stripped free of my sweaty tunic.

The royal longhouse was large enough to hold an impressive gathering. A stone inglenook heated the hall. The long table was always ready with ewers of ale and bread. But the back room is where I spent most of my time. It was private. A place where Valen could simply be him, and I could simply be me.

At the table, I traced my fingers across the opened parchment, smiling. I missed Junius since she'd returned to the Eastern Kingdom, but we'd sent missives to each other over the months. To know she'd returned to her Alver folk and her husband brought a swell of warmth to my chest.

Still, it would be nice to have her talent of tasting lies with us now. Stave came to mind. Would he betray Valen? No. Not in war. Not in the rebirth of Etta.

But killing his consort to make room for another? I had no doubt if one were to give the man a knife, he'd ask where I wanted the first blow.

This missive, though, stilled my heart like a dead weight in my chest when I first read it.

> ... *The Storyteller is returned to the west. I don't understand the child's joy at returning. The place, Raven Row, is more a slum than Skitkast, and when you come to see us someday, you will understand why I am repulsed.*
>
> *Elise, I've thought a great deal about what you last wrote, about the child's prediction. I didn't give it much thought, until I returned to my folk. Frankly, I'm embarrassed I did not think of him sooner.*
>
> *I know of an Alver who fits what Calista described. A breaker of night and fear. Elise lives here in the east. We call him, the Nightrender...*

To know someone, one of these Alvers had magic like Calista predicted in her trance before she left our shores was unnerving.

I shook my head. Truth be told, I didn't know what to think about this Nightrender.

Your battle ends when his begins.

Calista said the words before she left Ruskig. I didn't know if it meant we needed this Alver, but to know he existed was . . . confusing.

What battle would he face? How would ours end?

I folded the parchment again, desperate to stop thinking of blood, war, and battles. For a moment, I wanted to slip into a calm. Behind the fur draped over our bed chamber, I filled the wooden tub with fire heated water. Rose oils and moonvane petals added a bit of healing for the nicks and scrapes from sparring.

As I soaked, laughter nearby sent chills dancing up my arms. Stave kept close. I was certain he and his companions would drink well into the night simply to keep me awake. Then, the moment Valen returned they would bow and show respect as if they kissed my feet.

Perhaps I should say something about his blatant disrespect.

No. If I was to stand at Valen's side, then I needed to learn how to manage disruptions like petty resentment for being Timoran on my own.

I drew strength from thoughts of Lilianna Ferus, Valen's mother. Her journals hinted at a bit of upset when she was chosen to take vows with the Night Folk king. As a Timoran, Lilianna found her place in Etta. She was loved and wise.

Did Stave and those like him realize their king was half Timoran?

A grin spread over my lips, and I sank into the water.

I must've dozed off a bit, for I didn't hear the door creak open at the front. I didn't hear the scrape of boots over the floorboards. My heart leapt to my throat when hands dipped beneath the surface of the water, curling around my legs.

At the rumble of his laugh against my skin, I leaned back, wholly relaxed.

"Didn't mean to frighten you," Valen whispered against the slope of my shoulder. He left soft kisses across my skin, up my neck, to the curve of my ear. The rough calluses of his hand caressed my middle under the water as his other palm pushed aside my damp hair.

"You're back." I sighed, cupping one hand behind his head. "Please, frighten all you like if you keep doing this."

I leveraged onto my knees, and my chest squeezed at the sight of him.

His midnight hair was tied off his face. Dark eyes gleamed with a bit of green and gold up close. My fingertips left damp tracks down the edge of his jaw. I touched the tips of his ears, his lips, simply memorizing him again and again.

Valen curled his arms around my body, pulling me against his chest. One of his rough palms slid down the curve of my spine until he took hold of my naked ass, squeezing.

He drew his lips close to mine, pausing just close enough to cause a bit of madness. "I missed you."

"I hardly noticed your absence."

He narrowed his eyes and let out a little growl. I shrieked and laughed when Valen scooped beneath my thighs, urging my legs around his waist, as water dripped over the floor. In his arms I was safe, even after he dropped me onto our bed.

With a dark heat in his eyes, the Night Prince prowled over the furs, his body making a cage over mine. He pressed a kiss to the top of each breast, then grinned. "If I am so forgettable, allow me to remedy this, my love."

I trapped his face between my palms, each breath deepening, each touch a flame. "It might take a great deal of time, My King. Possibly all night."

He smiled, melting my heart to his all over again, then claimed my mouth. Deep, needy. Perfect.

CHAPTER THREE
NIGHT PRINCE

Elise drew small circles over my chest. Her skin against mine had become a comfort against the pressures of life, and I could not get enough of it. My fingers dragged through her hair; our legs tangled. These moments were too few.

"How many came with you?" she whispered.

"Over fifty. Some are from the Eastern Kingdom. Was all well in our absence?"

She hesitated long enough I didn't entirely trust what she said.

"Yes. It was fine."

"Was it?"

Elise laced her fingers over my heart and propped her chin on top, grinning. "Yes. Halvar trains us and most days I can't decide if I love him for it or hate him."

I laughed, holding her body tighter against me. "He's like his father. Dagar trained me to fight, and I remember wanting to run the man through some days, while still craving his praise. I respected him above nearly everyone."

She smiled, but it didn't last. With the tips of her fingers, Elise brushed my hair off my brow. "I worried for you. We expected you home three nights ago."

I gathered her over me, drawing her in so I could press my lips to hers. I kissed her, sweet and deep. When I pulled back, our foreheads dropped together. "I didn't think it would take so long. The scout delivered the message, didn't he?"

"He did." Elise coiled some of my hair around her finger. "And it is the only reason I did not lay siege to the land searching for you. Still, I worried."

"I think it is more that you missed me."

She smirked and settled her head against my shoulder. "Possibly. But only because it's colder when I don't have your body here to curl against. No other reason."

I speckled her in kisses until she laughed and tightened her hold around my waist.

"Valen," she whispered. "I miss you every moment you're away."

"And I, you."

I cupped her cheek, then urged her body over my waist until her thighs straddled my hips.

Elise's pale cheeks grew flushed when I took control, guiding her core over my length. Her gasps were a craving, her pleasure my delight.

When her lips parted, Elise reached between us, palming the hardness of my shaft and guiding the tip to her entrance.

Together we groaned as she sat over me, taking me in from tip to root.

By the hells, I would never get enough of this woman. From the first moments I spotted her outside the game hall in Lower Mellanstrad, a sort of heated light broke through the violence and hidden hatred in my heart.

As though her mere presence had power to tame the beast inside my blood.

Elise rolled her hips, taking me in deeper and deeper, until it felt like we might truly meld as one. Her breasts shuddered when I pounded up against her harder. I pinched one of her flushed nipples between my fingers, reveling in her soft whimpers.

"I love you," I whispered, arching my hips, slow and steady.

She looked down at me through a hooded gaze and smiled, drunk on pleasure. "And I, you. Always."

Elise dug her fingernails into my chest. Pleasure coiled low in my gut, heated and taut. Her breaths grew more ragged, more desperate, until together, we fell apart.

She collapsed over my chest, keeping us joined, her soft lips speckling the place over my heart in slow kisses.

"Are you quite finished?" Ari's voice rang out through the longhouse. "King Valen, I've need of you, and frankly, I've been more than generous by waiting outside."

I groaned and let my eyes fall from my perfect, stunning, very naked lover's body "No one pestered him this much when he wore the crown. He does this on purpose."

"I do," Ari answered, though he was at least fifty paces from our bedroom doorway. "It brings me such joy to pester you. Penance for all the grumbling and pouting done as the Blood Wraith, My King."

Elise snickered and pressed a kiss to my shoulder, unraveling herself from my body. "You are king during a war. There is never time for rest."

I rolled from beneath the furs and slid into a clean pair of trousers. As I adjusted my belt, I faced her. "Believe me when I say it pains me to leave you."

Not bothering with a tunic yet, I crept back to the bed.

Elise locked her arms around my neck, kissing the hinge of my jaw. "Such is the life as consort to a king. I'm sure there will be many times I will get used to the back of your head. But it shall make the front that much sweeter."

Consort.

We'd not spoken much about what the crown meant. There was nothing wrong with consorts, at least not in the Ettan court. Tor was a consort and held an honored position. My grandfather had been the queen's consort. It was a place of prestige, commitment, a place of love and adoration. But I wanted Elise as more.

I wanted her as my queen.

Vows, to Elise, once meant the end of her freedom. They'd been forced upon her when we met, and the bastard, Jarl Magnus, had forced her to take vows with him at Ravenspire not long ago. She held a distaste for them, and the notion she might hate to take vows, even with me, soured my insides.

Then again, I'd not asked her. She chose me. I chose her. Did we need more?

I offered her a quick smile, then finished dressing. "See you soon."

"Prepare yourself. Should you take too long or be too preoccupied after being gone for a week, I will kidnap you and toss you into dark corners just to put my hands on you."

"I look forward to it. In fact, now I demand it."

Elise smirked. With wicked intent, she dragged her fingertips between the cleft of her breasts, circling her hardened peaks. "I suppose, until then, I'll merely wait here. Alone. Naked."

"You are cruel." My voice was rough, too throaty and thick.

With a laugh, Elise tugged the fur quilt beneath her chin, smiling as I left the room.

I didn't need vows to know I loved Elise and wanted her at my side until my final breath. But I did want her as queen. A thought I couldn't shake, as if it had been planted inside my chest by a power outside of myself.

Ettan queens could rule without the word of a king. They could declare war, invade, build townships, attend council. A consort could only take power if a king or queen were incapacitated in the mind or body. The reason Tor would be able to take the crown if he wanted. Sol was not himself; his mind was not his own.

Imprisoned, or gone for an extended absence, and a consort had little power in strategy. Decisions fell to the royal council.

My parents had once shared the crown as equals. I'd always admired them, the way they worked together. The way my mother raised the armies when my father was taken by the Timorans. They fell together. Never breaking to the end.

True, I did not plan to wear the crown forever. Sol would return; he had to. He'd take up his place as the rightful king.

But until then, Elise should be queen. I felt like a bleeding child for the knot of nerves gathering in my chest at the thought of asking her. I loved her, wanted her, and had no doubt she felt the same.

"What are you smiling about?" Ari asked, tipping back a horn from the table. He looked tired, but always had a sharp wit to his tongue. His eyes flicked to the fur over the bedroom doorway. "Never mind. I'd rather not know. Farewell, my dear Lady Elise!"

"Pleasant day, Ari," she called back. "Although by taking him you have ruined mine!"

Ari grinned. "It is all part of my plan. Rid you of him, so I might make good on my threat to take vows with you." He dodged my fist, laughing. "A jest, My King. A harmless jest."

"I'm about to change my mind about taking your head."

"It is such a pretty head." Ari opened the door for me, his expression changing into something shadowed. "Forgive me for interrupting so early, but there are problems at the gates, Valen. They've weakened, and we're having disputes over food rations. Fishermen feel they do the work, so they ought to get the greatest haul. Townsfolk think since they keep the bustle of our miserly refuge running, they ought to be afforded more grains and textiles."

"Any severe arguments?"

"Nothing that would bring down the law, but some are getting close."

I clenched and unclenched my fists. More folk entering our borders meant more troubles with rations and space. The people were bound to get a little unsettled and discontent. "Have Stieg and Halvar speak to the folk with complaints. I'll see to the walls."

Ari dipped his chin. "One more thing. Have you thought more about sending a party to the South?"

I faced the south walls barring Ruskig from the sea. The idea had merit—send a scout party to the Southern Kingdom in search of allies. I'd never been, but knew my own father once had relationships with underground folk in the kingdom, and some of the royal lines.

Still, it had been centuries. In all that time rumors of overthrows, divided folk, and unrest reached our shores. I didn't even know who held the throne, mortal or fae. But the Southern Kingdom was said to be the kingdom most accepting of fury. A sort of birthplace of different Night Folk; nyks, forest folk, and mortal alike.

They might have answers I needed to help my brother. Truth be told, they might have stronger magic that could help us win this war.

Of course, if they had stronger magic, they could use it to take our land for themselves.

"If you still wore the crown, what would you do?" I asked.

He sighed, as if he considered each word of the question. Ari stood slightly taller than me but wasn't as broad. He'd pierced the points of his ears in silver rings, and as he tucked pieces of his golden hair behind his ears, the glint brightened the kohl runes marking his cheeks.

The Ferus line stood to inherit the throne, but I still considered Ari Sekundär a leader here.

Perhaps we did not begin as allies, but now, I trusted him as much as the Guild of Shade.

"The people of Etta are strong," Ari said softly. "But if we do not extend the branch of friendship first, how long before Ravenspire does? It is a risk, My King. We do not know what faces us on the shores of the South, but if it were up to me, I would take the risk. There might be fury we do not have here."

I asked my concern. "What is to keep them from overpowering us?"

He grinned slyly. "Our knives."

True enough. Ruskig grew weary of those looking to oppress fury. The people would fight until they met the Otherworld if needed.

A risk. One I didn't want to place on anyone, but such were the choices of a king. I placed a hand on Ari's shoulder. "We'll discuss it as a council."

"As you say. I'll go now to see if we can stop these petty battles over herring."

Whenever I stepped into the center of Ruskig folk bowed; they greeted me with respect. I'd yet to grow accustomed to it. Thank the gods, I never walked alone long.

Tor and Casper joined me at a cart of linens and fabric dyes. Casper, always eating, plucked cloudberries from a branch in his hand. Tor's jaw set, hard and unmovable. He never removed his weapon belt. Doubtless he bathed with it. As if a battle would begin at any moment.

"Where do we go today, Valen?" Casper asked, a bit of berry juice dribbling over his lips.

"The walls. How have the folk settled in since last night?"

"Crispin, Frey, and Frey's brother are finding shanties for families with young ones."

"Axel," I said. "Frey's brother. The people trusted him last night."

Tor nodded. "From what I understand Axel helped lead revolutions. They say he can sense the gods' will."

"What does he say?"

"He says he has a sensitive stomach." Tor chuckled darkly. "He stands with the Ferus line."

Good. One less potential traitor to worry about. Bringing in so many new faces put us on alert after Ulf's betrayal to Ravenspire. But if Axel was like Frey, he would be a skilled fighter and loyal to the end.

"The others without young ones will need to set up camps in the trees for now," Tor went on with his report. "Frosts are coming, though, and the false king keeps destroying what few trade roads we have left."

Damn Calder. He was cleverer than I gave him credit for. We never took main roads for our supplies. Ruskig routes demanded rocky terrain, precarious side roads the guards of Ravenspire despised using. Somehow the fool would find our roads, destroy our supplies, and push us that much closer to starving before Timoran slipped into a harsh winter.

At the far walls, stone and broken earth shaped jagged gates like claws from the bedrock. Moonvane grew in thick vines across the crags and crevices, as if the blossoms couldn't help but bloom over my fury.

But even built with fury, there were places where the walls crumbled.

"King Valen, over here."

At a large hole, Stave gestured for us to join them. I didn't remember Stave as a boy, but had learned his father was a palace guard during the raids. He'd proven loyal and hated Castle Ravenspire as much as me.

"Stave," I said, clasping his forearm. "Good to see you. My thanks in looking after Ruskig in our absence."

He grinned, slathering clay and sod over the edge of the wall. "I will always defend our people against threats, My King."

I clapped him on the shoulder and studied the break. A split shattered through the stone, wide enough for a man to slip through. Fury grew taxing, and I never wanted to be drained, never wanted to be caught off guard. But this was too deep to be repaired with mud and clay.

"Step back." I waved the people away.

Folk curved behind me, watching. I was unsettled enough over people bowing to me, but the way they gawked whenever I used fury drew a flush of heat to my face. A hum of magic danced through my fingertips, melting into the stone when I flattened my palms over the surface.

In a matter of moments, the earth tilted and shuddered. New jagged points scraped to the surface. The more fury pulled from my body, the hotter my blood grew. The burn was a comfort, a reminder of weapons we had that the Timorans didn't.

Then again, when the raids came, we had fury and the Timoran king overthrew our people. Traitors in the royal council could be blamed for our loss. Another reason I chose my inner council with care.

Sweat beaded over my brow by the time the wall was repaired.

"Fill in the cracks with the clay," Tor shouted.

The people wasted no time.

"Always a sight to see, King Valen," Stave said.

I scoffed. "It would be greater if I did not get so winded. I'm afraid being cursed for so long has left me lazy with fury."

He chuckled and followed Tor and me along the walls, filling in the gaps with a bucket of mud whenever we paused to rebuild weak points.

"There is a new confidence in the people of Etta," Stave said as we paused at a bucket of water. He ladled in a gulp and wiped a dribble from his chin. "You've restored the hope here."

I took the ladle from him. "Not me alone. There are many who have done more than me." Elise Lysander being one. Without her, I would still be a mindless beast, killing and suffering through blood and violence. Even after the curse was lifted, without Elise, I would not be here. I would never have taken my place. I wouldn't even know Sol still lived.

"All the same," Stave went on, "the people are pleased with you. But there is talk."

"What talk?"

"Of the future. For you, for our people, and for the kingdom." Stave smiled. "They wish to see the king settled, happy, with a strong Ettan queen to lead us through this."

At first, I laughed, imagining nosy folk planning a royal vow behind my back. Then, I came to a pause. "Elise is Timoran."

"Yes," Stave said softly. He didn't look at me as he slathered mud over the cracks in the wall. "It is well known the king's consort is Timoran. The folk speak of a queen. As king, you may have both."

I glanced at Tor, confused. Did the people take issue with Elise's lineage? She'd proved her loyalty time and again even before I claimed my place on the throne. Hells, I was half Timoran. If they took issue with Timorans, they took issue with me.

I thought of her pause, the slight frown over her lips this morning when I pressed on our time apart. A coal of anger stirred in my chest.

What happened in my absence?

"Keeping multiple lovers is a Timoran practice, Stave," Tor said. "Our king has made it clear he intends to follow the tradition of his parents and grandparents before him. To rule with his *hjärta*."

Stave dipped his head. "Of course. I simply have repeated what I've heard."

Had I been so oblivious to discontent with my consort? My jaw tightened. If the people did not accept Elise, then damn the crown. I would step down and return it to Ari.

Casper squeezed my shoulder as he passed, a reassuring grin on his face. "Be calm, my friend." He rarely spoke informally. I must look ready to slaughter everyone. "Do not listen to small minds. Elise is loved. Probably more than you."

Casper bellowed his deep laugh. Even Tor smiled. A bit of the unease lifted from my shoulders. I'd speak to Elise soon, insist she tell me the truth, and discover who—if anyone—had caused her grief.

If I gutted them for it was left to be determined.

"My King!" A woman cried.

The wail stirred me from my anger and set my nerves on edge. From the far side of the wall, a woman sprinted toward us, shoving through the repair crowd, eyes wide with fear.

"My King!" She fumbled to a stop, gasping. "Across the . . . across the ravine. Th-they've come! Ravenspire!"

Instinct drove my steps. Hands on my axes, I sprinted to the scaffolding we'd erected for archers to scale the walls. At the top, I leaned over the edge, and as the woman said, across the deep ravine torches and blue banners with the seal of the false king rose through the trees.

My fists curled at my side. What game were they playing?

A full unit of Ravens filled the gaps between trees, but in the front stood a man with one eye covered. Dressed in fine furs, standing straighter than I remember. He waved a white flag.

All gods I hated him.

"Tor," I said, voice rough. "Find Elise. Her father has come to call."

CHAPTER FOUR
ROGUE PRINCESS

"Elise!" Kari's voice shattered through the longhouse. Panicked, rough. Something was wrong.

I abandoned the plaits of my braid and raced out of the bedroom into the great hall. Kari was there, fiddling with a sword on her waist, breathless.

"What is it?" I reached for the silver dagger on the table as if steel and blades were a mere impulse now.

"At the wall, it's . . ." She struggled to get her breath. "It's . . . come."

"Kari, what is it?"

"Your father, Elise." Valen stepped through the door, face as stone.

My mouth parted, but no sound came. I fastened my dagger to its sheath with trembling fingers. Last I saw my father, he stood aside while Jarl Magnus forced me to take vows, then again as the same bastard stabbed my mother through the heart.

I had no father. Not anymore.

Valen crossed the room to me. One palm cupped the side of

my face. "He comes to speak to you. You do not have to do this. I will speak to him, murder him, taunt him—whatever you ask, I will do."

I licked the dryness on my lips, pulse racing, even as a smile curled in the corner of my mouth. He said the words lightly, doubtless to make me grin, but underneath it all there was truth to the Night Prince's words. He would do anything I asked of him.

It was almost as if he prayed I might give my permission for him to slaughter those in my family who had harmed me. Like it might be a gift I could bestow to him.

I forced a smile and brought my fingertips to his jaw. "I will speak with him."

"At my side. As half the heart of the king, Elise. You are not a second *Kvinna*—you are so much more. Make sure he knows it."

Valen pressed a kiss to the center of my palm, while sneaking a second knife into my belt. A silent vow between us. Do anything to fight, to defend ourselves. To return to each other again.

Kari handed me a fur mantle. Valen placed a black circlet that looked like the wings of a raven around his head. A symbol of the original crown from Ravenspire; a symbol restored to the true heirs of the land.

Outside, folk hurried with weapons, shields; the fae created illusions around the massive stone walls. Others twisted roots and earth until thick briars encircled the border of Ruskig.

Valen held firmly to my hand as we approached. The crowds parted, and soon the Guild of Shade fell in line with us. Tor had placed his black mask around his chin and mouth, Halvar circled one hand, stirring up a maelstrom of clouds and wind above us.

"We'll speak at the tower," Valen said, resting his hand on my lower back. He turned to his guild. "All eyes will be on their archers. If one damn arrow even looks like it might angle at Elise, you slaughter the archer. Understood?"

"Dead before he even thinks to load the arrow, Valen," Stieg said with a wink.

"For the king too," I said, glaring at the Night Prince. "Do not let this fool play my human shield or I will hold each of you responsible if he takes another arrow to the back."

"As you say, My Lady," Halvar said, laughing.

Valen smirked and led us toward the wooden stairs built into the tower. "I thought you liked when I played your hero."

"I like you breathing much more."

The top watchtower was wider than the others, and able to fit the whole of the guild with room to spare. I laced my fingers with Valen's and squeezed his hand until his smooth brown skin turned pink. Twenty paces from the border a line of darkly dressed Ravens held seax blades, or battle axes. Some held longswords, or short blades made of bronze and iron.

But my eyes danced across the glimmer of steel and landed in the center. My father stood beneath a canopy. His hair combed and glossy. Healthy. His beard was beaded in bone and silver, and across his left eye was a black patch where Runa had blinded him to spite me.

All my sister had done to destroy his family and he remained her pet.

I looked to my hand in Valen's. For a short, silent moment my heart smiled. I had no family outside this refuge. All my family lived here, with him. He was part of me more than anyone in the Lysander manor had ever been.

Valen stepped forward. He never released my hand, and I suspected he would've adjusted if I insisted on keeping his palm in mine. I cleared my throat and released him, allowing him his place to show his own strength as the rightful heir.

Head high. Do not falter. I was consort to a king. To cling to him like a frightened child would only give us a weakness to be exploited. It would give Valen a weakness. If he could stand tall, then so could I.

"*Kvin* Lysander," Valen said. The timbre of his voice rolled like a dark storm across the ravine. "What do you want?"

"I will not speak with you," said my father. "An imposter."

Valen laughed, a little wickedly. "An imposter? Yet you come here in service of a false king. A king this land did not choose. I believe we may understand the word differently."

"I am here to speak with my daughter. Move aside, little prince."

Arrows raised from our side at that. To insult the Ettan king, for our folk, meant death.

Valen held up a hand, a silent command to hold. He looked back to my father. "If Elise wishes to speak with you, then she will."

He turned his black glass eyes to me, a gentle smile on his face. I gave a subtle nod, then stepped forward.

"What is it you want?" I said, embarrassed how my voice trembled when Valen's was smooth and cutting.

"Daughter," my father said. "You have been manipulated by the fae long enough. I have come—in truce—to bring you home. To your people. Your family. Our blood is gods' chosen to rule this land, and if you remain here, I fear it will be your end."

Where hesitation had been a moment before, now a hot, strike of anger boiled in the center of my belly. I laughed and leaned over the ledge of the tower. "You fear for me? How strange. Where was your fear when you fed me to the wolf, Jarl Magnus? Where was your fear when your first daughter slaughtered half of Castle Ravenspire to steal the crown? Take your pitiful pleas elsewhere. They fall on deaf ears, *Kvin* Lysander."

"Elise," he snapped. "You will return."

"Why? Why fight for this? What am I to you? If this is all for control, then you have wasted your time and the lives of those men who stand with you. You control me no longer."

Even from a distance, the heat in my father's eye crackled between us. "You will be known as a traitor, Elise. You fight against your own people, and I will not leave this as our legacy. You were born to a duty, and you will see it through, or I would rather you be dead."

Silence dug deep into my skin. The folk of Ruskig kept the bowstrings taut. Not even the ravens moved as they waited for the next word.

"Elise," Valen whispered against my ear. "You are more than he says. Do not forget it, and do not let him forget it."

I did not feel more. To have the scrutiny of both Timoran and Etta on me left me reeling, wishing I could disappear in the ground.

Until I looked at the Night Prince.

Trust, affection, love lived in those eyes. I took his hand again, drawing him to my side, so all could see.

This time my voice didn't waver. "I wish all to hear—I am not of House Lysander any longer. I reject the False King Calder and his queen."

"Elise," my father warned.

I raised my voice above his. "I stand with the people of Etta, but also those of Timoran." I gestured at the ravens. "Look who you follow, who you serve. A king who murders for power. See the land around you. See how it is once more alive with fury. And you fight against it. My father says we are gods' chosen—he lies." I raised my voice, refusing to have anything I would say misheard. "I stand with the true king. The king of both people. Born of both Timoran and Etta, I serve, and will only serve, the Ferus bloodline. Stand with us or leave. This will be your only warning before we force you to go."

"Hells, woman," Valen muttered under his breath, drawing me into his side. "I have many plans to show you every improper thought rushing through my head the second we are alone. Prepare yourself."

My face heated. Only Valen Ferus would be indecent when we faced an enemy.

"Elise, if this is your choice, then I wash my hands of you, daughter." My father turned his back on me.

"I believe that is what I just said," I retorted, drawing a few laughs from the Guild of Shade.

Amusement was short-lived.

Down the gates, shouts rose and the whistle of our archers releasing arrows filled the space between both armies.

"Dammit," Halvar cursed. "They're breaching the wall!"

As the first knight, Halvar leapt into the chaos, shouting commands as a group of Ravens drew blades, attacking a gap in the stones.

More Ravens spilled from the forest. My fists curled tightly at my sides. All this was a ploy. A chance to infiltrate Ruskig again. To kill as many folk as possible. Maybe slit my throat if they got the chance.

Valen tossed the circlet from his head and drew his axes. He faced me, his eyes saying a thousand things. A gentle touch to my face was more than any word. We didn't need to speak, I already knew. Fight. Return to me.

Then he went after Halvar. The earth shook as his fury shredded the rock between us and a gap widened between the forest and Ruskig.

"Elise," Tor said behind me. He held out a bow. "We'll take the towers."

I nodded. Not as skilled as other archers, still I'd been working on aim for several weeks, and fared better with a bow than hand to hand fighting. Tor shouted at me to stay low, he commanded Stieg and Casper to prepare their fury.

"Where is the king?"

"Ari," I said with a sigh of relief when the fae climbed into the tower box.

Tor pointed to where Valen had gone. "Stay by him, confuse the Ravens until they go mad, Ari."

With a playful wink, Ari raced after Valen. Once adversaries, now they were practically inseparable.

"Down!" Tor rushed to me, covering my head as arrows rained over the wall in a perfect arch.

The sick thud of iron slicing through flesh boiled in my ears. Screams, shouts, curses, all of it spun as the arrows fell. Tor's arms surrounded me, holding me against the wall of the watchtower, unable to do anything until it stopped.

Once a shout from our walls roared to return fire, I shoved Tor away. "When I said I didn't want Valen as my shield, I thought it was understood none of you are easily sacrificed, Torsten!"

Such a rare thing, but Tor flashed a white smile. He tapped the end of his arrow, igniting the tip with his blue pyre fury, then pulled the string taut. "I think you like us, Elise Lysander."

Another battle was beginning. Fear grew potent until it left a sour taste on my tongue. Yes, I liked them. I loved the entire Guild of Shade like I would a family, like I would true brothers.

And every time the people of my birth showed their bleeding faces, they threatened those I loved most. I tired of it all.

Pulling the tail of an arrow against my cheek, I locked my sights where my father cowered beneath his canopy. He was a stranger to me. Today, he would pay for trying to harm them.

Both eyes open, I let the arrow fly.

CHAPTER FIVE
NIGHT PRINCE

WE WERE ALWAYS prepared for Ravenspire. They tried to breach the wall, but in every crevice, every gap, we had warriors at the ready. Now they held the hearts of more than a few Ravens in their hands.

I stood, buried in our archers, using fury to split the earth. To divide us further from the Ravens. The burn in my blood only deepened as the armies of Calder proved more cunning than I gave credit for.

With heavy bolts they shot rope across the ravine I'd carved. Like spiders to a web, Ravens worked seamlessly weaving rope and tethering it to thick trees, readying to shimmy across the gap.

"Cut the damn ropes!" Halvar shouted.

All around our folk worked on trying to pluck the bolts from the stone, or saw the rope, but some sort of coating glistened on the twine. It added a strength to the line and made it nearly impossible to cut.

We'd drop a few, but not all. There were too many.

"Halvar! The Divide—remember? The Divide!" I shouted at

my friend. During the beginnings of the raids, we'd trained side by side. Dagar taught us to use our fury together, to utilize our strengths, all to protect Etta and bury the Timoran raiders.

Halvar paused and studied the space between us. After a few heartbeats, a smile cracked over his lips. A vicious kind of smirk darkened and brightened his face all at once when he faced me. "It could work."

"Then go!"

"Back away from the edge of the wall," Halvar commanded.

Archers dropped their bows and backed away. In a crouch, I spread my palms across the stone; the heat of fury scorched the pale stone with blackened marks. A crack fissured under my hands. Stone scraped over stone. Soil tilled in thick, rocky mounds as I broke our wall.

Wails and cries of surprise went up when part of the wall slid toward the ground as if I shaved it in half.

"Follow the king," Halvar said at my back. "Go, you bleeding fools. Step only where I tell you."

It took a few moments before the warriors peeked over the edge of the broken wall, and saw there were now levels, like a stone staircase, I'd carved along the side to take them out into the deep ravine.

"Cover him!" Elise's voice rose at my back.

I grinned. She had a regal tone, and I did not need to even look to know my *hjärta* had two dozen archers at my back.

The Divide was a strategy to be used if the raiders ever crossed the canyons or peaks long ago. It would take all my fury; it would take unhindered concentration, but if we pulled it off, the Ravens would leave with massive losses.

Arms raised, my hands trembled. Fury pulled from my blood. From the bottom of the ravine, tall towers of rock and earth broke free and sprouted like stony fingers from the ground. The towers were flat on top, and wide enough our warriors could leap from top to top like stepping stones across the ravine.

We'd reach the other side, corner them, and they'd regret stepping into the sunlight.

Or, the better plan, they'd mimic our steps and join us on the tall platforms of stone and fight us there.

A thick Raven stepped forward; the captain of the unit, I presumed. He tossed back a hood, and for a few breaths studied each block of earth as it shot up from the ground.

At last, he signaled his warriors forward, demanding they cross the space on the stone towers I kept carving. My limbs ached, but I provided the Ravens with bits of stone platforms that were close enough it wouldn't take much for them to step over the darkness below.

And they did.

"Hold," Halvar shouted, and our warriors stilled wherever they were.

I took a place in the center of the ravine. The blocky pillar of earth I stood on was wide enough to hold four more men, but I was alone there. I could see all sides, all the steps that could be taken.

Steadily, the Ravens pursued us. Shaky at first, leaping from rock to rock, but their confidence gained, and they went faster.

"Ready, My Prince? King, I mean King. Hells, I'll get used to it, I promise," Halvar said, laughing a little maniacally as he raised his hands.

"Ready!"

"Go!" Halvar shouted, and chaos followed.

With most of the Ravens out in the open on the stone pillars, I waved my hand and crumbled their towers back into dust. Screams echoed on the long plummet to the jagged ravine floor.

"Fall back!" the captain cried. "Get back, you fools!"

Ravens scrambled to return to their side, to solid ground. Some pushed their own warriors off the ledges in their panic, but where a Raven would step, I would break the earth until the tower fell. Where an Ettan moved, I'd strengthen their footing with closer, surer slabs of stone.

We advanced.

Ravenspire fell to their deaths.

If Ravens did not fall from me bending the earth, Halvar took them by sharp, brutal gusts of his fury. No mistake, when we were finished, the bottom of the canyon would be soaked in blood and bone.

"Stop!" A bellow roared over the chaos.

My stomach tightened. *Kvin* Lysander, along with two Ravens, dragged between them what I feared would happen.

Sol.

Only this time, Sol wasn't stiff like he'd been carved as stone. He wasn't battered or lost in his own mind. No, the man before me, chained in heavy iron, grinned viciously. His blue eyes were filled with a rage I recalled only when Sol blinded the guard for taking Torsten away from him so many turns ago.

"Stop!" I shouted. My shoulders heaved, breaths came harsh and ragged. Fury ached in my veins, but I lifted my palms and shot a jagged spike of stone at Elise's father.

He cursed and glared back at me. "Cease this, Night Prince, or we will toss your brother over the edge."

I laughed, and something burst inside me when Sol did too. "Toss him. I will be there to catch him."

"All these turns and Timorans grow stupider, do they not, brother!" The Raven behind Sol kicked him in the back of the legs, bringing the Sun Prince to his knees.

I clenched my fists and at my back, Tor cursed all the gods, spewing threats I doubted any of the Ravens considered credible. In time they'd be proven wrong.

Kvin Lysander was a bleeding fool until a sly grin carved over his face. "You want the Sun Prince. He is a weakness to you, so we know how to cut you at the knees."

"They need us, Valen!" Sol shouted. A Raven struck him in the face. My brother laughed. What had changed? How had he escaped the catatonic state he'd been in not so many months before?

The hair lifted on the back of my neck. It could be a ruse, for all I knew they wanted me to believe Sol was himself, so I acted foolishly.

Painful as it was to stand back, there were too many lives to think of.

"Why else would we be alive?" Sol pressed.

"Shut up," *Kvin* Lysander hissed at Sol. My brother ignored him.

"Use the brain I think is in there, Valen."

Gods, my brother was still insulting me. But when a Raven went to strike Sol again, I didn't hold back. One step later, a point of rock skewered the guard where he stood. The unit muttered and stepped further back toward the trees.

"Beautifully aimed," Sol said, sneering at the other Raven at his side.

I looked at Elise's father. "Touch my brother again, and I will have each of you piked before you can take a step."

"I offer a trade, Night Prince. Your brother, for my daughter."

In my heart, I knew the moment her father showed his bleeding face, Elise would be used as a pawn. Clever and vicious, the man knew how to threaten, knew how to tug at my heart.

Sol was the only one unbothered. I was almost certain he rolled his eyes.

"No," I said, wholly aware a few murmurs rose at my back.

Kvin Lysander gestured with one hand, and the Raven at Sol's side had him pinned face down in the dirt in the next instant. The guard ripped out a large, glass jar filled with what looked like black smoke and held it over the Sun Prince.

"He is coherent now, little prince," Elise's father said. "But one dose of this, and he will turn into the monster you saw before."

"Don't be foolish," Sol grunted, his words muffled. "One life for many, Valen. One life for many. Don't be weak!"

Sol didn't deny something would happen to him should they dose him with whatever elixir they'd warped with fury, and he struggled as if the jar burned being so nearby.

"Valen." Tor's voice burned my ears.

I didn't turn around. Couldn't. I knew the pain he felt. When Ravenspire took Elise, I understood what it meant to watch the other piece of your heart be ripped to pieces.

Once more, though, I had no idea how to protect everyone.

"Night Prince, I'll amend my offer," said *Kvin* Lysander. "Allow me to deliver a message to Elise. From her sister. A warning, you could say."

"I wish to speak with her, brother," Sol said, his voice low, and rife in underlying meaning.

Her father snorted a laugh. "There. Would you deny your brother the chance to meet your whore? Would you deny a father the chance to behold his child before a family is divided forever?"

It wasn't worth the risk. "*Kvin* Lysander, you are no father, and she is no whore. Send the Sun Prince here to speak with her, and we will not lift a blade. You keep your lives. I keep my brother and Elise."

With a sneer, the bastard nodded his head, and the raven opened the jar, readying to pour whatever dark magic lived in the potion over Sol's head.

"Stop!"

Cursed hells. I turned around. Elise stood on one of the standing towers of stone, eyes furious as she looked at me.

"Elise," I warned.

She cut me with a gaze, then faced her father. "I will come to you, but you will not touch the Sun Prince, or I will tell King Valen to slaughter you all without a drop of mercy, and certainly no remorse."

The woman had lost her damn mind. I lifted my palms, molding a narrow bridge from my place to hers, and stomped over to her. She never faltered, not under my glare, and that reckless strength was one of the many things I loved about her. But this went too far.

One hand cupped behind her neck, and I drew her close. "You are mad if you think I will watch you go to Ravenspire again."

"And you are mad if you think I will allow Sol to be tortured in front of his people and his lover. If it were you over there, there are no lengths I would not go to stop your pain."

Foolish, beautiful woman.

She rested a hand over my heart. "I will not go with them, Valen. I will not. But I can offer a respite, perhaps a bit of a distraction so we can free Sol."

My jaw tightened as I looked over to where the raven forced my brother back to his knees. "I think Sol knows something. He's being coy and irritating on purpose, but the way he asked to speak with you . . ." I shook my head. "No. It's too risky."

Her warm palm rested against my cheek, drawing my eyes back to her. "Valen, trust me, like I trust you."

"It is not you I mistrust."

"I know, but trust that I will not be so foolish to risk being separated from you again. But there are wise, calculated risks that could lead to getting your brother back. It is worth it."

I closed my eyes, furious, and wishing she did not make sense.

"Moments," I hissed through my teeth. "Moments are all I will give them before they die. They make one move, and—"

"It won't come to that." Elise frowned, then faced the edge of the stone. "Now, if you please. I need a path to get there."

I let out a frustrated breath, then turned to our archers. "Keep your arrows on Lady Elise. Shoot and do not miss should they try to harm her."

With care, I shaped an arched bridge of roots and rock and dirt from our tower to the edge of the cliff.

Before Elise stepped onto the bridge, I curled an arm around her waist, and pulled her back to my chest. My lips brushed against her ear. "I love you, and you ought to know you are fated to be the death of me if you keep doing these things."

She bit her bottom lip, doubtless to fight a grin, then lifted one of my hands and pressed a kiss to my palm. "I'll return soon, My King."

CHAPTER SIX
ROGUE PRINCESS

At my back, Valen shouted commands. It was his way to keep his head, I'd learned. Barking orders when I had few doubts his body hummed in nerves and rage. The only way to sate the bloodlust would be murdering every one of the Ravens in front of me.

At the end of the bridge the captain stood like a stone. He held out one hand for me; muscles in his jaw pulsed. I refused his assistance from the bridge, and walked past with my chin lifted, eyes on my father.

The only break in my focus came as I strode past Sol.

Our eyes met. He resembled Valen now that his face was filled out and color had returned to his skin. The differences were in the eyes. Valen's were like black skies, and Sol's were blue, like the deepest part of the ocean.

"Elise."

I turned away from the Sun Prince and met my father's glare. "You have me. What is the message?"

"No message," he said. "I merely wanted to see your eyes, to know for certain you had not been mesmerized by the fae."

"I assure you I am more clear-headed than I have ever been."

My father's face twitched. "I will remind you, daughter, that you are vowed to Jarl Magnus. Anything you plan to do regarding the fae is void. The gods will not honor it."

I laughed. It couldn't be helped. He was utterly ridiculous. "The gods? You think the gods honor a vow that was done by force? I wore bleeding chains on my ankles, Daj. You think the gods smiled upon you when you allowed Jarl to slaughter my mother?" I stepped closer, my voice low. "You're a coward."

He raised a hand to strike me but stumbled when the ground shook.

"Lay a hand on her, and it will be the last thing you do," Valen shouted.

Leif Lysander pointed his rage across the canyon, then took a few breaths, composing himself.

"You will not succeed, Elise," my father said. "You do not know the secrets of Ravenspire."

He believed every word, and it sent a cold shock of fear down my spine. I hid it well. "I don't fear you."

"You should." My father dipped his head alongside my face. "You know I will not allow you to return to him, right? He will not be fast enough to kill us all."

I scoffed. "Yes. I knew the moment I stepped here I would not be allowed to leave. But I do have a compromise. I will leave peacefully; I will not fight. I will tell Valen to stand down if you allow the Sun Prince to speak to his consort."

I looked over my shoulder. Sol didn't turn to me, but he dropped his chin to his chest, and closed his eyes.

"Allow this for me, Daj. Let me stand with the Sun Prince as he, at least, gets a chance to bid farewell."

My father's face contorted in confusion, perhaps a bit of shock. It took several long moments before he gave a curt nod.

"If you try anything, I'll cut him until his blood stains the grass."

My father flicked his hand, excusing me, and left me to the captain of the unit. The Sun Prince was pulled to his feet, and we stood in silence as the Ravens backed away.

"You are brave, My Queen," Sol whispered.

"I am not a queen. I am your brother's consort."

"For now." Sol's grin was as mischievous as Valen's.

"Torsten needs you," I told him softly. "Speak to him."

Sol swallowed with effort and looked across the canyon. "What an odd request for a queen to make. Give me a moment to speak to those I love, but no request for yourself."

I didn't correct him on my title again, simply lowered my voice. "My hope is together we might think of a plan. I've read your mother's journals, and from her word you rival your brother in cunning."

Sol smiled, and it was a marvel to see him so alive. So changed since the curled, lifeless form in the dungeons of Ravenspire. "Rival him? My Queen, a lesson you should learn now is I best Valen in everything."

"Ah, how wonderful. Another sharp-tongued Ferus."

Sol chuckled, then sobered as he took a step toward the edge. Across the space, Ettans and Night Folk stared in silence. Halvar and Tor both stood beside Valen. Not one of them moved. I wasn't sure they even breathed.

Sol cleared his throat. "I've been given a gift from the Lady Elise." He paused, fists clenched, the pain in his heart on display for all. "Tor, I-I thought you were dead. They have kept me alive, locked in a state of madness, and I cared little thinking you were gone. Until I saw you. Now, I live for you. I live for a moment when there will be no chains, no space between us."

Tor dropped his bow and stepped as far to the ledge of his plot of stone as possible. He hammered a fist over his chest. "I lost you once. It will not happen again."

"No." Sol grinned. "It won't. I vow to keep living if you vow the same."

Tor shouted his frustration and paced. "Today. I will not leave you here, Sol."

A flicker of sadness crossed the Sun Prince's face. "I wish it more than anything. But I do not believe that is what fate has in store."

"I don't give a damn about fate."

Sol ignored Tor's insistence and smiled. "As if no time has passed, I love you. Even more than I did if it is possible."

"Sol—"

"I have a request, Tor. Please." Sol pointed at Valen. "Try not to kill him. We both know how irritating he can be. And Hal, I expect you to do the same."

Halvar had no crass remark. Truth be told he looked ready to break as he pounded a fist over his chest.

Sol looked to his brother, voice rough. "The Ferus line is strong. It is needed by these Raven sods. I may not have had my mind, but I always had ears. I trust you are being a wise king, little brother."

"Keeping it warm until you wear the crown."

Sol didn't correct him. "Be wise now and listen. You should know, I dream of the day the blood of the first, the middle, and the last will once more be reunited." Valen stiffened. I didn't understand and had no time to ask before Sol went on. "Be ready to bend, Valen."

A prickle of unease ran up my arms. Valen dropped an ax. Tor tensed. Sol was planning something, and he was coming for me.

"My Queen," he whispered. "Make the title official."

"What are you talking about?"

Sol glanced at nearby Ravens, a touch of caution to his voice. "Your title is needed. I can't explain more. Listen and repeat to Valen the things I'm about to say exactly as I say them. Tell Valen she is being used. Has been used all this time. Tell him to find her. Then, tell them to come home to visit me."

"I don't understand."

"And neither can they." He gestured to the approaching Ravens. My father suspected something as well. He commanded the guards to seize us again.

"I am proud to meet another sister," Sol whispered, a sly grin on his lips. "Elise."

"What?"

The Sun Prince dipped his mouth close to my ear. "Run."

The next steps came in a blur. Sol shoved me toward the ledge. He raised his palms the same as Valen always did.

"Tor, burn them with me!" he cried.

All at once, skeins of thick, wretched black pooled around the Sun Prince. A great cascade of blight chased me toward the edge. Time slowed. Shouts rang out. I heard my father demand Sol be taken alive, heard commands to retrieve me.

"Jump, Elise! Now!" Sol shouted.

He pushed more of his poisonous fury at my back. I had no choice but to rush to the ledge. All around dark shadows of blight readied to devour me.

I jumped.

Wind whipped against my face. Did I scream? I didn't know. My stomach shot to my chest as I plummeted through the air. As if every movement raced in my sight, I watched the black wall of dark fury meet a blue, fiery wall and surround the remaining Ravens trapped on Valen's towers of stone.

A deafening boom roared over the forest when they collided.

And nothing but ashes remained of those warriors trapped between the two furies.

My thoughts were muddled.

Why did Sol tell me to jump if I was to deliver a message? Would Valen keep his head and be king if he watched me die? Or would he give in to rage and bloodlust, becoming the Wraith once again?

I closed my eyes, bracing for the sharp points of the rocks below when something rough coiled around my wrist. Then another around my waist, slowing my fall. Roots tangled beneath me, around me, across the canyon weaving a makeshift web beneath my body.

In the next heartbeat, arms surrounded me. Valen fell with me, one hand keeping me close, the other controlling the earth until all at once we stopped.

I cried out at the jolt of pain when the roots and muddy threads broke the fall, giving enough to soften the blow, but by morning we would be bruised and battered.

The net bounced slightly, and the weight in the middle rolled me to the center. Into the arms of the Night Prince again.

Valen trembled as he smashed me to his chest. Heat from fury evaporated off his damp skin. His breaths were heavy, matching mine. I shook away the stun and curled my arms around his neck, holding him like every moment might be our last. My face burrowed against his neck, and I breathed all of him. The spice of his skin, the hint of earth and soil, the strange burn of fury I could practically taste.

"Did you do this?" I whispered. "You bend more than rock."

"Anything . . . in the earth," he said through heavy gasps as he caught his breath. His lips pressed firmly against my forehead. "Never, *never*, do that again."

I smiled against his skin, holding him tighter, longer.

I didn't know how long we held each other, trading kisses, touching as if we might disappear, but when we abandoned Valen's fury net and used his magic to climb our way out, Ravenspire was gone.

My father was gone.

So, to my dismay, was the Sun Prince.

CHAPTER SEVEN
NIGHT PRINCE

I didn't want to see anyone but my inner circle and Elise. The most trusted of anyone, and they all surrounded the royal longhouse table now.

We stared at drinking horns, silently reciting the events of the morning. Elise's face and arms were scraped, and Kari helped clean the gashes from the rough net I'd frantically pulled from the walls of the ravine.

Bleeding Sol—he could've given a bit of warning. Not vague hints. Then again, my brother was wisely calculated in how he spoke. It was his words that kept me quiet now. I still hadn't fully accepted the truth.

"I wish to say something," Tor muttered at last.

"You do not need my permission," I grumbled.

Tor turned on the log bench and looked squarely at Elise. "What you did—" He paused, clearing his throat. "It was a gift I can't repay."

Elise tilted her head. "Tor, it—"

"No. You don't understand. For centuries I lived cursed, but empty. My heart knew a piece was missing, and I did not remember what it was. When you released us, I remembered everything. The last time I saw the Sun Prince, he was bloodied, and risking his life to save mine while they dragged me away to be tortured. I could not speak to him for fear they'd kill him or me to bring more pain."

Silence thickened until it became a physical part of the room, as much as the stench of ale and smoke.

I could not forget the day. When the Ravens came, when they hurt Tor in front of Sol, I'd never seen such a rage in my brother's eyes. Somehow, fury or brute strength, broke him from his restraints.

We spent weeks in a snowy cage for it, but now that I had Elise, I understood the desperation to protect what is yours.

Tor took Elise's hand and went on. "Allow me to thank you for giving me a small moment. A new memory to cling to with different words, and a different sight."

Siv wiped away a tear on her cheek, taking hold of Mattis's hand a little tighter.

Elise smiled and dipped her chin. "You deserved it, Tor. I do have a question, though. What did you do with your fury and Sol's?"

"Yes," Stieg said, his interest piqued. "I've never seen such a thing."

"Nor I," said Ari. "In truth, you old folk have fury I've not seen . . . ever."

"It's not as if dark fae like Sol go around sharing their fury," Tor said with a touch of bitterness. "And we're not old, you fool."

"Spry as ever," Halvar grumbled.

Kari spared him a look; concern laced in her smile as she ran her fingertips over his forearm. My friend had been unusually somber since stepping back behind the walls, and it was unlike him. But I knew if he wanted to speak, there was never anything that stopped Halvar from putting words to thoughts in his mind.

He would when he was ready.

"I am curious as well," I admitted, looking at Tor. "I don't know what you did, but I've never seen your pyre mix with Sol's like that."

Tor shifted in his seat, rubbing his fingers over the bridge of his nose. "Because only Arvad knew our fury had an explosive connection. You know how everyone kept Sol's fury secret, but he and I liked to experiment. As it turned out, when my pyre touched his blight, something happened. A collision that could bring anything to ash."

My chest tightened. "The Ravens. They were—"

"Turned to ash," Tor said sharply. "Yes. A show to Ravenspire what can—what will—happen."

"That was reckless of him." I dragged my fingers through my hair and leaned over the table on my elbows. "He's proven how dangerous he can be to them; now what will they do? Kill him? Turn him back into the mindless fae to do their bidding?"

I slammed a fist onto the table, angry, frustrated, more than a little frightened for the thin thread dangling my once-dead family in front of my eyes.

"There comes a level of respect when one is feared," Ari said softly.

"Explain," I snapped, only stilling when Elise drew her hand over my leg. A comforting touch, a bit of magic all its own. Only this woman could bring the bloody rage still swirling within me to a calm.

I dropped my chin, squeezed her hand in mine, and gave her a tight smile.

Ari gestured at me. "As the Blood Wraith, you were feared, yet respected. Even from the Ravens. There was an understanding if they chose to face you, then they should be prepared to meet the Otherworld. They have kept Sol alive this long without knowing how fearsome his fury can be.

"True, I have no doubt they've experimented on him, but today they saw what will happen when Night Folk stand together and stand against them. He gave them a small show, planted a bit of fear in their hearts. Castle Ravenspire will have nothing to do but give us the respect our armies deserve. What our king deserves."

"So, you're telling me what my brother did was wise?"

Tor and Halvar shared a look, grinning.

Ari arched one brow. "Well, yes. I think it was a calculated risk that will give us an edge."

"I'm going to kick him out of here," I told Elise. She stared at me as if I'd lost my mind.

"What?" Ari glared at me. "Why?"

Tor laughed. Brutal, fierce, angry Torsten laughed. "You will come to learn the Sun Prince and Night Prince have the fiercest brotherly rivalry I've ever seen."

"True," Halvar said. "And I had four brothers once. But the way our dear princes bickered, only the queen or Herja could get them to shut up. Good luck, Elise. It falls to you now."

The light mood lasted a mere moment before we fell into a somber silence. More needed to be said, questions to be answered, and I didn't know if anything could be answered. Not tonight, at least.

How had Ravenspire manipulated our lives for so many turns? What power did they truly have? What fury? Did they have some connection with seers or fate that I didn't know? The next question would be why? I was told by the girl, Calista, that the storyteller who twisted fate to curse me did it to save my life. To stop more killing of my family.

Did that enchantress so many turns ago not know my brother and sister still lived? Or was there a reason the three of us needed to survive?

A hundred questions battered my head, and I despised the fear that burrowed in my chest. Perhaps, as they had threatened countless times, I didn't know the true strength of my enemy. If I had to guess, Sol had learned things in his captivity. We needed to free him. We needed to find Herja.

"You mentioned my sister." I paused until I found the words. "Herja is alive."

No one moved, no one spoke. A good thing. Such a statement needed time to settle right before being sliced to pieces.

Elise laid a gentle hand on my arm, her eyes wet with emotion. "How do you know?"

I took a drink, eyes on the fire. "Sol told me. When he said he looked forward to the time the first, the middle, and the last were reunited—he was telling me Herja was out there. Alive."

Casper lifted a hand. "Uh, care to explain how you got that?"

"It's what he used to call us as children—mostly to bother me." I shook my head, smiling. "He'd always say the first, as in him, was the strongest. A foundation to hold the others."

Even Elise laughed. "All the words he could've said to me this morning, and what he wanted me to know was that he bested you in everything."

I rolled my eyes. "He said that? While an entire unit of Ravens held blades to his neck, that was what he chose to say?"

"He was quite adamant about it too."

Hells, I missed my brother. "We'll see about that. Herja, he always called the middle. The piece needed to bridge the opposing first and last. The calm, dependable piece. Then, I was the last. I don't need to repeat what he said about my birth order."

A chuckle rumbled down the table.

Ari reclined in his chair and laced his fingers behind his head. "I look forward to getting to know the Sun Prince. He does seem entertaining."

I'd continue self-deprecating and raising Sol on a pedestal if it meant Tor's smile remained how it was. There and bright, when for so many turns it did not exist.

Mattis knocked on the table, drawing our attention back to the conversation. "How would he know she's alive? And, not to be crass, but *how* is she alive? As I understood it, Princess Herja was not Night Folk."

"My mother and Herja both went through *förändra*." The Change. A way for a mortal to become like the fae folk. At least in lifespan. As far as I knew, Herja, nor my mother, ever held fury. "My sister at her birth, and my mother shortly after she took vows with my father."

I flicked my eyes to Elise's hand in mine. Soon, I would ask her to do the same. If she desired it.

"Again, how would the Sun Prince know? Do you suppose she is in Ravenspire?" Mattis asked.

"I don't know."

Stieg shook his head. "It was almost like he was asking you to make it happen, in my opinion. He could've said the middle was with him, but he said he looked forward to when they were all reunited."

"If she's out there," Elise said, "then we do all we can to find her. I think . . . I think he was telling me something about her."

"What do you mean?"

"Before he told me to jump, he said strange things, then insisted I repeat them exactly as he said them."

Elise held the table captive as she retold Sol's words. What did he want me to pick apart from them? If Elise was specifically told to repeat it as he said, then Sol chose his words carefully. I rubbed my head, frustrated, wishing he sat beside me.

Until Kari shifted in her seat. "We should check the brothels."

I snapped my eyes up. "What?"

It took her a moment. Brant and Halvar exchanged a dark glance. A bit of protective anger only a brother or a lover could have. But Kari was no piece of glass. She took a deep breath and lifted her chin. "Used. He said she was being used, yes?"

Elise nodded slowly. "Yes. Sol told me she has been used all this time."

"When I was in the Ravenspire guard, when . . . they took me, each guard said I was theirs to use; they said I was like a pleasure mate at a brothel."

Halvar's jaw pulsed, and his hand rested upon the hilt of his sword as if he might burst out of the longhouse and hunt down each Raven that had ever brought harm to Kari.

If I were a better man, a better friend, I would sympathize with him. But a white, hot fire scorched in my veins as I rose from my chair. "You think, for centuries, Ravenspire has used my sister's body?"

To her credit, Kari didn't crumble under the darkness of my voice. She met my glare straight on. "It is one suggestion, My King. That is all. The first thing that came to mind."

"Valen," Brant said. "If this is true, they would keep her hidden where only nobility could have access. She would be too valuable to them. I know of some brothels used only by Castle Ravenspire, used only by the kings themselves over the turns."

"Then we tear them apart," Ari said, his hands fisted over the tabletop.

"Keep your head," Tor told him. "Used could mean something more. No one knew the blade like Herja. She could be used to fight for them."

"Let us hope that is all," I said, a dark threat in my tone.

Elise must've sensed the heat of bloodlust; she'd grown too skilled at reading me, and hurried to say, "What do you think Sol meant by telling you to come home to visit him?"

My stomach cinched. The final part, I understood exactly what my brother meant. I didn't understand why, but he would not say it without a great reason. I gave her a soft smile and pressed a kiss to the palm of her hand. "I'm not sure. I think he meant bring him to Ruskig. He always called this place our home."

Mutters ran along the table as if they mulled the explanation over until it made sense.

"There is something else I want, and after what Sol has said to Elise, I think if he were here, he'd agree it is long past time," I said, blood rushing in my veins. Hells, this was like the night at my old schoolhouse when I kissed Elise Lysander for the first time. Nerves rattled me, but I spoke with conviction. "I would ask you to take vows with me, Elise. Be my queen."

Siv was the first to make a noise. She drew in a sharp breath, covering her mouth, and shuddering as if she could not contain emotions well. Mattis chuckled and drew her against his side.

Elise squeezed my hand; her eyes bounced between mine. Slowly, a soft grin teased the corners of her mouth. She trapped my face between her palms and kissed me. Unashamed, unguarded. When she pulled away, Elise left little space between our mouths, and said, "It is about time you asked, Valen Ferus."

I smiled against her lips, and pulled her in, kissing her without thought to the audience at the table.

Elise's fingers gripped my hair, the sting of the pull spurred me to my feet. I took her with me.

"Go away," I said to the others.

"Rather unkingly of you," Ari said. "You could dismiss us better. Perhaps, say: be gone with you. Or we may adjourn, or—"

I pulled back from Elise to glare at Ari. "I could take your head if you prefer."

He blew out his lips but stood. "A pointless threat. You've grown too fond of me. I'll say it again, Elise. You may still choose me."

Halvar laughed, took Kari's hand, and shoved Ari away. "Leave, you fool."

I waved them out of the longhouse and dragged Elise to the room we shared.

Behind the furs, alone, I did not hold back. The fear of watching her cross the divide to those who'd harm her collided with the undying pride to have a woman who'd walk toward danger with her head high and blade ready.

This moment didn't demand sweetness, or tenderness. This was wild, fierce, unguarded.

Her body arched into mine. Her palms tucked in the belt holding my axes around my waist. I only knew it was gone from the clatter of steel on wood. I pulled away from her long enough to tug on the back of my tunic and toss it aside.

Her fingernails dug into my skin when I lifted her and wrapped her legs around my waist.

Our mouths collided again. Teeth, tongues, and heavy breaths as I pressed her back against the wall.

Elise sighed when I dragged my mouth across the soft, delicate slope of her neck.

"I've wanted to ask you for months," I said against her skin, nipping the top of her shoulder.

She shuddered, breathless, throat bared. "What took you so long?"

My hand snaked around her back, loosening the ties of her gown, splitting the seam, until her bare flesh was hot beneath my palms. I dragged my teeth and lips across her shoulder; I brushed my thumbs over her nipples, rolling the peaks between my fingers.

"You hated the idea of vows once." Where I touched her skin, I followed with my tongue. I covered one breast with my mouth, lavishing her sweet skin until Elise writhed and whimpered.

She held the back of my head, keeping my mouth on her body. "I hated the idea of vows until a rather irritating dowry negotiator was placed in my path."

I smiled and pulled away from her skin. "Irritating?"

"Very."

A kind of growl came from my throat. I let her legs fall long enough to rid her of the rest of her woolen gown which kept too many clothes—terrible layers—between us.

"Gods, Elise." I groaned when she kissed the place over my heart, my middle, until she lowered to her knees and took my length between her soft lips, sucking and licking away drops of arousal from the tip.

A hand braced against the wall, I could not form a coherent thought, could not make a sound. My teeth clenched, one hand tangled in her hair, and I was lost in my future queen.

Elise lavished me with her kiss, her hands, her mouth until fire pulsed in my veins, and I needed to make a choice.

With a trembling hand, I gripped her chin. Her eyes shone like the sea trapped in glass. I'd never seen her look so beautiful and was damn determined to keep that look in her eyes until the bleeding dawn.

At my pause, she arched a bemused brow.

"I plan to lose control," I said, voice raw. "But I will do it with you in my arms."

I tugged her to her feet. My pulse raced; the tips of my fingers needed nothing else but to touch this woman. I pulled her to the bed, pressing a hand to her heart, until she laid back.

Our eyes met. Blue fire with midnight.

Her chest lifted in heavy breaths as my fingers traveled across her skin, memorizing over and over the smooth curves of her body, the few scars across her ribs, the soft jut of her hip bones. I pressed a kiss to each one, my hands on her thighs, settling between her legs.

Elise lifted onto her elbows and stared down at me. A look that said a thousand things. I left her with a wry smirk, a challenge, a vow of good things to come, and dipped into the wet heat of her center.

My kiss drew out short, sharp gasps as I tasted all of her. Claimed all of her.

My name from her lips unleashed a primal need for more. I relished in every glassy look, every moan. Elise pulled on my arm, drawing me up from her legs, until she crashed her mouth onto mine, so we shared the taste of her still on my tongue.

With her hand on my hip, her body beneath mine, we slid together, breathlessly taking a moment of peace in a time of corruption, of war. She set a frenzied pace. My hands curled around the furs over the bed as I murmured her name, whispering secrets only meant for her.

When tension snapped, she clawed at my back and cried out my name. I shuddered, my body set aflame as my release built, then filled her in a beautiful fog that danced from my skull down my spine.

I sank against her. For a moment I remained still, sated, and happy. A sort of happiness I never imagined until a second *Kvinna* burrowed deep into my veins.

I kissed her sweetly, then pulled her against my chest, cradling her head to my heart until the soft, steady breaths of sleep took us both.

ELISE SLEPT SOUNDLY when I crept into the great hall of the longhouse. The snap and hiss of the fire in the inglenook drew my eyes and heated the flesh of my bare chest. With my eyes clamped tightly, I turned to the table to face Halvar and Tor.

I knew they'd be back.

"Come home to visit him," Tor whispered. "The blood of the first, the middle, and the last."

I nodded, an icy chill in my heart.

"Is this why you want to take vows?" asked Halvar.

"No." It wasn't. Now, it would be logical, but it was not my reason. "I wanted to take vows with Elise Lysander before I even knew my true name. It is long overdue."

Halvar seemed pleased. "She will be a fierce queen. Like your mother."

"And you both will stand with her, defend her, fight for her if I am not here."

"Valen," Tor said. "You cannot do this."

"I have no desire to, but Sol would not ask it if it weren't important. You of all people should know that."

"But—"

"Tor," I said softly. "My brother is asking that we return to Castle Ravenspire. He knows something and needs me and Herja. Our blood. Somehow, I must find a way to go home."

"And what of Elise? She will never agree to it," Halvar said. "You cannot hide this from her."

Bleeding hells I wanted to. I wanted to protect her from the truth of the risk, the pain, from everything to do with this war. "Elise will know, but we find Herja first. That is the first step."

"She will hate you if you get yourself killed for this," Halvar warned.

I sighed and stared at the table. "Sol knows what he's asking. He would not if there were another way. If whatever Sol knows protects Elise, you, and our people, if it helps us win this war, then I will do it. But do not mistake me—by the gods, I will not stop until I fight my way back to her."

CHAPTER EIGHT
ROGUE PRINCESS

As a girl I lived in a fantasy where I would take vows in the gardens of Ravenspire. Honey cakes, mulled wines, sharp ales, and savory pheasants would stack in mountains of food. Too much to eat.

I'd wear a gown sewn in imported silks with sea pearls in intricate designs. My match would be handsome, strong, a warrior desired by everyone. The whole event would make me the envy of every woman in Mellanstrad.

A fantasy.

My vows as *Kvinna* would've never been grander than Runa's. I'd never have a warrior. A pious nobleman would be my match. A loveless, painful union to benefit the royal Timoran house. Feelings, love, none of it would matter. I'd be expected to look away as my husband took consorts, visited brothels, loved everyone but me.

But what would there have been to complain about?

I'd live in sprawling manors. Have lands to my name. Attend galas dripping in sea pearls.

In the royal longhouse, tucked away in Ruskig, without pearls and fine gowns, I smiled as the hall bustled in folk preparing bitter roots and a wild boar over the spit. Siv and Kari braided my hair. I scrubbed dirt and blood away from my fingernails.

My gown was made of handspun wool, dyed a light blue, and simple. No jewels or jade.

But the moonvane blossoms pinned in my hair glittered like silver stars. The forged iron bracelets around my wrist were in the shape of sea serpents and vines. A symbol of the strength of the Ferus line.

This day was nothing like my childhood fantasies.

It was grander in every way. From the simple meal to the fidelity of the man who'd take me as his by the end.

I scrubbed my fingers harder, anxious to begin.

When Valen made the declaration, I soon discovered taking vows during a war meant hurrying any formalities along. A little over a week later it was arranged, and the square cleared for the vows.

We'd take one day, one afternoon to celebrate, and tomorrow we'd return to the table with strategy and battles to wage.

"It's the best we can do," Siv said, holding her hands away from my hair.

"Exactly the words every bride wants to hear on the day she takes vows." Kari snickered and added a final blossom to the long, detailed braid down my back.

"There are no pretenses here. We were drawing blood from each other yesterday. We do not do fine, dainty things," said Siv with a grin. She met my gaze in the silver mirror. "But you look exactly like the queen we need, Elise."

I rolled my eyes and tied the end of the plaits with a gold ribbon, edged in chips of sapphires.

"From Junius?" Siv asked, helping to tie the final knot.

"Yes." I grinned. "Her letter was strongly worded with her opinions about us not giving her time to return for the vows."

Kari laughed. "I'm surprised she'd want to return. This land held her prisoner."

"No," Siv said. "She was taken by her own folk in the East and traded here. To me it sounds like the Eastern Kingdom is as brutal as this one."

"I promised I would not ask her to ever return here unless it were a dire need," I told them. "Still, it was kind of her to send the gift."

"Pity Ravenspire hasn't sent anything. Ari and Mattis made sure to send their notice first." Siv winked as she secured a soft stole of fox fur around my shoulders. Her eyes misted when she took me in. She clasped my hands. "There. Perfect."

I pulled her into a tight embrace, the burn of tears stinging my eyes. "Thank you, Siv. For always being a true friend."

She buried her face against my shoulder and tightened her hold on my waist. To Siv, she had not always been a true friend. Sent to me as an Agitator assassin. But she never killed me, never tried. She was protective and fought for me every step of the journey to this moment.

She freed a shaky breath. "I wish Mavs were here."

"All gods, she'd be chattering nonstop, wouldn't she?" We laughed together and pulled away. After a moment my smile faded. "I miss her too."

Kari let us have the time, silently cleaning up the room until a heavy-handed knock thudded against the doorjamb.

Mattis peeked around the fur curtain. "Ready?"

Siv drew in a sharp breath, her eyes roving over him with a heated stare. Mattis didn't seem to mind in the least. I laughed but could understand the feeling. "You look handsome, my friend. I think Siv would agree."

"She would," Siv whispered.

Mattis rocked on his toes. Dressed in a fine black tunic, his beard trimmed into dark stubble, and his hair combed back. Even the dagger strapped across his shoulders and the seax blade on his waist gleamed brightly, polished and buffed.

I linked my arm with Mattis, smiling. "Siv, you'll need to wait until I'm through with him."

She clicked her tongue. "Then begone. Hurry. Our king will start to worry you've changed your mind."

"Or she will shove me aside simply to get her hands on you," I whispered to Mattis.

He clenched his jaw to keep from laughing and led me through the longhouse.

Siv and Kari stayed close, but out in the hall the bustle stopped. The women and men preparing the feast paused and dipped their chins. My face heated. It had been so long since I'd been treated as a royal, I'd forgotten how I hated the attention.

Outside, a cart awaited to drive us to the square. Blossoms draped over the sides, doubtless to hide the stains of blood and mud, but it was the best we had. No hansom cabs. No fine coaches. I'd take the muddy cart over them without question.

A pathway sprinkled in lilies, moonvane, and rose petals carved through the crowds of people all the way to the square.

Mattis smiled and squeezed my hand before helping me onto the front bench of the cart. Stieg controlled the reins. He winked as I nestled close to him to make room for Mattis on my other side, then gathered the leather harnesses on the two mares. "Ready, Elise?"

"Everyone keeps asking me that." I closed my eyes, the sun warming my cheeks. "Hells, I'm so ready. I've been ready for this day long before he was a king. Get a move on, Stieg, or I'm walking."

He scoffed and cracked the reins. With a jolt the cart moved forward. A wave of folk lowered to their knees, then followed us. Stieg kept the cart rumbling at an impossibly slow pace. My knee bounced. My stomach backflipped.

Above us banners of the Ferus seal and small lanterns dangled from tree limbs. It could've been my own excitement, but it seemed the moonvane glistened in sharper silver, with larger petals than before.

When I thought my heart might snap through my ribs if we didn't move faster, the cart rounded a corner, and we met the end of the pathway. My breath stilled in my chest.

At the square border an archway of colorful berries and ribbons marked the end of the path.

Beneath the archway stood Valen.

He'd kept his eyes on the ground, shifting on his feet, until the cart came into sight. The king lifted his eyes, and if I could bottle the smile on his face into a memory that would never fade, I'd cross all the kingdoms to find the magic to do it.

Tradition insisted the partner vowing into the royal line walk to meet the blood king or queen. But Valen Ferus was not one for following rules or traditions.

The instant the cart rolled to a stop, the king abandoned the archway and hurried to my side. Mattis purposely stood in his way, determined to serve his role as my escort. "Your future husband is crowding me, Elise."

"I am your king and want you to move," Valen grumbled.

"Today I serve the queen," Mattis said, taking my hand. "By the hells, you'll touch her in a few moments. I'm supposed to give her hand to you. Do it right, my impatient king, or do not do it."

I laughed loudly when Valen reluctantly took a step back. We had a rather strange kingdom, where Valen cared less about formalities than he did about loyalty. No king I ever knew would allow his people to speak to him in such a way, but most of his inner council did without a second thought.

Mattis held out his hand. "Lady Elise."

I ignored his hand and hugged him the same as I hugged Siv. "You are a true friend, Mattis."

He wrapped his thick arms around me, voice low. "As are you, My Queen."

With a smile, Mattis took my hand and turned us toward Valen. I met his eyes; a blur of tears distorted his beautiful face. He looked like a king. The light in his eyes caused the darkness to shine like a starry night. A heady hint of pine spice and woodsmoke on his skin drew me closer. Instead of his Blood Wraith axes, he wore a blacksteel sword on his hip, and on his wrists were the same iron bracelets as mine.

"You are beautiful." Valen lifted my knuckles to his lips, eyes never leaving mine. "I have wanted this since I first met you, Elise Lysander."

"Liar."

"Ah, you want the truer, less romantic version. Fine. I have wanted this day since I realized the woman I was using to break a curse had stolen my heart, and I suddenly cared a great deal if she lived. Better?"

I laughed and went to kiss him but was stopped by an arm that seemed to materialize out of nowhere.

"No." Halvar glared at us both. "Not until the end. Gods, do either of you know how to do a vow? Go. Walk forward and we will be done with it."

Valen kissed my hand again, then laced my arm through his. A hum of energy, from fury or the race of my pulse filled the space between us. My body trembled in anticipation when we stepped beneath the archway and into the square.

On either side of the arch, two women draped our shoulders in fur cloaks, then painted runes on both our foreheads.

Valen covered my hand on his arm with his other hand. We shared a look, one of meaning, one rife in excitement, in desire.

Together we stepped into the sunlight, eyes locked on the dais where Elder Klok stood, dressed in a black pelt and a bear head hood. The path was lined by our people. Herbs were tossed at our feet in blessings. Hands laced small bones and wooden runes on our clothing as we took the slow, steady steps to our future.

At the end of the path, Tor stepped out on Valen's side, Siv on mine. With a nod from Klok, we both bent a knee and our friends placed circlets of silver on our heads.

"Rise," Klok said softly.

My throat tightened as Valen helped me back to my feet. I didn't know if we were supposed to step away from each other, but I didn't care. I squeezed all my nerves into his hand and remained at his shoulder.

Klok laced his fingers in front of his body and looked between us. "Ettan vows are distinct and simple. But fiercely meaningful. I urge you both to hear each word and keep it in your heart until your last breath." He faced Valen first. "Valen, son of Arvad, son of Lilianna, King of Etta, by your mind and your heart you have chosen to walk this life with one who will be a helpmate, friend, lover, and companion. Do you make this choice of your own desire?"

"Yes," Valen said with the dip of his chin.

Klok faced me next. I didn't breathe. I didn't want to miss a word. "Elise, I have thought a great deal of what to say here. By your own word, you have denied any blood family—"

"Daughter of Mara," I whispered. "I am the daughter of Mara."

Valen tightened his hold on my hand.

Klok smiled with a nod. "Elise, daughter of Mara, consort and liberator of the King of Etta, by your mind and your heart you have chosen to walk this life with one who will be a helpmate, friend, lover, and companion. Do you make this choice of your own desire?"

"Absolutely. Yes." A rumble of laughter went through the crowd.

Klok gestured for our hands. He maneuvered us to stand in front of each other. Valen's eyes were bright and glassy. I took a step closer, and still felt too distant. Klok laid a linen over our hands with words of the final, sealing vow of Ettan ceremonies.

In Lilianna's journal I read the words once. Now, about to read them for myself, I thought my heart might swell three sizes too big.

Valen cleared his throat and said, "Elise, daughter of Mara, consort and liberator of my life, you are the choice of my heart. I vow to serve you, to love you, to honor you, to be your loyal companion for life and into the Otherworld."

He added another kiss to my knuckles.

My knees danced under my gown as if my legs begged me to run to him, to touch him, kiss him.

Only a little longer. "Valen, son of Arvad, son of Lilianna, My King, you are, and have always been, the choice of my heart. I vow to serve you, to love you, to honor you, to be your loyal companion for life and into the Otherworld."

"You changed it," he whispered. "Unfair."

I smiled, starting to bounce on my toes, moments away from screeching at Elder Klok to end the ceremony. I had a king to kiss.

Klok offered a toothy grin and looked to the crowd. "By the gods, I present King Valen Ferus and our new queen, Elise Lysander Ferus." Klok leaned into me and whispered, "Now, My Queen. You may touch him now."

I needed no more of a nudge than that. My arms wrapped

around Valen's neck, he trapped my face, and kissed me. Hard. Each taste of him left me greedy for more. I had loved him since he was Legion Grey, the Blood Wraith, and the Night Prince.

No mistake, I loved him more now.

I pulled away, tears on my cheeks, smiling as the crowd cheered. He kissed me quickly a few more times, a bright, genuine grin on his face. This moment, this was what I would hold to in the days to come. Days that would be trying, but in this moment I had never been happier.

Valen Ferus was my husband.

We lifted our joined hands to our people, and they lowered to their knees.

In my mind nothing could dampen the moment, until I caught sight of a group of men near the back of the square. Stave, and others. They lowered to their knees, slowly, reluctantly. But I could not mistake the loathing in their eyes as they looked at me.

Their new, Timoran queen. And they hated me.

CHAPTER NINE
ROGUE PRINCESS

There was no time to worry about Stave and his tantrum over a Timoran taking the throne.

Folk surrounded us at once, leading us back to the cart, tossing more petals, more bones, and herbs with their blessings until we were driven to the royal longhouse for the feast and celebration.

Fury must have stretched the longhouse. I had no other explanation for how most of Ruskig stuffed inside the walls.

Valen sat beside me at the head of the great hall, his hand possessively on my leg, my head on his shoulder. All around people laughed, drank ale straight from ewers, danced to lyres and hide drums. They were happy, and I could not look away.

Here, we could pretend there were no enemies beyond the walls.

Here, we could be at peace, even for one night.

Whenever someone passed where we sat, they'd bow, sometimes drunk and snickering, but they'd address me as queen. The word had yet to settle right in my ear.

I was not born to be a queen. Never aspired to be one.

In truth, I didn't know how to be one now.

As if he sensed the unease, Valen squeezed my hand and leaned close to my ear. "You look terrified of the word." He snorted a laugh, his thumb drawing seductive circles on my leg. "Queen. You despise the title."

"I don't despise it. I'm unaccustomed to it, and like another monarch I know, don't particularly enjoy every eye on me at every moment."

"I don't know what you mean," he said. "I love folk fawning over me. The more exuberant they are in their adoration, the more satisfaction I take from it."

"Pity," I said, taking a drink of sweet wine. "Your repulsion toward a royal pedestal is one of the things I loved so much about you."

Valen laughed and kissed the side of my head, drawing me closer. His breath teased the curve of my ear when he lowered his voice and whispered, "What troubles you about the crown, Elise? Tell me, and I will not stop until I take it away."

Brutal. Kind. Fierce. Gentle. A collision of opposites made up Valen Ferus. It was no wonder I loved the man to the depths of my soul. He could be all those things and leave me feeling safe and empowered in every breath.

I let out a sigh, running my fingers across his chest. "Timoran queens were figureheads, pretty trophies for their husbands, but power remained with the king. Your world, the world of your parents, all of Etta is different than the world in which I was raised. This crown—I have no idea what I am supposed to do."

"This is your world too. I assure you, the land we see now is not the land of my parents. It will be ours." Valen rubbed the ends of my missing fingertips, the only blood he'd ever spilled of mine when his mind was cursed and polluted with bloodlust. "You have always been my equal; titles mean nothing to me. But now, to these people, your word will carry the same as mine. When Sol, my father, and I were imprisoned by King Eli, my mother raised our armies. She and Dagar were the ones who created Ruskig as a refuge. You have the same power, and I trust you to lead here the same as my father trusted my mother."

Valen paused. A muscle tightened in his jaw as he watched the celebration unfold. "Elise, even as a child I knew my parents were equals. They worked together. No strategy was made without my mother's approval, and when they were able, decisions were made together. I promised your mother before she died, you would never have reason to fear me, and you would have all of me. You do have all of me. There is no one I would rather share this burden with, no one I trust it with more than you."

He tapped the silver circlet on his head.

I studied our laced fingers. "I am Timoran, and I am not convinced everyone will take orders from a Timoran queen."

Valen used his knuckle to tilt my chin up. "Then you do not give them a choice. You, my love, have a gentle image of my mother, I think. You've only read her writings as she speaks of her family. The woman came from raiders and warriors like you, and she was unafraid to gut a man if her family were ever threatened. She did, more than once." He paused and pressed the back of my hand to his lips. "You never were for Timoran or Etta, Elise. You were always for fairness, for people. Do not forget the first time I saw you, sneaking away from a serf gambling table. Or the first real conversation we had."

I scoffed. "I remember. You were rather arrogant, you know."

He grinned. "I was confused. You made no sense. A *Kvinna* hiding on the balcony, wanting to do more, be more. Not for herself, but for others. You mesmerized me that night, and you have never stopped."

"You say the right things, Valen Ferus." My fingertips touched the sharp line of his jaw. I leaned in to kiss him but jolted back when the slap of a hand on the table drew a quiet to the longhouse.

Halvar stood in the center, drinking horn raised. "To our king and new queen." The people cheered, some drank to us, some began to dance again until Halvar held up a hand. "We have gifts. Of course, keep in mind we are in the middle of a war and live in a refuge. Imagine we are in the old courts and are showering you in fine things."

Valen rolled his eyes. I laughed, as Halvar snapped his fingers and the Guild of Shade hurried to us. Casper and Stieg stepped forward first. In their hands were blades, both wrapped in skins.

"Been working on these since we left the fight at Ravenspire," Stieg said. "Figured this day was coming.

My mouth dropped as I gingerly fingered the polished edge of the dagger. The hilt gleamed in untouched bronze, and in the center a smooth, glassy crystal caught the firelight, breaking into a prism of color.

Valen was gifted its equal, but in the hilt was a black onyx stone.

"From a court of ice," Casper whispered, pointing to my dagger. "Your people were strong, resilient against the harshest lands."

"To a court of fire and fury." Stieg gestured to Valen's blade. "One burned to ash, but together, we have no doubt you will restore a land greater than what any Timoran or Ettan has ever known."

"These are beautiful," I whispered.

"I didn't know you two were so poetic. You ought to write the sagas." Valen laughed when Casper shoved his shoulder.

A council member shoving a king. I smiled, thinking I preferred our court of ice and ash over anything I'd seen before.

Halvar and Tor gave nothing to Valen, insisting it was penance for all the grief he caused them as boys, but they had a silver ring made for me. Shaped like a moonvane blossom with the crest of the Ferus line engraved on the band.

Valen slipped it over my finger, kissing the top, then returned his attention to the furs, the quilts, and herbs some of the people offered. Next Ari, Mattis, and Siv came forward.

"Have it known, this was my idea," Ari said with a touch of mischief.

"Untrue. You suggested them as a gift, that is the extent of your idea," said Mattis.

Ari waved him away. "The details don't truly matter. Elise, I know how fond you are of reading. With great effort I have—" He grunted when Siv elbowed him. "Several of us thought to gift you something of a relic from the courts of King Arvad and Queen Lilianna."

Valen sat straighter as they pushed a wrapped parcel to us. With unsteady hands, I pulled away the skins and held a stack of old, wrinkled parchment.

"What are these?"

Siv stepped forward, a sad smile on her face. "When Queen Lilianna was in captivity at Ravenspire, she wrote missives. We don't know who they were written to, but we thought you might find some comfort, maybe wisdom in them."

Valen touched the parchment with a bit of reverence. "I've never heard of these."

"Nor had we," said Ari.

"When did you find them?"

"Axel," Siv hurried to say. "Before either of these two sods takes another lick of credit, Axel found them and had them in his possession."

My eyes lifted to a place halfway down the long table. Frey chuckled and clapped his brother on his shoulder. Axel returned a gentle nod, his face buried in red heat. Going out on a limb, I'd guess the man would rather do without the credit.

But Valen wouldn't stand for it. "Axel, where did you find these?"

He let out a long breath, and when his brow furrowed, he reminded me a great deal of his brother. Axel stood taller, but with less bulk and brawn than Frey. He spoke softly and had a wickedly cunning mind from what I'd witnessed in the townships. Axel had a way with folk, he helped soothe skirmishes, and had already devised places to dig fresh-water wells to avoid trekking back and forth to the river.

"My time in chains was spent with many traders, My King. When I learned of the missives, I could not allow something so valuable to Etta to be traded between men who cared nothing for the queen."

"You stole them from a trader? Without being caught?"

Axel's face deepened with stark red. "Unfortunate, but the master who last owned them became quite ill that very night. I'm afraid he never saw the sunrise."

The room silenced for no more than three breaths. All at once deep, booming laughter shook the walls, and rattled the ale on the table. Casper, with his thick meaty hands gripped Axel's shoulders, shaking him. "You bleeding sod. Poisoned him, did you?"

Axel pinched his lips. "I admit nothing."

It only caused more laughter, more drinking. I cared little if Axel cut out the serf trader's throat, and I let my fingers trace the rough edges of the stacked parchment.

New writings, new words. Words Valen had never seen. Part of me wanted to slip away and read through them now. What was life like for Lilianna as Eli's prisoner, what did she know, what did she learn?

"Thank you," I said. "All of you."

Tor rose and came to Valen's side. "There is one more." He held a small box in his hands and regarded Valen with a touch of caution. "It was not from us and bears the mark of Ravenspire. Found at the walls."

The longhouse fell into an abrupt, unsettling hush. Only the crackle and spitting fire made a sound.

Valen rose to his feet and snatched the box from Tor before he could even set it down. His eyes flicked to me. "It is for you."

My stomach turned sour. "Runa knows."

"You don't need to—"

"No," I said, reaching for the box. "This is the game, Valen. She is beginning to set her moves, and I must meet her there."

He gripped the box for a long moment, before giving in and handing it to me. Ashamed how my hands trembled, I sat, desperate to hide them from the gawking eyes of the room.

Inside was a handwritten note placed over something small and wrapped in cloth.

Mother would want you to have her ring for your vows, sister.

I set the note aside, allowing Valen to see it, then slowly reached inside the box, removing the cloth.

A strangled noise came from my throat. I bolted to my feet. The box fell off my lap. My blood went cold in my veins. Frigid, wretched anger flooded my mind and body as a blackened, scabrous finger rolled onto the floor.

A sapphire and gold ring still attached.

Horrified gasps pounded off the walls of the longhouse as folk who'd seen blood and gore ran from the dead finger of my mother as it went still on the floorboards.

I wanted to retch.

Valen was at my side in a moment. Hatred and bloodlust burned in his eyes. I understood and felt much the same.

I did not know how long I stood there, staring at the ring, hating everything about Ravenspire. But when I looked at the stunned faces again there was sympathy written in some of the eyes.

I didn't want sympathy.

I wanted blood.

My fists clenched at my sides. Valen's hand on the small of my back fueled me.

"When we face Castle Ravenspire," I raised my voice so there would be no question, so no one would miss my words, "no one is to touch the false queen. Understand me—Runa Lysander of Ravenspire is mine to kill."

CHAPTER TEN
NIGHT PRINCE

My friend,

Betrayal has placed my husband and sons in the hands of a man I once considered a dear friend. Such hate fills my blood. Such violence.

I wish him the most painful death for what he has done to my family and our people. You once told me he is fated to strengthen the limbs of my family's legacy, but I refuse to allow it.

I will cut him from the branches, then watch him bleed.

I need you. Your guidance. I'm not strong enough to face what you insist is to come. I will not face it. The suffering, the pain. Help me save them. Help me save us all.

—Lili

For a week now, when the moon rose to its highest point, I'd wake to Elise standing at the window, studying the stars. Most nights, I gave her the peace, but no longer.

I vowed to be her companion, her friend, her lover. What a poor habit it would be to begin our life together by keeping burdens hidden inside.

Careful not to make any noise, I slipped out of the bed, and crossed the space between us.

She jumped when my arms curled around her waist, but in another breath, her head fell back against my bare chest.

"You are warm," she whispered.

"There is a warmer bed behind us." I kissed the slope of her neck.

"I can't sleep."

"I said nothing of sleep." Her elbow met my ribs, drawing out a soft grunt and laugh. "What's troubling you?"

"Herja. Ravenspire. There is a stillness, and I hate it. Like a calm before a storm, it feels as if we are simply waiting for my sister and Calder to make the move. I want to be steps ahead of them, but feel lengths behind."

I spun her around to meet her gaze. My palms cupped her face. "We are not lengths behind. Calder has no move to make. My brother is no longer in their control—"

"Why?" she interrupted. "What happened to Sol? How is his mind restored?" She paused to look at me. "Why are you all alive? I don't understand the purpose."

I shook my head. "I don't know."

"I think it's more. You didn't see Leif's eyes up close. He was angry they'd lost their manipulation over the Sun Prince, but he wouldn't kill him. He wanted Sol alive more than me. They know something," she insisted, "some reason, some fury—something— we do not know."

"But we can't dwell on what Ravenspire might know and what we don't. We focus on what we do know. Because my brother has his mind, we know Herja is alive. We must assume Ravenspire isn't aware of her, or at least they don't realize we are." I tucked a lock of stray hair behind her ear. "Elise, it is to our benefit if Sol cannot be controlled. Having him in Ravenspire gives him the chance to fight for us from the inside."

"Unless they're torturing him." I closed my eyes, stiff and cold until her palms touched my chest. "I'm sorry, Valen. Words are just coming out."

"It's the truth. It is nothing I don't think about myself." True enough, I knew Sol was likely mistreated daily, and it added a heavy layer of urgency in the pit of my gut, weighing each step. "I share your frustration, Elise. But exhausting yourself with no sleep will not bring us closer to Herja or Sol."

"We've been unable to learn anything of your sister."

"We will. We keep looking, keep searching. Ari and Casper will be going to a dock brothel tomorrow." The notion drew bile to the back of my throat. While half the Shade searched brothels, the others scouted Raven units. But as much as I hated to admit it, according to Kari and Brant, if a fierce female fighter were part of the Ravenspire guard, it would be known.

Unlike Ettans, Timorans had yet to realize their females could learn a blade as well as the men. To have a Ferus princess wielding a sword, at the least, there would be rumors.

In truth, enslaving Herja to the pleasures of Ravenspire was the sort of cruelty fitting for the bastards in the castle. And I could not think too long on it, or the dormant bloodlust simmered to the surface, and I feared I might slaughter anyone who stood half a step in my way.

I forced the thoughts to the back of my head. A furrow deepened over Elise's brow, and it would stop if I had any say.

I pulled us away from the window. "Come with me."

Past the bed, into the hall, I took us toward the door of the longhouse.

"Valen," she whispered roughly. "Where are we going?"

"Away."

Ruskig slept. Only the light of the moon and a few posts with lanterns lit the muddy roads and sod rooftops. The night was calm and warm. A few night patrols strode through the darkened shanties and walls, singing folk songs and staring at the stars.

Elise snickered, tightening her grip on my hand, when I led us into the trees. Thieves in the night in our own kingdom.

A back wall kept Ruskig from the view of the sea, but we had crevices and secret holes where we could send ships or trade to what few allies we had in the East and hoped to gain in the South.

Guards and archers tromped in a steady march atop the scaffolding overhead.

I held Elise against my chest, my back to the wall as a pair of our guards went by. She shuddered, and I took a bit of pleasure knowing she was laughing instead of locked in tension and worry.

"Hiding from your own guards."

"The life of a royal," I whispered against her ear. "You should know this more than anyone."

"I've missed sneaking past guards."

As the thud of boots faded above us, I turned us to the wall. "Go. Hurry."

Elise's white smile broke the syrupy night. She didn't hesitate, didn't question, and slipped through the narrow break in the wall until brine and damp filled our lungs. We ducked into the few aspen and spruce trees that led to the pebbled shores, and as soil transformed into sloped rocky water edges, Elise's smile widened.

A moment later, moonlight cracked over the black glass of the narrow fjord. A gentle push and pull of ripples on the shore soothed fear. The chilly, clean air of the sea chased away battle. Out here was empty of carnage and blood. This was where peace lived.

Even if it only survived by moonlight.

Elise released my hand and stepped onto the white pebbles, passing fishing nets and traps, drawing her hands alongside the few longboats we had. At the edge of the water, she slipped off her shoes, gasping when the chill of the water touched her toes.

A smile curved at the corner of my lips. In the light of moon, her pale hair gleamed. She looked like part of the starlight. Through all the turns of living a cursed life, all of it, every moment, seemed wholly worthwhile to be here with her.

I hooked a finger behind the neck of my tunic, tugging it over my head as I joined her at the water's edge.

She widened her eyes, drawing her bottom lip between her teeth, when I worked my belt, then sloughed off my boots and pants.

"I didn't see all this coming," Elise said, drawing her fingertips across the planes of my stomach. "Not that I'm complaining."

I grinned a little viciously and stepped into the water. "Come with me."

Elise hesitated. Her eyes following me as I sank into the water. Finally, she unlaced her chemise. Her body bared in the dimness. Beautiful. Perfect. She shivered when she treaded the shore until her skin was buried in the black water.

I pulled her against me, arms curled around her waist. She tangled her legs around mine.

"What are we doing out here?" She studied my lips with her fingers, adding seductive, gentle kisses to the point of my ear, my jaw, my shoulder.

"Those rooms, that refuge, is suffocating you," I said gently.

"When there is a problem I can't solve, stepping away clears my head. Thought it might do the same for you."

One hand stroked the slender curve of her back, the other on her thigh, higher and higher until Elise drew in a sharp, quivering breath. Her legs tightened around me. "I'm not so sure you brought me out here to clear my head at all."

"True. I came to swim." I released her, so she let out a shriek and sank to her chin. "I don't know what you're thinking."

Her laughter muffled when I dove under the water, swimming away from her. It took only another breath before Elise followed. Numb in the cold, alone in the night, we did forget about war and death. This night belonged to us. Playing, trading kisses, teasing.

When I fell in love with Elise, these nights were what I imagined; they were the ideas I clung to. A land where we had the freedom to love each other completely and unapologetically.

Elise had her arms wrapped around my neck, clinging to my back, by the time I started to swim back to shore. The closer we came, the trickier her mouth grew. Slowly, her lips teased the edge of my ear. She nipped at my neck, her hands roving across my chest and middle under the water.

"Elise, I will drown if you keep doing that." The wrong—or right—thing to say.

Elise put more passion behind her mouth. Her tongue and teeth teased my shoulder, her hand slid down my stomach, gripping my length in her fingers.

I let out a harsh breath and maneuvered so we were chest to chest as the gentle tug of the tide pushed us to the shore. When the sand and smooth stones hit my back, I pulled us most of the way out of the water, spread the crumpled pile of my clothes beneath me, and held Elise as she leveraged into a straddle over my hips.

I kissed her; my fingers twisted around her soaked hair. A

sharp heat from her fingernails scraping my wet skin drew out a rough groan.

"I don't want gentle, My King," she said when I took a soft nip of her neck.

Gods, this woman.

I tugged on her hips and slid inside her with a grunt.

Elise clung to my neck, gasping over my shoulder as we rocked together, taking and giving. Free to unleash.

I gripped her jaw and drew her face into my line of sight so I could hold her gaze. Her fingers tangled in my hair as I answered her plea for passion, not gentility, and ground our hips together until no space was between us.

Elise tossed her head back. "Valen . . . more."

I rolled her onto her back. One hand beneath her head and the pebbled beach, I hooked one of her legs higher on my waist, filling her deeper, harder.

Elise bucked her hips. She took all of me. I thrust into her wet core in a frenzy, losing myself in my wife, my lover, my friend. Pleasure numbed my mind. All I could do was sink into a rough, primal instinct to feel, to please this woman who'd captured me, body and soul.

"All gods," I said, voice dark and low as Elise's whimpers turned to breathless, ragged gasps next to my ear.

Elise drew in a sharp breath, shuddered, and froze. Sound strangled in her throat. Her fingers dug into my hair, the bite of pain on my scalp was the final push to toss me over the edge.

One heavy thrust, two, and my length twitched, spilling my release inside her. It was blinding, powerful, like the crash of waves beyond the fjord, setting the whole of my body on fire.

I lifted my gaze to hers. The icy gold of her hair was sprawled across the dark beach. Moonlight revealed the pink flush to her face. Elise's lips were parted, her fingertips gingerly touched my jaw, like she wanted to relearn everything about me.

I kissed her, nipping her bottom lip. Words for how much I loved her escaped me in the moment. I would burn every piece of this land for her. I'd slaughter anyone who brought her heart pain.

I once told her my heart beat for her, and I meant every word. My name breathing off her lips. Her eyes closing. Her touch heating my body.

All this beat for her.

It always would.

A SLIVER of pink sunlight crested in the distance. Elise nestled against my chest, head on my heart. My eyes closed, wholly at ease.

"Valen."

"Hmm."

"I think I know how to find Herja."

I lifted my head from the pebbles. "How?"

Elise's jaw tightened. Ah, I had a feeling I wouldn't like it. "You keep sending men to the brothels posing as patrons. But I don't think that's going to work. The pleasure mates won't speak to patrons. They don't trust them."

True. "What do you suggest?"

She swallowed with effort. "I go instead."

"Elise—"

"Hear me out." Elise sat up. I propped onto my elbows, fighting every impulse to instantly refuse whatever she was about to say. Elise hugged her knees to her chest, voice soft. "Send me,

Kari, and Siv into the brothels as new mates. We'd be trusted faster and might be able to learn something."

I shook my head but stopped when she placed a palm on my cheek.

"Valen, we are equals, right?"

"Yes, but—"

"Then why are you the one who takes all the risks while I keep our bed warm, tucked safely away in Ruskig?"

"I recall you leaping off a cliff after crossing into a unit of Ravens not long ago."

She chuckled. "And did the risk pay off? I believe I came bearing messages from the Sun Prince."

"I could've done without the leaping off a cliff part."

"Me too." Elise's smile faded. "This would not require leaping off cliffsides, and I wouldn't be alone."

"Elise, you're asking me to put my wife in a position where a patron could purchase her. Then what?"

She smiled a violent sort. "Have more faith in my ability to draw blood, my love." Elise kissed me slowly. Hells, this was pure manipulation. She knew how to wreck any walls, any reservations removed with her wicked touch. "Admit it, Night Prince," she whispered against my lips. "You see the brilliance in my plan."

I hated to admit sneaking into brothels from the other side made a bit of sense. Doubtless the pleasure mates knew more about the inner workings of the wretched system than anyone. If Elise could learn of secret brothels, or rumors of anyone who could possibly be Herja, we would have a direction.

And as the sun broke through the night, I had to admit we did not have much of any direction. The longer we remained here, unmoving pieces in this game, the more of an advantage Ravenspire would have.

Still, I didn't have to like it.

"We are there," I said. "As patrons, in the trees, under the beds, I don't bleeding care. If anyone puts a hand on any of you, they die."

Her eyes brightened. "Agreed. But you must give us a chance to play the part. You cannot be cutting out eyes if a patron looks at me."

"I refuse to promise such a thing and reserve the right to take at least one eye as a warning."

She laughed and curled her arms around my neck, holding me close. "We'll find her, Valen. I swear to you."

I buried my face in her neck.

Yes, we'd find Herja. We'd rescue Sol.

I had to hold to the hope of reuniting with my brother and sister, of learning why we were kept alive, but I could not lose Elise in the process.

I would not.

CHAPTER ELEVEN
ROGUE PRINCESS

"They wear more paint on the lips," Frey said. He flushed when half the men standing around watching, speared him in sharp looks. "What? I don't patron the brothels. I liberate them, but I've seen plenty of pleasure mates."

"There are some things better kept private, little brother." Axel gripped his brother's shoulder and offered a forced sympathetic look.

"I don't use brothels," Frey insisted. "I don't need them."

"Right," Ari muttered and turned back to where Siv finished painting my face.

"Bleeding fools." Frey shook Axel off and slammed his fist into his brother's shoulder, moving to the back of the crowd, enduring a few chuckles at his expense.

A group of us remained in our camp beyond the hills of a northern township called Bordell. The wretched little place was tucked on the outskirts of the kingdom, in the crosswinds of the pass that would lead travelers to the wastes of Old Timoran. Here, even the brownest, driest grass struggled to grow. Trees were naked, like the bones of a corpse, and every corner reeked of piss and dried skin.

The Guild of Shade would surround the brothel, near enough we could call for help should anything go awry inside, but far enough they wouldn't be suspicious. Some of the inner council—those who'd served in distinguished homes or had lived a more distinguished life—would enter as patrons.

Crispin and a few of his men had once been serfs for noblemen. They'd be the eyes outside the brothel, and it added a bit of relief knowing Frey and Axel would be inside with us.

"I still think you should let me inside," Ari insisted. "I was once a king after all."

"Your face was seen too much among those who know Elise," Brant said.

He kept rubbing his head like it ached but insisted he could not make sense of the magic in his blood tonight. Junie had named him an Alver like her, one who could predict or see visions. I didn't let on how Brant's uneasiness added to my own. If something weighed heavy on him, odds were there was danger to be found here tonight.

"We can't risk anyone recognizing you, Ari," Tor added.

"I am an illusionist."

"And will be kept busy enough concealing all the damn fae ears," Stieg insisted, flicking the sharp points of Casper's ears.

Ari muttered under his breath but turned away. There was a part of me that shared his disappointment. If Valen could not be at our sides, Ari, Halvar, or Tor were the ones I'd want in his place. But they would not be inside the brothel. They'd remain with the king.

I trusted most of the council but could not shake the unease that continued to ripple over my skin every time too many of them were near.

But at least we had Frey and his brother; they would be loyal.

Valen had been reluctantly convinced to remain by the trees. His temper when it came to his queen reared too fiercely and with too much of his former bloodlust. He was more a liability should he come inside the brothel.

Valen frowned in the back, arms folded over his chest. I gave him a significant look, warning him to stand back. To trust me.

His frown carved deeper lines into his face.

The king had said very little since Halvar and Tor returned from the barter. I'd officially been sold as a pleasure mate to the Bordell brothel. Kari and Siv along with me.

"They did not think my price was fair, but I would not sell my love for anything less," Halvar had teased Kari.

I'd learned as much about the first knight that he hid much of his disquiet behind witty words and laughter. Still, the way he remained close to Kari I suspected he had the same worries as our king.

"We're out of time," Casper insisted. "The meet is within the hour."

Valen cursed under his breath and cut his way through the group, taking my hand. "I don't like this."

"We're only going to be with the mates." I flattened a palm over his chest. "And once we find out what they know, we'll leave. Be ready to catch us."

He kissed me deeply, lingering as though it might be a final touch.

"No cutting out eyes," I whispered, stroking my fingers down his cheek.

"No promises." Valen gave a curt nod to Casper who'd drive us to the meet with the Mistress of the House.

Mattis took Siv's face between his palms, whispering against her lips, careful not to disturb the disguise, then pressed a kiss to her knuckles. It took longer for Halvar to release Kari. He cared little if her red lips smeared, and devoured her mouth until she laughed and had to shove him away.

"Try not to kill them all," he called after her. "We may need to question some."

"That man will ruin me," she said as we walked away.

"But it will be enjoyable as he does it," I returned.

Kari grinned, gifting herself a last look. "Very."

In the back of the cart, I held Siv's hand on one side, and Kari's on the other. The wheels seemed to fumble over every notch in the road; each divot bounced us around until my back ached.

"There will be a dominant pleasure mate," Kari said. "They survive by being popular. Don't speak to the leader. They will not be helpful; they'll view us as competition. Go for frightened little pups. Understood?"

Both Siv and I nodded at once.

At the base of the hillside a black coach, lined with three burly men in waistcoats, awaited our arrival.

The center man stroked his long beard and fiddled with a strand of bone beads braided along the ends. He held up a hand for Casper.

"Mistress DeMark will inspect the trade here."

Casper grunted. He moved like a man with stones in his boots and too many cricks in his back. Better to look feeble and roughly made around folk as this. Dignified traders didn't spare serfs and warm bodies to brothels tucked in the slums of the kingdom.

With a breathy rasp, he uncoupled the back of the cart, and whistled at the three of us to move.

"Apologies, My Queen," he whispered as I stumbled out the back of the wagon.

I ignored him and lifted my chin to face the underbelly of my former home.

Until Siv jutted her elbow between my ribs.

"Head down," she hissed. "You're nothing here."

I obeyed, watching the sludge squish between the thin leather straps serving as tattered shoes. When one of the brothel's men grabbed my arm too forcefully, instinct demanded I shirk him off, perhaps ram the dagger hidden on my thigh through his belly. But I froze. Complied. Truth be told when the door of the brothel coach groaned open, it didn't take much to tremble with a bit of fear.

The rustle of satin. The reek of too many roses. A smoke-eaten voice. "Let us see what you have purchased, Mikal."

A woman's touch—in my experience—had always been gentler than most men. Not the Mistress of Bordell. Her spindly fingers dug into my chin, lifting my gaze. The mistress had red painted cheeks and too much kohl surrounding her sharp, icy blue eyes. Her hair was ratted and piled in old, musty-looking curls atop her head.

She boasted a fine dress, but on a closer inspection there were clear signs that seams had been restitched more than once, and she attempted to hide snags in the fine satin with false gemstones and bone beads.

"Skinny," she said. "But good teeth and no pocks."

She went on to inspect Siv and Kari. Siv had her dark hair inspected for sores on her head, Kari was named broad and too strong, to be reserved for large patrons to manhandle.

Halvar would tear out their throats. No mistake, Kari would, should he take too long.

"Good enough," said the mistress. "Load them. We have appointments."

Without a backward glance at Casper, we were tossed into the spacious coach and commanded to remain silent.

My heart raced, stirring my blood. I dug my fingernails into the meat of my palms, desperate to hide my disquiet.

We were surrounded by those who loved us.

Valen would swallow the brothel whole should anything go wrong.

This was for Herja. For Etta.

The house came into view. A ramshackle building made of wood and wattle. A tilted roof covered the numerous rooms and great hall where patrons gathered. The coach rounded a long dirt drive and rumbled past the house toward a stable where a few lanterns cast gilded shades over stacks of straw and ragged goats.

"Get out," the mistress barked. She clacked a wooden rod she pulled from the edge of her seat against my ankle.

I bit down on my cheek to keep from giving her the satisfaction of crying out at the sting and stumbled out of the coach first. Two of the men who'd come to the meet opened the wide doors of the stable, and the third ushered us inside.

The walls were thin and brittle. Too many gaps in the laths welcomed in a harsh north wind. Musty air and dust clogged the back of my throat. At the back of the stable was another room. One man tapped the door, waited two breaths, then opened it to a lighted room with too much flowery perfume.

More than the old stalls, the reek of sweet and rose turned my stomach.

Girls and boys of all designs huddled in a makeshift dressing room of sorts. Tall, plump, bony, broad. The mates who'd seen too much in too short of time slipped into the muted colors of the Bordell Brothel. Their skirts, trousers, and tunics reminded me of a storm rolling in over the sea. Gray and black with a stripe of blue tagging them as property of the mistress.

"In you go," the man said in a grunt. He nudged Siv between the shoulder blades, waiting until the three of us stepped over the threshold. A few of the pleasure mates glanced our way but said nothing. "Get your coats on. You'll be viewed within the hour. Should your company be required, you'll be taken to the main house. No fuss, no protesting."

And with that, he left. Not another word, simply a door slammed behind him.

"Look at this," a tall woman facing a cloudy mirror said to her reflection. "Looks like old Mistress DeMark is wasting shim again. I give them two nights."

"At least a week for the strong one," said a boy, probably not much younger than me. He was slender, but the curves of muscle on his arms hinted at strength buried underneath the drab tunic he wore.

Together they laughed and returned to preparing for the night.

"Remember," Kari whispered, "the pups."

Heart racing, I nodded. My eyes skipped over the two who'd addressed us and studied the others.

Most mates were uninterested. A few took us in, eyes narrowed as if we'd crossed an enemy line. But some cast nervous glances over a shoulder.

One by one, we separated. I drifted through a few pleasure mates whose faces seemed locked in permanent scowls until I reached a girl with golden hair tied in a nest on her head.

She avoided my gaze. Her entire skinny body curled away from me as if she'd rather turn into mist than look my way. Tonight, she wouldn't have a choice. I cleared my throat and pointed to the kohl rub in her hand. "May I use some when you're finished?"

Her body shuddered and with a trembling hand, passed the kohl over. "Done."

"Thank you." I pretended to line my eyes for a few heartbeats, studying her jerky, stiff movements. She was young, but the weight of life curled her shoulders and sagged in dark pillows beneath her eyes. "How long have you been here?"

The girl flicked her eyes up, regarding me with suspicion before turning back to the stockings she held in her hands. "Lost track."

She had no interest in talking. Then again, none of the mates had any interest in talking. If Herja were trapped in a place like this, she needed us. Think. Make this work. If we did not signal in time, Valen would make himself known in bloody ways.

"I've never been to this side of the kingdom," I whispered, dabbing some of the kohl around my eyes. "In truth, I thought I'd be taken to one of the exclusive houses. Traders kept talking about places where only the noble folk go."

I was reaching, but if Kari's theories were true, Herja would be kept out of sight to the common folk.

The girl wrinkled her brow. "What's so special about you?"

"Nothing. Just what I heard. Guess they changed their minds." I closed the top on the kohl and handed the jar back. "You ever see any of those houses?"

She blew out her lips. "What's so special about me that I'd see those?"

"I wasn't sure they existed."

The girl shrugged. "Castle Ravenspire has exclusive houses. From what I hear, mates eat better. Even get to wear what they want."

This was all ugly, but I needed to adopt an indifference the same as all the mates. A way to survive perhaps. I forced a laugh. "Hells, what would a girl need to do to get in there?" A grin teased the girl's mouth. She shook her head, more at ease, but didn't answer. She needed a bit more of a push. "You ever know anyone who got out of a place like this and made it to the top?"

"Why you asking so many questions?" she snapped. "Did I look like I needed to gossip?"

"Sorry." I cowered as if she'd bitten me. "I'm new to all this. Had to be sold when my master's house burned by all the uprisings from the Night Prince."

Another stretch, but I never pretended to be good at lying.

Still, I must've said something right because her eyes widened; her voice lowered to a low rasp. "He's real?"

Did folk not believe Valen was real? He'd made his name known in front of all the nobility of Ravenspire. He'd been leaving his mark across the kingdom for months since. I leaned in closer. "He's real."

A bit of light brightened in her eyes. "I hear things, but they tell us s'not true."

"It's true. I saw the armies. He's going to bring down Ravenspire; he cares about the lesser folk, places like this."

She snorted. "No one cares about places like this."

I needed to give her some hope. Squaring my shoulders, I took a different route. "I keep asking about special houses because word has it the Night Prince plans to take one. A special one, with a special pleasure mate. I guess I hoped I'd be there when he came." Less hope. Be despondent. I let out a long sigh. "Probably doesn't exist. Such a place, I mean."

Silence packed between us. Only the sounds of the rest of the pleasure mates readying for their night in the hells surrounded us. Low murmurs rose. Maybe Siv or Kari were having better luck, but I didn't want to risk looking and breaking this weak connection.

At long last, the girl stepped against my shoulder. She lifted her chin, voice softer than a summer breeze. "It exists."

"What does? A royal brothel?"

She shook her head. "No. A prize mate. A challenge hidden

away that draws the wealthiest of folk from across the kingdoms. They call her the Silent Valkyrie."

"A gods' warrior?" How many times had Valen made it clear his sister was deadly with a blade? "Why?"

The girl cast a nervous glance over her shoulder. "To win her you must defeat her. She is a bringer of death. As in Valkyrie sagas, this mate is so formidable she has the power to choose who she will kill and who will take her. Folk pay to win. From what I've heard, few ever do."

"Where is she?" Before I could think, my fingers gripped her arms. I didn't mean to sound so desperate, but if ever there were a whisper that Herja Ferus might be alive, this Silent Valkyrie had to be it.

The girl retreated, shirking me away.

"Sorry." I held up my hands. "But if we can get to this place, the Night Prince will come. We could be free."

"Free." She laughed with a touch of bitterness. "Freedom doesn't exist. Not here."

"With the Night Prince folk will be equal."

She shook her head, clearly unsure if she should trust me. "Even if it were true, the Valkyrie is not kept at a pleasure house. She is a prize; one kept under guard at an estate."

"An estate?"

"You think such a game would be wasted by giving power to a mistress? No. Rumor says she's the property of a high noble. Perhaps the king himself. I don't know. All I know is the appeal of defeating a woman of the gods has added to a thick purse somewhere."

A scuffle in the back of the room drew us to turn. My fists clenched. The woman who first addressed us, shoved Kari against the wall. Two young men gripped her arms.

"Who are you?" the pleasure mate snapped. "You've asked too

many questions. If you think you can come on your first night and take control, then you are sorely mistaken. This is my house."

Survival. She wants to survive. She'll devour anyone who gets in her way.

"Wait." I held up my hands, stopping her from striking Kari in the face. "We're not here to take anything from you. We're not here for that."

The pleasure mate cut me with an icy glare. "You speak as if you have a choice."

Kari and Siv shook their heads at me, but I could not let these folk stay here. This woman, she behaved like this was her home, but it was based on fear. On desperation. She could be free. They all could.

At my word they would be. Was I queen by name alone, or by action?

"You can leave here tonight," I said, voice rough. "We can free you all."

The woman laughed. "They're mad, and they'll get us all flayed."

She made a move for the doors, doubtless to signal for a guard. Murmurs followed her. They were turning on us. Even the girl who'd told me about the Valkyrie backed away.

I would not fail here.

"Listen to me. We have come with the King of Etta, the Night Prince."

A few gasps met his name, but most looked at me like I'd lost my mind completely.

"We've come in search of something, but he is out there," I said, pointing to one wall. "If you stay with us, you all can escape this place tonight."

"She's lying. A test from the mistress to prove our loyalty," said the tall woman.

"No. Let the mistress bleed for all I care. Do not signal the guards. Let us call our people and we will take you with us to Ruskig."

"Believe her," Siv said. "She is Elise Lysander, former niece of the dead Timoran king, now the Queen of Etta."

Silence had a way of rattling the nerves, of deafening the ears. No one moved. No one bleeding breathed.

The woman, who I took as the head mate, shook her head. "Mad. You're mad."

She said the words, but there was less venom in her tone. Buried somewhere in each word lived the slightest bit of hope.

"No king would send his queen to a pleasure house," said the boy who'd laughed at us at the beginning.

Siv and Kari grinned.

"Then you do not know Elise, nor the devotion of Valen Ferus to keep his queen satisfied," said Kari.

"Valen Ferus," the girl behind me whispered.

"He's here, and we need to find this Valkyrie. We believe she is important," I said, unwilling to give up too much of our plan. "Do you know what manor she is kept in?"

The girl started to shake her head, but all thought, all words died when the door slammed open. One of the mistress's guards stood in the doorway, grinning viciously. "We have an early request."

All the pleasure mates stiffened. A few closed their eyes, muttering prayers. But when the man's gaze turned to me, my insides froze.

He raised a finger, pointing. "You. Timoran. You've earned your first patron."

CHAPTER TWELVE
ROGUE PRINCESS

My hands were bound. The brothel guard led me out of the stables with enough time to give Siv and Kari a quick look, a silent signal to get free, to get our people. To get Valen.

This was not in the plan. We'd studied when the selections began at this brothel. It took place in the main room, where patrons could inspect their potential pleasure mates, then make their purchases. We were to slip away and make for a blot of spindly trees before we stepped foot in the main house. There, Stieg and Ari would meet us and take us away.

I couldn't get away when it was only me.

Certainly not with big, meaty hands on my arm and ropes on my wrists.

Plans would change. No doubt they'd draw blood and death soon enough. I was not a damsel to be rescued, and Valen did not see me as anything weak or helpless. Warrior blood flowed in my veins, but my husband knew better than most how to succumb to bloodlust. Even with the curse lifted, he had—more than once—

admitted the draw to blood, violence, and slaughter tugged at his soul like a disease he could not cure.

Perhaps it was more he did not wish to cure it.

This guard—this gods-awful fool—did not know what he was doing and the lives he'd put at stake.

I told him as much.

He laughed and tightened his grip. "You've been sold as a pleasure mate, Love. You think anyone is out there willing to fight for you?"

"You deliver me into that house, I vow on all the gods, on all the fates, it will not stand long."

"You've been requested personally."

"How? No one has seen me?"

"You're a feisty one," he said with a laugh. "I don't ask questions, Lovey. I do my job and deliver the pleasures is all. A new, blue-eyed Timoran was asked for, and you fit the bill. Almost like he knew you'd be here."

My insides coiled, hard and fast.

If anyone knew I was here, then they were no friend of ours. All hells! What did that mean for our folk in the trees? Valen, did he know? Was he surrounded and about to be ambushed?

I had no time to wonder before the guard shoved me inside a narrow doorway at the back of the house.

Inside the air reeked of pungent herb smoke and heavy ale. Laughter rose as patrons gathered in the great hall engaging in their own self-important debauchery before the pleasure mates were even brought inside.

"Put this on," said the guard. He held out a thin pearly sheet of lace. When I did nothing but stare at it, he made a gesture like placing a hat on his head. "Put it over your bleeding head. To hide your face. You've been bought. No one else gets to see you. Rules of the house."

Think Elise. On my leg, the dagger burned my skin. All in my mind, but the heat became a reminder of a promise to Valen. I'd fight and defend myself. I promised long ago, and I'd keep it. But to grab the blade now would be reckless. Too many patrons, too many guards, too many enemies stood around.

With a long breath, I slipped the lace over my head.

In the room, alone with the bastard who thought he could buy my flesh, I'd deal with it swiftly. Wooden floors would run red by the time I finished.

The guard led me into the hall. All around tables were stacked with men and women. All of different status. Most appeared to be stone workers. Bulky shoulders with arms thicker than my waist. So close to the peaks, folk up here were used to harsh winds and hard labor. Scattered throughout, though, were a few finely dressed people. Likely travelers or traders from other kingdoms or townships merely stopping through.

Vulgar shouts roared in my ears when I was brought into the room. Men barked, some pretended to reach for my skirts, others commented on my shape and figure.

The dagger scorched my leg. What I would give to dig the point in each chest.

Through the filigree on the lace, I took note of a table in the corner, of familiar faces. My heart leaped into my throat as I strode past Axel and Frey, drinking nervously, scoping out the space, waiting for any signal the plan had gone awry.

Covered, they wouldn't notice me. They were too focused on the far door, or the windows.

Think Elise.

I did what I could and fell forward. Nothing graceful, and utterly disruptive.

"Cursed hells, Lovey." The guard reached for my arm. "Clumsy little thing. Best tell your buyer the night ought to be spent off your feet."

The guard pulled on one arm, and with the other I used the edge of Frey's table to help me find my feet.

Discreetly, my hand covered the warrior's. I squeezed once.

His eyes shot to my covered face. The guard pulled me away, apologizing to Axel and Frey. As I left, I splayed my left hand, praying to any gods listening Frey would notice the missing fingertips and know it was me.

The last I heard was the scrape of chairs over floorboards.

All gods, I hoped it had been Frey and his brother taking action.

"As promised," was all the brothel guard said before he nudged me into a small, musty room, and slammed the door behind me.

With the breeze beating against the walls, wood groaned and creaked. Movement in the corner was the only indication I was no longer alone.

Hastily, I removed the veil and turned to face the patron.

A Raven.

Dressed in his dark tunic with the seal of Ravenspire over his chest and a silver short blade crossed over his back, the man grinned. As if he'd found the greatest prize, he flashed his yellow teeth with each step.

"I hate patrolling in the north. Bleeding cold and boring. But tonight, it would seem, the gods have smiled on me."

"I will warn you once, do not come closer," I said.

All the lessons from Halvar reeled through my head. How to duck, how to dodge, how to thrust a blade between the ribs. A dozen scenarios played out in my head. I'd need to survive long enough for Siv and Kari to find a way out, or if my distraction worked, for Axel and Frey to make a move.

As if I'd summoned them, shouting rang out somewhere outside.

The Raven noticed, but his smile didn't fade. He kept coming closer.

"I wish we had more time. But I'm sure it won't be long before your fae arrives, so we really ought to be on our way." He chuckled at my stun. "You think I do not know you? Elise Lysander, traitor of her own people and blood."

"How . . ." I let the words die. What was the point in asking the guard anything? If he knew who I was, then he was here to take me to my sister. That, or kill me.

My fingertips teased the hilt of the dagger tucked beneath my ratty skirt. I met his viciousness with my own. A sneer curled over my mouth. "If you know me, then you would be a fool to think you can walk out of here alive should you put a hand on me."

"I do plan to leave here with both of us still breathing." His body drew closer. I could smell the days-old sweat on his clothes and skin. He reached for my throat. I swatted at him, but he pinned my wrist to the wall, using his hips and body to trap me.

I didn't blink, didn't falter. So be it. Drawing so near gave me more opportunity to pierce his body deeper. Truth be told, I embraced my own bloodlust the same as Valen, and as the Raven breathed his rank breath on my face, I imagined a hundred ways I could make my bloody mark.

"Trust me—"

"That'd be foolish."

He sneered and tightened his grip around my throat. "Your fae friends will be plenty distracted," he rasped. "Too much to notice us. Then you, my little *Kvinna*, will be my gift to the king. I'll never see these bleeding peaks again."

"Someone told you about me," I said, giving myself enough time to slide the hem of my skirt up, to reach for the dagger.

"Careful who you trust, Elise. I hardly had to pay anything for your name." He pulled the short blade from his back. "We're going now."

"I'd rather not."

The sting of his hand didn't hurt nearly as bad as falling to one side and knocking my hip on the hard floor when the ground rolled like the waves of the sea. The Raven stumbled backward, his back striking the foot of the haggard bed.

Even with the sharp burn of pain shooting down my leg, I laughed and withdrew the dagger from the sheath.

The Raven looked to the door, eyes wide.

I rose to my knees. "Too late."

He locked me in his glare and took up his sword again. "He won't reach you in time. If I must, I'll take your head myself."

From the knees, I could slice up, strike his belly, his groin. What did Halvar say to do against a larger blade?

My head spun. I studied his feet. Watched his hands.

Vulnerable places in the Raven armor were joints and a small seam over the ribs. Duck at the first strike, then reel back and cut behind the knees. Take him down to my level.

Sure enough, the Raven lifted his short blade, ready to maim me enough I couldn't run. As the blade fell, I rolled onto one shoulder. Steel split the wood into splinters. The blade caught enough into the floor, I had time to spin back.

My dagger's edge sliced through the roughly spun trousers. A point above the top of his boot, but below the joint of his leg guarder.

The Raven cried out as hot blood soaked his leg, and he crumbled to his knees.

I scrambled to my feet, ready to strike again, but he fisted my skirt and pulled me back. A sharp cry came from my throat as I slammed backward onto the floorboards.

Roars of an attack boiled in my brain. Our people—Valen, Ari, Tor, Halvar—we did not come with the numbers to hold back a unit of Ravens. If one guard from Ravenspire was here, how many more had been patrolling the northern roads?

In my distraction, the Raven made a sloppy strike with his blade. A sharp, blinding burn scorched my flesh when the edge of his sword cut into my thigh.

The Raven tried to tighten his grip on me; he aimed for the newly opened gash above my knee. I swung my dagger, catching his cheek. He roared his pain, dropped his sword, and retreated.

I staggered to my feet and kicked his sword aside.

This wasn't over.

As if the wound unlocked fury that didn't exist in my blood, I turned away from the fight outside. Blood oozed down my leg, but I ignored the pain. All that mattered was this moment, this Raven, this life.

The man's pale eyes lifted to mine as a shudder shook the house. Perhaps he saw something in my eyes that frightened him, for he scurried away on his backside, eyes darting side to side, searching for anything to serve as a weapon.

He wouldn't get the chance.

"You will visit the false king," I rasped. "As a message from his doting sister-in-law. Unfortunately, you won't be living when you arrive."

He narrowed his eyes, a shadow pulling away the blue. He would not go down without a fight. Then again, we were Timorans. Bred from warriors.

But, no mistake, we were about to see who was the greater of the two.

CHAPTER THIRTEEN
NIGHT PRINCE

A GREAT, suffocating unease took up space in the deepest part of my gut. It had been there all day, all last night, and it swelled until now I might retch.

Whatever it was, something did not settle right about this plan.

I kept my distance. Reluctantly.

I could not risk being recognized and putting Elise and the others in danger. Not unless it was necessary. In truth, I was not the only one who looked ready to split their skin in disquiet.

Halvar hadn't blinked. Truly, I didn't think he'd dropped his eyes once from the land surrounding the pleasure house since Casper had driven the women away. Next to him, Ari held the sides of his head, focusing. He grew paler with each passing moment as he fought to hide fae features from those inside the house.

"This is a good plan," Tor said.

"Convincing yourself, or me?"

"It is a good plan, but it doesn't mean things will go as we expect." Tor paused, then stared at the grass. "Elise is as needed in this fight the same as you, Valen. I've believed it since Sol spoke with her. Fate brought her to us for a reason. We will all fight to keep her safe."

"All of them safe. We fight to keep them all safe," Halvar snapped, still without turning away.

"Hal, if you think for one moment anyone could get the upper hand with Kari, then she will make you pay for it when she returns."

"A man can hope." He almost grinned, almost broke his stare.

I looked back at Brant. His forehead wrinkled in a deep furrow.

"Brant? Anything?" His magic was strange. Perhaps it was his discomfort that added to my own.

Brant shook his head. "I can't get a handle on this bleeding fury—mesmer—whatever they called it. I see shapes and shadows in my head, but nothing clear. It is more a warning, heavy on my chest. But I can't say if it is worry for my sister, or if it is a true warning. Either way, Valen, I don't want to wait much longer."

Agreed. No need to convince me. If I did not see my queen's face in mere moments, I would level the rickety walls of the pleasure house before another ewer of ale was poured.

"Dammit." Halvar's curse added a layer of cold to the air.

I reeled around in time to watch my friend unsheathe his seax, Tor and Ari at his shoulders. My gaze locked on a fiery glow against the black night. In the stables where the pleasure mates readied for the night, a cloud of black smoke rose through the sod roof.

"It's the bleeding signal," I said. Trouble. Something had gone wrong. Elise, Siv, or Kari were to signal us with fire if anything went off our plan.

Why did I stay so far away? I could've kept hidden, as promised, in a damn closet inside the house. Almost without control a wave of fury burned through my fingertips, rolling the soil and bedrock.

Shouts rose from the house, glass shattered, part of the roof tipped slightly.

"Don't waste energy," Tor said, scolding me. Never mind that his palms were already alight in blue pyre.

"Go." I whistled toward the trees even though the fury blast would be enough to signal the others.

We sprinted toward the stables. From the corner of my eye, shadows moved. More of our folk joined the ranks.

But we weren't alone.

Brothel guards and a few Ravens sprinkled the lawns. I took out one axe, catching the end of a spiked rod from a house guard. He grunted, slashed at my ribs. Sloppy. Lazy. Almost insulting.

I allowed the swing and as the strength of it pulled his body forward, I cut the curved edge of my battle ax through one half of his face.

There were few guards in the north. We'd chosen a shabby brothel for a reason. Fewer patrons. Fewer interruptions. But the Ravens did patrol here as if the ghosts of the dead wastes of Old Timoran might slip through the mountain pass. Those sods from Ravenspire spilled out of the shadows and held a good fight.

A large Raven met my eye. He rolled his sword in hand. I took out my second axe. Ready and willing.

But when the back of the stable burst open, he and I both turned as smoke and flame ignited the night in a wash of gold and red. The lawns were overtaken with a huddle of pleasure mates. At the head, two women—Siv and Kari—directed them to the trees.

Without a moment of hesitation, Halvar shouted at Kari,

tossed her a sword, and gave her the means to fight. She didn't pause, and took the battle I'd planned to take with the Raven in my place.

Where was Elise?

As if she sensed my scrutiny, Siv raced—pleasure mates at her back—to me.

"She's in the house, Valen," she said breathlessly. A few of the mates stared at me with wide eyes. I hardly noticed them; my head swam in shadows. A pull to slaughter anything that moved grew potent enough to taste. Until Siv touched my arm, drawing me back to reality. "Someone purchased her."

My jaw pulsed. I jerked my head, voice low. "Take them away."

She dipped her chin and shouted at the pleasure mates to take cover in the trees. Around me my people fought. Pyre engulfed Ravens from Tor. Stieg and Halvar used fury to keep the air breathing life into the flames. Mattis fought beside Brant. Kari shouted in the face of the Raven as he fell to her feet, bloody and battered.

My eyes locked on the house.

This ended now.

Another shudder of fury seeped into the soil when I took my first step toward the door. The fight outside faded, but inside furniture toppled. Women screamed. Men shoved through hallways, desperate to escape.

I didn't stop. Some folk knocked into me as they ran. I shoved them aside. The house mistress whimpered by a writing desk; Stave and another of Crispin's men held their blades at her throat. If they acknowledged me, I didn't stop long enough to notice.

"My King." Axel shouted from the center of the great hall, blood on his face, light in his gaze. "They took the queen to that room!"

He cut a kneeling patron's throat as he spoke and pointed the bloody knifepoint at a sealed door.

The axes in my grip heated with fury. It took a mighty level of focus to keep my magic from splitting the soil beneath our feet, but if Elise's face did not greet me behind that door, this hovel would sink in the ground.

If a patron had touched her, when my hands found him, he'd pray to the gods to end his life to stop the pain.

In truth, I should've done as Elise asked. Had a bit more faith in her ability to draw blood.

When I rammed the door open, ax raised, my eyes fell to the thick Raven sprawled on the floorboards first. His eyes stared lifelessly at the wall; his throat cut deep enough it nearly exposed his spine.

Blood soaked everything. The walls, the floor, the hems of the tattered quilts. That was where I found her. Elise sat in the middle of the bed, paler than she'd been an hour ago, blood in her hair, on her hands, her lips, an open wound on her leg.

My stomach turned.

Beside her on the bed were bloodied fingers. Bones and flesh mangled on the ends, still dripping onto the floorboards.

Much like her sister had done with their mother, for the first time I noticed she'd sliced the beringed fingers off the Raven, the silver bands a mark of his status as a guard remained in place.

Her blue eyes met mine. She lifted her chin, but a tremble lived in her voice. One only her husband might notice. Because only her husband knew how often brutality and compassion collided in her heart.

All she said was, "We've been betrayed, My King."

CHAPTER FOURTEEN
NIGHT PRINCE

Smoke from the burning brothel hid the moonlight. As we gathered in the trees, no losses among our folk, I watched without a word as those closest to me organized blades from the dead Ravens, or shim from the mistress's coffers. To the side, the pleasure mates kept close together, watching every move, likely trusting no one.

I could understand the feeling.

Elise stood beside me, stoic and silent. She hadn't washed her face of the blood yet. Truth be told, she hadn't said a word about the fingers or the dead Raven who'd purchased her.

Later. We'd work through it together, preferably alone. Now, there was more blood to be spilled.

"Enough." My voice carried and everyone froze. I narrowed my gaze at the inner council. At Stave, Crispin, Klok, at men I suddenly realized I knew very little about. There were no more than ten who'd joined us, but they all backed away from the blades and stood with a touch of caution.

"Line up," I commanded, using my ax to point my directions.

With a nod at Axel and Frey, I demanded they join as well. I doubted the brothers were traitors, but I would not take any chances. Without needing it, even Casper and Stieg stood in the line.

Everyone inside or near the house joined the long row in front of me.

I rolled the ax in my hand, pacing down the line, jaw tight. "Someone among us has been making deals with Castle Ravenspire."

"My King—" Stieg began, but I held up a hand. I trusted him as a member of my guild.

"I hate traitors." My voice hung in the air like a sharpened knife, jagged and deadly. "Now, who would like to confess to betraying your queen to Castle Ravenspire? Confess, and you die a warrior's death to join the gods."

No one moved. I doubted anyone breathed.

Elise rested a bloody hand on my arm. She didn't need to say anything; I took a step back.

"My name was purchased," she said in a tone so unlike her typical warmth and kindness. "Someone sought out the Raven, intrigued him, then sold my name."

All gods, I wanted blood.

She stalked the line meeting each eye. The men stiffened under her watch, and I embraced the moment with pride. Like the last Timoran queen of Etta, Elise could shock fear into the hearts of the most formidable warriors.

I'd never forget the first time my mother commanded a unit of our warriors when my father had been absent in delegations over the peaks.

Elise was even bolder. Fiercer.

She paused at Stave. He met her eye, but I couldn't read his expression. My blood boiled with each beat of my heart. Did he do this? Did she know? And if she did, how? What had I missed?

Before the spin of my thoughts faded, Elise moved on. "There would be evidence of the purchase," she said. "Shim. I'd like to see what I'm worth to you. Strip, and turn out your clothing."

There was hesitation, a few uncertain glances.

"Did you not hear your queen?" I shouted. "Move!"

The line jolted, and one by one the men began to remove their clothing. Tor, Halvar, and Ari set to work searching every thread of fabric. Stieg didn't blink as he dropped his trousers and tunic. Casper pounded a fist over his naked chest, smirking. "Your name is too valuable to sell, Elise."

She fought a smile. I did not feel the same lightness. Did the Guild of Shade betray her? No. Instinct rolled through my senses and told me Stieg and Casper were in line but enjoying their nakedness without an ounce of guilt.

Still, there was a bit of relief when nothing was found on them, nor on Frey and Axel.

"We stand with the king and queen," Axel said, dipping his chin.

Tor shoved Stave aside. He looked at me, shaking his head. Nothing on Klok. Three of Crispin's men were cleared.

Then . . .

"What is this?" Halvar's tone was playful, but the dangerous kind. A sound I only heard when my friend planned on killing someone and laughing as he did it.

The pleasant clatter of coins scraping together turned ugly. I almost didn't want to look.

Almost.

"Crispin." My voice was devoid of any feeling as I approached the naked, old man. A few whispers filtered through our people. I tilted my head until his slate eyes dared meet mine. "What have you done? After all we did for you, this is how you stand with Etta? Or perhaps you were always for Timoran."

His gaze turned wickedly cold. "I have never stood with Timoran. I would gladly watch it burn. My loyalty lives in the crown of Etta, and I am loyal enough to protect its king, even when he is blinded."

I'd peel his skin away layer by layer. "I have never seen so clearly."

"Why?" Elise's softness returned. Hurt was there. I wanted to take it away. "Crispin, we helped you. I helped your people."

"Helped me? You overruled me." His nose wrinkled in disgust. "We have no business working with Timorans. I knew it from the day you insisted those Ravens be given a second chance at life, not only to live, but to join us. Ravens? You have manipulated the heir of Etta and have worked your way to be queen of a land that will never be yours."

I made a move to strike him, slaughter him, one of the two, but Elise stopped me.

She didn't look away from the man, simply shook her head. "You are the blind one, Crispin. You cannot see beyond your own prejudice and have become nothing but a coward. It is not so painful to know you betrayed me; I can see the looks, the mistrust around me. But you put our people at risk today. You put us all at risk."

I'd heard enough. With a flick of my fingers, I gestured to Tor and Halvar, standing by as they bound the old man.

"Etta will never rise strong if we do not rid it of all things Timoran," Crispin shouted. "They robbed our people of the fury from this soil. They do not deserve to walk it now! I am not alone in my thoughts."

His cries muffled as Casper took over. His bulky hand closed around Crispin's throat as he wheeled him through the trees.

I watched him disappear into the shadows. Cold. Detached. Vengeful. Without a look at our men, I followed into the trees. "We return to Ruskig. We have an execution to attend."

THIS TIME, I sat by the window. Cold dawn spread over Ruskig as I sharpened the curved edges of my battle axes.

Lost in my own thoughts, I didn't hear Elise slip from our bed. But as if her touch had a bit of fury in it, the instant her arms curled around my neck from behind, my shoulders slumped. Relaxed.

"I love you, Valen. I am loyal to you."

I stopped drawing the stone over the edge of my axe, and turned to her, pulling her onto my lap. "If there is one person whose loyalty will never be questioned, it is yours. Have you kept things from me? Mistreatment of you that I haven't seen?"

Her lips tightened, but her fingertips kept stroking the side of my face. "Not since our vows. But . . . as consort, some folk didn't seem to approve."

"Who?"

She buried her face in my neck and shook her head. "Until there is reason to cut them open, I think it's better if your bloodlust does not know their names."

I pulled her away so I could meet her eyes. "You are queen here, Elise. My equal. I don't care if you came from the slums of the Eastern Kingdom, you are the queen; you are the better half of my heart. Do not accept treatment any less than that. And if it happens—damn my bloodlust, let it spill out."

She offered a sad smile, holding me tightly. A quick glance down and my gaze found the dark, rusted blood of the bandage wrapped around her leg. My hand fell to the wound, but she covered it with hers quickly. "I'm fine."

"The Raven could have killed you all because of a traitor."

"But he did not, and I took his fingers. If our messenger is swift, Runa and Calder will receive a gift I hope ruins their evening meal."

I kissed her neck, breathing in her goodness, her viciousness, trying to soothe a bit of my darkness. If I did not calm the race of my heart, I would take all my anger out in the square today, and I would dishonor the crown through wretchedness and brutality.

A knock on the wall drew us apart. Ari stood in the frame of the door. His typical blithe way of looking at life was missing. Today he frowned and his gilded eyes looked blacker. "It's time."

Elise slipped off my lap and pulled a fur cloak over her slender shoulders. While she bundled for the chill of the wind, I stripped my chest bare. Across my skin was painted runes. Traditional curses and prayers for what was to come. Deep inside, beneath the anger and lust for gore, I hated this. To know a man I'd respected, a man Elise and I had befriended together—or so I'd thought—had tried to sell my wife to her bleeding sister. It wouldn't stand.

Examples needed to be made.

Already crowds gathered outside the royal longhouse. Long lines of our people stood, much like the day of the vows, except today they were dressed in dark clothes, their faces painted in blood and kohl. Some wore skins over their skulls, some with horns and antlers from wild rams or deer.

Together, Elise and I stepped into the light. She was every bit as formidable with her hair braided in intricate designs around a black iron circlet. Her fur cloak made her body seem broader than true.

The lines of people led to the square of Ruskig. From here, I had a clear view of the ropes tethering Crispin's arms out from his body like wings.

I gripped an ax in each hand and walked briskly toward a stone basin at the edge of the square. Blood filled the bottom. A symbol of what was to come, a tradition from my grandmother's rule.

My father once told me the blood was an acknowledgment to the gods that a life would be taken, and the one who lifted the blade accepted the consequences of taking it. Good or bad.

Elise dipped her fingers into the basin, then faced me. With a gentle touch, she dragged the bloody lines down my face, from crown to chin, and stepped aside.

All voices died when I stepped into the square.

For a moment, I scanned the edges of my people, allowing them to meet my gaze. As if my stare might draw out any others who felt the same as Crispin.

I hated this and craved it in the same breath.

"We are at war. There is no time for such petty things as betrayal. I have little patience, and no mercy to give such cowards." I turned in a slow circle, voice raised over the heads of the people. "Our kinsman betrayed the crown by betraying its queen. The reason? The blood in her veins." The axes burned in my palms. My voice darkened. "Blood that runs in mine!"

A few gasps interjected. Folk lowered their eyes, but I was not near finished.

"Have you forgotten? Cut me and I bleed for Etta and Timoran. Have you forgotten, long ago a Timoran huntress saved the life of an Ettan prince? You worship Queen Lilianna the same as you worship King Arvad—but have you dimmed their history in your minds, or the truth of where my mother came from? Have you forgotten so soon that without this woman—" I pointed an ax at Elise, "without our queen, I would still wallow in blood as a mindless beast? And you despise her, and those like her because they wish to unite all people. Because they do not hate as you do."

I took a deep breath, lungs burning. "I tell you this—if you do not stand for all people, if you plot against those born of Timoran so much you would betray your crown, then I have no business being your king."

Each word rattled against the stone walls surrounding Ruskig. No eye turned away.

"Cut me," I said again, hoarse and angry, "and I bleed Ettan and Timoran. Cut me and I bleed for her."

I pointed at my wife once more, letting the finality of my voice pierce every heart. No one moved. No one looked away.

"So, tell me now," I went on. "Am I to be your king, or should this burden fall to another?"

It took no more than a few breaths before people kneeled in a great wave, heads bowed, fists crossed over their hearts.

I gave a stiff nod. "Then let us be done with this." Clearing my throat, I rolled my shoulders back. "For the crime of treason, I have condemned Crispin Vänlig to meet the hall of the gods this day."

A roar of acceptance lifted from the crowd as folk staggered to their feet.

With careful steps, I approached Crispin from behind. "*Farväl en älskade.*" Farewell once loved.

His muscles tensed. I let the first strike fall.

Moments blurred. I did not know how long I carved him to the bone, but by the time I finished, Crispin's body was bathed in blood. I severed the bindings tethering his mangled arms to the posts and let his broken body fall in the pool of blood at my feet.

Hair stuck to my forehead. Drops of hot, sticky blood fell from my lashes. My eyes lifted to the reverence of my people. Their eyes clashed in horror and respect as the Guild of Shade moved to gather what was left of a man I thought was loyal.

A man who'd reminded me to trust few.

I handed the axes to Tor without a word and went to Elise. There was nothing to say to anyone else. I slipped my fingers into hers and walked away. She didn't falter, didn't tremble. She stood by my side, eyes ahead. Focused. Prepared for what we still had to do.

We would go to find my sister. Then, Ravenspire would at last be met with our blades and fury.

CHAPTER FIFTEEN
ROGUE PRINCESS

My friend,

By the gods, why did you give yourself over to the Timoran King? Do not deny it—you are too clever to be caught sailing so near a shore. You intended to be found and taken.

I cannot deny having you so near me brings comfort, but also severe unease. My future and fate must be dire, indeed, if you have so willingly sacrificed your own freedom to come to my aide. Tell me the prophecies are not written on my threads of life. I am not certain I can see it through if it is as you say.

Tell me what I must do to free them, to save them, to heal this land, and I will do it. Even at the cost of my own life. I will do it all to keep my children from suffering. To keep my husband breathing. Tell me and it is done.

I anxiously await your reply. Leave the missive beneath the third ewer on the highest shelf in the kitchen, and my maid will deliver it to me.

Your loyal friend,
—Lili

Two weeks after the execution, the Silent Valkyrie remained lost to us.

Not even Lilianna's mysterious letters brightened my spirits. How were we to press forward when we could not find our footing? Valen agreed it was the best lead we had to Herja. If such a woman as this Valkyrie existed, she was mightily hidden.

Still, the waiting and searching had left us all rather restless.

"You don't need to be here doing this, Queen Elise," an old, wizened woman named Gretel said.

I tugged with a bit of annoyance on the twine and needle. "If you can repair nets, so can I." Siv snorted, but turned away when I shot her a glare. With furious fingers, I finished knotting my twine. "No, I mean it. Why is net making beneath me? We cannot attack Ravenspire, not yet, so I am not needed in battle strategy. I can barely show my face outside these walls since everyone recognizes me. So, I shall sit here, repair nets, and be useful."

"I think our queen might need to eat," Kari said in a soft, sing-song voice. "She seems irritable."

More than a few snickers rippled through the small room. If I were not so irritated, I might laugh. This was the sort of court I always wanted to be part of, one where leaders respected the common folk. Leaders who sat with them in their shanties by the sea. Leaders who knew their names, their families, their fears.

But being trapped in Ruskig while the Sun Prince withered in Ravenspire, while a princess might be chained and battered in a manor I was not sure existed, my greatest impact on the day was mending fishing nets.

I did not even want to be in the royal longhouse.

The man might own my heart, but it did not mean we always stared at each other with longing.

I scoffed at the thought. No, there was no longing this morning. In fact, I'd snapped at Valen not so many hours ago for staring too long at a map of the kingdom.

He'd looked at me with a touch of Blood Wraith, so I lifted my chin, stalked out of the longhouse, and took my leave with the hope salty air might do me some good.

I picked up another net, searching for holes, ignoring everyone and their aggravating grins. I'd barely taken up the needle when Klok entered the shanty, stomping mud from his boots. "My Queen, a missive arrived for you from the East."

Once, I'd been a royal of Timoran; I'd been taught how to behave with dignity, but there was no dignity when I bolted from the chair and snatched the parchment from Elder Klok's hand. His eyes widened, but no one questioned me as I tore the seal, scanning Junius's delicate writing.

> E,
>
> I've done as you asked. There is no one by the name Silent Valkyrie in any corner of this land. I assure you the Nightrender and his Guild of Kryv hold unique skills to get such a job done, and they found nothing.
>
> By the by, you asked of him, but I have heard nothing more from you on the Nightrender. What is happening there? Should we come to you? There is something you're not telling me.
>
> I could taste it in your last missive, my friend. Do not keep things from me.
>
> Remember your allies in the slums,
> —J

I folded the parchment and slumped in the chair. I'd known it was unlikely, but with vast travel between kingdoms, it was worth it to see if perhaps this Valkyrie prize was shipped to and from distant lands.

"Disappointing news?" Siv asked.

"Yes. Again." I passed her the note. She frowned and showed Kari.

"It's possible she doesn't exist," Kari said. "I never heard such a name when I was in the guard."

I rubbed the bridge of my nose, unwilling to accept we were chasing a myth. If true, we were a dozen deadly steps away from finding Herja. According to Valen, she was necessary, and Sol would not have mentioned the first, the middle, and the last if their sister were not alive and utterly crucial to this fight.

Hells, even if she were not, we still needed to find her.

Siv dragged her stool closer to my side and lowered her voice. "Maybe you ought to tell Junius. We don't know this husband of hers, and she made him out to be dangerous. In a way we might need. They could help."

I shook my head. "Not yet."

In truth, I wanted to tell Junius of our lack of progress. She had connections to strange magic I didn't know, but she'd only earned her freedom not long ago. I did not want to put more people I cared about in danger when I had no bleeding direction.

She'd used this Nightrender to search for me. Why? What sort of man was he to do such a task?

I forced Calista's warning of a breaker of night and fear, of battles—present and future—out of my mind. This unseemly acquaintance of Junius might not be the one the storyteller meant anyway.

I wasn't sure if I thought it more to convince myself, or if I truly believed our battle was nearing its end.

To end it meant there would be an outcome. A victor. In truth,

I wasn't sure I was ready to learn if we would rise victorious or find ourselves dead.

Valen stared at the flames in the fireplace, his fingers lazily clutching a drinking horn. One leg was outstretched, one fist held up his head on the arm of the chair. I studied him for a few moments, memories of long, unburdened conversations with Legion Grey rippled through my head.

A smile curved over my lips. He'd been cursed, I'd been trapped in a world I hated, but we laughed often. We had few true burdens. To think, once our paths collided, the things that would unfold.

My heart warmed.

To know this would be the outcome—war, blood, death, fear—for him, I'd do everything again.

With slow steps, I crossed the space to him, my fingertips gently touching his shoulder. Valen lifted his eyes, a smile on his lips.

"I wondered if I'd gotten too far under your skin." He pressed the back of my hand to his lips.

"Oh, you did," I said as I nestled in the chair, leaning my head against his shoulder. "You are aggravating and always have been. But I have a confession—I love even your aggravating qualities."

He chuckled and scooped his arm around my waist, holding me close. Valen offered me a sip from the horn and together we stared mutely at the flames for a time. There wasn't much to say. Raw assurances that we'd find his sister? I said them often. New places to search? We'd scoured the land.

Sometimes silence was all we needed.

"Elise," he whispered, his fingers in my hair, softly playing with the tresses. "Sol needs me to return to Ravenspire. With Herja."

"What?"

A muscle in his jaw pulsed. "With all that has been happening, I never mentioned it. When he said to come home to visit him, he meant Herja and I needed to return to Ravenspire. Our old home. There is something there, I don't know what, but he needs the three of us together."

"But you said you didn't know what he meant."

"I wanted to be sure," he admitted. "After some thought, I'm certain Sol needs us there."

I shook my head. "You're not going there, Valen. You'll never come out."

"So little faith in my abilities, Wife?" He grinned in a way that weakened all my resolve. A sly smile unique to him. When I did not return a grin, he sighed. "We knew the fight would reach Ravenspire eventually, but I do agree we should try to get Sol out, get him to us, then we find a way to attack."

Yes, I knew in the depths of my heart we'd return to Ravenspire, but the thought of Valen being taken before our growing army had a chance to rise against them added ice to my blood.

I lowered my forehead to the side of his. "We return there together. After we have Sol and Herja."

"But how do we get Sol without going to Ravenspire?" He was thinking out loud, rattling ideas with me. A habit I loved.

I mulled the question over for a few breaths. "They bring him out to manipulate you. Maybe we can set a stage they cannot resist, and they will bring him again. We take him there."

Valen watched the fire, the glow of it like red stars in his dark eyes. "It could work. We lie, draw them out, force them to make a move."

I gripped his shoulder, straightening. "Valen! What if that is how we find the Valkyrie?"

"What do you mean?"

"The same as drawing out Ravenspire, we could put word out that some wealthy sod is seeking the legend of the Silent Valkyrie, then see if any slimy traders emerge from the underbelly. You were a trader, am I wrong? Dark deals are done through word of mouth, are they not?"

Valen stood abruptly, a wicked kind of smile on his face. "It could work, and as you said, if word reaches Ravenspire, they might come if she is Herja."

"They might not bring the Sun Prince, though."

Valen scratched his face. "Perhaps not, but we might kill a few Ravens in the process. And if we have Herja, our next move would be retrieving Sol anyway. We fight them, we free him, we take back what is ours." In a few quick steps he had my face trapped between his palms, lips close. "Have I told you I think you're brilliant?"

I grinned. "No, but I am completely open to any ideas you have in convincing me."

Valen kissed me, freer than before. There was a fire behind his touch, as if hope burned through his veins and came out through his kiss.

We were close. We'd find more answers, more strength at our backs. I might learn the answer to a toiling question I couldn't shake: why keep the Ferus children alive all this time? What purpose did it serve to curse Valen, enslave Herja, to poison Sol?

Timoran could've guaranteed its survival if they'd slaughtered them all.

I understood a past storyteller convinced King Eli to keep

Valen alive by lying about the land being cursed if he died. But had she done the same with the others?

I was all at once grateful to a fate witch from the past. She'd risked a great deal to keep a vicious Timoran king satisfied in the Ferus suffering, while keeping them alive for . . . this moment?

A wash of hope filled my heart. If fate wanted them alive, then it was more possible fate wanted them back on the throne.

Another week behind the walls of Ruskig, but at least we'd taken steps forward. Once more, I sat beside Valen in the longhouse, well after lights were doused and the quiet of midnight overtook the refuge. Beside the fire, Siv slept, her head on Mattis's lap. He fought mightily to keep his eyes open but was failing.

Stieg and Casper shuffled a game of wolvyn and crowns, but neither seemed interested in playing. Kari sat beside Halvar in front of the fire, her fingers massaging the point of his ear until the tension in his neck melted and he closed his eyes, leaning into her touch. Tor and Brant remained at the window, watching.

Everyone moved with such nerves, I could hardly breathe. The only tether I had to peace lived in the few touches Valen offered as he paced around the table. He was lost in thought, but every few moments he'd curl a finger around mine, run his hand across the back of my neck, or gently squeeze my hip as he passed.

I suppose I served as his anchor too.

Once the plan was placed, we quickly discovered delivering word about the Silent Valkyrie drew more attention than we imagined. The woman was a game, constantly on the move. She'd be well guarded. By Ravens? I didn't know. But it was nothing but a sport to the house who owned her.

A vague messenger greeted Ari at Sven's alehouse not three nights ago. A courier for the owner of the Valkyrie.

The match was set. The challenger accepted.

Now, we were to wait for word on the final meet. Directions to where we were to play the game of defeating the Valkyrie or dying at her hand.

It was a twisted game, and if this woman did not turn out to be Herja, there was no telling what could happen.

Not soon enough, the door swung open, banging against the wall. Ari tossed back a wool cowl, shaking off dust and a bit of frost from his hair. He looked weary and travel worn. Without a word, he reached for a tall ewer and poured a horn of sharp, warm ale.

Siv and Mattis were awake now. In truth, everyone was on their feet before the door closed at his back.

At the table, Ari took a long drink, some ale spilling out the sides and down his chin. He gasped loudly, probably to annoy us before speaking. "It's done."

"You're going to need to give more information than that, you bleeding fool," Tor said.

"Always so irritable." Ari reclined in the chair and met mine and Valen's gaze. "They've accepted the payment amount and will set the match where you will face their Valkyrie. The rules are you draw blood, you earn the right to take her. But if she guts you first, then you meet the Otherworld."

Valen clenched his fists. His face contorted in red rage. We all thought the same—how many patrons had faced this woman, tortured her, used her, fought her?

"You're positive these people are who we're looking for?" Kari asked.

Ari gave a firm nod. "It's a deliciously twisted network of secrets hiding this game. We never would've found it without putting our interest in the wind. It is as if they have eyes everywhere, waiting for a glimmer of willing players. Without doubt they span throughout all the kingdoms. Which reminds me—I have made you a dignitary from the South, My King. The ears—they'll be expected."

Tor crossed his arms over his chest. "And they simply believed you?"

"I created a very convincing illusion of a documented noble line, thank you very much. Your tone of mistrust is rather irksome, Torsten. In need of a drink? A gentle embrace? Tell me how we can ease your frustration when it is I who have been traipsing across this gods-awful land arranging this game."

"We're grateful," I said, smirking. "Ari, you are magnanimous in your abilities, and we don't deserve you."

"Thank you. I completely agree." He tugged on the sleeves of his tunic. He lifted his eyes to Valen. "I will go with you, to make sure you are not recognized. They will set the encampment in three nights on the east side of the Nightwood."

"And we will be alone?" Valen asked.

"No one goes into the Valkyrie's chamber but the patron. I should warn you; the courier was quite insistent that you understand she has never lost in his entire employ with his master."

A curl tugged at the corner of Valen's mouth. "Good."

"Who are the masters?" I asked.

"Ah." Ari took another drink. "The final piece of this wretched game. The Valkyrie belongs to Ravenspire's most trusted warriors. A noble house. A brutal one, made of many generals of war, of raiders, of—"

"All gods," Stieg snapped. "Who is it?"

"All gods, let me explain," Ari hissed back. "If she is Herja, I am not convinced these nobles know it, or they would not risk her in such games. They simply believe she is a gift from Ravenspire for their service. Their brutality in war is well known and should not be discounted when we go to them and trust me—they are as close to Ravenspire as we can get without setting foot inside." Ari didn't look anywhere but at me. "She belongs to House Magnus, Elise."

I closed my eyes, chest tight. Jarl's house. His cruel, wretched family. If they suspected our ruse at all, they'd end us before we drew our blades.

CHAPTER SIXTEEN
NIGHT PRINCE

"When we are no longer living in a hovel of a refuge, I demand you do not allow your servants to wear this drab." Ari tugged on the scratchy burlap tunic for the hundredth time. "I was once a king."

I shook my head, trying not to smile. Dignitaries did not tease with their serfs. While Ari dressed in rags, I once more had donned stiff collars and trousers spun in soft thread.

"You are soft, Ari. I thought you were a warrior."

His eyes flashed in anger. "Test me, My King, and you will know if I am soft or a warrior. Now, be gone with you. Bid farewell to my queen, and we'll go."

I scoffed and shoved him aside to mutter about the rags he'd be forced to wear and went deeper into the trees until I found Elise. She was dressed all in black, from her knee-high boots to the dark lines of kohl painted down her face.

Without a word, she pulled on the back of my neck, kissing me fiercely. Time paused and gave us a moment. A chance to breathe as one, for me to taste her, to touch her. For her to hold fast to me, as if I might disappear for good. Her fingers tugged on my hair; her body molded with mine.

I never wished the moment to end.

Tonight would be dangerous. Getting into the Valkyrie was handled—getting out would be made of knives and blood and fury.

"There are Ravens," she whispered against my mouth when I pulled back.

My brow fell to hers. "I know. Keep watch on your backs."

"We'll look out for Sol."

I nodded. For all we knew a unit of Ravens arrived out of sheer curiosity. There was no telling if they were sent by the false king to protect my sister.

I lifted her fingers to my lips. Her glassy eyes soaked me in. "Return to me, Valen."

"I always will."

From the trees Halvar and Tor flanked Elise. Their faces were painted much like hers, and they watched me with a somberness that added to the unease in my gut.

Brant came to my side, voice low. "This is a necessary step."

I lifted my brow. "You see something?"

His magic confused him, it confused all of us, but Brant nodded with a surety now. "I feel it fiercely. But not everything will be as it seems in there."

"What do you see, Brant?"

"Only those thoughts. I'm sure it was less than helpful, but they're coming stronger. In time, I hope to decipher what is vision and what is thought. For now, I know you need to do this, but also be on guard and be ready for anything."

The unease stacked like heavy stones. I hid it well and clapped him on the shoulder before turning back toward the edge of the clearing. Not half a length away, the encampment where the Magnus family set up their bloody game awaited.

I could not look at Elise, or I might not leave. She was queen. She could lead here, and if I took a misstep whatever warning itching in Brant's magic might take me from behind.

Ari stood away from me and did not move when I joined him at his side. "Ready?" he asked.

"Yes. Let's get it over with."

The journey wasn't far, but with every step through the Nightwood, my body tightened, ready to strike at the slightest shadow. At the sight of the first gilded wash of a flame, we were met by four burly men, strapped in knives and axes.

They weren't Ravens, but I had few doubts the Magnus family had personal guards.

I looked down on them. Easy to do, but I would need to play my role well enough to convince the fiercest military men of Timoran I was no fraud. I certainly needed to convince them I was not their enemy in disguise.

Now would be the test of stamina for Ari's illusions.

"*Herr* Lönger?" one guard asked, holding up a hand to stop us.

Ari bowed at the waist and held out a clean piece of parchment. I nodded. "My travel papers. See for yourself."

The guard inspected the falsified document. It had been a happy discovery that among his other talents, Axel had a gift for forgery. With his time spent with traders in various kingdoms, he'd mastered some of the seals from the wealthy in the South.

I fought the urge to swipe my sweaty palms on my trousers as we waited. My shoulders ached by the time the guard returned the parchment and ushered us forward. "You have a blade, *Herr*?"

I nodded and revealed a seax with a gilded hilt.

"You are allowed two." A man with a rotund belly over his belt stepped forward from a small, white canvas tent. "I am Stor Magnus."

He clasped my forearm. The senior Magnus. I'd gut him the same as I planned to shred the skin from his bleeding son the next time I met Jarl Magnus. "A pleasure, *Herr*."

My voice came out wrong. Strangely accented. Ari. He winced through the pain of his fury. If I liked him less, I might dawdle to make his life miserable, but, alas, I considered the former king a friend.

"When do we begin?" I asked.

Stor barked a laugh. "Anxious to die?"

"I have no plans to die tonight."

"Yes, patrons always say the same, but my pearl is a fearsome creature." He gestured toward the large tent at the back. There was a drawn circle around the space and on the outer ring a row of the Magnus personal guard stood still. Next to the large tent were three coaches and another guarded canopy.

Perhaps Magnus's wife or mistresses stayed inside that one?

I walked toward the largest tent. "Where did you come by her?"

"A gift from the former king for my service. She has been in my life since I was a young man. The woman is of the gods, I assure you, *Herr*. As if time does not pass with her, she remains fair and lovely and . . . deadly. Should you be so blessed to draw her blood, your prize will be unlike any woman you've ever had."

Young after decades. Herja—she had to be Herja. His insinuations did not fall mutely in my mind; I merely stacked each vulgar word away for later when I carved out his innards.

"I have longed for this day all my life," I told him when we stopped at the edge of the circle. "My serf will stand here. I want to see to it this is done fairly."

Stor raised his hands. "Who am I to deny a dying man his last wish?" He rasped a laugh again and handed me an extra dagger from a sheath on his leg. "I thank you for playing our game. Remember—draw blood, she is yours. But if the Valkyrie chooses you in death, your money and your serf belong to me, and you meet the gods."

Stor Magnus signaled to one of his guards to cross the circle and lift the flap of the tent.

I gave Ari a final glance. Shoulders back, hand on my blade, I stepped into the tent.

The flap fell behind me instantly. Dark nearly swallowed me whole but for a small flicker of light guiding me forward through a narrow corridor. I rounded a corner into an open space in the center.

The ground was covered with wooden boards. Against one canvas wall was a table with a tallow candle. A bed covered in fine pelts and furs took the other side, and in the corner . . . my heart stopped.

A woman—tall, wet straw-colored hair to her waist, underfed—faced away from me. She wore nothing but a white nightdress, her feet bare, her fingertips danced across the tip of a silver knife.

I thought my heart might snap through a rib. My tongue danced behind my teeth, ready to speak, ready to scream her name, and beg her to face me. I had to be sure. Disbelief grew potent. How could Herja be alive? Then again, I had been certain I watched Sol dragged to his death.

I didn't get the chance to speak.

She tilted her head to one side, her voice a soft, dangerous rasp. "You must be brave. Or perhaps you are a great fool."

My jaw tightened. Every impulse demanded I run to her, draw her close.

I remembered details of my past. Cherished them. My mother's sly way of stealing bites of my father's honey cakes at meals.

Sol's confident strut through the hallways of the castle. His love of mornings and laughter. My father's scent of hickory and cedar from his long rides in the hills. And Herja's rough voice. A playful sound. When she laughed it scratched and wheezed and made the rest of us laugh even harder.

She was kind and loving, but brutal and deadly all at once.

But I would never forget her voice.

"I have stunned you," she went on, stopping me in my place. "I am supposed to be silent, yes? Strange things have gone on, and not long ago my voice found itself again. I admit, there is a bit of pleasure knowing I will be able to tell you exactly how you will die tonight."

She had been unable to speak?

Would she recognize my voice? I licked my lips and took a step closer. "I do not plan to die today."

She chuckled and held the knife into a skein of moonlight from a gap in the canvas. "They say confidence is important, but I'm afraid the odds are stacked against you. Only one man has ever succeeded."

I'd find him and pick the bones from his body one by one.

Herja snickered, voice low. "Shall we play our game, *Herr*?"

I wheeled back when she spun around and sprinted at me, knife raised. I lunged aside, half stunned at her speed, half stunned this truly was my sister. Alive. Strong. Fearsome.

Alive.

She sneered, clearly not recognizing me. But she was not exactly looking into my eyes, she focused more on my middle, my heart, my throat, and slashed her blade again. I ducked.

A grin spread over my lips. "Have you begun your game?"

Her brown eyes burned like fury pyre. "I urge you not to taunt me. I might take my time killing you, and you are already keeping me from where I truly wish to be."

"You always did talk so mighty." I dodged another strike.

"You know nothing of me." Herja shrieked and lunged, ready to tear out my heart. She was swift, but I had always been the fighter with surer footing. My sister could use a blade like no one I knew, but she had always lacked patience in learning the dance of swordplay.

I used it against her. My feet stamped out an intricate pattern, causing her to stumble long enough I swept my arms around her body from behind, locking her arms against her chest. Herja screamed and gnashed her teeth.

"Stop," I said, holding her tightly. "Stop. Herja, please."

She shuddered, then froze. "My name."

I held her tighter, eyes closed, embracing her for all the years apart.

"Herja," I whispered. "Forgive me for taking so long to find you."

She whipped around and looked at me, really looked at me for the first time. Tears glazed over her eyes. She lifted a trembling hand to her lips, the other dropped her knife and reached for my face.

"V-Valen?" She shook her head violently. "No. No. You're . . . you're dead. Have . . . am I dead?"

I brushed the hair from her eyes, cupping her cheeks. "No. I can't explain it all now, but I have . . . not been myself. Sol is alive. We're alive."

She broke into a haggard sob, her head falling to my chest. "Sol?"

"*Herr* Lönger?" Stor Magnus's voice boomed through the tent walls. "Have you met the gods? You are to signal if the fight has ended, and you still breathe."

Herja's breaths came jagged and rough. She looked to me with fear in her eyes. I retrieved her knife and withdrew my blade. "Our people wait for us outside, but we will need to fight our way through Magnus's guards. Hurry, we must go now."

"No." She pulled back on my arm.

"Herja, we must. This is the only way. I will stay beside you; I swear to you."

"No, you don't—"

"We have no time," I said fiercely. "They will not touch you again."

I pulled her toward the entrance of the tent, and by the hells, my bleeding sister pulled back. "No, I cannot leave, Valen. I will not go with—"

"Will not?" My eyes narrowed. "My people, my wife, are out there risking their lives for you. If I must sling you over my shoulder, I will. Do not doubt me."

"Listen to me!" She shoved my chest. "I cannot leave without them, Brother."

My heart stilled. "Without who?"

Herja wrung her fingers together like they were boneless, she looked through me, as if she saw something I could not see.

"They keep them under guard outside, a reward for me when I win. I must get to them." Two tears fell onto her cheeks. "I have children, Valen. My children are here."

CHAPTER SEVENTEEN
NIGHT PRINCE

Children.

I stared at my sister's face, looking for anything to indicate I'd misheard. Herja met my glare with one of her own. Whatever she'd suffered, it paled in her determination now.

"*Herr* Lönger." Stor's voice came again, and it carried a sharper edge. "Enter," he muttered to someone, no doubt a guard.

I shook my head. The time to stand here mindlessly was over. I gripped Herja's shoulder. "Where?"

"The smaller tent."

So, not Magnus's wife or mistresses. No. The guards at the smaller of the canopies guarded my sister's children. Her children. A dark, hot anger boiled in my chest. She had admitted one man won this game...

I forced the thoughts back. I would embrace the swell of bloodlust later, but now our plans would change.

Returning the seax to the sheath on my waist, I lifted my palms. Fury would reveal us, but it would signal Elise, Tor, and

Halvar that our plans had gone sideways. The flap to the tent rustled and heavy footsteps slapped across the planks.

In a crouch, I touched the earth. A fiery hum burned through my fingertips. The boards cracked. A fissure split the soil. The tent swayed as rock and dirt erupted from the narrow gash. Our guest shouted a cry of surprise, and his thick body stumbled into view around the corner. Herja did not need me to instruct her and had her blade buried in his chest in another breath.

I shredded the earth at her back.

Fury opened my mind, as if I gained a third omniscient eye. Sol, Halvar, Tor, they'd all described a similar sensation when using their magic. Though I did not literally see what was not in front of me, there was a knowledge that came from my power. I knew where to bend and mold the earth against our enemies; I knew where to leave it intact for our people.

The more focused I was with my strikes the more taxing fury became. I could go for hours if I simply bent everything and took out my people while taking out the Ravens. But homing in on enemies and allies added a level of exhaustion and left me unable to use magic for long without resting.

I pushed deeper. Each surge divided parts of the Magnus camp, smashing stones against guards, tripping those who tried to flee, toppling trees over carriages.

All the chaos magnified once I stepped into the light of the camp.

Stor roared commands at his guards as the ground tilted and swayed and split into jagged pieces.

His eyes found me. I grinned and swiped my hand over my chest. A jagged shard of rock and soil rammed to the surface. The man was plump and awful, but he still moved like a warrior.

In the corner of my eye, I caught a glimpse of Ari striking at a guard. He was outmatched in the sword, but it wasn't long before the guard clutched his skull, shrieking of some sort of pest stinging his head.

Ari turned his satisfaction to me, a cruel smile on his face. Shouts rose from the trees as our people surged into the camp. Steel scraped over steel. Grunts and cries filled the night as Magnus's protection faced our greater numbers.

"There!" Herja pointed at the distant tent.

The guards around the tent had scattered, leaving us a clear entrance. Together, we sprinted across the camp, avoiding blades. I pushed inside, and smashed into a thick, armored body. A guard stood in the neck of a narrow space before a large room much like Herja's tent.

His eyes widened for half a breath, then he reached for his sword. He wouldn't get the chance to strike at me before I had the dagger Stor Magnus offered me shoved through the bottom of his chin.

As he gulped and spluttered through the blood, I shoved him aside and rushed into the room.

"You want to leave!" A young, but deep voice shouted at me.

"No, Gunnar." Herja shoved around me, darting into the room. "No, he's safe."

Something itched in my head, a deep, annoying jab of desire to turn on my heel and abandon this tent. I rubbed at the spot and glanced around.

Herja stood on her toes, her arms wrapped around the shoulders of a tall boy—at least sixteen turns. His bright, brown eyes were locked on me, threatening me silently. He shared my sister's scowl, no mistake, but the sharp edges of his face belonged to another.

A man I looked forward to meeting someday.

Behind the boy's legs a pale, innocent face peeked out. A small girl with the same, big eyes, but golden hair like Elise's.

"Laila." Herja sobbed and clutched the girl to her body, joy carved into every line of my sister's face. "I shall never tire of saying your names out loud."

I was an intruder on a private, loving moment, but we had no time.

"Herja," I said.

At my voice the boy, to his credit, stepped in front of my sister and his. Brave. Like his mother.

"Gunnar," Herja said, touching his arm. "This is my brother. Valen."

The boy lifted his brow and studied me under softer eyes. "Your brother?"

"The Night Prince of Etta. Remember me telling you of him?"

Gunnar nodded slowly. "But . . . how—"

"We have no time to explain," I said. "Boy, do you know how to fight?"

He didn't hesitate. "Give me a bow and I will not miss."

I didn't have a bow, but I tossed him the dagger. "A blade will have to do for now. We fight our way to the trees."

"Gunnar," Herja said. "Do not reveal your Talent."

"Maj, I will—"

"Do not. Not here," she snapped.

"You have fury?" I stepped closer.

The boy opened his mouth to respond, but Herja stepped in front of him. "He is not Night Folk but has strange magic. I am told he is called an Al—"

"Alver." I interrupted, studying my sister's son. "I've met several. You did something to me, didn't you?"

"I had only just begun." He smirked with the same arrogance as my sister.

I knew little about the magic of the east, but according to Junius it could manipulate bodies much like Night Folk could manipulate the earth. I rubbed the spot where my head still ached.

"Don't make him use it, Valen. It is painful for him and drains him of his energy too quickly."

"*Maj*." Gunnar's youth betrayed him. While cries of battle waged around him, he still managed to whine to his mother. "I'm getting stronger. I can use it."

"Fight with a blade," I told Gunnar. "Do not give them any other reason to take you. Herja, take the girl, make for the trees. If we are separated, look for Elise. My wife."

A faint smile teased my sister's lips as she gathered her daughter in her arms. "Seems we both have much to share with each other."

Oh, I had many questions. Most pressing, who the father of these children was and how I could find him.

Gunnar accepted Herja's knife. She held her daughter. I offered my nephew a single nod, then blades raised we abandoned the tent.

Blue pyre ignited the night outside. Tor and Halvar worked side by side, devouring the Magnus camp in their fury. But there were more guards—the Ravens we'd spotted had arrived. More than we thought.

My blood heated in my veins. My first thought was of Elise. Where was she? As if she sensed my desperation her voice carried to the stars. "Guard the king! Guard the princess!"

Blood and death littered the camp. Fallen guards were still warm at my feet, but I grinned at the sight of her.

A wildness, a ferocity had taken hold of the soft-spoken *Kvinna* I first met. She pointed from her place between Siv and Casper in my direction. Dark blood stained the short blade in her hands, and her icy braids were damp with sweat and gore.

She was a damn queen.

And her command carried. Folk from Ruskig moved their stances, driving a line of guards away from us as we kept to the edge of the camp.

At the soft cry of a young girl, I was drawn back to the reality that my sister was unarmed and everything about our plans changed the instant young ones were brought into the battle.

I needed to get them out of sight, to safety.

I'd already used a great deal of fury. To use more would make me useless with a sword. But I did not need to drag them into the heart of this fight.

One hand cupped the back of Gunnar's neck as I drew him close. "Take your mother and sister to the trees. No magic, understand?"

He nodded briskly, doubtless a little stunned at the madness around him. I gave him the extra dagger.

"Go. Quickly, now."

Gunnar turned to his mother, took her arm. Herja gave me a worried glance. So many words hovered between us, questions, stories, memories. We would have time to reconnect soon enough.

We had to have time.

As they ran, a Raven came. Then another and another. The cuffs of my shoulders ached the more I used the blade, but it was working. Little by little the camp quieted. Stor Magnus was nowhere in sight. I had plans for the man.

Elise fought her way closer. There was a drive inside me to use fury and shove her back into the trees, protected and guarded. The way I'd divided us once the curse had lifted. But there was a fine line on what I feared more: her safety or her wrath.

She is queen, I reminded myself over and over, uncertain how my father ever survived watching my mother step into battle without losing his head in fear.

Keeping her in my sights, I fought my way toward her as she fought her way toward me. Halvar's lessons were paying off. She had a new viciousness in her strikes. Imperfect, but effective.

But all at once, the world tilted.

"Night Prince!"

A familiar, wretched voice rang out over the camp. I did not need to look to know our plans were about to shift even more. With a slow turn I faced the edge of the camp. Jarl Magnus stood beside his father, lines and lines of Ravens at his back.

But the only sight that mattered was the grip he had on Herja's hair and the knives he had leveled at her children's throats.

I dropped my sword and lifted my hands. "Release her, or I bury us all. This war will end before it truly begins. I have the strength, and I will do it."

"You would not do it. I have learned at least that much about the gaps in your armor—your blood, your family will always be your weakness." Jarl looked down the line to the guard holding Herja's daughter. "Kill the girl first."

"No!" Herja and Gunnar shouted together.

"You don't want to do this," Gunnar shouted, but it weakened. He leaned forward, almost like he might retch. Still, he said the words again. "You . . . don't want to do this."

There was a pause, as if the guard hesitated. A gift from the fates, and I would not slap it away. We were severely outnumbered. Fury had weakened us, no doubt, and Elise, my sister, her children, our people would not die. Not if I could stop it.

Hands raised I lowered to my knees. "They go free, and you shall have me. No fight. No resistance."

"*Valen!*" Elise's cry cracked through my chest, but I had Jarl's attention.

He raised a hand to stop the Raven against little Laila. "What is this? Surrender?"

"The children and the woman go free. Elise, and my people leave this place without harm, and you take me as a trade."

"No." Elise's voice grew closer but muffled. Good. Someone in my guild had the brains to hold her back. Still, I heard her cries of rage as she lashed and kicked and fought to me. "Valen Ferus, you bleeding fool. What are you doing? Do not do this."

Jarl chuckled and told the Raven to keep his blade at the throat of Laila. The little girl whimpered but did not cry out. She clenched her tiny fists. Brave for a child.

"It is a fair trade," Jarl said, "but I know who the woman is, Night Prince. I can't simply allow the second born of the Ferus line to go free."

"She is a woman, nothing more," I insisted, intentionally diminishing her value in their eyes. "You want our fury, take me. Herja has none to give you."

"But she has the blood of your line."

"She stays, or there is no barter, no trade, and many lives will be lost. Hopefully, yours." He would die. Slowly. Painfully. Somehow this snake who always managed to slip through my fingers would die for what he had done to Elise, and now what he threatened against my sister.

"She is skilled with a blade. Too great a risk to run free."

I scoffed. "A choice must be made, Jarl Magnus. I have set the terms. Choose wisely."

Any arrogance faded. Now, blind hatred painted his features in an ugly twist. Jarl Magnus had been backed into a corner, and it was a dangerous place to put a man like him.

"She is of Ferus blood," he shouted, more to himself than anyone, the dilemma stewing in his skull.

"Take me then," Gunnar shouted.

Bleeding hells. My smile faded.

"Gunnar, stop," Herja begged.

He ignored her. "You want Ferus blood with magic, take me and leave my mother and sister. I have the magic you want. I have the bloodline you want."

"Shut up, boy," I snarled. Stupid, stupid, reckless fool.

Jarl tilted his head, wholly invested in Gunnar now. He released Herja into the hands of his father and stalked over to her son. "Is this true? A little Ferus pup?"

"They are her bastards," Stor said, nodding.

Jarl laughed, a deep bellow from his throat. "And who is the father?"

"A man from the East with the strange body fury of their mystics."

"So, fury does live in these veins. Interesting. No doubt more valuable than a woman without a hint of fury."

"Leave him." Herja rammed her elbow into the ribs of Stor and earned a strike to the face.

"Touch her again and you will know just what fury can do before you die," I said in a tight snarl.

I was not the only one who had raised their hands to defend the princess. In my side view Ari gasped through exhaustion and held out his hands. Stieg, and Halvar beside him, awaiting my simple command to strike.

Jarl frowned, but flicked his fingers, so the guards pulled Gunnar forward.

"No!" Herja fought against Stor. She nearly broke free, but two Ravens rammed her head with the hilt of their blades.

A slab of jagged rock split the spine of one of the guards. A stillness creeped over the camp as they shot their stun at me.

"I said do not touch her."

"Maj." Gunnar's voice cracked. "Let it be."

Jarl glared at the dead Raven. "Leave the woman."

"She knows the blade too well," Stor argued.

"As do we." Jarl narrowed his eyes. "We have the blood of the three Ferus heirs. It is all that is needed." He abandoned his place, leaving Gunnar to his Ravens, and stalked across the space to me. On my knees, I met his eye. His smile was gone, his voice low. "I've waited for this moment, Night Prince. Now your poor brother will not be the only one who bears the weight of my frustration."

My jaw tightened as Jarl commanded I be bound, my fury blocked.

"No," I said. "I will not be bound until my people have been given the freedom to leave."

Jarl let out a long breath of frustration but nodded with a jerk of his head. "So be it. Let the traitors pass. For now."

"The Valkyrie is mine," Stor said.

"And the Night Prince belongs to your king. You will not interfere." Jarl outranked his father now.

The sod had no choice but to clench his teeth.

"Valen!" Elise shrieked her fear when the Ravens came toward me, and I did nothing. "Fight for the king, you bleeding fools."

A shift through our people stirred at her voice.

"Keep my bride silent, Night Prince," Jarl said. "Or I will take her as well, and she will never leave my bed until she stops breathing."

Fury raged in my blood. How I yearned to crush his bones with the weight of the earth. I lifted my chin and shouted, "From your king, you will stand down. You will go."

Hesitation halted the attack. Elise raged more as Tor began to pull her away. Ari and Stieg looked at me, as if they weren't sure if I meant it. I gave the nod to Halvar. His fist slammed against his chest, and he urged them to retreat as he went to Herja.

I held my breath, waiting, ready to crumble the earth in one last surge should Stor and his guards do anything to my sister. Silent tears streamed down Herja's face as she gathered her daughter in her arms, and allowed Halvar to hold her against his side, then start the slow retreat to the trees.

The Ravens tossed Gunnar to the ground. His gaze twisted to me. Fear lived there yet he said nothing. I held his eyes, silently reassuring him I would watch him, be with him.

Herja cried his name. Elise cried mine.

She struggled against Tor, murder in her eyes. "Valen, you promised me. Do not do this."

A heady rush of fear could be felt from every man, every woman who'd come with us against the camp. I could not go to her, but I could speak.

"Raise them up, Elise. Command them!" I shouted at her as she was dragged into the shadows of the night. Our people followed into the trees, final glances found me and fueled the heat beneath my skin. "Bow to your queen! For Etta. Rise for Etta!"

Elise's cries faded as Tor and the Guild of Shade forced their queen away from me.

I slouched forward. This was not the end. This was a misstep. One that would separate us, true. But as promised, I would not stop until I fought my way back to her.

Ravens bound my wrists and Gunnar's. Bindings would do nothing against his Alver blood, but a hot sting scorched my wrists where the silver bands cut into my skin. They lifted me under the arms and forced me to my feet.

Jarl faced me, smiling. "I look forward to our time together, Night Prince."

"As do I." I returned the grin. A silent promise of all the plans I, too, held for him.

My heart left with Elise, my fears, my hopes, my love. I replaced the emptiness with dark bloodlust and imagined every way I would crumble the gilded world of the false king over his head.

Not as I imagined it would happen, but we would go to Ravenspire. Sol would get his wish.

I was coming home to visit him.

CHAPTER EIGHTEEN
ROGUE PRINCESS

My friend,

I fear the battle is lost. Our refuge is filled to the brink. Eli has made his demands. I do not know what more I can do. If I refuse him, my sons, my husband, and my daughter will die.

But if I accept, they still suffer, and my soul dies. Perhaps death for us all will be sweeter. At least we shall dine with the gods together. I know you said we must live—to save this land—we must live, but you ask too much.

I will not watch them suffer. And I will not be a betrayer's and false king's consort.

By refusing him it will be the end of the Ferus rule. Do not mistake me, I will see to it we are all dead by morning before they get the chance to torture a hair of my family.

Farewell my friend. Be well. Be safe.

—Lili

Numb. Cold. Nothing.

I stared blankly at the velvet sky above me, softly rocking with the movement of the cart we'd used to travel to the encampment.

Where I should rage, I was silent.

Where I should cry, tears ran dry.

I recognized faces of those I loved around me, but only Valen's face filled my head.

Part of me hated him. Part of me mourned for him. Part of me loved him so fiercely I thought I might break in two. But I said nothing, did nothing, simply stared at the soundless stars above my head, alone and numb.

Cold.

Nothing.

When the cart rolled through the walls of Ruskig, a hand rested on my shoulder.

"Elise." My gaze turned to Tor. He would know, he would understand. His *hjärta* was lost to him too. A crack of pain jolted my heart from its stillness and tears brimmed in my eyes, blurring his face. Tor squeezed my shoulder and shook his head. "No. Not yet. Not here. Keep your head, My Queen, and think this through."

How Torsten knew what I needed to hear I could only guess. With a quick swipe of my hand, I buried the sting of emotion away and rose from the back of the cart. My mind whirled. What steps came next? How did we get to Valen? Where did we strike?

"One action at a time, Elise." Now Halvar's voice melted through my silent hysteria.

"One action." I cracked several knuckles. Every eye turned to me. Haggard, desperate, frightened folk looked to me now.

The pressure was crushing.

I nodded my head at no one, eyes on the back of the cart. Herja Ferus was alive. She rocked a sleeping child in her arms. Her eyes were swollen from quiet tears. She was weak, too thin; she shivered in a thin linen nightdress.

I licked my lips and faced Halvar. "Take the princess into the longhouse. Get her food, get them warm."

Halvar nodded his approval. "As you say."

I quickened my step in the same direction. Soon enough my flanks were marked by Siv, Brant, Ari, and the entire Guild of Shade but for Halvar who remained with Kari and Herja.

"Keep everyone who is not part of the king's inner council from the longhouse," I told Stieg and Casper.

They bowed their heads and rushed to the doors, barking at curious folk who came looking for answers. I would need to prepare our people soon enough. We'd fight. We'd bring war to Ravenspire. How and when, I didn't know, but more than I knew I had to breathe, I knew war drew near.

Ari held the door for me, and I stormed into the great hall.

"I need a moment," I snapped, and hurried to the bedroom.

Alone, hand pressed to my heart. I gasped through a sob as it ripped from my throat. Still on wooden shelves were Valen's clothes. I grabbed one of his black tunics and held it to my face, breathing in the woodsmoke and freshness of him. His battle axes—he'd left them to avoid being recognized—were polished and set neatly on a table near our bed. My fingers traced the curved blades.

Once I'd despised these weapons, now I wanted nothing more than to see him here, tying them to his belt, laughing, or teasing. Anything so long as he was here.

"A woman told me to bring her in here."

I whipped around. Herja stood at the fur covering the door. Her little daughter's head on her shoulder. With furious swipes, I rid the tears off my cheeks, and I gestured to the bed. "Yes, here. Take this for you both."

Up close I noted the similarities of Herja to Sol and Valen. She was not Night Folk, so her ears curved like mine, but her skin was a soft chestnut like theirs. Her hair like summer berries in the sunlight, and her eyes like tilled soil.

Her cheeks were sunken, and shadows circled beneath her eyes, but Herja Ferus had a fierce beauty about her.

"Clothes." I fumbled around the shelves of my own dresses and tunics. Herja stood at least half a head taller than me, with longer arms and legs. I gathered the longest dress I had and placed it on the table, hands shaking. "I'll . . . I'll find more. And food. You should eat. I'll get you—"

"Elise." Herja's hand stopped my fumbling and rambling. "We will get him back."

My jaw pulsed. Heat flooded my neck, making a slow, tenuous crawl to my face. "He wanted to go to Ravenspire. I want to scream at him, for I don't know if he did this on purpose."

"Why would Valen want to go to Ravenspire?"

My body trembled, but I was as stone. "The Sun Prince. We believe he has found something, but . . . we had plans to bring the Sun Prince to us, not put Valen behind the walls of Ravenspire."

"Plans often change. We would've been slaughtered had he not done what he did."

I didn't want to hear it, didn't want the rationale of a king who made the best—perhaps the only—choice for his people and family. I wanted him here to shout and scream and hold. Alive and warm. Safe.

I turned away from the bed and stared at the stars as if they might hold some sort of answer.

"You are Timoran," Herja said after a long pause.

"Does it offend you?"

"Do you love my brother for his heart and not his crown?"

Hot tears sprang to my eyes. I bid them away, but they

resisted violently. "Valen Ferus stole my heart and soul before I knew his true name. He could be a pauper and my heart would bleed as fiercely for him as it does now. Truth be told, I'd prefer the pauper to Ravenspire endlessly seeking to separate us because he is king."

"King." She scoffed with a bit of disbelief. "How long has he held the throne?"

"Since the beginnings of spring."

Herja's face shadowed, a groove formed between her brows as if a thought pummeled her head. It was a look gone in an instant, fast enough I wondered if I'd imagined it. When I looked again, a faint grin played with her lips. "To your question, I am not offended by the blood in your veins."

"I am the great-granddaughter of King Eli." I didn't understand why I spewed all the rotten pieces of my lineage. Perhaps from a desperate need to have the brittle pieces exposed, a desire to hide nothing, to be accepted by the only Ferus I had with me.

"Ah. Am I supposed to hate you because of this? Is that what you're getting at?" She shook her head. "I suppose I should despise my mother then. She was his most cherished friend, after all. Probably knew the bastard better than anyone. Oh, and she was Timoran. How horribly selfish of her."

Three. There were three sharp-tongued Ferus's in my life now. A smile would've come if my heart were not a pile of ash in my chest, but her dismissal of my fears helped ease the tension cramping my muscles in knots.

"This is what matters to me: if you love my brother as you say you do, then I will trust you to lead us back to him and my son with every beat of my heart."

I blinked, unsure what to say. No words seemed fitting. I said nothing.

She turned away, tucked her daughter beneath the furs, and

pressed a gentle kiss to the child's forehead. Herja paused, stroking the girl's cheek for a few breaths.

"I've only been able to kiss her to sleep a few times in her entire life."

My heart tightened in my chest. "They kept you from her?"

"From both my children. Perhaps once every ten days I would get a few cherished moments with them. To be able to sit here beside her and hold her until she sleeps—I hardly know what to do."

I held my stomach, eyes closed. "I'm sorry about your boy."

Herja stiffened. "He is too bold. So like his father." She glanced over her shoulder, an empty smile on her lips. "Their father is not what you might think."

A patron. A rapist. If not that, what would he be? Where was he? I did not have a chance to ask the questions or press at all before the fur over the door was pulled back.

Tor and Halvar stepped inside the room.

Herja stood and rushed to them. Her arms hooked around both their necks. "I finally have a moment to breathe. Let me look at you both. By the gods, I never thought I'd see you alive."

She kissed Halvar's cheek. He grinned at her like a brother might. Herja paused at Tor, her palm on his cheek. "Torsten. Sol . . ."

"Yes, I know. I was just as surprised," Tor said, voice rough.

Herja let out a quivering breath and embraced him again.

"It is good to have you returned to us, Viper," Halvar said.

A raspy chuckle burst from the princess. "Hells, how long has it been since I've heard that name?"

Halvar looked to me. "We never knew when Herja might leap from the shadows and attack, all to practice and prove she was the greater fighter. We started calling her Viper."

I forced a smile, but as delightful as the reunion might've been, my heart was hardened and scabrous and cold.

"Elise," Tor said softly. "I understand this is trying, but you are queen and needed. The council is waiting."

By the skies, I wished Valen were here. His presence added a strength to me. One I would need to summon now. For him. For our people. For Etta. I did not bother washing my face of the blood or kohl running down my cheeks and followed them through the doorway.

Frenzied faces filled the hall. Elder Klok held up his arms trying to calm all the shouting and desperate opinions on how to proceed. Stieg and Casper stood beside Brant, Mattis, and Kari near my doorway. They stiffened when I stepped into the room, looking to me for guidance. I came up dry.

The only person who seemed at ease was Ari. He drank in the seat beside Valen's.

At first glance, the former king might've appeared wholly unbothered by the events of the night, but if one took the time to look closer, they'd notice the untouched, full drinking horn at the king's seat. As if Valen might come and indulge at any moment. They'd notice the way Ari slumped over, losing himself in his cups.

"We need to act now!"

My stomach twisted at the voice. Stave, red-faced and furious, shouted back at Elder Klok when the old man told them to be still.

"We will not be going anywhere tonight." I surprised myself when my voice carried over the madness.

Stave's slate eyes pinned me against the wall. A wild, seething frustration marred his face. He held me there, locked in his disdain for several breaths before looking back to Klok. "We should act now, or we risk losing the king to Ravenspire once again. The princess is a warrior, she can lead us—"

"The queen," Ari muttered through a hiccup. "I think you mean the queen."

From the corner of my eye, Herja came into view. She leaned against the wall, silently watching the conflict. Would she push me aside and lead here if enough of the people wished it?

Valen's request was for me to raise these people. I did not know his sister, nor her desires toward the crown. But while Stave started his rant about action again, Herja remained silent. Her eyes landed on me, a soft smile on her lips. Almost like she wondered what I might do next.

Stave narrowed his gaze at Ari, then flicked his eyes to me. Bold. Foolish. "I serve the Ferus line. Their blood brings life to this land, they are the gods-chosen to heal Etta. Not a royal of our enemies."

For too many months I'd allowed Stave and his hateful stares to bubble under my skin, adding to the layers of inadequacy I already carried for the crown. Tonight, my blood burned in such anger the room shaded in a crimson heat.

Taken in a bit of madness, I hardly noticed the dagger in my hand, but I let it fly. The point sailed the short distance between us and lodged deep into the wall, a hairsbreadth from Stave's ear. I crossed the room, lost in the same maelstrom of rage, and shoved another knife I carried across the small of my back against the soft skin of his throat.

"Enough, or I cut out your ability to speak." Each word peeled from the back of my throat. "I will hear your dissension no more; it is well past time for you to choose your place and serve your queen."

The room went silent.

For the first time Stave looked at me with a degree of reverence, maybe fear, but he clenched his jaw.

I pulled the knife back, a line of fresh blood beneath his chin, and I faced the stunned council.

Except Ari. He showed no stun, and once again grinned through a long drink of his horn.

"I am the queen of Etta, and my crown is not up for negotiation. You stand with me, or you are nothing more than a snake in the grass, and I will crush your head." I turned back to Stave, voice harsh and fierce. "Disloyalty ends now! We will act, we will burn Ravenspire to the ground if needed, but tell me now, do you stand with your Timoran queen who bleeds for this land and its king? Or do you see nothing but your enemy in my face?"

One breath. Two. More. Tension gathered like a storm on the horizon.

"Bow to the queen!" Halvar roared. He took the knee first, Tor following straightaway. They hung their heads, fists crossed over their hearts.

It was a wave of kneeling. Mattis, Siv. Next, Kari, Brant, the Guild of Shade.

Herja's smile widened. "I stand with the Ferus line the same as the fool in the back."

I hated the idea of killing Valen's sister, but if she betrayed us now, I would not hesitate. When it came to freeing him, I could not afford any added risks.

But Herja turned her smirk to Stave. "I stand with my sister, Elise Ferus. The *hjärta* of my brother. I would give my loyalty to no one else. And you are fortunate you have such a forgiving queen. Had you spoken to me in such a way, the point of that knife would be pierced into the back of your throat, not a slab of wood."

At that, Herja lowered to her knee. It took no time for the rest of the hall to bend the knee. Stave lowered his head in, what I hoped, was a bit of shame.

After the room spent a few heartbeats on their knees, I

embraced the fire in my blood and nodded. "Rise. And let us begin."

I barked orders for the council to gather our weapons, to prepare our warriors for battle. A new wave of confidence took hold. The frightening strength Valen often showed came out in me, and I reveled in it. Without a sure plan, I would not see my husband again. And I refused to accept that outcome.

By the hells, I refused to accept it.

"Halvar," I said.

"My Queen?" His voice was playful, but attentive.

"You will lead us in our strategy. Work with Brant, Stieg, and Mattis—develop a plan of formation around Ravenspire. Where we strike, what weapons to use, what bleeding time of day we move. I want any detail marked and noted. I want every blade of grass on the lawns of the castle covered."

Halvar dipped his chin.

I had one final request. "Ari, Casper. You will board a ship tonight. Sail to our friends in the east with haste. Use water fury until you cannot stand, until you cannot breathe, I don't care. But get to Junius without delay."

Ari rose at once. "What message do we deliver?"

I had already started scratching my directive on a battered piece of parchment, but as I wrote, I repeated the missive out loud. "Tell her we need them now. Tell her, we need the one she calls Nightrender. His fate is here with us, so our battle might finally end . . . as his begins."

CHAPTER NINETEEN
NIGHT PRINCE

Being kept face down in the barred coach had caused part of my face to go numb, but what I knew of Jarl Magnus, I'd expected to be dragged behind the wheels all the way to Ravenspire.

Beside me, Gunnar was on his belly. For the first time since meeting my nephew, he appeared terribly young. Alone here in the dark, with the stink of vomit on the laths from past prisoners, his boyish features bled into me. Each wince of fear, each wrinkle of his brow when a Raven slapped at the bars drew out a wild protectiveness of my sister's son.

"Gunnar." I waited until he opened his eyes. "When we arrive at the gate, do not speak to them, but if you must—tell them you have fury. Our magic."

"I don't have fae features."

The ears. Dammit. "Then insist you lied about your gift to save your mother. Do not let on you are one of these Alver folk."

"They'll kill me."

"They won't touch you."

"My maj told me of those bindings on your wrists. I know they kill your magic. What can you do?"

"Know this about our family, we fight for each other. I will fight for you. Bindings will not stop me, boy. I swear it."

The coach rolled to a stop. Blood rushed to my head. Alone, I would have little fear. I would find Sol, and we'd work our way out of these damn walls. Now, we had the weight of keeping Gunnar alive when his magic would draw a fine price in the East.

"Follow my lead," I hurried to say. "They're like bleeding dogs and will smell your fear. They'll use it against you, Gunnar. This is when you must be strong."

He nodded briskly; fists clenched in the chains behind his back.

"They'll take us to dungeons. Be ready for pain, but you can do this. You are Herja Ferus's son. You are made of substance that does not break easily."

Gunnar visibly tensed when the back doors hauled open and greedy hands tugged at his legs and arms, wrenching the boy to his feet. A swell of pride tightened my chest at his instant resilience. In front of the Ravens he did not wilt. His head was lifted—he was from royal blood and the boy showed it.

Three Ravens reached for me. They were anything but gentle as they dragged me by my legs from the back of the coach. My head slammed onto the ground, and one guard kicked at my hip, a signal for me to stand.

Before I could, two thick boots stomped in front of my face.

Jarl towered over me. "Welcome home, Night Prince." I braced, knowing a coward as him would kick to show his dominance, but the sting of his boot still shocked my system. "Get up."

Jarl was shorter than me, but still gripped a fistful of my hair, forcing my face close to his. "I see so much of Legion Grey in you, the man I tried so desperately to impress. How cunning you must think yourself. Fooling a kingdom. But you don't know any of the true secrets Ravenspire keeps. You don't know what we already know."

I grinned wickedly. "I assure you, when you knew me as a dowry negotiator, you were neither my first choice for the *Kvinna*, nor did you impress me."

He struck my jaw. What a bleeding fool. Showing how words crawled under his skin by losing his head at a few biting remarks.

"I do not think it bothers you that I fooled a kingdom," I said, spitting blood. "It bothers you that I fooled *you*."

His eyes darkened. I wasn't finished. If this sod craved power, but crumbled under words, I would slash his innards with every taunt, every jab until he could not escape his own fragile mind.

I lowered my voice. "What really bothers you, though, is Elise. A woman—a lesser in your eyes—did not choose you. That even after my lies, she still chose me. You will never win her."

"I will break her, and I will make you watch."

Unlike Jarl, I'd learned to conceal reactions. While his threat burned in the deepest parts of my soul, I kept my face smug and aloof. "I doubt that. You met your match in the Queen of Etta, Jarl Magnus. You cannot break her, but she will undoubtedly break you."

Jarl's pale cheeks burned in a flush of red, but he turned his rage to Gunnar. "Did you know your mother is dead, boy? That little mouse of a sister too."

Gunnar blanched.

"He's lying," I told him.

"Am I?" Jarl chuckled. "We no longer needed her. One direct link to the princess was plenty. Why take the risk of her blades finding us again? She's dead, strung from a tree. Naked. So the entire kingdom can see what a pathetic, shell of woman the legendary Herja Ferus became."

Gunnar made a move for Jarl, but a Raven swung the blunt end of a hilt against his stomach. I ground my teeth together as he doubled over.

"You don't believe me, Night Prince?" Jarl asked.

"Not at all." Truth be told, I wasn't sure. They could've pursued everyone after we were taken away.

"Then you are a fool. Take them to the holding chamber."

An entire unit of Ravens surrounded us through the portcullis of the main courtyard. Gunnar wiped his mouth, torment carved in the lines of his young face. I nudged his shoulder. "He's found your weakness. They will now use your mother and sister against you. Do not let them."

His voice cracked. "What if she's . . ."

"Hells," I hissed. "Do you know your mother at all? You think she would not slaughter half a unit to defend your sister? The only reason she did not take up arms before was because you had to play the great defender and get yourself chained."

"You should talk. You got yourself snatched too," he grumbled.

"Bury your fears." I practically snarled the words. "I'll not warn you again."

"I've dealt with Ravenspire my whole life. I don't need warnings."

"Am I supposed to be impressed? You survived a fat, out-of-commission warrior. This is the bleeding snake pit. Now keep your mouth shut."

I already held a chest full of affection for this boy I'd just met. But he would need to meet fire with fire. I would not coddle him, not when his life depended on cunning and the will to fight.

Gunnar took me at my word and pinched his lips, trudging silently toward the tower.

Castle Ravenspire was less of a stone and brick castle, and

more wood and wattle built tall and in wide towers. It had withstood the turns of battle from my great-grandparents to false kings.

Eli had reshaped much of the grounds to suit his endless consorts and wives.

Villas and longhouses speckled the lawns that once were open and lovely with gardens my mother loved so much. There were wide open fields where we could ride horses, or spar, or use fury to feed this land with magic and the gods' power.

I did not recognize this place any longer.

Golden sunlight was buried behind gray, somber skies. Lush grass and wildflowers had wilted into cold, wet earth. Once these grounds breathed with sweet blossoms. Now a constant burn of standing water and mildew soaked the wood panels and mud beneath our feet.

Wizened branches of moonvane struggled to live, until I strode past.

I didn't miss the few murmurs between the Ravens when the silvery blooms burst to life; the boughs seemed to reach and arch for us as we were shoved into the far tower.

"Up. Move." A Raven pushed my shoulder when I turned toward the lower levels of the tower.

Up? Why would they place us in the upper levels? Hells, I despised not knowing what these sods were planning. I could brave the face for a time, but Jarl did speak true that Ravenspire—that Calder—had games to which only he knew the rules.

One Raven gripped Gunnar's arm, wrenching it too high up the boy's back. "Move your feet."

It was swift. A simple adjustment of my stance, my chained arms, and I soon had the heavy iron fetter laced around the guard's neck, a dozen short blades pointed at my back from his companions.

"Don't touch the boy again," I hissed in the Raven's ear. "If you think a few chains will keep me from snapping your neck, you are mistaken."

The point of a blade jabbed my back. "Stand down, Night Prince."

"Do we have an agreement?" I looked at the bold guard behind me.

"Release him. No one will harm the bleeding boy."

I sneered and pulled the chains off the neck of the Raven and stepped back. "Was that so hard?"

"For now." The Raven added. "The boy will be left alone for now."

"As you will be left alone. For now."

Gunnar stood a little straighter, a faint smile pasted on his lips as the Ravens kept a healthier distance from us and led us to the highest room in the tower.

"Windows are warded with magic you don't have, little prince," the lead guard said at the door. "Rooftops, doorways, it's all warded and you can't use your earth fury to get out. Don't try. We'll know."

"Ah. Clever of you. Don't you think?" I glanced at Gunnar. "They are so impressive with their little tricks."

I was going to get struck again, but I'd say it over and over if it drew the wide smile on my nephew's sober face.

The lead Raven pointed all his disdain at me as he unlocked the door.

I made swift mental notes of everything. Heat. There would likely be a stove or small fire inside. Thick walls. We'd be unable to hear goings on in the towers or hallways. A flicker of light. Could be from lanterns, or the fire. They didn't plan to torture us with darkness and cold. Then it'd likely be through pain.

I could summon the bloodlust inside; I could tolerate pain. It was Gunnar I feared for.

A final detail. The door key—a rune stone. One I couldn't read or understand. Dammit. The Raven spoke true, and fury didn't guard these walls. Distant magic or manipulated fury from the experiments at the quarries held us in here.

But what the Ravens didn't know was we had an Alver on our side. I didn't know the depths of Gunnar's abilities, but maybe he could help somehow.

To my surprise—no, my suspicions—the Raven turned me and released the chains on my wrists and ankles. The bindings remained, but I wasn't shackled. What games were they playing?

"Get in and do us all a favor and be good, little prince." The Raven chuckled and slammed the door behind him.

I didn't understand this. In all my turns in the captivity of Timorans, a warm, comfortable room without chains had never been part of their strategy.

I trusted this less than a dank cell below ground.

Gunnar and I stood shoulder to shoulder, unmoving for at least four heartbeats before laughter stirred me from my puzzlement.

When I glanced over my shoulder, my heart sank to the pit of my stomach. "Sol."

A smile on his face, a mischievous gleam in his eye, my brother stood from the edge of a large bed.

In five wide strides, I crossed the room into Sol's open arms. I'd always been broader, while Sol was the tallest, but my embrace seemed to swallow him whole. All gods. I clenched my eyes shut; my forehead fell against his shoulder.

Sol's big hand gripped my tunic. The both of us kept slapping the other on the back, the sound a constant reminder this was real. He was real. No longer a face I saw at a distance. Here, I didn't feel a drop of shame at the sting of tears. When I pulled away, Sol even batted at his face, laughing sheepishly.

"Hells, Valen." He cupped the back of my neck, forcing my brow to his like our father used to do. "I've missed you."

"Have you? Seems you've been living well while we freeze in Ruskig."

Sol scanned the large room. "A play in their game. Simply another play. You've joined a gilded cage."

I cleared my throat and patted the side of his face.

Sol adjusted, sniffing, and clearing away his emotion. "And well done. You must be a little wise if you figured out my message. Though, you are an idiot and came without a much-needed piece. Where is Herja?"

"Safe. With Elise."

"Grand. Why the hells is she not here?"

I gestured to Gunnar who remained by the door, shifting on his feet. "Because her son has the same hero complex as you and I."

"Son?" Sol gaped at me, then looked back to Gunnar. He took a few strides across the room before the truth hit him square in the face. Sol was the brother who loved best. He'd been happiest, kindest, probably the most wicked depending on the day. But when his family or his *hjärta* were ever threatened, the eldest Ferus became the deadliest. "What do you know of the bastard who fathered him? Where is he?"

"We'll find him."

Gunnar's eyes flashed in a bolt of anger I'd not seen. "My daj isn't like those other men. I know you must think he hurt Maj, but he didn't. They've loved each other for turns, and now they took him." Gunnar's breaths came deeper, more ragged. "All he wanted was to keep us safe and . . . they took him."

Sol was nearest, and cautiously put a hand on the boy's shoulder. "Who took him?"

Gunnar's eyes were red, but he fought mightily to steady his voice. "My father is Alver folk. From the Eastern Kingdom. They forced him to play for the Valkyrie, but he only pretended to. He always told me he fell in love with Maj that first night. She listened to him, didn't kill him, and for hours all they did was learn of each other even though Maj could not speak."

"Herja couldn't speak?" Sol looked at me.

I didn't have answers, so I simply shrugged.

"The first time I heard my mother's voice was only months ago. Something changed, we all felt it, and her voice returned," Gunnar said.

Sol glanced at me. "It was the same with me. All at once, I could think clearly again, and their manipulations began to fail. What changed?"

I racked my mind, trying to think. "Nothing. After we left you here when I came for Elise, we returned to Ruskig, and I suppose the only difference was . . ." I paused, eyes wide. "I took the throne."

Half Sol's mouth curled. "The land chose you. There is much to be said about the fury of this earth. These curses placed upon us, perhaps they could not withstand it. Etta is fighting back, Valen."

A thrill raced through my blood. If true, then we had the power of the purest fury on our side. The bleeding power of the fates themselves.

Sol looked to our nephew. "Boy—"

"My name is Gunnar," he muttered. "Are you the Sun Prince? My other uncle? Maj often spoke of you both. She always wanted us to know our history, our people."

"I am," Sol said. "But tell us of you. How old are you now?"

"Sixteen this past summer."

"You have magic?"

"Yes. I . . . I can manipulate the mind."

"Not earth magic?"

"Alver folk," I started, "their magic is over the body."

"Fascinating," Sol whispered. "What can you do with this manipulation?"

"Convince people to do things. Plant ideas in their minds," Gunnar said. "But . . . it hurts. I can't hold it long."

I recalled the itch in my skull when we met, the desire I had to leave the tent. He'd told me I wanted to leave, and I *had* wanted to leave.

"I can fight, though," Gunnar insisted. "I'm better than Maj with a bow. Rarely, if ever, do I miss."

Sol laughed. "I have no doubt your gifts will be very useful."

"Possibly. I don't want to expose him to the false king, though." I folded my arms over my chest. "I want to know more about your father. You say he was a good man? He cared for Herja?"

"Yes. They have been together for nearly eighteen turns. They played the charade of defeating the Silent Valkyrie well, so as a reward, Magnus allowed Daj to visit twice a turn."

"Did Magnus harm you?"

"My father's family is nobility in the east, and I believe Stor Magnus does trade with them. He did not beat us or torture us out of fear one word from my father would ruin their civil business."

"If he has such power, why did he not free you?"

Gunnar's jaw pulsed. "He tried. All my life he's tried. I don't know the Eastern Kingdom well, but he fought against his folk, and ours here. The best deal he bartered was for Laila and me to remain unharmed and unable to ever be sold. He tried to use his magic to break the bonds that held Maj captive. When they found out, I did not see him for an entire turn. He is nobility, but not as free as you might think."

It would not surprise me. If this man was an Alver, Junius hinted magic was as brutally hunted on her shores as it was here.

"But when Daj returned months ago, my mother had her voice. She told him something had changed. Begged him to take us away. She knew something dangerous was happening in the land. He promised he'd return for her, but we only made it as far as the north fjord before they caught us.

"He wouldn't let me use my mesmer—that's what he calls it. He didn't want them to know I was Alver folk and made sure they didn't. His Alver magic is blocking and snuffing out other gifts by a simple thought. I could've protected him." Gunnar closed his eyes and shook his head. "A man from the east was there at the docks, almost like they knew we'd run. I . . . I think it was his father. My daj told me all would be well, but I know it isn't. He always writes to us, but we've heard nothing since he left. We don't know where he is."

This was . . . unexpected. Part of me wondered if Gunnar was shown only what this man wanted him to see. He might appear to be a doting lover to his children, but perhaps alone with Herja he was cruel. But it didn't fit. Herja would never allow him to live or go near her young ones if he were vicious.

I looked to Sol. "Magnus pretended not to know the man, called him a mystic. If they have correspondence, we might be able to find him."

Sol scratched his chin. "Add finding Herja's lover to the list of tasks we have yet to accomplish. A name would be helpful, Gunnar."

"Hagen Strom," he said, eyeing us with caution.

"Do you know anything about his life or family?"

"Not much. H-He didn't like talking about his home, but he

mentioned once if ever we came to the Eastern Kingdom, he'd introduce us to one person. A younger sister, but he didn't say her name. All I know is she is an Alver, and he was hesitant to speak of her. Said she was one of those valuable Kinds that would be traded if anyone knew what she could do."

"It's not much, but it's something to search out," Sol said.

Gunnar wrung his fingers in knots. "You . . . you really would help find him?"

"What did I tell you?" I asked. "This family fights for each other. If your father is Herja's *hjärta*, then it means a great deal." I closed my eyes against thoughts of Elise. One task at a time. "It makes your father family. When we win back this land—and we must—we will do what we can to find him."

"Agreed," Sol said. "But for now, we have more pressing issues. Did you make Elise's title official?"

"She is queen. Why?"

"I don't know, but her sister and the false king feared greatly if Elise took the title as queen. I don't understand it, and now her sister will want her more than anyone."

"You put a target on Elise?" My voice rumbled dark and low.

"Me? You took the vows. Did you take them only at my word, or do you love the woman?"

I cracked a few knuckles. Words were flying, and I needed to keep my head. I'd already planned to take vows before we found Sol. "Sorry. I cannot stand that I've left her to raise this fight alone."

"But she will?" Sol asked. "She is a woman who will bear the burden of queen like our mother?"

I smirked. "Elise will tear this kingdom to the ground soon enough."

"Good. I look forward to seeing the fear on her sister's face."

"What do you know, Sol? Why did you need me to come?"

My brother hesitated. "When my mind had returned to me, I did not let on for some time and played the part of insanity well. I've overheard many things, Valen. Careless words spoken amongst the guards when they did not think I could understand. The false king was desperate to trap you, to have your power here where he could keep watch on it. He did not know Herja lived at first, but when he discovered the truth, he came for me."

"How did he learn she was alive?"

"I think when the curses lifted from us, she could no longer hide her bloodline and word was sent to Ravenspire. Did strange things happen around her when her voice returned?" Sol asked Gunnar.

The boy took a breath, then nodded. "Yes. Now that you mention it. The land around our manor where they kept us changed. The flowers always pointed at her, as in they moved when we walked past."

I chuckled. "The land gave up her secret. It is because the fury of this land chose the Ferus line to rule here long ago. You will see it do the same for us."

"Magnus pressed her when they took note of it," Gunnar said with a deadened voice. "It was one of the few times he hurt her. They chained me, but I could hear her try to fight him off until they took Laila and threatened to cut off my sister's ears. Maj finally gave up her true name. She'd been known as Breeta until then. Only we knew her as Herja Ferus."

By the dark glare Sol pinned on me, it did not take much to guess he had the same thoughts as me. House Magnus would burn for what they'd done to our sister.

"The false king lives in his bleeding library," Sol said after a pause. "He spends his days searching prophecies and sagas. Perhaps he has slipped into his own bit of madness."

"What did he do?" Gunnar asked. "You said he came for you when he learned my mother lived."

Sol dragged a hand through his dark hair. "He shouted at me, said he knew my mind had been restored. He said the curses were dead and insisted I tell him what I knew of a tomb, to explain how the land would die if we died. For once I had no idea what he was talking about." Sol rubbed a spot over his chest. "No amount of torture gave him answers."

I closed my eyes. How long had they hurt my brother all because their king was losing himself to old writings? But, unfortunately, Calder's rantings held a degree of understanding for me.

I despised fate. She never did make life's path simple. "There is a tomb I know. The Black Tomb, and it is a wretched place, Sol."

His eyes widened. "You've been?"

"I died there. Nearly twice."

Sol arched a brow. "I'll expect that story later, but for now, we need to figure out a plan on how we can get there. The false king insists our mother hid powerful fury in this tomb and only the blood of her heirs will be able to open the doors. If they do not, the land will slowly die in time, and our curses will shift to Timorans."

"And Calder believes this?"

Sol grinned darkly. "More than he believes in his own name. Before he knew my mind was no longer dark, the false king ranted for hours, cursing his dead father for telling him nothing of the fury secrets passed down between Timoran kings. He is discovering truths as he goes and will be weaker for it."

"Unless we cannot find the answers before him," I said. "The Black Tomb is wicked. We don't want to go there."

I hated the Black Tomb. It'd become a bleeding curse on its own. But this didn't make sense. I'd been to the tomb too many times for one lifetime, but there was no grand door with fury.

Then again, the bleeding place was rife in the darkest, deadliest fury I'd faced. Who was to say there could not be greater secrets?

"We may not have a choice," Sol said. "If this is the false king's move, we must beat him to it."

I shook my head, an ache building behind my eyes. "What is it he mentioned about heirs again?"

Sol nodded. "He spoke of our mother's heirs. Their blood can unlock the fury of the tomb. We're the heirs, tell me I'm not misinterpreting."

"If he wants three heirs, then yes," I said. "He doesn't know what is hidden there?"

"The way he looks ready to slit his own throat when he tries to get answers, no. I don't think the false king has any idea what is at this tomb. But it explains why we've been kept alive," Sol insisted. "They fear us, but they bleeding need us for some reason. Either to keep us from discovering this or using us to help them take it. I feel it in my bones—we're the only ones who can open whatever Maj hid away."

I glanced at my nephew who stood somberly by the wall. "Gunnar has Herja's blood, do you think it will be enough?"

"I can't say," Sol admitted. "But we need to try. Prepare for him to come for you, Valen. He wants answers, and he will hurt you to get them."

I steeled myself as if Calder might appear at any moment. We were interrupted by a knock. I froze, expecting the king, but a broad serf opened the door. Not Ettan, and one who hardly seemed ruffled by our faces as he pulled a cart of food behind him. "The king and queen insist you keep your strength up."

I gawked at my brother. "Ravenspire feeds its prisoners now?"

No doubt there would be attempts to poison us.

Sol rolled his shoulders back and clapped me on the arm. "Ready yourself, Valen. The games have begun."

CHAPTER TWENTY
ROGUE PRINCESS

My friend,

What you suggest, could it truly work? Do you have such power? What will become of my family?

Forgive the many questions, but I do not understand this fury. You insist the false king must remain part of this land, that he will help bring about four queens of fate. I do not understand the purpose of four queens, but if the false king is to live, the thought sours in my mouth.

After the pain he has caused, I would like nothing more than to see him gray and bloodless on a battlefield. Still, if keeping his life means my family will see sunrises again, then let him live until he is nothing but brittle bone.

I'll be at the meet tonight. We shall talk more.

—Lili

"May I join you?"

I looked up from the cryptic letter. Herja stood behind me. "Yes. Please."

With a gesture at the empty space on the log, I scooted over.

She nestled beside me and stared at the gentle flow of the creek. Nine days in Ruskig had added more color to her cheeks, more meat on her bones. She was strong and lithe. I understood the many tales of Herja Ferus and her blade as she took up a position training our warriors while Halvar developed our strategies over rough maps and drawings of Castle Ravenspire.

"What are you reading?"

I studied the rough strokes of the pen. As the letters went on, Lilianna's desperation grew clearer in each missive. I handed it to Herja. "From your mother. I take comfort in her writings. Always have."

Herja read the page, a wrinkle above her nose. "This is when she was locked in Eli's tower?"

I shrugged. "I don't know."

"I would imagine it is. He kept her parted from us, demanding she be his consort. He threatened to take me if she did not comply. Until I slaughtered his guards." She scoffed bitterly. "Then, I think he felt it wiser to keep me locked away, untouched."

"Do you know the friend she is writing?"

Herja shook her head. "I don't. She had many friends across the lands. It was my mother's great strength—her ability to unite people despite differences. The only one she could not convince was King Eli."

I folded the parchment and gently returned it to a pouch on my belt. Tears blurred my vision. In quiet moments, when the stars brightened the sky, I would allow thoughts to turn to Valen, of his gentle touch, his soft words he spoke only to me. Then, when the harsh sun rose day after day and those tender thoughts became only dreams, I'd return to a dark despair that we were parted.

He was being tortured, no doubt.

"Elise," Herja said, one hand on my arm. "We are making progress."

"It is not enough. Not until Valen is free."

"Halvar is cunning in his positions around the castle, and when your men return with allies—there is no telling what gains we will have. I know something about Alver folk, after all."

I stared at my hands. "You speak of Laila's and Gunnar's father?"

"I do. Alvers are tricky, like fae, but at times more fearsome. Their different gifts are truly terrifying and wonderful. Trust me, if your allies are Alvers, we will have the advantage when they couple with Night Folk and the sheer will of Ettans."

"Where is he? Your lover, I mean. Wouldn't he like to know you are free?" I was doubtful about the man. Perhaps he liked his family in captivity. They could not depend on anyone but him if they were locked away.

But my doubts faded when Herja's face paled. "I fear something terrible has happened to him. Fury we didn't understand kept me locked in the hands of Stor Magnus. For turns Hagen and I tried to break whatever magic kept me there, but nothing ever worked. When my voice returned after living with the curse of silence for so long, I knew—deep inside—I knew something was shifting in the land. Something dangerous.

"I forced Hagen to flee with our children. Hells, the man can argue, and he fought me to the end. But he also fiercely loves his young ones and seeing them free was worth every risk to him."

"But what risk? Why could he not take them from the beginning?"

Herja played with a few blades of grass for a few moments.

"Alvers might live the life of a noble, like Hagen, but they walk a dangerous line if their gifts are rare, or if they step off the line in the slightest. They are traded and used for entertainment, especially the women. But Alver men are taken as well, and from what Hagen described they are turned into monsters. It is the reason he was brought to play for the Valkyrie to begin with. If he won, his family would gain a new level of prestige from the winnings, and they would not fall under the scrutiny of Alver hunters at such a position."

"So, he played." My lips pinched into a tight line. "And clearly, he won."

"No, he did not play. I prepared to kill him the moment he stepped into the tent, but what he said stopped me: *May we just talk a while before you kill me?*" Herja chuckled. "Silent for turns, and at last someone wished to speak with me."

"But he kept returning."

"Yes. He would speak, I would write responses." She smiled at the trees with a wistful glance. "I fell in love with him."

"But they would never let him remain with his family?"

She shook her head. "When he survived the first night, they assumed he'd defeated me. As the first—and only—victor, Hagen was allowed to return twice each turn. After our children arrived, Hagen fought to have all of us released. Hells, the coin he paid Magnus to simply consider the thought. But he could only do so much, remember, or risk stepping off the dangerous line in his own kingdom."

Herja freed a quivering breath and hugged her middle. "Until I forced him to step so far off the line. He planned to run with the children to the South, the West, anywhere to keep them safe. And now he's been returned to his land and . . . I fear the worst, Elise. I fear I have doomed him to a life of pain and captivity."

With a quick swipe of her hand, she brushed tears from her

cheeks. "If you need another who understands not knowing where the second half of her heart is, then you have me. I know you love my brother the way I love Hagen. But we must believe we will see them again or the fight inside will wither and die. I will not give up on Hagen, and you must not fall into hopelessness over Valen's absence."

I grabbed her hand and squeezed, tears on my cheeks. "I won't accept a life where we do not see them again."

"Then keep fighting, My Queen." She smiled softly. "We are close."

Herja Ferus must've had a bit of a visionary in her blood because in the hours before dawn, the bellow of a horn announced approaching ships to the walls of the refuge. I'd given the bed to Laila and Herja and had taken a place on the rug near the inglenook in the longhouse. I did not remember falling asleep, but when the horn sounded, I snapped awake, buried beneath a thick bear pelt.

I rarely dressed in nightclothes now. When war knocked at the gates, keeping blades and boots nearby seemed more prudent.

The belt with my seax and dagger was barely secured when the door slammed open, and the hall was filled with the Guild of Shade.

"Ships," Halvar said breathlessly, adjusting his own belt.

"Ari?"

"Looks to be," Tor said, handing me my silver circlet.

"Elise, have they come?" Herja pulled back the fur, half dressed.

"We're going to find out."

"I'm coming."

"I'll stay with the child." Kari materialized from behind Halvar and stepped into the royal longhouse.

Hells, was everyone fully dressed and ready to leap at all

times? It was as if my most trusted friends had the fury to appear at my side in a matter of breaths at the slightest change. Truth be told, I took a bit of comfort knowing they were always there.

On the way to the walls, Stieg, Mattis, and Siv joined us. Atop the posts that faced the sea, Brant spoke to the archers, then waved us through to the shore. Beyond the walls the expanse of the Fate's Ocean filled the brimming dawn.

In the sliver of morning light, four swift longships maneuvered into the fjord. The steady thrum of drums announced their approach. My chest squeezed. On the lead ship, Ari hugged the stempost, blowing into a curled ram's horn. At his side, Casper rolled the tides to lead them into shore with haste.

The nearer they came, the more folk from Ruskig came out to greet the fleet.

Only then did I catch sight of something different. At the back point of the ships' formation, a cloud of pitch rolled behind them. Darker than a moonless night, skeins of black slithered across the water like sea serpents.

"What is that?" Siv breathed out.

We were about to find out. I hurried to the shore as the first ship banked and Ari hopped onto the rocky beach. No hesitation, I flung my arms around his neck. "I beg of you to bring us good news."

He laughed and ran a comforting hand down my back before he pulled away. "I bring you intriguing news, My Queen. And old friends."

I looked to the second ship as it skidded over the smooth stones on the beach. A man leaped over the keelson. Atop his thick mat of russet hair, he wore a napless cap. A canvas coat draped over his shoulders, and on his belt were rows of pouches and vials tucked among three knives.

He drew in a long breath through his nose. "No smell of piss here."

Herja snorted a laugh as we watched him turn back to the ship. Handsome. Young. An unending grin of mischief on his face. The man reached up and held out a hand.

I let out a childish squeal of delight when Junius took his hand and accepted his help onto the shore.

"Junie!" I rushed to her, wrapping her in my arms. She laughed and held tight. "Look at you. You look . . ."

"Fed?" She lifted a playful brow. True enough, she seemed healthier than before. Two silver piercings dotted her cheeks in the divots of her smile, and her long, glossy black hair was braided in gold chains. She wore a flowing tunic and silver bands on her wrists. A different woman than I saw last.

I hugged her again. "I can breathe now that you are here."

"Elise," she said sternly. "We should've been here long before Valen was taken. Hells, you people are so bleeding stubborn, and you've caused a great deal of strife at home. I've had my own battle keeping Niklas at bay. Not an easy task since the man has wanted to join this fight since I returned."

She looked back at the man who'd helped her down as he fitted a strange band of what looked like gold rings around each finger, then flexed and clenched his fingers a few times until the row of rings stayed in place.

They stepped aside with me as the three ships unloaded with men and supplies. Most of their folk dressed like Niklas. Less furs and tunics, and more trousers, boiled leather belts, and heavy boots.

I kept a wary watch on the approaching shadows and eerie beat drums. Doubtless most of these people were Alvers if they lived with Junius, but it still drew a level of unease as the cloud approached.

"Nik." Junius's voice interrupted my thoughts. "Meet Elise Lysander. The new queen here."

"Ferus," I corrected.

"Ah, right. Your vows. The ones I was not invited to attend," Junie said, pouting.

"I'm sure you've heard a great deal about me." Her husband stepped forward. "The formidable guild lead of the infamous Falkyns of Skìkast."

"I've heard some," I said, smiling.

"Only some? Didn't Junie tell grand tales of my brilliance?" Niklas winked and kissed the back of my hand. "I suppose it is better to see it firsthand. You helped keep my wife alive, Queenie, so you have my thanks and loyalty."

Junius snickered and elbowed him. "Proper titles. She's a bleeding queen, my love."

"Afraid I don't know much about proper," Niklas said more to me. "The Falkyns' kingdom is made of the slummiest of slums."

I grinned. For the first time since Valen was taken, a wash of hope filled me. "I care little about propriety. You have my thanks for answering our call."

"Hells, a fight for a bleeding crown," Niklas said, stretching his arms over his head. "How could we refuse?"

"As I said. He's been begging to return." Junie's smile faded. "Tell us about Valen."

I closed my eyes. "There is much to tell. Come back to the longhouse, we'll explain everything."

Another horn blasted in the wind. My blood chilled. I'd dropped my gaze for a moment and now the shadows had engulfed the shore. Our people scattered, but they were the only ones.

Niklas, in fact, balked, crossing his arms over his chest.

"Always insists on making an entrance. I'm starting to think he enjoys the attention."

"What is it?"

Junius glanced at me like I'd slipped my mind. "The Nightrender. As you asked."

At her word the shadows drew toward a center point, like a cyclone pulling them away. Between them a dark longship appeared with two young ones beating rawhide drums, and only a few crewmen unloading blades and bows.

When the last drop of shadows died, a man emerged, as if his body had absorbed the darkness. In truth, I was certain it had.

Hooded, dressed in black, he cut a path through everyone on the shore. His movements were swift, sure, and demanding. I held my breath, too captivated, perhaps too afraid to move. At my side, Herja, Tor, and Halvar took a protective stance as the Nightrender pushed forward.

Two paces away he stopped. The hood concealed his top features, but his mouth was set in a sharp, harsh line.

We remained this way for two, ten, a dozen breaths.

Until at last he spoke. His voice came in a soft, eerie rasp. "Are you the queen who is fool enough to think she knows my fate?"

"You'd be wise to show some respect," Tor threatened. "You do speak to a queen."

The Nightrender chuckled. There was little affection in it. "Not mine. I serve no royal and never will."

"I am Elise," I said, a hand on Tor's chest when he reached for his blade. "I do not pretend to know your fate. But I will also not pretend your existence was not made known to me through a speaker of fate. Every prophecy she has given has come to pass."

"And you believe I have some role to play in your war?"

"I don't know, but you came. You must've wondered a little yourself."

If possible, his frown deepened, but he pointed at the small skeleton crew around his small ship. "I came because the majority of my guild voted to come. I was overruled. As I said, no one stands over another in our world."

He hated me. Or everyone. But we didn't need to be friendly allies. We simply needed to find a way to work together to save the king. Then he could disappear into his shadows again. "Will you tell me why you are called the Nightrender?"

He paused. How much could he see beneath his hood? For it felt a great deal like he was peeling into my deepest thoughts with eyes I could not see.

"I could kill you," he said. "Right here. Without moving."

Tor and Halvar stepped forward, but I held up a hand when the Nightrender chuckled.

"Because of them," he said with a nod at the two Shade. "They fear for your life. I could make their deepest fears reality. You. Dead."

"Always pleasant, my friend," Niklas said, rolling his eyes.

Friend? Looking at the Nightrender, friendship, allies, the lot of it seemed wholly impossible. He radiated distrust and disdain for anyone who breathed.

"Are you an Alver? I thought their magic had everything to do with the body."

"Is fear not fed from our deepest emotions? Reaction to circumstances and experiences? It is those impulses, those thoughts, those rushes of adrenaline where my power lies. I can break into your deepest fears and make them real. Do you know what folk in the east call me? My Kind of Alver, I mean?"

I shook my head mutely.

He closed the space between us. His nearness made me freeze as he pulled back his hood. Wavy, brown hair, mussed over his brow and ears. But it was his eyes that shocked me. Not a glimpse of whites, nothing but pure, inky black.

"A Malevolent," he whispered. "That is my Kind. Wicked, evil, made of darkness. So sure you want my fate tangled with yours, Queen?"

He was testing me. I'd learned enough to know people like him needed to share a level of confidence in their allies. Weak and brittle would turn the Nightrender away in an instant. I butted his chest with mine. It was only us on the shore. Nothing mattered in this moment but convincing this dark magick to stay.

"I do not care if the hells themselves spat you out. If you question the lengths I am willing to go to save my husband, then you have never loved the way I have—the way I do."

A small twitch of his cheek proved something about what I'd said lashed at him. But he covered it well, adding more questions I doubted I'd ever see answered.

The Nightrender studied me, scrutinized me, then closed his eyes in an extended blink.

A small gasp came before I could stop it. Where swirling ink had been in his eyes, now bright gold stared back at me. Eyes that made him look utterly normal, but for the sadness. The heavy burden that hinted to a hard existence.

"We do nothing for nothing." He narrowed his eyes. "We are not warriors, we are dealmakers. Make this worth our time, and you may consider the Guild of Kryv willing to listen to your plans."

"You wish to be paid?" I arched a brow. This was war, not a bleeding trade deal.

The Nightrender's mouth twitched. "I do nothing for nothing. I do a great many things if it fattens my purse."

"You're serious?"

"Welcome to the Eastern Kingdom, Elise," Junius whispered,

hardly surprised by the barter. She nodded her head at the Nightrender who seemed entirely too pleased with himself.

I scoffed and looked to Tor. "See to it the Guild of Kryv and the Nightrender are paid well for their trouble."

"We take weapons, coin, and anything worth a good trade," the Nightrender said with a wink. It wasn't playful, it was arrogant. As if he'd placed us in the exact position he wanted.

He turned to make his way to his guild, but I stopped him. "If we are to do this, don't you think I should know your true name? Trust begins at the simple things, Nightrender."

His expression was unchanged, but with the gold of his eyes exposed the glimmer of light he tried to hide. "We came to fight in your war, Queen. Not trust each other."

Our conversation was at an end for now. The Nightrender abandoned us for his guild.

"Elise, are you sure about this?" Tor asked.

"No." True. I didn't know what the Nightrender, or what the Falkyns could do for us, but I would trust this was the person Calista meant in her daze. I'd trust this was the path fate had chosen for us.

Niklas chuckled and patted my arm. "Don't fret over him too much, Queenie. He likes you."

"Oh, does he? Is that why he talked about killing me?"

That only made Junie's husband laugh harder. "He winked. It's practically a warm embrace from the likes of him."

"Can we trust him?" Halvar asked.

Niklas looked at the Guild of Kryv as he slung a canvas travel bag over his shoulder. "Understand the Falkyns and Kryv are not honorable, not in the ways you are, I'm sure. In the east, being an Alver means you are taken by the rich and used until you die. The only trade skill for those who manage to avoid capture? Thieves. Smugglers. Criminals. Or wealthy bastards who can buy silence.

Can you trust any of us? Eh, if you have glittering things, we might snatch them. But if we say we fight for you, yes. You can trust that. We'll stand with you. But we'll likely rob you blind as we do it."

With a final wink, Niklas took Junie's hand. She shoved Halvar's shoulder, chuckling at his furrowed brow.

Herja was the only one who seemed amused. She folded her arms over her chest and leaned in to whisper next to my ear. "Aligns with what Hagen always told me about his homeland. But what do you think?"

"I think our new thief friends are going to be rather put out when they find we have nothing of real worth to pay them with or for them to steal." I snorted and linked my arm with hers as we followed the path back to the wall.

CHAPTER TWENTY-ONE
NIGHT PRINCE

I WAS MISTAKEN.

Even in a comfortable, warm room with food aplenty it was still torture.

We were no closer to finding a way out of whatever fury guarded the walls of our tower than we were ten sunrises ago.

Even Sol was disheartened. He'd taken to staring blankly out the window of the tower in long stretches.

Through the days, between our attempts to plot, I told Sol of the curse. How my memories of who I was were lost to me all this time. Of the wandering turns where I succumbed to vicious bloodlust like a rabid wolf in the trees.

The Black Tomb, the storyteller, and the part she played in my path to Elise Lysander.

It wasn't much, but Sol took some comfort that I knew Calder, knew Runa, before they hid their true selves from me as the Night Prince. When I was no one to them but Legion Grey I did not realize how many traits I noticed.

Not until Sol pulled them out.

Calder craved power. He loved no one but his own ambition. But his weakness lived in debauchery and praise. If his people did not see him as the dog with the sharpest bite, it would grate at the false king.

Kvin Lysander was a spineless fool who would follow anyone on the throne. He'd be as loyal to me if I'd claimed the crown months ago as he was to Runa now. Weak and not a threat in my eyes.

Runa, however, was dangerously ambitious. Perhaps more than her husband. I'd always believed she had some affection toward her sister, but as time went on, I started to believe Runa tolerated Elise because she was not a threat to her.

Now, my wife was her greatest threat. And I was Elise's weakness. Runa would use me against her.

But we still hadn't seen Jarl Magnus. Nor Calder, or even Runa. It unsettled me. I imagined they'd revel in drawing our blood, torturing us endlessly, but this absent game was confusing. I didn't know how to retaliate. And I hated the helplessness more than anything.

As the sun faded on the eleventh day, I went to Sol at the window.

"I was so sure we'd think of something, Valen," he said, voice rough. "I knew it to my soul if you were here, it would unlock the way we could take Ravenspire back from the inside. Now, I see I've simply gotten my brother—the king—captured."

I scoffed. "Always making things about you."

For the first time that day, Sol released a smile. Weak, but it was there all the same. "Will you tell me of Torsten? How is he, truly?"

He hadn't asked until now, and I hadn't pressed. Heartache needed to be treated with care.

"Ill-tempered as ever." One shoulder against the wall, I went on. "But loyal as ever too. Knowing you are alive has brought out the Torsten I always knew."

"Stubborn. Deadly." Sol grinned with a touch of longing. "Determined."

"Yes. He'll refuse to leave this world before he can at least touch you again."

"I keep thinking how, as boys, Tor and I would mock Daj because of how much he spoke of Maj. Back then love and things of the heart were for weaklings, of course."

"Of course."

Sol rubbed the back of his neck, staring at the golden sunset. "Daj always told us grand tales of how loving her saved him in more than one way. He'd tell me how much he wished nothing more than for his children to find someone they could love like he loved his queen."

I dug through my own conversations with my father. He often said similar things in different ways. But he was like that. Arvad Ferus always spoke to each of his children in ways that connected with our individuality. While Sol loved the Wild Hunt, I sparred with my father. Herja went for mountain rides with him on their favorite horses.

"I think he'd be pleased," Sol said, "to know we've all found that love. It will be what pulls us through this. We fight for those we love, and they fight for us."

"Love has always fueled the strength of Etta." I squeezed his shoulder. "It always will."

"Someone is coming." Gunnar scrambled away from the door. "Let me use mesmer. I need to try again."

"No. Last time got us an added guard and extra bindings." I held up my wrists, now banded in two burning silver rings.

Days ago, we thought to have Gunnar convince one of the

serfs to let us free. It worked. Next, he manipulated the guard, but his magic burned in his head so fiercely he nearly retched.

No one from Ravenspire knew exactly what had happened, but they suspected one of us had broken through the bindings, so they promptly secured our tower room even more.

Then Gunnar had been pale and ill for an entire day afterward.

Gunnar cursed under his breath, wishing for his father for the hundredth time. According to the boy, Hagen Strom had been teaching him about his magic. Another reason to find the man. His son needed him.

Our nightly serf was different each time. Tonight, a skinny woman with black curls kept her eyes on the floor, but when she lifted them, I had to blink. Her eyes were slit like a cat's and greener than spring grass. No taper to her ear, but perhaps a bit of nymph or forest fae lived in her blood.

"You've been requested to dine at the high table tonight," she said.

Ah. The game was changing.

Hair stood on end on the back of my neck, but I buried my disquiet beneath a sly grin. "And if we refuse?"

"I am to tell you there is no room for refusal." Her eyes flitted to Gunnar. "Unless you do not care for your nephew. May I leave now?" Her voice squeaked like a soft breeze.

The two Ravens who stood at our door did not give her a choice before they shoved the woman aside and crowded the doorway. "What is your choice, Night Prince? I hope you refuse; I'd love to experiment on the boy. We have new methods we've been wanting to test."

I locked my jaw. Not out of fear of this bleeding fool, but at the rush of dark violence, corrupting my desires in something sinister. With each new sunrise remnants of my curse simmered beneath the surface. Like waking from a long sleep, the desire—the need—to kill heated at every harsh word, every threat.

This Raven, like others, was locked in my mind, and I imagined a dozen ways I could draw out a scream. More than anything, I feared the bloodlust. By the time this was over would I still be the man Elise loved, or would I once more be a beast who lived for death and hate?

The Ravens were joined by five more at the top of the staircase. They surrounded us in a tight formation, making the trek down the tower difficult not to step on toes.

We remained silent, doubtless the three of us all puzzled through what was happening, preparing for anything. Runa and Calder played sly moves, but we'd been surviving this long. It'd take a great deal to break us by now.

The great hall was empty. Wooden shades were pulled over the upper windows near the eaves. Light came from the few torches in the corners and the candles on the massive table in the center of the room. Already plates had been set, and I hated how my body reacted to the savory hint of roasted meat and the warmth of hot bread and clean, fine ale.

Seed bread and boiled roots had kept us alive so far.

I frowned, almost disappointed. If food and fine things was the best manipulation they could manage, the false king and queen would need to play a different hand. Sol and I knew how to live on melted snow and tree bark for weeks at a time.

Doors swept open in the back.

My stomach soured. I'd waited for this moment. Hells, I'd been yearning for it, if only to gauge our enemies a little more. Even still, at the sight of Calder and Runa, rational thinking fled and all I saw was hate.

It did not help that Runa Lysander looked a great deal like her sister.

Calder wore an ostentatious crown and a black fur cloak that dragged behind him. Runa was draped in gold. From the sheen of her gown to the circlet secured with braids in her hair. Since we last met, Calder had aged his beard, allowing it to grow past his chin, and Runa's eyes had lost even more feeling.

Unfortunately, the false king and queen were not alone.

Jarl Magnus strode into the hall, followed by Leif Lysander, and half a dozen women wearing fine woolen gowns. Courtiers, or mistresses for the king, no doubt.

At the sight of me, a few of them whispered and snickered as they followed their king.

"I half expected you to refuse us," Calder said. "You've been so disagreeable to our hospitality thus far."

"Room is a bit cramped." Sol stepped forward. I might be king, but he would always be the older brother. An innate need to defend his family flowed through his blood and I think he might cuff the back of my head like he did when we were boys if I tried to stop him.

Calder chuckled without a drop of humor. "Would you prefer your old cell, Sun Prince."

Sol didn't falter. "My dear false king, you do not want to know the things I prefer."

A few moments of silence settled between us, but it was enough to set the room in unease.

Calder's lip twitched. He gestured to the table. "Sit. Please. You are our guests tonight."

We had few choices and took places—Ravens watching our every move—in chairs as far from the Timoran king as possible. Jarl sat on the right hand of the king and sprinkled between us were the courtiers.

"So," one woman whispered to me. "You are not *Herr* Legion?"

I studied her face. She looked at me with total sincerity. I supposed the bindings on my wrists, the points of my ears, and the guards aiming blades at my back were not enough evidence.

"Not today, *de hän*."

The woman managed to giggle as if any of this were enjoyable for me. "I can hardly believe it. You look so much like him."

"Because he was Legion Grey, you bleeding idiot," Runa hissed at the woman, causing the mistress to hang her head in shame.

"That's enough talk of past things. Eat. Enjoy," Calder told everyone. His grin was cruel and twisted as he lifted a glass flute in the air. "We're honored by fellow royalty, after all."

His courtiers had no trouble following orders. But we remained unmoving. I stared down the table where Runa kept me in her sights. *Kvin* Lysander studied his plate, but every few breaths he would flick his eyes to Sol, to me, at times Gunnar.

Calder noticed and snorted into his ale. "I believe you make my father-in-law uncomfortable, Night Prince."

"The best news I've heard all day." I gave a significant look at Elise's father.

"But I suppose he is your father-in-law too." Calder sneered when Leif blanched. "Isn't that right?"

"No."

"No?" Calder's puckered his mouth. "I was certain you had illegally taken vows with my poor, deranged sister. I thought you a fool, but perhaps you are wiser than I thought."

"Don't mistake me, False King," I said. "Elise is my wife, *my wife*—" I repeated simply to watch Jarl fist one hand on the table. "But she has made it quite clear, she has no father here. So, you'll forgive me if I do not honor him with such a title."

"I see." Calder sneered. "Well, it is about your so-called wife that we wanted to see you tonight."

Sol shifted at my side. My insides numbed against any lies

they'd tell me about Elise. She was dead—I wouldn't believe it. She was captured—I'd demand proof.

Calder's eyes narrowed. "Night Prince, I'll not mince my words. Your brother and your sister's son go free in exchange for Elise."

I didn't have time to take a breath before Sol laughed. "What a pathetic offer. I'm insulted you did not take the time to learn of the Ferus bloodline. If you had, you'd know that bargain would never stand, False King."

"I'll not be traded for anyone," Gunnar said.

"There you have it." I gestured at my brother and nephew. Loyalty, love, and honor were thrust into our heads as young boys, and it was clear Herja had taught the same to her children. "We do not sacrifice our family. Do what you will. Elise will never be part of the bargain."

Calder sighed and slouched back in his chair. "I'd hoped you wouldn't be difficult. We've treated you so well."

"Well?" Sol's voice darkened. "Ten days of a bed and a meal does nothing to erase centuries of curses and bloodshed after your people stole this land. Hells, the only reason it still blooms at all is because our bloodline still lives. You should be kissing our feet, you bastard."

Ravens moved in, a few gasps rippled around the table, but Calder's raised hand stilled the room.

"What would your people think," I said, low and raw, "the ones who starve and freeze in winter while you eat such a feast, if they knew the land survives because their kings have kept the true royals trapped all this time?"

Calder's fist slammed onto the table. "Those are lies. You speak valiantly, but how would those people react if they knew the one who robbed them of their goods and supplies is the Night Prince of Etta and his band of thieves?"

I glanced at the curious courtiers. Rumors and gossip thrived in the Timoran court. I would see to it talk ran like an uncontrolled flame after this night.

"Think hard at the strange events you've seen. Barren pieces of this kingdom now bloom with life. The Sun Prince escaped the centuries of Ravenspire control, and the princess regained her voice after being silent and captive all this time." I slowly stood, leaning over my fingertips on the table. "Care to know why?"

The woman beside me seemed unable to control her voice and let out a breathy, "Yes."

I looked nowhere but at Calder's cold eyes. "The fury, long dormant in this soil, awakened when, once again, a Ferus took the throne."

Calder's jaw pulsed. "You spin the truth. Or have you forgotten another king took a different throne? I have raised Timoran from the failings of my father, restored mighty trade; I rid this land of his futile, foolish policies and laws. I have saved Timoran."

"Yet you still keep us alive. Your enemies, the greatest threats to your throne." My lip curled over my teeth. "Why take the risk? Admit it, False King, you keep us breathing because you know if our blood spills, your people will be thrust into the frigid wastes of my mother's childhood when fury abandons this land forever."

Violence flashed in Calder's eyes. For a moment I thought I might have pushed him too far, and he might make good on my bluff and cut us down where we sat. But to my surprise and distrust, Runa rested a hand on Calder's arm. She smiled, a kind smile on first look, but buried under her pretty face was a viciousness more cruel and wicked than her wretched husband. "Tell him, Husband. The Night Prince should know."

Calder hesitated, but soon his expression softened. He kissed the back of Runa's hand, but the way they looked at each other showed there was no love there. "My queen is right. Since House Ferus is so fond of prophecies and twists of fate, you might care to know you were not the only ones to receive a curse from the ancient storyteller."

Calder snapped his fingers and a serf hurried forward, a wooden tray in hand. From the tray, Calder removed a pig skin purse. He handled it carefully, but from inside removed aged parchment sleeves, protected, and bound together by thin leather.

"Ettans and Night Folk have their sagas, but so do we. From the life of King Eli. Seems he was given his own predictions of his fate."

"Why would I care about a dead false king?" I hated King Eli. Loathed him. Remembered him. The way he smiled, the way he desired my mother, his brutality.

"Because this dead king has a great deal to do with our current predicament, and its outcome if we do not come to some arrangement."

"Is that what this is?" Sol said with a bitter scoff. "A peace meet? Brother, I think we have them scared and we have not even raised a blade."

Calder frowned at the Sun Prince. "This is our last attempt to stop needless bloodshed—of your people." He looked to me, voice unnaturally soft. "You think we beg for Elise because we wish her harm. We ask for her to save her, Night Prince. She will not survive this fight."

His fingers deftly touched the parchment. Hells, I despised how my curiosity piqued.

"Valen," Sol warned. "They lie."

"See for yourself." Runa stood with the parchment in hand. "We have the writings of the Fate Witch of old. Perhaps you will recognize some."

She rounded to our side of the table. Jarl rose to his feet, hand on his blade. I made no move to look at Runa as she placed the sheets in front of me.

"What are they?" Gunnar asked after a long pause.

Jaw tight, I blinked my curiosity to the musty parchment. Sharp, hurried writing scrawled out on the pages. Faded with time, but still readable. My heart stilled in my chest, as if my body could not function as I read the words. Words I heard in my head during the night. Words of nightmares.

"The curse she wrote for me. But Sol's and Herja's too. We were all cursed." Bloodlust. Silence. Madness. Why?

Perhaps Calder held a bit of magic and could read minds because he laughed and gestured to the parchment. "Eli had a brutal mind. He chose your suffering. Did you know that? The warrior of the two princes—" He pointed to me. "You'd wallow in the blood you might've spilled against him. I believe his original hope was you might be his fury weapon, but you never did cooperate, did you Night Prince?"

"Not when enraging the dead false king was such fun," I snapped.

Calder's gaze spun to Sol. "The clever prince. You'd lose your mind. And the princess—well, as I understand it Eli was not fond of female talk after keeping so much company with your mother and sister. She would be silent and learn that her place was on her back."

Gunnar bolted from his seat, fist slamming the table. Sol gripped his shoulder and shoved him back down. My brother shook his head, silently urging the boy not to listen to their cruelty.

I pushed the parchment to my brother and nephew. I did not want to read them another moment.

"Until the crown is in place," Sol whispered. "That is how mine ended. Herja's too." Sol tossed aside the parchment. "Proof my brother's ascension is powerful enough to break this strange fury."

"But which crown does it mean?" Calder pressed. "I took a crown, and you have not read King Eli's curse."

Runa took the liberty of removing a final sheet. She placed it in front of me and leaned over my shoulder. "Read it. Out loud."

I hated them, but I recognized my curse. It was authentic. These were from the storyteller long ago, and curiosity, desperation, perhaps both were too much to resist. "From desire and greed, this land will live in a broken state of weakness. The kingdom you sought will never be yours before the Otherworld calls you home."

"Which it never was," Sol interrupted. "Timoran kings have smothered this land for centuries, and it is dying."

"Go on," Calder said, ignoring my brother. "Keep reading."

I locked him in a glare but looked to the parchment. "Through the blood of the heirs from the bond you shattered, will the tomb of fury reopen. On that day, one queen rises to end another, and at the fall of the second will your kingdom at last be."

Calder rose from his seat. "This is why you are unharmed, little prince. This is how you keep your brother and the boy safe. Give me what is in that tomb, tell me how to find it, and I vow not to kill them, and to let Elise live."

It struck me from behind, and I didn't know whether to laugh or rage. Calder had been to the tomb, or someone from Ravenspire had. When they placed the Lysander flags to signal to Elise Ravenspire knew of her involvement with traitors.

The fool didn't know he'd been close to what he sought all this time.

I leaned back in my chair with an exaggerated sigh. "Forgive me, False King, but I know nothing of this tomb."

Calder's face twisted into hard stone. "So, like your brother, you need to be persuaded to speak."

I laughed with venom. "Do what you will. My answer will not change."

Calder's skin heated to a deep, blood red. He muttered something low to Jarl who seemed rather pleased when he stood and left the room. The false king turned away, ignoring his wife, and gripping the arm of a mistress as he stormed from the hall.

Sol was right—Calder was slipping in his desperation.

We'd exploit it.

I jolted when Runa pulled the parchment away. "My husband focuses on the wrong motivation with a man like you. The part of this that really matters is obvious, isn't it?"

Nothing was obvious. It was as if a dozen points needed to be made and the storyteller decided to be vague on purpose. My fist curled over one knee.

"I suppose it isn't," Runa went on. "Two queens. The second will fall, and the kingdom of King Eli will rise. Second *Kvinna*, second to be crowned." Runa leaned forward, her lips against my ear. A dozen violent thoughts filled my head. She grinned as she spoke. "Elise's blood will secure this kingdom, but she will not leave the battlefield alive."

CHAPTER TWENTY-TWO
ROGUE PRINCESS

"She is taking too long." I paced, unsure why I was such a fool and listened to strangers, to thieves, when it came to strategy.

"She is taking the right amount of time." At my side, the Nightrender picked at a handful of nuts and berries. He no longer wore the dark cowl over his head, and his eyes remained the sharp golden hue. He watched the empty shadows in the forest, awaiting his guild member to return.

Behind us, the rest of his guild remained close, but behaved as if they were as unbothered as him.

I hated it. A constant frenzy rolled in my veins, desperate to attack, to retrieve the King of Etta, shout at him for being so determined to play the hero, then to kiss him until a thousand mornings passed by.

My eyes drifted over the new faces in our refuge. Dozens of Falkyns joined Junius and Niklas, but the Guild of Kryv, there were not even ten. And two were bleeding children.

I questioned the Nightrender's sanity if he trusted young

ones. Herja had taken a liking to the girl, Hanna. She did not use her voice, but her hands to speak. In all her turns as the Silent Valkyrie, Herja had used similar gestures. The boy, taller and skinnier, had spent the time since he'd arrived schooling Laila and young Ellis all about tossing knives. And how to do it well with more skill than a boy his age ought to know.

"Why do you fear for your king so much?" The Nightrender asked, brushing the crumbs on his hands. "I can hardly focus on anything but your fear when I stand beside you. It's aggravating. So, tell me. Is this husband incapable? A weakling? Does he crumble under torture? What is it, Queen?"

I was going to kill the man.

"Valen Ferus is no weak thing. I fear for him because I love him, Nightrender. An emotion, I'm discovering you, clearly, do not grasp. And if anyone will not crumble it is him. If he were here, he could split open this very earth and swallow you whole."

"Impressive. I've heard a great deal of your Night Folk. From what they say, he is the only true bender of the earth in a thousand turns, yes?"

"Yes. But it is not his fury that makes him great. He has survived curses, brutality, and still remains the gentlest man I've known."

He chuckled. My fists clenched.

How could he be so . . . tranquil when his own guild member took such a great risk today?

"Then stop fearing for him," he said with a taunt in his voice. "Get angry for him, hate for him, seek blood and bone for him, but hells woman, stop fearing for him. If he is all those things, he'd be ashamed to know you did not think him capable of surviving this."

"I don't like you." Rather childish of me, but I couldn't help it.

"I've been told much worse before." He deepened his smirk.

I rolled my eyes and returned my gaze to the trees. The Nightrender was younger than I thought. Well, I suppose he could be ancient for all I knew since Alver Folk lived the lifespan of Night Folk. But he seemed young. A few turns older than me, perhaps.

But he had a knack for irritating me.

"I don't see how this is wise," I said at long last.

"Elise." Halvar joined us and I breathed in relief.

What the Nightrender didn't know was that I was the weak one, not Valen. Without Herja, the Guild of Shade, without Siv, Kari, Ari. Without my friends, I would not be standing here now.

"To send in the Kryv woman was a sound idea. We need the layout of any changes they might've made on the inside. And we need to know where they're keeping him before we make a solid plan of extracting him."

"Listen, Queen," the Nightrender said with a new briskness in his tone. "You may not like me, you may not even trust me, but you asked me to bleeding be here, and you will let me do this my way, so my guild will live to see another sunrise."

"Your guild is not the only thing at stake," I snapped. "An entire kingdom could fall. Perhaps you do not care, perhaps this is a game to you, but this is our future and freedom."

The Nightrender paused, a bit of his shadows returning to his eyes. "You're right. This is a game, but you ought to know—no one plays games as I do." He crowded my space, but I didn't cower. I held my stance and met his eye. The Nightrender lowered his voice to a dark rasp. "This is what I do. Scheme. Plot. Thieve. To me, stealing a king is no different than stealing a purse of gold, understand? You plan the battle; we'll plan the score."

I parted my mouth to argue Valen was not some score from a

wealthy man's purse but silenced when one of the Kryv shoved between us.

"She's coming." He was tall, with tanned skin like Valen's, and had few cares about knocking me aside.

"I see her," said another Kryv with scars littering his arms. His fingers twitched at his sides, and from what I'd seen of the man, he rarely stopped moving.

"I heard her first."

"Wrong, Vali."

I had no idea what they meant. The trees were empty. I heard and saw nothing but a fading sun.

A snicker drew my attention away. Junius stepped beside me, looking at the arguing men. "Vali and Raum," she said. "Both called Profetik Alvers. Their mesmer gives them inhuman senses. Vali hears the smallest sound, while Raum can see through the thickest fog. But they also have the most intense need to compete with each other."

"It is a matter of principle, Junie. Val needs to know I exceed his Talent and always will. Keeps his head the right size." The one I assumed was Raum said. He rubbed a hand over the scars on his arms, and winked at his fellow Kryv, who frowned and stared forward.

A snap of a twig broke the quiet forest. Another, and another, until through the brambles a woman emerged. Her dark curls were tied off her neck, and those eerie cat-like eyes brightened in the sun. She pointed between her two guild brothers. "Which of you discovered me first?"

"Me," Vali grumbled.

"Like the hells you did. I saw you, lengths back, Tov," Raum insisted.

"Tova," the Nightrender interrupted, almost lazily. "The queen was beginning to doubt you."

The woman snorted and held out her hand until the Nightrender supplied her with some of his nuts and berries. "I'd be offended, but I've lived through the impoliteness of those castle guards. They're just unnecessarily rude."

The Nightrender offered a half grin. Ah, he could show amusement. Strange.

In a few quick steps I stood directly in front of the woman, Halvar beside me. "Did you see him?"

"Oh, I saw him." Tova's strange eyes gleamed. "He's quite handsome, Queen. Rather sharp-tongued too."

"Well?" Halvar grumbled. When it came to Valen, his family, it was unwise to keep him in the dark.

Tova popped a few nuts onto her tongue. "He's alive, unharmed. For now. They all are. The royals at the castle have kept them in a warm tower room and have hardly touched a hair on their heads."

They've been unharmed? My heart swelled in relief, but also disbelief. What were Calder and Runa planning with them? This distance was driving me to madness.

"Did you clue him in on who you were?" I asked.

"No. I was there to scout out his position. No sense tipping off those bleeding guards to anything amiss. To them I was nothing but a meek serf."

I rubbed the sides of my head. "I don't understand what Runa is doing. I thought without a doubt they would be tortured."

"Things could be changing. I believe your sister's patience is wearing thin."

"Then we need to get to him. No more waiting." I squeezed Halvar's arm.

"I'd agree." Tova nodded and picked out a few undesirable things from the food in her palm. "They were given some prophecy that seemed to unsettle everyone, seemed to add a bit of urgency. Never did take much stock in prophecies myself, but there was no time to linger around to see the outcome. All I know is it had something to do with you, Queen."

"Me?"

"That's what I said."

"Any talk among the serfs?" the Nightrender asked.

"A great deal." Tova untangled her wild curls, letting them fall down her shoulders. "Serfs chatter endlessly in that bleeding place, but the good news is most feel a great deal of loyalty to your husband. The bad news is they are too frightened and spineless to actually free him."

I hugged my middle and waved the thought away. "What did you hear?"

"Mostly bits of conversations about a tomb of some kind. I am told the wicked king has a great obsession with it. Mean anything?"

Halvar and I both groaned.

"The Black Tomb," I said. "It's a terrible, cursed place."

Tova shrugged. "Doesn't matter. According to an old kitchen serf, the only way anyone sees the inside is if they are connected to fate or fall into a . . . sort of fae sleep. I don't know what that is, and frankly, she wasn't the most reliable source."

Halvar lifted a brow. "A fury sleep?"

"Yes." Tova snapped her fingers. "That's what she called it. Heard her saying the princes ought to sleep, and at last find peace and quiet in the tomb."

"The tomb is nothing," I said, looking to Halvar. "There were no actual graves in the place. Right?"

"That we could see," he said softly. "Elise, if there are sleeping fae there, it could be why it is so heavily protected. Fury sleep is a strategy used long ago. A curse placed upon others, or oneself, as a protection against enemies. Night Folk kings, queens, and warriors would slip into the fury sleep to hide their deepest, most dangerous secrets from enemies. It was a risk, and one not commonly used anymore."

"Why?" the Nightrender asked.

"There's a chance the one asleep might never wake. A true eternal sleep."

"The point is," Tova went on, "your husband, his brother, and the boy are alive, and by now they're likely getting tortured. That is my report, now if you'll excuse me, I'm famished for more than bird feed."

She turned and left as if she did not knock the breath from my lungs. Each interaction with the Falkyns and Guild of Kryv left me surer they truly had no respect for royalty, or truly had no idea how to interact with them.

Halvar touched my wrist. "This will help. I need to see to Mattis and Brant and adjust our battle lines."

"Go," I said.

Alone with the Nightrender drew a somber quiet. With a heavy breath, I stood at his shoulder. The man said nothing as he stared at the distant walls.

"Does her report help you?" I asked after a long pause.

"Too early to know. I have more questions, but there will be plans to make."

He started to walk away, but I grabbed his arm. His eyes landed on the spot I touched him. Let him glare, I would make myself clear. "I am trusting you with my heart and with the lives of my people. Why did you come? Why do this? Help me understand you, so I may trust you completely."

His eyes narrowed. "Get used to disappointment, Queen. I

owe you no explanations. Trust me or do not, it matters little to me. I have been given a job to do, and I will do it. Now, are you coming to the table? Niklas and your surly warrior friend will want to be updated, no doubt." He shirked me off. "We are moving forward. Are you with us, or not?"

CHAPTER TWENTY-THREE
ROGUE PRINCESS

I was with them. Of course I was with them. Junius was a trusted friend. She trusted the darkness and ill-temper of the Nightrender, and so would I.

Even if the next day the final plans seemed nearer to a whim, a guess, and pure lunacy than actual plans. I paced in great strides across the floor of the longhouse, thumbnail between my teeth, half-listening to Tor and Niklas argue the details. Halvar was already busy working a battle, but the Alvers' plan—no—their scheme, ploy, anything but an actual plan would be acted out first.

In Valen's chair at the head of the table, the Nightrender slouched, watching me with an amused expression. "What is it that upsets you most, Queen? That you did not think of this first, or that you do not control the outcome?"

I ignored him and glanced at his guild who hovered close. There were so few, I wondered how they could really be called a guild. Then again, the Guild of Shade once was a trio.

How were the Kryv all brought together? They seemed so different, so odd to be a family of thieves.

By the inglenook, a bulky Kryv who reminded me a great deal of Tor with the constant frown on his face, stood beside Tova, eating flatbread and muttering something to the woman.

Another pair kept close to the Nightrender, a red-haired man and a man with a scar carving through his brow. The way they whispered together, the way they touched, I wondered if they might be lovers. I didn't ask, didn't care.

In a corner, the young boy, Ash is what the Kryv called him, twirled a knife in his hand, describing it in detail to Ellis. Hanna giggled mutely with Laila over moonvane blossoms. Giggled. Like children ought to, but the girl was in a bleeding guild. A thief in the making.

I leaned over the table, voice low for only the Nightrender to hear. "Children? You plan to send children in first? How in the hells will that help at all?"

He cast a smug glance at the young ones. "Never underestimate a child who is desperate to survive."

"They are children."

"And capable. Have you even asked what sort of mesmer Ash and Hanna have? Why they might be useful to protect the young boy as he goes in?"

I pinched my lips into a line.

"Ash, he can break a man from the inside out," he said with a touch of venom. "Crush his bones, fill his lungs with blood. Shatter his skull. Hanna, now she is unique. She can block magic. Stop it dead in its tracks. We've tested it on your fury here. No mistake, if your king were here—he would not be able to break the earth with Hanna nearby. I've only met one other Alver in my lifetime with the same Talent."

The Nightrender leaned back in the chair again and laced his fingers over his stomach. "Now, a child who can break bodies, and another who could block any curses, spells, any dark fury or mesmer, don't you think those inconspicuous children might be useful with little Ellis there?"

It was both terrifying and captivating to learn of the Alvers' abilities. "Why Ellis, though?"

"The boy insisted the king would recognize him. He will need to know we are coming and be in position for the rest of the plan."

"They are children," I repeated.

The Nightrender stood abruptly. "And they have lived a life that demanded they learn to survive. It well may be that children in your land live comfortable, coddled lives. But in the east, Alver children fight for freedom from their first breath. Do not underestimate them, and do not think I'd put anyone in my guild—especially Ash and Hanna—in a risk if I were not confident they'd succeed."

"You are terribly disagreeable."

"With you, yes. I am not accustomed to someone so filled with doubt in me."

"I don't know you. I am allowed to doubt. We're going to war, Nightrender."

"And you will have an advantage if we pull this off."

If. I did not want possibilities. I did not want chances. But there were no guarantees, there never would be.

"You're certain your people saw Valen?" My stomach soured again. A disturbing report that Valen's comfort was at an end at Ravenspire.

The Nightrender looked to Vali and Raum as they spoke to Mattis and Brant. He nodded slowly. "They saw the square and the racks where they have them. I understand it was not what you wanted to hear, but it is better that he is kept in the open. The children will reach him easier."

All day Raum and Vali had been absent. I only learned they'd been sent to the hills near Ravenspire to scout any activity pertinent to Valen or Sol or Gunnar. The distance was at least twenty lengths away. I didn't understand their mesmer entirely, but they had not stepped foot in the Lyx township, and still reported back as if they were seated in the courtyard.

Blood was spilling.

Our time to act was now. Trust, or do not. For Valen, as I told the Nightrender, I would risk it all.

I moved the sheets of parchment scrawled in our plans, formations, in the dimensions of Castle Ravenspire and the Black Tomb in front of him. "Do you need to review these again?"

Truth be told, I had not seen him glance at the plans once.

He tapped the side of his head. "I know my marks."

Yes, that is how Junius and Niklas described every movement. As if this plan were more a dance than a rising battle. We all had marks to meet.

First, a nudge to the Night Prince that his people were coming. Delivered by Ellis. I hated it but had no better option.

Second, Niklas, Junius, and Tova had the burden of finding a way to get Valen through the guards, and out of Ravenspire. Niklas had magic like Bevan's. An Elixist, a worker of poisons and spells and potions that could aid or harm. Tova was some kind of healer, which meant they believed Valen would be in need of healing, which sickened me even more.

Third, we'd meet on the battlefield and take back our kingdom.

Simple. At least in theory.

Why, then, did my stomach twist at every repeat of the plan?

We'd skipped something, overlooked a problem. Calder could have plans we simply couldn't foresee.

I dragged my fingers through my hair, staring at the parchment. When I thought my knees might give out under my weight, a gentle hand touched my shoulder.

Herja took hold of my hand. "Elise, you fear. As do I. But I feel in my heart that joining Alver folk with Night Folk will do remarkable things. I know you have not had experience with their magic like I have, but it is remarkable."

I squeezed her hand in return. "If only we could have the storyteller with us and harness the power of fate, then I might not rattle out of my skin with worry."

"Hold fast to the knowledge that Ravenspire has kept us alive all this time. They need Valen and Sol. And as much as I hate the thought, Gunnar is an Alver and of the Ferus line. They will believe they need him too."

A glimmer of a tear filled the corner of her eye. Herja had gone silent at the report of the treatment of Ravenspire's prisoners. I wished to comfort her, to tell her the boy would be fine, but I didn't know.

At her word, the Nightrender stood. He moved like a shadow, and I hardly heard a sound until his shoulder brushed past me. But his eyes were on Herja. "What did you say about your son? He is an Alver?"

She nodded. "I thought you knew."

"I hadn't heard. What is his Talent?"

"His father called him a Hypnotik. He can change thoughts, but it pains him terribly."

"Because he has not learned how to embrace it. His father is an Alver?"

Herja winced and nodded.

"Where is he? Dead?"

"I-I don't know. He was taken back across the sea." She gestured at Hanna, smiling. "The child, she does what he could do. He could block all kinds of magic."

His typical disinterest was what I expected, but instead the Nightrender paled, eyes wide. He took a swift step closer to Herja. "What is his name?"

She took a step back. "H-Hagen Strom."

Hadn't he just told me he knew one other Alver who could use magic like little Hanna? My fingers dug into the meat of my palms. All gods, what if he knew Hagen? What if this was part of fate's plan? To join the two kingdoms through powerful magic?

For at least five breaths the Nightrender stared, dumbfounded, and unmoving.

"Do you know him?" Herja took hold of his arm. "Please, we must find him."

"Strom," he said under his breath. He pulled back with a shout of frustration, a dark glower on his face, and stormed away.

Herja's empty hand trembled. The Nightrender knew her lover, I was sure of it. I took a step to demand he help her, even telling her he was dead was better than wondering what had become of him, but the Nightrender was lost to the shadows.

In the next moment it didn't matter. The longhouse fell into a hush as Halvar stood, clapping his hands, demanding silence.

"We have waited for this moment. A rebellion first brought by Ari Sekundär."

Ari lifted a drinking horn to a bellow of applause. He, along with so many others, was dressed in battle leathers and guarders. His waist lined in blades; a shield propped against his leg. His golden hair was tied back in braids. With a nod to me, Ari pressed a fist over his heart.

Together we'd stand on, what I hoped, would be the last battlefield.

"We finish it with our queen." Halvar stepped aside, nodding to me to take my place.

My skull throbbed with my pulse, but I would not falter. Not here. Not now.

With a lifted chin, I stood before the crowded longhouse. "We go into this fight for the Etta of old, the land of plenty under the rule of King Arvad and Queen Lilianna. We take back what is ours, what belongs to all people. We take back our king! Our homes. Our fury. And we do not falter. We do not fall. Together we will rise for the enslaved among us and across the seas. We rise for the magic blessed by the gods. We rise for freedom!"

I lifted the dagger from my vows. Roars shook the walls, blades sliced from guarders.

A smile tugged at my lips. We're coming, I prayed to the eaves with the hope Valen would know it.

The time had come at long last.

War was calling.

CHAPTER TWENTY-FOUR
NIGHT PRINCE

STRIPPED OF MY TUNIC, the Ravens worked on tethering my wrists to the posts, so my arms stretched at my sides. Bound away from my fury, weaponless, surrounded by half a dozen guards, there was little I could do but allow it.

Calder stood two paces from me, grinning. "This could stop, Night Prince. Tell me what you know of the tomb, and it ends. Was yesterday not enough?"

The open wounds on my back still boiled in pain. Sol was pale beside me as they forced him to lie back on a board, arms splayed to his sides, burns across his chest.

"I know nothing of this tomb," I lied. "If I did, do you really think I'd tell you?"

"Have another go, you bleeding bastards," Sol snapped, as if to drive the point home. "We've only just begun."

"If that is your wish." Calder flicked one finger and five Ravens jumped into action.

Sol lifted his head. My body went numb. For the whole of the torture yesterday, the false king took a great deal of pride forcing

Gunnar to watch Sol and me be brutalized. They taunted the boy, laughed when he winced, shoved him around, but never drew blood.

A tactic, no doubt, to make Gunnar break. They thought him weak, and he proved them wrong.

But now they hoisted him away from the narrow bench where he'd been chained and dragged him to the podium in the center of the courtyard.

"What are you doing?" Sol spat, unable to keep quiet.

Calder went around Sol's table, leaning on the edge with one elbow. Relaxed, enjoying every twisted moment. "Oh, I don't think it is fair to keep leaving the boy out of all the fun."

The Ravens shoved Gunnar to his knees. His jaw tightened, but if I looked close enough the slightest quiver took hold of his chin. With more force than was needed, two guards extended his arms, tying his wrists across a board, as if he were reaching over a tabletop. The snap of leather woke my senses to a Raven approaching my nephew, and to the braided ribbons of tanned pig skin hanging from one hand.

"Gunnar, look at me." I waited until his golden eyes landed on me. "We are with you. You have the bravery of both your parents. Both of them."

I didn't know his father, but the boy valued him, and he'd risked captivity to save his family. He was brave, and words mattered. Gunnar's chin stopped quivering. He nodded and narrowed his eyes at Calder. "W-We're not giving you anything."

"Such a brave little Ferus." Calder laughed, drifted to my side, and patted my face.

My cheek twitched. "I will not hand over my wife. This tomb you want remains closed. We will not stop our fight. And you will not kill me because you do not believe your own threats and fear the consequences if we die. So, stop stalling. Get on with it."

Calder's sharp features shadowed in hate. "Very well." The false king nodded at a place behind me. "Let us try again and see if we can draw out that bloodlust, Night Prince. I rather like the idea of having a mindless beast at my disposal."

I'd say nothing more. I wouldn't make a bleeding sound.

The same threats were made yesterday. The hope of Castle Ravenspire was to enrage the simmering violence in my blood until I became lost in my own mind once again.

In truth, watching Sol and now Gunnar suffer added a dismal fog to my brain. A desire to tear the limbs from each raven slowly. Thoughts too dim and violent to ever share out loud belonged to Calder. To Runa. To Jarl Magnus.

As if my mind drew him from the air, the captain of the Ravens approached. I'd memorized his sound. Heavy steps, with a slight drag of his toes. The table to my left was lined in weapons of all kinds. Carving knives, shivs, iron spikes, chains.

"Valen," Sol said. "You are king here. The land chose you. Fury will see you through."

My brother closed his eyes as Jarl fingered the weapons.

He fisted a handful of my hair, yanking my head back, so I met his eyes. "I wanted to be the one to deliver your punishment for your crimes against Timoran. It is an honor to do this for you, Night Prince." He leaned his mouth against my ear. "When this war ends, when your folk are obliterated, the law will recognize Elise as my wife. Should she live, I swear to you, Night Prince, I will take very good care of her."

Axes to his heart.

Dagger to his throat.

Perhaps I'd take each finger one by one.

I closed my eyes, imagining each deliciously bloody sight.

Then, came the pain.

Jarl was methodical in his torture. It thrilled him. The way bodies clenched and tightened against the agony only added to his brutality.

I closed my eyes, fists clenched. Each dig of his knife opened the faded scars of my life as the Blood Wraith. A hot, tang of blood burned my nose, filled my lungs. Bile teased the back of my throat.

Endless jabs, cuts, slices of different blades carved down my back, my arms, my legs. He carved out a piece of my ear. Burned the palms of my hands.

When the knife eased back, my muscles convulsed. I gasped, spitting blood on the wood laths. Through it all crowds gathered to watch, but it had been sickeningly silent. They craved sobs, the cries of the tortured.

I would not give them the satisfaction.

Jarl moved to the front; his hands soaked in my blood. With careful movements he dragged the tip of a bloody shiv down the length of my fingers. "You are accustomed to pain. But your armor breaks when those you love hurt, isn't that true? It makes your mind spin with madness, with bloodlust."

Hair stuck to the sweat on my face, but I glared at him through the gaps. Knives. Broken teeth. Fire.

So many ways to end him.

My dreams of slaughter were dashed at Sol's groan. My brother flinched, gritted his teeth as Jarl pressed burning stokers against his bruised chest, branding his skin with symbols of Ravenspire.

"Sol," I rasped.

I couldn't be sure if it was a reaction to the pain, or a response to me, but my brother shook his head, silencing me.

A cry broke. The first, and it muffled quickly. When the second crack of the braids fell, I watched as Gunnar opened his mouth and curled forward. A Raven lashed his forearms again, and again, and again. Welts raised. The boy clenched his eyes. He tried to stay silent.

Sol and I knew what to expect from Castle Ravenspire. Maybe Gunnar did on some level, but he'd never been tortured with Stor Magnus. Isolated, locked away from his mother and father, yes. But physical pain, this was his first experience.

More than my brother and me, I ached for the boy. I raged for him. My body pulled against my restraints like a reflex to try to stand between him and the endless lashing.

He could stop this with his magic. He could twist the Raven's desire. But Gunnar had vowed not to reveal his magic. Doubtless life would be worse should the boy reveal he was no fae, but something else entirely.

Until a stink filled the air when Gunnar's skin at last split.

No.

That damn rank Alver blood. Even without using his power, he'd be found out. Blood dripped over his wrists, down the table, a steady stream to the boards of the podium. Sickly-sweet, a sort of fetid cloying smell surrounded him.

The Raven covered his nose with the back of his arm, sniffed, then lifted the whip again.

He wasn't the only one to notice. All around folk wrinkled their noses. Even the false king. "Is that from his blood?"

"Valen," Sol said through a gasp. No one paid us attention, they'd taken curious glances at the potent boy. "Mask him. Do it. Please."

Frenzy tightened in my chest. My vision blurred from loss of blood, but I followed Sol's gaze. All around the courtyard were weak blooms of moonvane.

"The land chose you," Sol whispered. His skin was so raw, so broken, but he wouldn't break. Until the last threads of his life, the Sun Prince would not break.

The land chose its king. Fury strong enough to break the curse of my family brought us here.

I was bound against fury.

There was nothing I could do.

The truth did not stop me from begging. In my mind, my heart, I pleaded with whatever fury the gods placed in this soil long ago to answer my calls. Sol could kill the earth, but I could make it bloom.

My body clenched. Fury trapped in my veins burned. I let out a cry of frustration as I battled the bindings, as I begged for a glimmer of power.

Torture, I could survive. But this, this pain of digging through fierce magic, searching for a thread to hold to despite the bands on my wrists drained me of energy, of my will to keep awake, faster than anything.

How many moments passed before my body could give no more, I didn't know.

My chin fell to my chest when the gasps came, and my heart thudded against my ribs, too fast, too wild. Through the haze, a woman's shrill voice lifted over the crowds.

"All gods, look!"

"By the hells."

More voices hummed, but I heard them as through a wall of water.

Whatever had begun didn't matter nearly as much as sleep. Or death. I'd take either. My legs couldn't hold me any longer. I slumped, and the ropes around my wrists wrenched against my joints as the weight of my body fell forward.

"See your true king!" Sol's voice roared. "Bow to your gods-chosen king!"

"Shut him up," Jarl hissed.

I cracked one eye.

The podium was not the same. Tables of weapons, the ropes around our bodies, the entire expanse of the bloody floorboards was covered in moving, growing, blooming vines of silver moonvane.

Like spindly fingers, the branches had stretched and overtaken the rack. Moonvane coiled around every piece of wood, every table, every post. Thorny branches had cocooned the weapon tables and covered all the knives and blades, rendering them untouchable.

Each blossom opened to the fullest, casting the sweet milky scent into the air, masking Gunnar's blood, and pointing their blooms to where I struggled to stay conscious.

A Raven went to Sol and stuffed his mouth with a dirty linen, gagging him.

Calder and Runa stood at the head of the podium, glaring at the show of fury. Their people stared in a bit of disbelief, in doubt.

I grinned, or at least tried.

"Kill it," Calder's dark command flowed over the rack. "Leave them out here tonight. Heal no wounds."

The next moments were a blur. Ravens poured inky black onto the branches, a bit of the manipulated poison they'd gained through Sol's torture.

At once the moonvane shriveled away, the blooms died. More guards ushered folk out of the square, demanded they return to their lives.

Jarl broke his weapons free of the dead brambles. Before he left, he whispered, "Until tomorrow, Night Prince." He struck my face, so my teeth cut into my cheek, adding more blood dripping down my chin.

But when it was done, when we were left there, bleeding and aching, I found a bit of peace. I could finally rest.

My body jolted, and when I blinked my eyes open it was dark.

The frosty winds from the north peaks roared. A shiver danced down my spine.

"Sol." My voice cracked.

He groaned. Alive. Gunnar twitched and turned his haggard eyes to mine. Alive. We were alive.

I tried to leverage off my knees, but the shredded skin on my shoulders and back protested. With a wince, I tried to give a bit more pressure to my knees instead of my bound arms. Dried blood coated my lips and my mouth tasted foul. Hells, I craved a drop of water.

"Get back, boy." A Raven stepped away from the podium, hand out. "Get on home."

"I just want to see him. Hate him so much. So much."

Did the Ravens laugh? Or was it more they snarled at whoever approached.

"Our sympathies, but it changes nothing." The glide of steel from its sheath tightened my focus. "I said get back."

Three children stood around the guard. In truth, I might've been seeing things. No, they were there, and they were bold. From what I gathered, they had plans to throw spoiled fruit pits at our heads.

"Lemme have one shot, please *Herr*? Just the one," one boy said again.

The Ravens around the podium laughed and waved the young ones away. They didn't budge.

"You have ears?" With a touch of frustration, the guard nearest the children took a quick lunge at the young ones, then let out a shrill cry of pain.

He crumbled to the ground, clutching his leg. The other three Ravens rushed to him.

"*Herr*, you should be more careful. Tricky steps are enough to snap bones around here." A boy said with a wicked grin. He was paler than the moon with hair like a raven's wing.

Guards surrounded their fellow Raven, leaving a window of distraction for one of the trio to rush onto the podium. I braced for whatever rotten sludge they planned to stuff us with, but the mouthy boy kneeled in front of me.

"Short on time, My King—"

I knew that voice. "Ellis?"

The boy's eyes locked with mine.

His grin lifted with a heap of mischief as he forced a rolled piece of parchment into my hand and what looked like a roasted tree nut. "No time to explain, eat this." Before I had a chance to protest the boy pressed the nut against my lips, forcing me to open my mouth. "Eat it."

I coughed, and tried to swallow the lump as a bitter, rotted taste soaked into my throat and tongue.

"Good," Ellis said briskly. "Make sure when it hits, they put you back into your tower room."

"When what hits? Ellis, what's—"

A whistle from the pale boy drew Ellis back to his feet. "You will not have a good night, King Valen. But the queen comes, something good to think about I s'pose."

"Come on." The new boy tugged at Ellis's arm. I didn't know him, but he took a moment to meet my eye. "I hope you live. I want to see your mesmer crack the ground."

Mesmer? An Alver. Had Elise gathered Alver folk?

They were gone before I could ask. A few Ravens shouted after them, but at the groans of the broken guard they let the children go.

My skin prickled in a feverish heat. I shook away the unease and leveraged the parchment in my fingers enough I could read the few words. A smile curved over my lips.

Meet me on the battlefield, my love.
—E

"Valen," Sol's weak voice broke the night. "What is it?"

"Blood called," I said, voice hoarse. "Our people have answered."

CHAPTER TWENTY-FIVE
ROGUE PRINCESS

THE SOUND of war rang through the shanties of Ruskig.

To some this meant pain, death, fear. To me, I embraced the whole of it. I stepped with more confidence, more desire to move forward than I ever imagined. In the trees, just beyond our walls of protection, stone on steel scraped in the dark as men and women sharpened their blades. The clatter of thick wood knocked together as Casper, Stieg, and Ari shifted the stacks of shields, handing them out to the foot warriors.

Even the scents in the air were different.

Instead of the fresh spice of the forest, woodsmoke floated from small personal offerings to the gods. A breath of leather, the sharp tang of heavily painted kohl. Sweat and a touch of fear masked the new rain on the leaves and soil.

From our vantage point, the slope gave up the distant lights of Castle Ravenspire.

My grip tightened on the handle of one of Valen's battle axes. Soon, I'd return these to his hands. It was the only plan that kept me fueled with the adrenaline needed to see this through. I was armed heavily and ready to face the path of fate. Both daggers, Ice and Ash, from our vows were sheathed across the small of my back. His battle axes on my waist, and a seax on my left hip.

At my back, Halvar, Brant, and Kari directed the warriors into their positions. Archers, foot warriors, those who'd approach by river, blocking the backside of Ravenspire. Niklas talked to one of his Falkyns, a tall man with a reddish tint to his golden hair. The Falkyn clasped Niklas's forearm, nodded, and turned to the rest of the guild.

The Alvers would fight with us. They'd use their strange magic, and I didn't know if their desire came from a love of battle, or loyalty to their guild leads.

"We fight the same fight." His low, dark voice caused me to jolt.

The Nightrender appeared at my side. His eyes were lined in kohl, with red and black streaks down his face. The hood he hid beneath was pulled over his head, and a few mists of shadows followed him like a dark, diaphanous cloak.

"Your pardon?"

He gestured to the Alver guilds preparing their weapons. "You looked quizzical. I assumed you were once again trying to figure why we are here, risking our necks for folk we don't know. For a fight that is not on our land."

"Perceptive, Nightrender. What do you mean we fight the same fight?"

He propped one foot onto a fallen log and leaned onto his elbows over his knee, staring into the night. "What this comes down to is stupid folk fearing the magic of this land and trying to muzzle it. Or, in your kingdom's case, steal it to keep the throne. It is the same at home."

"With your power to destroy bodies, I wonder how Alver folk have not taken control in your kingdom."

He scoffed. "With your power to crumble mountains, raise tides, and command the ground we stand upon, I wonder how Night Folk have not taken back the throne long before now."

Point made. "You have leaders who persecute those with magic?"

The Nightrender dropped his gaze to his fingernails, though I doubted he was truly interested in them. I'd learned that much about the man—he did not like to discuss his homeland, unless he thought it necessary.

"At home mesmer—magic—is turned into a healthy, glittering trade. But don't be fooled—there are Alvers in places of power. In plain sight, they trade, manipulate, and torture their own folk. Mesmer is studied like your fury, but it is also revered in a twisted sort of entertainment to make those who own it wealthy and give them power to search for a way to harness the gifts of the Fates."

I furrowed my brow. "Is that what you believe? That the Norns of fate give the powers of our world?"

"I don't take stock in mystical beings who ignore the cries of their people." His eyes flicked to me. "But if I did, it makes a bit of sense. For centuries folk have studied, tortured, exploited magic to steal a chance at controlling fate for themselves, and it will not end."

"We can end it. Here. Today."

He scoffed and looked back into the night. "Perhaps in your world. I hope the fae rise here, that your kingdom's magic reigns. I have few hopes it'll happen in the East."

"What is your battle there? What do you fight against?"

When your battle ends his begins.

I had few doubts the Nightrender didn't believe Calista's prophecy. Then again, there were moments when his gaze went distant, and he looked as if he thought of something he wouldn't say out loud. As if he knew more about why he was tangled into this fight than he let on. His eyes pierced me in place when he looked at me again. "The Masque av Aska."

"The . . . what?"

"Have you ever heard the tale of the four queens?"

My stomach flipped. Hadn't Lilianna written something about four queens to her mysterious friend? "No," I admitted. "I don't know what that is."

"A folk tale," he said. "Four queens who would one day restore the balance to all the fates' gifts: choice, devotion, honor, and cunning."

"Those are fates' gifts?"

"The lore makes the vicious Norns sound gentle, doesn't it?" He smirked. "According to the tale, these queens are the rightful gods'-chosen, you could say. So, in the east, Alvers are made into performers at a grand masquerade each turn to celebrate the legend. It is said each gift bears a relic or a sign that will prove the true queen has risen. Perhaps something simple as the bloom of a dead land."

I widened my eyes as he pointed out a few moonvane blossoms. I had not noticed, but they pointed their silvery petals at . . . me.

The Nightrender clicked his tongue and went on. "Our wealthy have created a contest of it, where women can stand for a simple task and if they succeed, well then, they must be the queen of legend."

"I would assume no one has won."

"You'd be correct." He shifted, cracking the knuckles of his fingers once. This unsettled him, and I wanted to understand why. The Nightrender had a great many secrets, but this discussion seemed to bring him the most unease since he arrived.

"If no one wins, why does this masquerade continue?" I asked.

"Because it is a grand fete. A beautiful nightmare. Over the turns it was believed those with strong, unique mesmer could be the one to win the crown someday. So, Alvers are taken, controlled, put as puppets for a wealthy celebration. At first glance they appear revered, enjoyed, but the Alvers taken by the masque are turned into loyal dogs who will kill for their masters.

"Our kingdom is not a kingdom. Not really. We have four regions, all led by different amounts of greed. Like here, it is the throne they fight for. But not in the same way. They fight to keep it empty. Those old folk tales and prophecies have the powerful fearing what might happen if one of our unique Alvers took the throne. What is the best way to ensure that doesn't happen?"

"Kill them?"

He shrugs one shoulder. "One way, perhaps. But back home, they've discovered it is quite lucrative to use those strange Alvers to line their own purses."

"You could rise the way we are. Take away their trade."

"Our land is not like it is here where the lines between Night Folk and those in power are clearly drawn. This is a battle between magic and mortal, yes? Where I come from, those with magic fight against those with magic. Loyal dogs who kill for their masters, remember? If an Alver wants to live even half a life, it is better to stick to the underbelly with thieves like us."

"So, is that why you're fighting here?"

A curl twisted over his lips. "We cannot win in our land, but perhaps we can help free some of the Fates' magic for your people. Perhaps some can live in the peace we will never know. And," he paused, "as Junius keeps saying, it'll be of use to be allies with a king and queen."

The moment was calm enough I almost smiled, almost dared venture back into what he knew of Herja's lover, but we were interrupted by a throat clearing.

"Queen Elise." Stave stood in front of us, dressed like a warrior from head to toe. "We're beginning. The Alvers are preparing to leave."

I nodded. Stave could not leave fast enough.

"He fears you," the Nightrender whispered.

"Good," was all I said as I tightened the straps of my belt.

"More than others." The shadows thickened over his eyes. "Fears death from you."

"He was once only loyal to my husband, not me."

The Nightrender narrowed his eyes. "Want me to make his fear reality? It would be over quickly."

I snorted a laugh. "No. I made my point to Stave, and doubt he'll be so foolish as to be disloyal to his queen now." I glanced at him as we walked toward the gathering in the center. "You truly can kill folk based on fear?"

"I can do many things besides kill." The shadows surrounding him thickened. Darkness so powerful I could taste it. Then they recoiled. "Illusions—the one gift that seems to link all those with magic across the kingdoms."

"I always thought it was a fae gift."

"I'd guess folk in the South, the West, everywhere have some illusion in their magic. Since my power is found in the rush of fear, I can use it. For example, folk here fear the dark, so the shadows come through illusion. I've tumbled buildings, created monstrous sights. Death is always a fear, and it is the simplest to use."

"Then I am glad you fight beside us, Nightrender."

He dipped his chin, and by the time we joined the others in the clearing, any hint of gold in his eyes was once more swallowed by night.

Junius and Niklas finished tying pouches to their belts. No doubt each leather purse was filled with some sort of Niklas's potions. He'd assured me time and again his magic was impressive, and he was more than a poisoner. I prayed he'd prove himself right soon enough.

Ellis, Ash, and Hanna had returned hours before. The two boys kept repeating what they'd told Valen to Niklas, almost like the Falkyn asked for the image again and again to better guide him to my husband.

My heart cinched deep in my chest. Children, at times, didn't understand subtlety, and at Ellis's graphic report on the state of the Night Prince, I'd retched when no one was around me.

Then came the report of his feat with moonvane.

The land chose Valen Ferus. It answered him even bound and bleeding. I had to believe it would stand with us now.

"Ready?" I looked to Junius. She was dressed in dark robes, but underneath she wore a simple woolen dress.

Junius took my hand and squeezed. "We're ready. Watch for our signals, Elise."

I nodded and looked around at the faces of our warriors. "Our friends go to free our king. We will be there to greet him, blades ready to fight for him and for our people."

Swords slammed against shields. I blinked through the sting of tears and found those who held my heart, as if it might be the last glimpse. Mattis adjusted Siv's belt, then kissed her palm. Kari held the sides of Halvar's face as he whispered something that drew out her smile. Stieg, Casper, and Brant burned a few runes to the gods.

Ari stood beside Tor as they finished securing their blades. He winked at me but didn't smile.

I went to Herja's side. The princess of Etta was formidable. She'd donned her slender figure in black, braided her hair off her face, and held more throwing knives than anyone.

My heart cracked as she crouched in front of Laila. The girl's eyes were wet with fat tears as her mother brushed her hands over her childish cheeks, kissing away her fears.

The Nightrender looked at the girl, then to the young ones beside her. "Ash, Hanna. You look after the littles of this land, yes?"

"We can fight," Ash said with a stiff pout. Hanna nodded mutely.

The Nightrender looked ready to smile but fought against it. "Who says you will not fight? What do I always tell you?"

Ash kicked at a few pebbles, flicking his fingers over and over. "Be ready for anything."

"And it's true. Be ready. You have the weight of these folk on your shoulders to look after their young ones. Will you let them down?"

To me it was a great deal of responsibility to lay at the feet of a child, but Ash puffed out his bony chest and twirled a black steel knife in his slender fingers. "I won't."

Ellis, Laila, and the other children of Ruskig would be left to the care of Elder Klok, Ash, Hanna, and anyone else unable to lift a heavy blade. They would keep behind the walls, and if the signal came, they'd abandon the Northern Kingdom in the ships waiting at the shore.

By the gods, I hoped the signal would never come. If they left by boat, it would mean one thing—we failed.

Herja pressed a final kiss on Laila's brow before she sauntered into the trees with the other children and faded into the night. I dropped a hand to her arm. She met my eyes and gave me a curt nod. "We take back our king tonight."

"We take back our kingdom."

The Nightrender came to my side again. "Your units have gone to the rivers, the archers are making their way to the peaks, and Junius, Tova, and Niklas are leaving now."

"This is it," I whispered. My insides hardened.

"Ready, Queen?"

I looked to the Nightrender. Such a simple question with a dozen answers. I grinned with venom. "I was ready long ago."

I took hold of my blade, ready to step into position with the rest of the foot warriors.

We'd storm the grounds of Ravenspire. We'd take the most blood, see the most death. I'd meet Valen there. A battle between our different people would reunite my heart with his.

Fate led me here, and now it was time to face whatever wicked plans she had in store.

CHAPTER TWENTY-SIX
NIGHT PRINCE

FEVER RAGED THROUGH THE NIGHT. Aches, spasms, delirium. I moaned, wishing the cruel gods would end me here. I held firmly to Ellis's words. *The queen comes.*

Elise. I needed to see Elise at least once more before I met the Otherworld. Too many words still needed to be said.

A boot to the ribs sent a bright spark of pain careening up my spine.

Jarl Magnus stood above me, the knife he'd used to cut the tethers on my wrists in his hand.

Through the night, frost coated the ground and the slick boards of the rack dais. Fevering, dying, no doubt, and still the sight of him sent a blinding rage through my veins.

"He looks half in the hells."

"Worried?" I croaked, trying to lift my head, but it was too much exertion. I closed my eyes and let the cool, bloody boards of the dais soothe the heat in my skin.

"Summon mediks." Jarl barked a cruel laugh. "Get them up to the tower. Can't have them dying. Yet."

Jarl signaled for the Ravens to gather us. It took over a dozen guards to drag our battered, frozen bodies into the heat of the castle tower. We stumbled. I could not focus on a single spot; everything spun in a maelstrom of fog and darkness. When they, at last, tossed us back into the upper room to await a meeting with the king, Sol scrambled to me.

"Valen." He scooped one arm around my shoulders. "All gods, you're a flame. Hells, when did you get so bleeding heavy?"

I thought I might've laughed. "Jealous of my strength, brother."

"Never." Sol laid me on the furs of the bed, mopping my brow with as much gentleness as expected from a man who'd lived centuries alone in madness.

"Will he live?" Gunnar's voice had grown soft, burdened.

"Yes," Sol said with a certainty. "Fever will not take the Night Prince."

I scoffed, the room spinning. "I think it is safe to say, little Ellis poisoned me."

Sol's jaw pulsed as he covered me with the furs and tried to get my boiling body to stop trembling.

By the time the sun bled into night, the fever worsened. The Ravens left us alone, never returning with Timoran mediks. Likely another version of torture.

"Don't die, Valen." Sol's whisper fluttered against my cheek.

Somewhere in the sweat and chills I must've fallen asleep. I smiled through dry lips; a weak chuckle scraped from my throat. "If I do d-die, tell everyone it was in a mag-magnificent battle that saved your l-life."

Sol and Gunnar pounced to my side. My nephew looked paler, the dried blood on his arms from the lashes red and raised. But Sol's blue eyes brightened like a summer morning. "Perhaps, I will tell everyone you died whimpering in your bed."

"You w-wouldn't dare."

"You know I would."

I snorted, weakly, but it was a delirious sort of laugh.

"What is funny?" Gunnar paced back and forth near the bed. His voice cracked. "You can't die. You can't."

"Ah, Valen, I think our nephew is fond of you."

I shuddered, but forced a grin, my head in a haze. "Boy, when we s-stop taunting each other, then it is time to f-fret over one of us dying."

True enough. During the raids the only moments I truly feared for Sol had been when he stopped calling me names, when he spoke of my attributes. Those moments meant he thought time was short.

The handle clicked on the door, drawing any talk to die a swift death. Sol stood protectively in front of the bed as two Ravens pushed in, but two others followed. A woman in a dingy woolen skirt and apron, and a man with a pipe, a thick woven satchel, and a sharp tongue pointed at the two guards.

"All I'm saying is you bleeding well should've summoned us long before now. I do not make miracles, and if he already be stepping into the Otherworld, the only thing we can do is wish him well. Next time, a summons before the chills set in would be better."

The Raven's lips pinched. "Do your duty medik. Quickly."

The man with the pipe, tipped his napless cap, and placed his satchel on the edge of the bed. His eyes were a rich brown, like new soil. Odd eyes. Not Timoran. And the hint of accent in his voice, I could not place it.

"Looks awful." The medik let out a long sigh, then clapped his hands together. "Well, no time to waste."

I did not trust Timoran mediks, but had no energy, no desire to fight him off. In truth, Sol would never allow me to.

But the medik did not approach me. Through the blur of my fevered eyes, I watched with horror, perhaps a bit of awe, as the medik cracked his neck to one side and rushed the two Ravens.

With a skilled grip, the medik twisted one guard's neck in a sick crack, the Raven's body crumpling on the ground. At the same instant the woman had a silver dagger in her hand and buried in the throat of the second Raven.

She watched him choke on his blood.

The medik drew in a long breath, grinning with violence. "Well done, Tov."

Sol stood in front of the bed and Gunnar, body tense. "Get back."

The medik—who, even in my feverish head, I did not believe was truly a medik by now—chuckled. "If you wish me to reverse the elixir and give him a bit of relief, I think you really want me to get close."

Sol didn't budge.

With a sigh of irritation, the man tilted his head. "Were you particularly fond of those little guards? Apologies if so, but I thought it might prove we are not here to harm you, and in fact, have come to help you."

Sol regarded them with suspicion but relented. Barely. He remained close as the man plucked a vial from his belt and the woman darted to the window, catching the moonlight with a piece of glass she moved side to side.

I lifted my head as best I could. Soon she tore off the apron and slithered out of the dress. Underneath her clothing she was dressed in a mottled tunic and pitch trousers. Sheathed to her leg were two more daggers, a bow strapped across her shoulders. When she faced us again, I took note of the green cat-eyes at once.

"The serf," I muttered, out loud or in my head, I didn't know.

"He's still lucid," she said. "Move aside, we need to heal him quickly. By the hells, Niklas, how much did you give him?"

"Oh, beg your bleeding pardon," the man, Niklas, said with a bite. "I did not know his stature and had to guess. I imagined a bit of a giant, I'm afraid."

"You'll not touch my brother until I know who and what you are." Sol hissed.

"Cut us and we might smell a great deal like him," the woman said, pointing to Gunnar. She overruled Sol and clambered over the bed from the opposite side.

"Alvers?" Sol said.

"Yes," Niklas said. "How is your mesmer boy? Painful?"

Gunnar hesitated but nodded.

Niklas rummaged through the satchel and tossed him a small phial. "Take this. It'll help keep your focus and dull the pain. I'll give you more when this is done. Afraid your Kind with the mind tricks must cope with wretched headaches."

"What is this?" Gunnar asked.

"Specialized herbs, a few crushed roots, and a dose of pure brän ale." He clapped Gunnar on the shoulder. "Drink up and get a little drunk."

I chuckled softly, recalling moments as Legion Grey, when I'd introduced Elise to the burning drink. I did not know my name, but it was one of the earliest memories I had of when I'd been stunned by how much I wanted to remain in the company of the *Kvinna*.

The woman nestled behind my back and leveraged one knee under my hip, nudging me onto one shoulder. She blew out a curse. "Sliced you up good."

"Get on that, Tov," Niklas said. "I'll draw out the ettrig poison. You'll feel better soon, King." He patted my shoulder and placed the vial with the murky smoky substance beneath my nose. "Old Bevan sends his regards."

"Wait," Sol said. "Tell me how you managed to pose as mediks."

"Simple," Niklas said without looking up. "You'd be amazed what you can do by paying off a few greedy folk. You think mediks particularly enjoy healing the tortured of Ravenspire? Gave the sod a few pieces of coin and he gladly turned over his robe."

Resourceful. Fascinating in a way. No blood drawn. Simply cleverness.

The pungent hint of maple leaves and tarnished steel awakened my brain and jolted my senses. I coughed, the burn in my lungs chasing away the fever. Horribly so. A slow hiss radiated off my skin. Poisonous clouds of white smoke faintly rose from my pores, taking with them the aches, the fog, the sick.

What did this man . . . had he mentioned Bevan?

"Elixist?" I asked, voice rough. The old man had used his talents many a time to keep me well during the curse, and he'd called himself an Elixist.

"Right, Fae King. A rather brilliant one, if I'm honest."

The woman snorted as her fingers gently touched my back. "You're the only one who says it."

"Untrue." He scratched his chin. "Junie thinks I'm remarkable and tells me often."

"Junius." I bolted up onto one elbow.

"Stay still," the woman demanded.

I ignored her. "You know Junius?"

"I should hope so." He tipped the hat. "Niklas Tjuv. I owe you a great deal of thanks for keeping my wife breathing." Niklas stood and looked to the cat-eyed woman. "Thoughts, Tova?"

"Could use a bit of help with the wounds."

I cried out when her hands touched certain places and an unnerving tug of my skin pulled toward the center of my back. As if a hundred small needles with thread stitched my skin back into place.

"What are you doing?"

"Healing." She grunted. "Though, admittedly, I am not all that particularly skilled with my mesmer."

I winced and shuddered against the sick feeling of pulling, rapidly healing skin. While Tova worked, I looked to Niklas. "Where is Elise?"

"Ah, if your queen has hit her mark, she will be declaring war on this bleeding castle shortly."

Sol stiffened. "They're coming. Tonight?"

"Oh yes." Niklas spoke as if nothing bothered him, as if everything were amusing. Perhaps he did it for us, he killed as well as anyone. If he smiled through it, let him.

"Valen, we must get to the tomb."

My skin didn't ache anymore, and before Tova could give me permission, I pulled away. "Heal Gunnar's arms."

"No." Gunnar pulled back. "This is not a time I wish to forget. I want to remember the folk who harmed my maj. But give me that bow. I won't miss."

He pointed at the bow around Tova's shoulders.

"He's rather confident in his abilities," Sol said. My brother held no qualms at being healed and accepted a pungent paste from Niklas for the burns and welts across his chest and ribs.

"You will be, too, once you see them." Gunnar grinned, and I could see a bit of Herja's mischief there.

At my next step, a thundering boom shook the walls of the tower, of the entire courtyard.

"That'll be Junie." Niklas clapped his hands together. "We need to go, King. War is coming."

"What was that?" I followed Niklas to the satchel.

"Elixir powders. Combustible, but we needed to mark the time, so why not take out the bleeding gates while we're at it?" He sneered and dug into the pouch. "Now, your delightful queen thought you might be wanting these."

My chest tightened when he removed my battle axes. I took them with a bit of reverence, a clear heat building in my palms. Niklas handed Sol a seax and a dagger. Tova gave up her bow and quiver of arrows. Gunnar tugged at the bowstring, grinning.

Commotion outside the tower drew us to the moment. Niklas frowned for the first time. "The guards will be suspecting us by now. Time to move. I hear you can bend the bedrock. I would be most interested in you using it to get us out of here."

"We're bound," I said, spinning an ax as Sol tossed me my bloody tunic.

"Ah, foolish of me, forgetting such an important piece." Niklas lifted a rune stone out of his pouch. "Wrists out. I should've led with this."

"How do you have the key to the bindings?" Sol stared at him, wrists out, aghast.

"Not a key. Another trick of mine. Created it after Junie reported how your mesmer—fury—whatever, is bound here. Since we're joining a war with the fae, thought it might be useful to you. I've many more. We have something similar in the East that blocks mesmer, so we prepared."

His magic could counter bindings? Not the time to think too long on it. Niklas ran the smooth stone over the silver bands. The heat dissolved and my fury rushed in my veins. Sol and I both curled over our knees, but we both managed to keep from vomiting.

"Pays to have allies, wouldn't you say?" Niklas winked. "Now, we need to meet at the back wall."

"No." Sol grabbed my arm. "We must go to the tomb, Valen.

Whatever is there could help end this. For Elise. For Tor." He looked to Gunnar. "For Herja."

I closed my eyes, fists clenched around my axes. All I wanted was to stand with Elise, to fight beside her. But something about the Black Tomb itched in my skull. If it gave us any sort of advantage, we needed to take it.

I let out a frustrated shout. "Come on, then. It is only a few lengths from here."

"Wait," Niklas said. "What are you doing? We must meet the mark."

"There is strong fury hidden away," I said without stopping. "We need it to win this war."

Tova shook her head. "He will be put out."

"Who is he?" I cracked the door, checking the corridor for Ravens. Footsteps below us hinted we had moments before they ascended the staircase.

"The Nightrender. He fights beside your wife," Niklas said. "The breaker of fear and night, as you lot described him. This is his bleeding plan, and he gets irritable when plans go awry."

My eyes widened. He existed. Part of me believed him to be a myth, or a misspeak, or another slip of the tongue. It didn't matter. I slipped out into the corridor. "He'll need to be irritable."

"Suspected as much." Niklas joined me, moving like a shadow. "Junius will be at the gate. Offend the Nightrender all you want, but we will take the time to get my wife."

I gave a nod. Eyes forward. Ravens pounded up the stairs. I held both axes in one hand, then raised my empty hand. Fury grew potent. Each beat of my heart pulsed more magic through my blood.

The walls shuddered. The stone and wood making up the foundation of Ravenspire cracked and shattered.

Tova prayed to the gods, her hand braced against the wall. Niklas chuckled villainously.

In a matter of moments, the stairwell started to collapse. Ravens cried out, shouting to retreat halfway up. One guard had nearly reached the top when he locked eyes with me. My lips curled. His face paled as I closed my fist and the roar of stone and rubble crumbling blotted out the screams of the men crushed beneath it.

Dust covered the bloody mess of bone and flesh, but Sol and Gunnar wasted no time and rushed forward, gathering what blades were still visible.

I drew in a long breath and let fury take hold. A dark desire for battle grabbed hold like a tangible being.

Tonight, bloodlust was welcome.

CHAPTER TWENTY-SEVEN
NIGHT PRINCE

WHATEVER POWDER NIKLAS used to set off the blasts sent Castle Ravenspire into a frenzy. Below us Ravens and serfs collided as one half tried to gather to defend the walls, and the other tried to flee for cover.

We climbed over the rubble of the staircase, using my fury to bend more walls, break more pieces of the castle until we had sure ground to step.

"They'll be setting the archers on the east hills," Niklas said, informing us of Halvar's battle strategy as we scrambled forward. "We were to meet them from the south gates, but that, obviously, is changing."

"What about Elise?"

"And Tor," Sol pressed.

"The queen leads with Ka—I mean the Nightrender—on foot from the north forests. Archers will aim first. But there are plans for your consort, older Prince. As I'm told, he uses fire well."

Sol smirked. "Just well? He is terrifying."

Niklas grunted and helped shove Tova over the last barrier of stone and debris. "Good. Then your water fae leads ships upriver. We shall have the castle at all sides. But for our missing mark, of course."

"How long do we have?"

"Not long," Tova said. "They'll be on the march at Junius's signal. Didn't want too much time for these sods at the castle to gather."

By the gods, we were doing it. We were at war. For too long such a thought had been more fantasy than a possibility. And I could not shake the tremble of fear of King Eli's last prophecy. Damn Runa. Damn Calder. Doubtless they told me such a tale to spin me in doubt.

Elise would not fall here.

Runa. I'd kill her on her throne before she stepped foot on the battlefield. I'd half parted my mouth to suggest finding the false queen when a half unit of Ravens rushed past the broken stairs. At first, it seemed they wouldn't stop to even look our way until the second to last guard shouted.

"Bleeding gods!"

I had one ax buried in his neck in the next breath. Sol took the last guard. My brother had never held my interest with the blade, but it hardly lessened his ability to kill. The Raven gasped, blood on his teeth, as Sol's dagger entered the side of his throat.

But it was the arrows I could not ignore.

Swift. Sure. Deadly. One arrow pierced a Raven between the eyes, before I could take another breath two more lodged deep into the hearts of two others. By the time I wheeled around, Gunnar already had a fourth arrow notched and aimed.

He finished the last guard and faced me. "I told you I did not miss."

"Hells," Sol said. "Your father taught you that?"

Niklas clapped Gunnar on the shoulder. "I think it's two abilities. One of fae, one of Alver. You control all those wonderful earthy elements in those arrows with your head, boy. Or that is my guess. I'd love to puzzle it out to know for certain. But later. War, battle, and bloody things are dawning."

I'd never considered Gunnar might have two veins of the Fates' magic. Herja was not Night Folk, but half her family was. She held the blood of the fae the same as her lover held the blood of an Alver.

Gunnar ran beside me, a new confidence in his movements, as we darted through the corridors of Ravenspire. Outside shouts of units assembling kept the inner walls free for us to run.

But one voice drew me to stop.

From an open window, Jarl Magnus shouted his demands, his orders, at his units. Ready for battle, he held tightly to a short blade, an ax on his belt. The fool planned to go against Elise. My sight shadowed in red. Fists tightened around my axes. One thought bled through my brain, his life leaving his eyes under my blades.

"Valen." Sol shoved my shoulder. "Not now. Savor him later."

Leave him? How? A violent need for his slaughter held me in place.

Sol muttered next to me, shoved my shoulder again, and in another instant, murky black creeped like a serpent in the grass from the window to the lawns, toward Jarl's units. Everywhere the black touched the earth transformed into something wizened, dried, and dead.

"Move!" Jarl shouted, catching sight of the syrupy blight.

"No!" I shouted at my brother. "He is mine."

Sol's eyes darkened the more he pushed his fury, ignoring me, watching as Jarl fled out of my sight with his units. The backline of his guards was not so fortunate. My bloodlust faded with Jarl out of sight, and as Sol's poison slithered beneath the feet of the guards.

They gasped and clutched their throats as black veins sliced across their skin. Their eyes lost color, faded to a silky darkness, until they could no longer draw a single breath.

Dead. Like the earth beneath them.

"Fascinating." Niklas shook his head with a smile.

Sol struck the back of my head once we started running for the back gates again. "You keep your bleeding head. Finish this and find your queen, Valen. Be the damn king."

Parted for turns and he still knew how to reprimand me better than anyone.

Torches lit the night. Smoke from bon fires roared over the towers of Ravenspire and around the outer gates.

We wove through satin canopies covering tables of sweet fruit and berry wine, abandoned now. The back gate was tucked behind the gardens, beyond the backdoors of the old schoolhouse where I fell in love with a Timoran.

"Niklas!"

The Alver blew out a breath of relief and took the lead. From the shadows, Junius appeared, dressed in a flowing blue tunic, dark hair braided off her face. Her soft brown eyes brightened when she caught her husband's quick embrace.

I moved forward and stole her away the second he released her. She chuckled in my arms. "I never took you for a warm sort."

"It is good to see you," I admitted.

Junius pulled away, one hand on my face. "Glad to see you put your bleeding head on straight and took the crown. A thing I always told you to do. Niklas will tell you, it is wise to simply listen to me the first time."

I smiled. For the first time since parting from Elise, I smiled in earnest.

"I'll remember that."

"Let's go," Tova whined.

"Where is this place you insisted we find?" Niklas asked.

"A few lengths through the trees." I used the point of my ax to direct us. Niklas hurriedly explained to Junius we'd be altering whatever plans this Nightrender had in place, and we cut into the shadows of the forest.

"Valen," Junius called out. "How do you plan to get by those creatures no one can see but you?"

"Creatures?" Sol said in a gasp, quickening his pace.

"Fury guardians," I said. "Beings cursed to defend the tomb. They are the ones who bleeding killed me. Broke my curse, of course, but when we returned again, only Elise and I could see them."

"Perfect," Sol grumbled.

Gunnar gripped his shoulder. "After all that has happened, did you think this would be any easier, Uncle?"

At our backs, the shouts of Ravenspire faded into the night. Smoke from their pyres clouded the moonlight, but when we reached the thorny walls of moonvane and rune pillars, silence swallowed us. As if we were the only ones remaining on the land, sounds of war died. All that remained was the somberness of the Black Tomb.

The mounds were lit by torches. Tattered flags of the Lysander crest were windblown and scattered across the thick grass.

I held up a fist, stopping the others at my back. My eyes scanned the gently sloping land of the tomb. The stone blood circle. It seemed almost peaceful, as if this place did not call for death.

"Elise went into many of the tombs," I said and pointed to one near the center. "But Ravenspire kept the storyteller in that one."

"The girl?" Sol stepped to my shoulder. "Even in madness I spent a great deal of time with her. Hells, she could talk."

"Did she say anything about the tomb?"

He paused, then nodded. "She spoke of her other cage. Called it a well-guarded grave." Sol rubbed the sides of his head. "It's difficult to wade through, I was not always aware of her, but she often spoke of how it frightened her. She told me once when they left her in the dark, she felt something."

"What something?" Tova whispered as she pushed forward. She crouched, knife in hand.

"I don't know. More like she was not alone in there, and it frightened her because she saw nothing. The child was one of many storytellers, and only knew of us in our present state. She did not know much of the war between King Eli."

"Yet she led us to this moment," I said.

Sol smirked. "She was no friend of Ravenspire. I don't know if she did it because she had a good heart, or if she wanted to irk them."

I didn't care what Calista's motives were, she helped break the fury curses, she helped us bring this battle to fruition.

"Good place to start, I'd say," Niklas said. A soft, steady beat of drums broke the silence. His jaw pulsed. "And we better hurry. Our friends are coming. I have every intention of standing with my guild."

I had every intention of standing with my wife.

Axes in hand, I rolled my shoulders back. "Prepare for the fury guardians. If you are blind to them, I will do what I can to guide you around them."

"Fighting blind," Tova muttered under her breath, "my favorite way to fight."

Gunnar notched an arrow and took a gulp of whatever elixir

Niklas had given him in the phial. The Alvers readied their blades, Niklas a few vials, and Sol stood at my shoulder, blade in hand.

Two steps into the Black Tomb the shrieks of the guardians awakened.

"Do you see them?" I shouted.

"I see them," Sol said through his teeth.

"Run to the mound. It takes blood," I said as the shadowy guardians raged. They rose in their haunting shapes, golden fiery blades at the ready. Their cries were pitiful, desperate, wicked.

"Go!" Niklas tossed one of his pouches in a murky cluster of the shadowy guardians.

A bright, spark of white ignited the tomb in a hissing mist. The guardians shrieked and faded. No time to wonder, no time to ask. All I could do was thank the Fates they'd brought us tricky allies with magic that rivaled our own.

Shadows would dissipate at the strike of our blades, the points of Gunnar's arrows, but they came without end.

I hated this bleeding place.

After slashing at too many, Sol cursed the gods and dropped his blades. Blight coated the palms of his hands. The poison filled spaces between the guardians, devouring moonvane, grass, trees, but also the fury keeping the guardians attacking.

Their shrill cries rattled in my skull, but I laughed. Sol's blight devoured them the same way it devoured the earth.

With a breath to act, I reached for Gunnar's hand and sliced him with the edge of my axe.

"What are—"

"Blood." I did the same to my hand. "Niklas, we will make for the door. Hold them back when Sol breaks."

The Alver gathered vials and pouches, handing them to Tova and Junius. "Move quickly and don't bleeding lock us out."

I let out a long breath, focused. We'd have moments. A few heartbeats.

"Sol! Now!"

My brother dropped his hands, blight fading, and wheeled over his shoulder. Gunnar sped beside me as Sol caught up with us. I slammed into the door of the mound Elise had once entered. My blood dripped over the basin near the door. Gunnar splayed his bloodied palm beside mine. Bursts of color and fire erupted around the guardians as the Alvers used the elixirs to give us time. Sol used a thick thorn from a dying moonvane branch to slash his hand.

The guardians hissed and spat their rage when the heavy door slid aside and we toppled in.

Niklas, Junie, and Tova sprinted for the door, shadows at their backs. When they reached the entrance, they flung inside and helped slam the door behind us.

Gunnar slid down the wall until he met the ground and let out a nervous laugh. "This place is like a nightmare."

I nudged his head. "Welcome to the world of your mother's people."

He snorted and gathered his bow again. Niklas and Sol scanned the space. There was a small cage made of iron bars. Doubtless Calista rotted in there many times.

"How did they get her inside without the right blood?" Sol asked, eyes on the cage.

"I don't know, but Elise opened the door once. We thought it was royal blood." Perhaps there was more to the storyteller than we knew, or perhaps it had been done by false kings in the past. "I don't think that is the door the prophecy spoke of anyway."

We dragged our hands across walls, searching for anything that might lead us to a door, something that might hide lost fury my mother never wanted Eli to find. Sod, dirt, and packed clay was all I found.

My fists clenched and unclenched.

"Blades, books, no door." Sol slapped a leather-bound book of parchment closed. "We might've chosen the wrong mound."

Drums pounded fiercer in the distance. We were on the losing side of time.

"Unless we are not looking low enough." Tova lifted her strange eyes from where she kneeled on the floor. She pulled back dusty woven rugs and revealed a row of blackened rune symbols scorched into the floorboards.

We scrambled over to the space. Niklas and Sol ripped back the rugs. A clear circle surrounded the runes, but it looked nothing like a door. No hatch, no breaks in the wood. From a pouch on his hip, Niklas removed an empty vial. "You say blood is the key here. Hurry."

He gestured to the opening in the vial. There wasn't a need to explain more before Sol, Gunnar, and I held new open wounds over the top until the bottom was covered in our mixed blood.

Niklas swirled the vial, then tipped it over the runes. I held my breath.

Nothing.

At first.

A few silent, wretched moments passed before a flicker of red heat brightened the line of runes. As it had the day my curse broke, blood swirled across the surface of the wood. The runes burned brighter. A heavy groan and shudder rippled through the mound; I let out a curse when the boards dissolved away as sand on the shore and widened to a tunnel below ground.

"All gods." Junius gaped at the pit.

My pulse raced in my skull. I took hold of one ax and glanced at my brother. With a nod, Sol took the first step into the dimness.

I followed, Gunnar at my back. The Alvers kept a cautious watch as they slowly descended a few paces behind.

A cold wall of earthy smells with an underlying rot burned my lungs. The tunnel expanded into a cavern. No light, no openings, nothing but stone and earth. Niklas clicked what sounded like glass stones together and soon a spark of pale fire ignited over the lip of one of his glass vials like a candle flame.

Sol scoffed. "You Alver folk are wise to keep around."

"We are impressive," Niklas said, a little breathless as he moved the flame around, studying the marks on the walls.

"Valen," Sol whispered a few paces into the cavern. "What is that?"

I followed his gaze. What little light Niklas's trick provided revealed something in the center of the open space. Dark shapes, possibly a table? I snapped a finger and held out my hand until Niklas gave the flame to me.

Together, Sol and I approached. My foot struck a barrier, a stone ring around the long shapes. With care we stepped over the edge of the ring. Part of me expected a new wave of guardians to pierce us with their blades, but nothing changed.

Until Gunnar joined us and all at once fierce wind hissed through the long tunnels, igniting a ring of torches, brightening the tunnel in ghostly shadows.

I looked around, ax at the ready, fury burning. No guardians came.

"Who are they?"

Gunnar's voice dragged Sol and I back to the center of the ring. It took a single heartbeat for my mind to accept what I was seeing. Then a jab to my chest stole the air from my lungs. I was not the only one. Sol fumbled next to me. He used my shoulder to keep upright; I braced against him.

"All, the bleeding, gods." The words came in soft, slow gasps.

Two stone tables were placed in the center of the ring. A gilded shimmer of fury shielded the surface, almost like a glittering canopy over two bodies.

"What is it?" Niklas hissed.

I went to one, Sol went to the other. My throat tightened, choking my every breath. Her face was peaceful, pale, burdened. The shallow rise and fall of her chest made no sense, how . . . how was any of it possible?

"Valen?" Gunnar pressed gently.

I shook my head and reached a trembling hand through the glowing shield over her features. It kissed my skin with a shocking warmth, a fury that spoke to my own.

I looked at Sol. He was on his knees, hands on the edge of the second table, breaths harsh.

"The true king and queen," I whispered. "They are . . . our parents."

CHAPTER TWENTY-EIGHT
NIGHT PRINCE

My friend,

I have done as you asked. Illusions have been believed. Vicious fury has been dealt. My warriors, my friends will seal the entrance as you instructed. They stand ready to sacrifice for their kingdom. To wait for the time the gods-chosen will rise.

My family is scattered, and all trust, all hope lies within you now. Your assurance that one day I will look upon their faces remains my solitary light.

I hope there comes a day where I shall walk the gardens with H, where I will read until sunset with S, where I will laugh until my heart aches with V, where I will feel my lover's kiss. But if next I wake it is in the great hall of the gods, so be it.

I go now, to sleep. May the Fates be with you.

Your eternal friend,

—Lili

"Your parents?" Junius stepped beside me, her eyes on my mother's face.

My mother.

She breathed.

She lived.

But she didn't move. Didn't make any hint she knew this sanctuary had been undone. My thoughts reeled. For weeks I'd scanned the strange missives from my mother with Elise. In the final one, when she said sleep, I assumed she spoke of death.

A heady panic rose through my heart. "No." I whipped my head to Sol. "No. I . . . This is wicked fury. I-I saw our father's bloodied body at my feet."

The memory was one I buried deep in the recesses of my mind.

"Valen," Sol said, his voice heavy. "As did I, but . . . he's here. He breathes."

Illusions have been believed.

No. Our mother, she . . . she wouldn't have deceived us. Or had she meant the false king had been deceived?

I dragged my fingers through my hair, pacing beside the edge of the table. What were we supposed to do? Was this even possible? Illusions lived in pieces of fury. I was not convinced I was seeing the truth.

"All right." Niklas held up a hand, stopping my furious steps. "Let us keep our heads. A war still rages, and we must act. What do we do?"

I shook my head, looking at my mother's face again. "I've never seen this."

"They appear to be sleeping," Gunnar said. He studied my mother's face. "Maj looks like her."

I hardly heard him. Too many thoughts tumbled in my head. Until Sol cleared his throat. This, *this* was why Sol deserved the crown. His stun took him for a few moments, then he collected himself, and faced the cavern with a calmness I couldn't find.

"Fury sleep," he said. "Dagar often spoke of it. A dangerous strategy. Fury can place one in such a state of sleep, they are unable to wake unless one has the correct element chosen to end it. Sleep could grow endless." Sol took in the room. "Look at this place. Look at what they wear. Their court gown and cloak. They were placed here as a burial."

"By Eli?" I suggested.

"I don't know, he might've thought they were dead. They were enemies, but I have no doubt he held some respect for Daj to bury him as a king, and some twisted love for Maj."

The idea that King Eli would keep my father alive did not make a great deal of sense in my mind; he must've thought he had succeeded in killing the Ettan king to place him here. If ever there were greater enemies than Arvad and Eli, I did not know of them. Calista spoke of the storyteller who cursed me; if she had a role to play in my brother and sister surviving, perhaps fate had played a role in my parents' lives.

"We can speculate, or we can wake them and get some bleeding answers," Tova's brisk voice broke through my stun.

"I don't know how," I snapped. "You heard Sol, we need a token, an element designed to break such a sleep."

A thrum of drums sent a chill dancing down my spine. Beyond the tomb a boom shook the ground. Niklas glanced at Junius. I understood the shadows in their eyes. We were out of time. Our people were beginning their fight.

"This is the fury," Sol said softly. "The fury locked away. She said the land would rise when it was unlocked. Valen, when the heirs open the door. We can wake them."

"How? Tell me how and I will do it."

Niklas sighed and held out his hand. "Hands. Give them to me. Yes, all three of you." He twirled a small knife in his fingers. "Might as well stay true to what's worked so far. Blood."

Blood of the heirs. When I looked at Sol, the small twist of a grin on his face hinted he'd thought the same as me.

Niklas gathered drops of blood from us and handed me the vial. "I'm unsure what to do with it from here. I know it is difficult to believe, but this sort of magic is something I've not seen."

I took the vial, as unsure as the Alver on what to do. My hand shook as I hovered the vial over the glow of fury hovering above my mother's face. I watched thick drops fall straight through, splattering across her cheek.

After a pause, I handed the vial to Sol. He did the same to my father.

We waited.

I hardly breathed.

Sol cursed. Gunnar stared forward without blinking. Nothing changed, and an ache of disappointment bloomed through my chest. I closed my eyes, desperate to find a new way. Blood would be the answer, I was sure of it. How much, though? Was there a chalice, another basin, we needed to fill?

I would...

Thoughts faded when a soft touch curled around my wrist.

My eyes snapped open. The gold fury had faded, and I was met with the sharp blue of familiar eyes.

A strangled cough ripped from my throat. I blinked as through a daze.

My mother studied me, almost as if she did not recognize me, then a slow, cautious smile played at the corners of her mouth. Her hand abandoned my wrist and touched the side of my face.

"You are a beautiful sight, my son." Her voice was dry and coarse.

I covered her cold hand against my cheek and smiled. "How is this possible?"

She didn't answer. Both of us looked to the other table. Sol laughed. All gods. My father had sat up, using one elbow to brace himself, and hooked an arm around Sol's neck, holding him close.

"Arvad," my mother breathed out.

Sol stepped aside, and at once my parents' locked gazes. Their movements were slow, perhaps a little weak, but in a few breaths King Arvad and Queen Liliana found a way back to each other's arms.

My father kept checking her face, brushing her hair aside, as if she might disappear.

"Valen."

I blinked my gaze back to them. My father looked at me. I shared his eyes, most of his features. The man had taught me how to hold a blade, how to value my mother, my family. He taught me of my fury. And he was here. Alive. Reaching for me.

Much like my brother, it took a matter of moments before his arm was curled around my neck, pulling me against him. We stood at the same height, but in the moment, I felt a great deal like a small boy. My fists curled around his gambeson. I buried my face against his shoulder.

"You're alive."

"You think that bastard could kill us?" he whispered.

I scoffed and pulled away.

"Herja." My mother's voice strengthened. "Where is Herja?"

"Alive," Sol said, taking her hand. "But not with us."

"Then how—"

"Gunnar." Sol signaled for our nephew who'd scurried to the edge of the ring, a look of fright on his face. "Come here."

My mother studied him as the boy approached. She took in his golden hair, the ugly welts across his forearms, the blood on his hands.

"Herja's son," I said. "Gunnar Strom."

Now it was our parents' turn to be taken back. My father rested a hand on my mother's shoulder as she reached for Gunner's cheek like she had mine. "Herja's son."

"Maj spoke of you both," he said, voice low. "Often."

"I expected battle and bloodshed if ever I woke, but not a new boy to love," my mother said, smiling at him.

Niklas cleared his throat, his eyes on me. With a silent nod he brought me back to the crushing reality we faced. We could not stay here.

"There is a battle," I said. "We must go. Our people are rising against the Timorans as we speak. We must go to them."

My father faced me. "You raised armies?"

"Valen did," Sol said with a touch of pride. "He is king."

Inadequacy reigned here. I stood before my father—the true king—and my brother, the expected king. "I've kept the crown polished for you," was all I said. "But they need us."

My father took hold of my mother's hand and gave her a nod. "This is the final stand, as we always knew it would be."

She pressed his palm to her face, tears in her eyes.

"How are you alive?" I asked again before I could kill the questions.

My father guided us away from the stone tables. "It is such a long tale, with so much sacrifice. The swift explanation? King Eli grew too strong; we'd suffered too much betrayal. We needed to take drastic measures to protect our people, and our land."

"A prophecy at your birth, Valen, had come to pass," my

mother said over her shoulder as we ran. "Where the land of my childhood would destroy the land of my heart, but the heirs of both would find a way to heal it. A dear friend with the talent to twist fate wrote the path to bring a halt to the war, then she rewrote a new path where we could return to the battle stronger. But it meant convincing Eli our children must not be killed; it meant convincing him he was the lone king. That your father and I were dead. Once the war ended, this land would be in a state of sleep, waiting for fury to rise again."

My mother and father had put this in motion. This intricate game of fate and blood. All for this moment. When the heirs of both lands would face each other on a battlefield. Both believing the land belonged to them.

I pushed the stun away. There was a battle we needed to win, then more questions could be asked. "Sol, do you have the strength to use your fury against the guardians?"

"I'm offended you even asked."

"No." My father stopped us, his stern, deep rumble a thing of my memories. A sound I never thought I'd hear again. "We go to the stone of the sanctuary. Those guardians—we're not leaving without them."

"What?"

A sly grin curled over his lips. "You want an army, King Valen? You shall have one. Move swiftly, it will take all five of us to rid this place of the final curse."

Niklas and his fellow Alvers had said little, but once we'd returned above ground, they were the first to the door of the mound. He held out a hand and gathered a few final pouches he had tethered to his belt. "We shall distract them. Run to where you must go. We'll fight them off."

"Don't die," I told Junius. "There is too much fighting to be had still."

"Wouldn't dream of it," she said. With a mute nod, Niklas, Tova, and Junius slipped out the doors first.

The creature within me breathed in the tang of blood, carried on the wind, I yearned to join whatever fight had begun. Wished to look upon Elise. To fight with her. To keep her breathing. A yearning for another had never been as fierce as it was with Elise. Like those surrounding me, she was my family. My heart. I would not rest until these bloodied hands touched her. Even once more.

Smoke filled the breeze. The wicked glow of fire flicked high against the velvet night. As soon as Niklas entered the open space of the Black Tomb the shrieks of the guardians raged. Their ashy bodies rose from the shadows, from the soil.

"Go!" Niklas tossed one of his elixir pouches, setting off deafening booms and blasts as the Alvers took up the fight.

"Quickly." My father took my mother's hand and sprinted toward the stone circle at the top of the slope.

At our backs the shrieks of the guardians descended upon us. The Alvers tried to fight them, tried to keep them, but more and more slipped around them, aimed at us. I'd raced to this spot too many times. Enough to have my bloodied hand ready to touch the symbol. Gunnar and Sol bled as much as me, and we paused as my father sliced my mother's palm before he sliced his.

"Together."

All at once, the five of us pressed our palms to the stone. Swifter than the night I died, the night I broke the focus the guardians had on Elise, a flash of blinding light burst from the stone. The dome surrounded us, then split into hundreds of sharp skeins of light. Each point struck a guardian through the place a heart might be if they breathed.

The guardians wailed, shrieked, then faded beneath a second, final burst of light.

The guardians were gone, the mounds making up the Black Tomb collapsed. But we were no longer alone here.

All around Niklas, Junius, and Tova, darkly clad bodies sprawled out over the grass. Like a battle had been waged in a moment's time and hundreds were dead.

Until they moved.

Groans and gasps rose from the field as every figure shuddered, and slowly clambered to their feet. Men. Donned in furs, seax blades, axes, and daggers on their belts. Shorn heads with braids down their skulls, or runes inked on their scalps. Some with tapered points to their ears, some with beards braided to their chests.

Warriors.

Two men approached. They bore the symbol of the Ferus line across their chests. Long blades clacked against their hips. Their eyes were dark as pitch, and their smiles were familiar and white.

"Kjell," Sol said in a long breath. "Dagar."

Tor's father stood in front of my brother, but soon had him against his chest, the same as our father had done. But as consorts, Torsten's family would be Sol's as much as Torsten was ours.

My mouth hung open like a bleeding fool as Dagar Atra grinned and lowered to one knee, fist over his heart. "Night Prince. It is good to set eyes on you again." Then, Dagar caught my father's eye. "Arvad. Lili!" He hurried to them, embraced them. "By the hells, it worked."

"It worked," my father said, one hand cupped around Dagar's neck.

"Our armies . . . were the guardians?" My head was beginning to ache with all the fury I knew nothing about.

My mother touched my arm. "If we ever met this day, we would need an army. They were willing."

"You did this, didn't you? All of it."

She winced. "I saw no other way to survive but to curse the land. I tried to save so many, but... I could not save everyone."

"The queen protected the courts," Dagar said. "Sacrificed greatly for your family's line to live on. It was the only way to keep what was left of Etta alive."

"By hiding it with fury." My mind resisted this. Twice I'd crossed into this cursed place, twice I'd walked over my parents beneath my feet. All this time, all these turns, our people have been alive and hidden in plain sight. "Why did you attack us then?"

Dagar barked a laugh. "We had no minds, Night Prince. Only instinct. Defend our king and queen from discovery."

"The curses were placed with great care, Valen. Many lives were lost to give us a chance to reclaim our land," my mother said. "I knew my children would be divided but had every faith you would rise together again. Etta needed to survive for this battle. This is where fate wanted us to stand with you." She looked to Dagar and Kjell. "Our Night Prince has raised an army that fights for us now. Hear the drums."

"An army?" Dagar said. "Made of what?"

"Night Folk, Ettans, folk of the Eastern Kingdom, a few Timorans who despise Ravenspire," I said.

"And if you are here, then who leads them?"

"Halvar and Tor." I paused. The names of their sons settled differently. Kjell grinned and looked to Sol, who nodded. Dagar's jaw tightened, he blinked too much, then cleared his throat and pointed a small smile at the grass. I stepped closer, voice low. "They lead beside the Queen of Etta."

"The queen?" My father raised a brow.

"My wife." I swallowed past the scratch of smoke in my throat. "A Timoran by birth; an Ettan by heart."

No one spoke. What did they think? Would they, after all this, hate my mother's homeland too much to accept Elise? I'd only gotten them back, but there was no bond, no blood that would keep me from my wife.

"Then we go to the queen." My mother stepped forward, a knowing look in her eyes, a grin that said a hundred things. "Now my son, as king, what is your word for our armies?"

A heady relief ignited a new fire to my veins. Fury coated my palms; without trying the ground shuddered as I scanned the field, the warriors, once thought dead and gone, now at the ready to fight for Etta once again.

I lifted my chin and raised my voice. "Etta rises against the people of Timoran. They fight at Ravenspire now! Take up your arms, we go to war."

CHAPTER TWENTY-NINE
ROGUE PRINCESS

Brant took his sister's hand. "Kari. If this night is my last, send my pyre to the sea. Know that you are stronger than me, and I am pleased for you to have found Hal. If you ever wondered if you had your brother's blessing to make him an honest fae, you do."

"Brant, quiet," Kari said, a slight tremble in her voice.

"Agreed," said Halvar. "No death talks until our innards are spilling out on the battlefield. It is more poetic and meaningful."

Brant pinned him in a look. "All the same, you are honorable, Halvar Atra, so tell me you'll look after her if I cannot."

My stomach turned over. I hated this line of talk, hated the thought of losing a single face in our numbers, but I could not turn away.

Halvar's playful smirk faded. He clasped Brant's forearm in a tight grip and nodded. "When Night Folk love it is for life. She is who I love."

Kari frowned, not at Halvar's words, but at her brother. "Enough. We focus. We fight. We return. Do you both understand me?"

She did not let them finish before Kari turned and stormed back into the trees.

I closed my eyes, feeling the heat of the Nightrender's stare on my back. He was furious. They'd gone to the post where Niklas, Junie, and Tova were supposed to be with Valen and the others.

Nothing had met them but a strange copper coin.

"A sign left by Niklas. They've changed plans," the Nightrender had grumbled before going silent, eyes black with shadows. He'd seethed in silence ever since.

"The rivers have been taken." A low voice stirred me from my moment of pause. Raum, the Kryv who saw distances, stepped next to me, a strain on his face. "Hells. Nightrender, they've seen the ships on the rivers. Plans must change."

"You're sure?" I straightened.

Raum nodded. "I'm sure, Queen."

The Nightrender cursed. "This is why Niklas was meant to be at the mark. They were to distract the Ravens off the rivers."

"Do not make the mistake in thinking the king did not have good reason to alter this design," Ari said, a bite to his tone.

"Enough." I shouted, silencing their bickering. "If they were not at the post then there was a reason they were forced to change plans. But we move forward. We help our people at the rivers, we begin this fight."

I'd waited to see my king long enough.

The archers were led by Herja and already in place on the peaks. They'd rain fire over Castle Ravenspire, and we'd bring down the gates. I raised my sword, embracing the heat and energy of the armies at my back.

I could give a fierce cry to battle, but no more words could be said that had not already been said. It was time.

I gave a curt nod to Tor. He shot a spark of blue across the night. It pierced the center of the sprawling field, beside a fountain shaped as King Eli. Tor waved one hand and at once the entire stone figure was engulfed in fury pyre.

Archers shouted from the peaks. More fiery arrows arched across the sky. Deep in the trees, to either flank, warriors shouted as the pyre roared below, the flames reaching for the silver moon like a beacon leading us forward.

The Nightrender drew a blacksteel sword and covered his black eyes away beneath his hood.

I dropped my sword. Before it reached my side, I was swallowed by the rush of our warriors.

The flood of our armies shuddered across the damp soil. At the castle, horns blared from the towers, warning of our approach. They were forming their units, but we came swiftly.

Another wave of burning arrows assaulted the tower guards and Ravens lined across the walls of Ravenspire. Screams mingled with falling bodies off the walls. A collision of steel and blood burst between two sides.

I braced, seax at the ready, and leapt into the fray. My sword struck a Raven's short blade. We locked, and spun, and dodged until I sliced the back of his leg. At my back, another came. And another.

Focus forward. Halvar's lessons reeled through my brain. I was shorter but moved swifter than most Ravens in their bulky guarders and armor.

I'd use it.

My cuts and stabs went to ribs, to thighs, the back tendons of the knees.

In a matter of moments, my face was splattered in hot, sticky blood, and my muscles throbbed for more.

Ari fought nearby. Ravens dropped at his feet screaming in terror. His fury molded their brains in illusion and left them defenseless against Frey and Axel as they slit their throats from behind. Halvar, Tor—they used the blade first. But their strategy would always be to conserve their fury until the right moment.

Doubtless if it was a last resort, they'd burn this field with wind and pyre.

The Nightrender remained furious over Tova and the missing Alvers. His anger written in the sharp lines of his face, but it served us well. All his rage was pointed at Ravenspire on our behalf.

Blacksteel blade in hand, the man fought with a finesse I envied. As if battle were a second nature, he broke Raven after Raven with his cutting edge. Scattered nearby, the Guild of Kryv proved why their numbers did not need to be great. The muscled Kryv stood off ten paces. From the corner of my eye, his fists raised and seven Raven guards staggered on their feet, then fell back as if asleep.

He rid them of life with the next swing.

Raum and Vali laughed. They laughed as they slashed their blades. As if battle and bloodshed were the greatest part of their day. Falkyns who remained with us fought much the same.

Alver magic was thrilling, odd, and deadly.

A shout at the gates kept me moving forward and sent a chill through my blood at the same moment.

From the back of a roan, Jarl shouted my name. Hells. Halvar had warned me of this moment. When the ruler is plucked off the battlefield.

"Bring her to your king!" Jarl was shouting.

A panic filled my chest as nearby Ravens didn't hesitate. Soon one, then two, then more and more guards converged on me. Tor fought his way closer to me. Halvar shouted commands to defend the queen. Ari held out his hands, twisting some Ravens in illusions that left them wandering blindly, but more came.

More always came.

The space I could fight lessened as guards came at me from all sides. One would strike. I'd block. Another would aim to take out my feet. I chopped my seax and cut into his shoulder.

We needed to get closer to the gates. There was more fighting to be done, and by the gods, I was not being removed from this battlefield now. But Ravens were a disease, ever spreading without end.

As much as my people fought for me, I would not be able to fend them off forever.

A blade sliced across my ribs. I cried out, fumbling. A Raven took hold of my hair; another gripped my wrist.

In the next breath, inky shadows curled around my legs, scaling my body like a dark cloak. They filled the spaces between me and the Ravens. My heart stilled. I watched in a bit of horrid wonderment as the Nightrender stepped nearer. His hood back, palms raised, eyes the blackest black.

Shadows abandoned me, then curled around dozens of guards like dark ropes. A few Ravens cried out, trying to bat them away.

For a moment, the Nightrender did nothing. His eyes took in the field, his darkness, and he simply studied it. He took a long breath, shoulders lifting, then all he did was tilt his head to one side.

A great snapping of bone echoed in the night.

Ravens choked and fumbled, blood on their lips, necks twisted in wretched ways. A wash of bodies fell to the ground.

By the hells. He'd . . . he'd killed at least two units of Ravens with what? One nod? Twenty paces on all sides of me, dead guards bloodied the battlefield.

The course of the battle shifted. Ravens gaped at their fallen armies in terror, some backed toward the walls of Ravenspire. But Jarl demanded more units forward.

Ravenspire would regroup, but the stun offered up a single moment to take the advantage.

Our frontlines slammed into the gates of the castle. I cut a Raven across his spine, ignoring how young he was, and sprinted to the first wall.

"Elise!" Ari shouted, his bloody sword pointing to the back gates.

A vicious smile curled over my mouth. The archers above us cleared their path by a blast of arrows at the backlines of the Ravens. Ari came to my side with Frey and Axel. They helped shout orders to push through the gates, to create a shield barrier as we'd done not long before at the fury quarries.

Our warriors gathered into tight, boxy units, shielding sides and heads as lines of our people rushed through the barriers with ladders and rope to begin the scale.

The Ravens atop the wall flung balls of straw coated in boiling tar and flames, desperate to keep those taking the walls from reaching the top.

I caught sight of the Nightrender shoving forward with his sword in one hand and a curved knife in the other.

"You killed so many!" I shouted with a fierce laugh. "And I worried you'd prove worthless, Nightrender!"

"I am worth too much, Queen. Fear is potent," the Nightrender shouted back. He looked paler, his eyes were returned to gold, and he rolled his blacksteel in his grip.

"I vote he takes out all of Ravenspire for us while we watch," Ari said, grinning.

"He's weakened now," I said.

It was obvious, the Nightrender used his blade, and no shadows remained. Clearly, Alver magic drained energy the same as fury.

We made it to the walls, but our advantage was over. At Jarl's command, the Ravens pulled back in the towers, and the portcullis lifted to hundreds of warriors. At the head of the new rush—Runa and Calder.

The false king and queen entered on horseback, blades on their leather gambesons. Their first knights rode beside them, dropping a sickly black powder across our frontlines. Dark, gray veins slithered over the faces and necks of our warriors. Eyes darkened, they screamed and scraped at their skin.

They flailed with a bit of madness much the same as the cursed Agitators who'd attacked the Lysander manor last turn.

Their cries dug deep under my skin. For centuries Ravenspire had manipulated fury, now they'd fight with their manipulations until half our people were lost to the warped blight.

"The riders!" Halvar roared, blade raised, facing the peaks.

Arrows flew at the knights, but Ravenspire warriors rode next to them, shields raised.

Runa and Calder pressed their armies forward. Calder was a bleeding fool, but he was not unskilled with the sword. The false king brutally took the heads, the throats, the hearts of Ettans as he barreled his horse through our lines.

All around, men and women groaned in agony. Wounds bled. Their hands clutched their middles, their necks, trying to stay upright. Ravenspire returned to cut them down. With a crushing truth it was clear we were outnumbered.

"Slaughter them!" Calder roared.

A new energy latched onto the Ravens. They fought brutally. They fought without mercy. I let out a scream of frustration and rage, pushing forward. Fate would not bring us this far to fall now. It would not happen. It could not happen.

The ground trembled.

My heart flipped in my chest, but nothing more came. There were armies clashing, doubtless I'd fooled my hopeful heart.

Valen wasn't here.

Across the field, I found the icy gaze of my sister. She'd learned to fight. Not the same as Calder, but in her time as queen, clearly, Runa had learned how to wield a sword. Still, she remained timid on her horse as my father led a charge ahead of her.

Leif Lysander was once a man like Jarl. A nobleman who led units of Ravens. He would know how to fight and how to win. I never thought I'd embrace a bit of my own bloodlust in such a way, but watching them now, I'd never wanted to kill anyone so badly.

Tor released a blast of pyre. A signal to Herja. Our archers were needed here more than on the peaks. When the flames faded into the sky, I raced toward my sister.

"Queen!" The Nightrender called behind me. He'd insisted, along with Halvar and Tor, that we remain close, and now I was changing his plans again. "Dammit. Elise!"

All I saw was a fight ahead of me.

I cried out, slashing my blades against Ravens as I battled closer to Runa and my father. If I fell, then I'd see to it Runa fell too.

The moment I stepped on the slope of a berm, I stumbled forward. A deep fissure shook the earth apart.

An eerie hiss fell over the field.

The ground shuddered violently. My skin tingled in anticipation as a smile cut over my lips. A guttural cry from my people rose to the silent stars. On the ridge of the south end of the field a dark figure stood alone.

My heart dropped to my stomach. Valen.

He stood alone for mere moments before an entire line of warriors filed in behind him. All gods. Where did he find warriors? The quarries? Were they our folk from the river? It didn't truly matter, and the sight sparked a new wind into the lungs of our people. Battle cries changed for their Night Prince.

The army behind Valen roared in response.

For the first time, Calder, Runa, and the whole of Ravenspire looked afraid.

"I assume—" the Nightrender materialized behind me, a little breathless, "this is the king we came to save."

I raised my blade, unsure if Valen could see me from such a distance and shouted, "For your king!"

At the second wave of shouts, Valen shook the earth and raced into the fight.

"By the hells," Tor said. "He has Sol and . . ." Tor narrowed his eyes. "No. It's . . . it's not possible."

"What?" I snapped. There wasn't time to be vague. "Say what you see."

Tor blinked his eyes to me. "Beside him, I . . . could've sworn I saw Arvad."

What? I turned back to Valen's army. They were melted into the fight now, too buried among Ravens and Ettans to pull out individual faces.

"Who is Arvad?" the Nightrender asked in a snarl.

"Valen's dead father."

The Nightrender looked at me like I'd gone mad and shook his head. "I don't understand this place."

I felt much the same.

At his direction, a few Kryv abandoned my side with the Nightrender and followed Ari into an onslaught of riders carrying more poison blight. I wanted to watch their every move, wanted to see the poison destroyed, but forced myself to turn back into the fight.

Battle waited for no one.

A Raven with a crooked nose and two short blades rushed for

me. I blocked his strike and twisted in a way to avoid a slice to the back from his second sword.

His blade cut a path toward my chest. I leaned back, narrowly missing the point. My dagger cut his ribs; my boot smashed against the side of his knee. He seethed at me as if he didn't feel a thing.

"Daughter!"

A wicked laugh came from behind the Raven. I gritted my teeth and kept slashing at the guard, ignoring that my father stalked me.

His face twisted my insides. All those turns I'd done my uncle's bidding. Submitted to his desire for an advantageous marriage, became a silent face in my household, all to keep mediks for Leif Lysander.

Here he stood, healthy, vicious, and without care if I lived or died.

No. He watched as I struggled against a boar of a man, a warrior with more skill than me. In truth, I think my father enjoyed watching, for the sport of it. No doubt he looked forward to the moment when the Raven's blade carved out my heart.

The guard slammed his thick fist into my mouth, tossing me backward. I coughed blood, gripping my blade to lodge it in his chest. Or at the very least, slash him in a weak joint of his guarders to run away.

Over the cruel laughter of my father a swift rush of air grazed my face. Followed promptly by another. The Raven grunted. I wheeled around as two arrows sunk deep in the throat of the Raven and he crumbled.

I smiled. From the trees, Herja had her bow raised, another arrow notched. She winked and fired into a new cluster of Ravenspire forces, arrow after arrow.

I adjusted my grip on my blade and spun around to meet my

father's blade. The clash of steel shattered a piece of my heart. This was never a moment I envisioned in my life. Blood fighting against blood.

A look of surprise shadowed his one eye for the briefest moment when the edges of our swords collided. Did he think I'd be the same? An obedient girl filling her days with books and distant dreams?

"You have learned the sword," he said through a grunt.

"Better than you." I lanced the edge over his body, causing him to reel back and meet the edge of my dagger. I sliced the smaller blade across his arm.

My father hissed his pain, quickly inspecting the gash. He was quick on his feet, as if the blood fueled him. Before I could move, he had his hand curled around my braid.

Dammit. Foolish Elise. I fumbled for my dagger, fingers slipping.

"Elise!" Herja screamed, but it sounded too far. I doubted she'd take aim swift enough.

My father yanked my face close to his. "You are not my daughter. You are nothing."

The words didn't hurt. I'd resigned, I had no family left in Timoran. "I am Valen Ferus's wife. I'm a bleeding queen, you bastard."

I rammed my dagger at his thigh. The tip nicked his skin, but it had to be said of Leif Lysander, he did not relent easily. His grip remained; pain written on his face. But he was too stubborn, too awful to give in. If anything, he tightened his hold. "After today you'll be scratched from the family sagas."

"Gods I hope so," I spat through my teeth. I readied to yank out of his grip, even if it meant losing a clump of hair. To die at the hands of this man was not in my fate. I refused to accept it.

Before I could move, Leif was yanked backward.

I went down with him, but instantly rolled aside, scrambling to get control of my blade again.

"I've so wanted to meet again." The voice came sharper than jagged ice.

Blood dripped in my face, but I saw clear enough. Sol Ferus had my father scooting backward. The Sun Prince appeared stronger than ever. Tall, broad, ferocious. He stalked my father like a wolf to a wounded deer.

Black fury bled from Sol's hands.

"For all those nights you visited me in the dungeons," Sol said, a dark rumble in his voice. "Consider this my repayment."

I shuddered. Had it been my father who'd tortured Sol?

"Burn him with me! Sol! Burn him with me!" Tor shoved through a cloud of smoke, sprinting toward his consort.

A wide white smile crossed Sol's face. Relief, brutality, love. All of it collided into one terribly fierce expression. Tor's pyre ignited. The blight darkened. I watched it all with a strange awe as Leif Lysander dropped his blades, went to his knees, and held out his arms.

Resigned to his fate.

The two furies collided as they had at Ruskig. A thunder of magic and fire exploded into the sky. A few warriors raced away from the Sun Prince as he and Tor pulled back their magic and nothing remained of Leif but ash.

I was left stunned. A tumble of emotion. Relief? Disgust? I couldn't place the tightness in my chest.

But it only took half a moment and three strides for Sol to drop his hands and cross the space to Tor, pulling him into his arms. They swallowed each other in the embrace. Tor held the back of the Sun Prince's head, kissed the side of his neck, his lips. Nothing was gentle. They were greedy and wanting.

Sol trapped Tor's face, pulling back, studying him for a few heartbeats. A tight laugh tore from his throat, he kissed him, then rested their foreheads together.

My heart broke for them. Endless turns apart and a sliver of a moment could be theirs at long last.

I needed to find Valen.

"Elise!" Sol's voice dragged me back to reality. He pointed to the walls. Runa chopped furiously at a few stray warriors who slipped past her guard. "Two queens are on this field. Only one leaves. Make sure it is you."

"Where is Valen?"

"We all have our parts to play. Finish this, Elise," Sol said. "You can finish this."

We were out of time. Sol and Tor were forced back into the fight when a raspy bellow from a Ravenspire captain launched a full attack on the Sun Prince. The way both fae used their fury, I doubted the Ravens would last long.

I looked across the field. It was a haze of smoke and warriors. In the distance I caught sight of Jarl. He dismounted his horse, eyes focused on a particular point on the field. I couldn't see where he was going, but my heart raced. Had he found Valen?

We would meet on the battlefield. I would stand with him. But the Sun Prince was right.

I locked my narrowed gaze on the false queen.

There were two queens on the field. Only one would be leaving with air in her lungs.

CHAPTER THIRTY
NIGHT PRINCE

Blood was calling.

During the raids our folk never made it to a battlefield as this.

Betrayal upended Old Etta before we had the chance to stand together, to unleash our fury as we'd once planned. Eli overtook our courts in the trickiest of ways. Using our own people against us.

An innocent ride to the forest ended in my brother, my father, Tor, Halvar, and me captured and tossed into the fury quarries. Herja and my mother, taken to the towers where they were tormented with the prospect of being enslaved for the use of the false king until their last breath.

To be here now, with Dagar, with Kjell, with all our warriors from those dark days fighting for the land we never forgot, my bloodlust turned into more than rage. More than remnants of a curse. It was an intoxication. A purpose.

Every corner, every wall, blood sang its song to the wretched desire inside. I caught sight of Elise near the walls long ago and had since lost her in the slaughter.

I had two objectives in this battle. Kill as many Ravens as possible, and find my wife.

Niklas proved as formidable as his wife. The Elixist tossed strange powders, scorching skin, blinding Ravens in bright flashes long enough for Tova and Junius to cut from behind.

At my feet a Raven held up his hands, muttering for his life. I drew my axes down into his chest.

With a deep breath through my nose, I straightened, blood dripping from the curves of my blades. A blast near the walls stunned the battle for a few moments. Black and blue rose in a wall.

A wild grin spread over my lips.

Sol and Tor had found each other. They'd bring this field to ash soon enough.

At my next step, a deep, hot spark of pain exploded across my ribs. I stumbled, glancing down where a bolt had rammed into my side. Blood coursed down my tunic. My hand went to the wound, eyes scanning the field.

Damn.

The moment I locked gazes with his unfeeling blue, I wrenched the bolt from my side, ignoring the sharp jab.

I rolled the axes in my grip. I'd waited for this moment.

Jarl was a coward. He stood twenty paces off with at least a dozen Ravens at his side. Fury burned in my hands, but I wanted to savor his death. Crushing him beneath stone would be over too soon.

Jarl stopped. His hands and face were coated in blood, but his teeth gleamed from the carnage. "I warned the foolish king there was something more at that bleeding place. I warned you Ravenspire had secrets, Night Prince."

"Secrets not even you knew, and secrets that have no benefit for you at all. You've boasted all this time over your power to win this fight. Seems it is in our favor now."

Jarl frowned, clearly without a rebuttal. "Do not forget the only way to get the one you truly love off this field in one piece is to surrender. I'm sure the king will be merciful. Give you a villa, so long as you feed this land with fury. You could live long, quiet lives."

"As slaves to a dying land. I am pleased you admit this land needs us, though. Denial was getting exhausting."

Jarl rolled his blade in his grip. "So, we fight? You choose this kingdom over your queen? She goes to her death as we speak. Go to her, let me walk free, or fight now. End this between us and let her die."

"You talk too much, Jarl Magnus." I lowered to a crouch, ready to cut his tongue from his head if need be.

"See for yourself." He pointed, and like a bleeding child, because I could not resist when it came to Elise, I looked.

My heart became as ice. Across the field, Elise carved a bloody path toward the walls. Her sights pinned on her sister, but what she did not see, what no one bleeding saw was the way Calder pursued her from behind with a unit of his top knights.

The false king had stripped his crown, made himself more like a warrior to remain elusive, but the way the guards huddled close to him, he was no ordinary warrior.

"Let me walk away, Night Prince. And you will have your chance to stop her, to save her from fate."

Jarl Magnus was the slimiest underling I'd crossed in my life. If I turned from him now, he'd be gone. If I did not turn, Elise risked facing her sister and cousin unmatched.

A thunder shook the ground as my fury raged. I had a choice. And I was not alone here.

"Gunnar!" I shouted. My voice drew my nephew's attention.

He fought close by, but it also lifted my mother's head. One thing I'd forgotten was how terrifying Lilianna Ferus fought in battle.

"The false king." I pointed toward the battlefield. "Your arrows."

Gunnar muttered something to the Raven he'd been fighting. The man had stilled, standing as if in a trance, then as Gunnar walked away, the guard took his blade and slit his own throat. By the hells, his magic was gruesome.

I lifted my palm and shook the earth, desperate to knock Calder off his course. Jarl didn't run like I imagined the coward would; he stayed. From the corner of my eyes, he shouted to attack. He came for me.

I winced as I pulsed exhausting fury into the ground. It was not reaching Calder. I doubted Elise could even sense the power of it. Energy seeped from my blood, and Jarl and his Ravens were mere paces away.

A violent hand knocked me back.

My father shoved me away from the earth, eyes flashing in his own magic. "Stop. Pick up those blades and fight, Valen!"

"Elise." Maybe ten paces and Jarl would be here, he'd meet us both. Calder would take Elise. My words wouldn't form. "The false king."

"See to your fight, then join us," my father hissed. Then he ran after Gunnar. My mother behind him.

I didn't have time to wonder if they were going after Calder, didn't have time to pick myself up to chase them before I raised one of my axes and blocked a swift strike from Jarl's sword.

He cut a dagger across my middle. I kicked his leg, forcing him to back away to give me enough time to stand.

The Ravens cut at me without end. But turns as the Blood Wraith served me well.

I crossed a foot in front of the other. Exact. Careful. Strategic footing. To handle this many opponents without footing would need sure strikes. A blade came at the front, one at the back. I crouched between them. One ax cut at the ankle of a guard; my foot kicked out the feet of the other. A third guard cut across my wound from the bolt.

A hiss slid through my teeth.

The Raven tried to strike my chest. I swung my ax up, cutting the inside of his leg. His body crumbled. Blood burst from the side of his thigh with each beat of his heart.

I'd let him suffer.

Skilled as I might've been, there were too many Ravens. Expend my energy by opening the earth, and be useless to Elise? Or fight until I had no blood left.

My options were piss poor, but only one clear path. Fight my way to her or die trying.

I took up my blades in a firmer grip, resigned to end this here, if fate would proffer me at least one more moment to see her face. But I didn't get the chance to strike.

Ravens dropped their blades. They scraped at their faces. Blood dripped over their lips, down into their beards, over their gambesons. From their ears, their eyes, rivers of hot, dark death masked them until they collapsed in a heap.

I whipped around, ready to strike whatever fiend had attacked.

A figure—a man, I thought—came nearer. Perhaps he was a spirit of the hells, I didn't know. He was dressed in pitch, and inky shadows curled over him like a mist of storm clouds. Once the last Raven finished choking on his own blood, the dark shadow lowered his hand, and the ribbons sank back into his skin.

Jarl muttered curses under his breath.

His guards were gone. He was alone.

"I'd like to move this along, King." It was the man in shadows.

"You want him?" He pointed to Jarl. "He fears you greatly. I could rid him of breath now, but I have an inkling you'd like to do it yourself. Hurry it up. Some of us would like to leave this bleeding kingdom."

"Kase! Oh, damn. I mean Nightrender. Pleasure to have you join us, my friend." Niklas waved from twenty paces away.

The Nightrender. Breaker of night and fear.

He was no myth and seemed entirely frustrated at the Elixist. From his grimace to his clenched fists, it didn't take much to assume the man was not pleased his name had been outed.

He pinned me in a black glare, darker eyes than Night Folk, and jutted his chin. "Your target is running away, King."

Jarl abandoned the fight, aimed at the trees. I scrambled to my feet and sprinted after him.

Ten paces at his back, I let an ax fly. A wave of violent delight rushed through my veins when the edge sliced into his shoulder. Jarl fell forward. He groaned, and tried to crawl away, blade in his back.

I stepped onto his spine. With no thought of pain or damage, I ripped the ax from his flesh. He cried out in a throaty whimper. This would not be the slow, torturous death I wanted. But to reach Elise stood before any desire for death.

I kicked Jarl, forcing him onto his back.

Blood stained the grass beneath him as my boot pressed down on his throat.

"You failed," I said, voice harsh. "Today you'll die alone, unloved, despised. A bane in the sagas and histories. The gods will never welcome you at their table." I picked up the bloodied ax beside his head. "Go to the hells, you bastard."

With both fists gripping the handle I burrowed the ax blade in the center of his skull.

Each breath burned as if torn from my lungs. Jarl was soaked in his own blood, nearly unrecognizable. The ax dug deep, and I would leave it there, marking him on the battlefield.

"We go to the walls!" I shouted, lifting the second battle ax. "We fight with the queen!"

Ettans shouted to my call and rushed behind me down the slope. I couldn't see Elise. I couldn't see Calder. The smoke and pyre blotted out everything. *She lives. She must live.* I repeated the same thought in my head as I led the warriors forward.

Jarl was dead.

Only Calder and Runa remained in this battle.

And blood was calling.

CHAPTER THIRTY-ONE
ROGUE PRINCESS

SMOKE BURNED my eyes to tears. I swiped the back of my hand over my face, smearing blood and sweat. Runa remained tucked away near the walls, sword in hand, but untouched on her horse. A forgotten foe by others. The entire focus for me.

I forced my eyes to keep open, to blink through the burn.

This was the ending. This was the final step in the path of fate. Only one crown for one queen would be won today, and it wouldn't be Runa's.

Cries of battle were fading. Little by little the slide of steel against steel weakened. Roars of attack were more laments of pain and exhaustion. I did not know our losses. I did not know where Valen was.

Soon horns of retreat and respite would sound, but I would not return to fight another day. My path ended at my sister.

I knew it to my core.

At my next step, a blinding light flashed through my vision. My head rang, and I fell to my side.

Struck. I'd been struck. My head spun as Halvar's battle

lessons grew hazy, but Valen's voice insisted I bleeding defend myself. He wouldn't accept the excuse to die because of a blow to the head.

My fingers curled around the hilt of my sword, and I hurried to my unsteady feet.

Night coupled with smoke and ash made it difficult to make out any faces. But the gleam of torches and firelight glowed over the pale, sharp angles of my cousin. Calder tossed back a dark hood, his face as stone.

His eyes held nothing but disdain for me.

"Kill her!" Runa's cry cut the last link between sisters. She raged from her post, watching with a twisted kind of gleam as her husband stalked around me.

"I tried to stop this, Elise. But you insisted on continuing this damn idiocy. This is on your head," Calder said. He moved as a lithe warrior. Skilled and deadly.

I gripped my sword tighter to hide the tremble in my hands. On impulse, I studied his movements and watched his footing. Calder would deliver strong blows. He'd strike at the sides, come from the top. I blew out a long breath, ready to block each blow.

All the lessons did not prepare me for cowardice.

Hands gripped me from behind. Calder's top knights held tightly to my arms, one kicked out my knees, forcing me to kneel. A guard snagged my braid and wrenched my head back. They kicked my seax aside.

Arms out, heart exposed, a perfect target for Calder's sword.

No. No. I cursed the gods. What a cruel trick to bring me so far, give so much hope, and end it all in a weak death.

"Think so poorly of your talents with the blade that you must render me defenseless, cousin?"

Calder tilted his head. "One queen leaves this field today. I'm afraid there is too much at stake to take any chances that it might be you." He paused a few paces away. "I'll always have fond childhood memories of you, Elise. Those are the ones I'll keep, where you were not such a thorn in my side."

He closed the space between us, sword raised. I wanted to close my eyes but forced myself to look at him. He'd see my eyes before he ran me through.

Calder took his strike.

The clang of blades rattled in my brain. Where I thought I'd lose my head, two swords crossed in front of me, locking Calder's blade from moving. Grunts and gasps followed. The knights holding me tightly stumbled backward, arrows in their backs.

Calder stared in disbelief as a tall, broad fae cradled the edge of his sword with two of his. The man flicked his eyes to me. Dark eyes, but wise. His skin was rich and brown. His hair was braided off his face, and two polished onyx stones pierced the lobes of his pointed ears.

He looked like Valen in so many ways, I did not know what to think of it.

This . . . this couldn't be his father?

What felt like many moments of staring at each other ended. No more than half a breath before who I thought might be Arvad Ferus shoved Calder out of the blade lock.

"You have the misfortune of paying for the sins of many false kings," he said in a low timbre.

My cousin's face was cut in furious rage. He held steady against the swords for a few paces, but the fight was outmatched in skill and steel.

An arrow broke through the haze. The point thudded into one of Calder's shoulders. He cried out, slouching to one side. Soon enough a second arrow met the opposite side. Through the smoke, Herja stepped forward, her son at her side. Both had bows raised, arrows notched.

Calder roared his anger and made a weak swipe at Arvad. He could've, but Arvad didn't swing a killing blow. Instead, he stood by as a woman came from behind.

My eyes widened. Light hair, stained in dark blood; she was no Ettan. Small in stature, hardly an obvious threat on the battlefield. But the way she clambered up Calder's broad back, arm curled around his neck from behind, knife at his throat, she became the most fearsome warrior on the field.

"Tell Eli we won," she snarled into his ear before she dragged her knife across Calder's throat.

He gasped for three heartbeats, then staggered to his knees, falling face forward onto the grass.

Dead.

More than one Raven noticed. They seemed to freeze in their places. Some dropped their weapons, some continued to press against our armies.

"Elise!"

My heart jumped. Valen. I didn't see him, but his voice carried in the wind, alive. He was coming. He was alive.

Perhaps to the Ravens, the king was the final word, but the murderous shriek at my back drew me to the truth. I turned away from the distant shouts of my husband, jaw tight, and slowly found my feet.

This would not end until all those who claimed the throne of Timoran were in the hells. Runa gripped a sword, eyes flashing with hatred. She screamed my name, then sprinted down the slope toward me.

I met her pace. No hesitation, no second thoughts.

The rest of the field fell away. If fighting remained at my back, I didn't know it.

With a strangled cry, I landed a blow against the edge of hers. A quick strike, one that tossed us apart nearly as fast. We circled each other. The vibration of the steel prickled up my arms. Runa's eyes flashed like a storm over the sea. No longer the sister I knew, then again, I was no longer the quiet second *Kvinna* of our past.

We said nothing. There was nothing to say.

The Lysander daughters were here to kill each other.

I rushed at her again. She met my strike with a ferocity I didn't anticipate. My sister landed a cut to my arm that reeled me backward. Adrenaline masked the pain, and I met her downward strike with more strength.

A kick to her ribs. A jab to my leg. Back and forth we pushed. Sloppy strokes, desperate blows, we fought with a finality, a knowledge this moment would change the course of this land forever.

Runa slammed her sword against mine, and promptly drew a fist against my jaw. I fumbled forward. The tang of blood grew hot on my tongue.

Stand up, Elise. Be ready. Do not fall.

"Elise!" Valen came into my sights. He shoved through the masses, dodging strikes, fighting his way forward.

He was too far.

Fear lived in those beautiful eyes. The realization he would not be able to reach me now.

This fight was mine to finish anyway.

I lifted my sword and faced my sister. Her breaths came heavy, her face twisted in pain. But my body protested too. Each step limped, my skin was riddled in burning cuts and gashes. I was certain I'd broken at least three fingers. The tip of my sword dragged through the grass, too heavy to hold up when no strike was coming yet.

"You have no kingdom here, Runa," I said. "It is over."

"I am chosen by fate! You are wrong." It was all she said before a new wind filled her lungs and she flung her sword again.

Blades met. Runa screamed as she tried to hack at my neck. I parried and shoved her back.

Another blow came to my lower spine. I dodged. She met my strike over her head. Each clash, each blow lost power but gained hatred. A breath of steel hit my guarder, cutting into the leather.

Runa's boot slammed into my knee. I cursed her and fumbled backward. In the haze of my mind Valen's furious shouts fueled me on. Runa made a sloppy cut at my heart, but weak steps fumbled over the uneven soil.

Now.

Her body curled forward, off balance. With haste, I adjusted my grip on the blade, point down. A scorch of hot air burrowed in my lungs. I spun on my heel, let out a wretched cry, and leveled the tip of my sword against her, carving out the base of her throat.

In a wash of dark blood, the steel tore through her skin.

Runa's pale eyes flickered in stun, remorse, hatred. Until light faded. Blood fountained from her neck, and for a moment Runa stood still. Her brow furrowed in a wince as if she might shed a tear, but nothing came before she fell back, lifeless eyes locked on the dark sky.

The seax fell from my hand. My body trembled, and I could not draw a deep enough breath. Weak steps took me away from the unmoving form of my sister.

Over. The world reeled in my head. It was over.

Armies stared at the bloodshed, stared at me in horror, awe. I didn't care. I saw one face only. My leg throbbed, my head screamed, but I quickened my step, limping forward.

"Valen." My voice croaked. I tried to run, and only stumbled more.

The Night Prince shoved through the last line of warriors and raced for me. In the next step, he caught me as I jumped into his arms. My legs wrapped around his waist. His embrace tightened, choking air from my body.

The tip of my nose burrowed against his neck. All gods. I breathed him in. Real. Alive. He was here. Valen gripped my hair, my neck. His lips pressed against my skin, hands roamed any surface of my body as if he, too, couldn't make sense that we were both standing, both breathing.

He pulled back, brushing bloody, sweaty hair from my face. His own features were blotted in smoke and bruises, but his grin whitened it all.

The Night Prince kissed me.

No tenderness. No gentility. This kiss was raw, pained. Perfect.

I was breathless when we pulled away, my forehead pressed to his. "You're done playing the hero, Valen Ferus. I will not allow it from this day on. No sacrificing yourself for another person again. I will not watch you die; I will not watch you be captured. You will be the king who hides in his castle when war calls. Do you hear me?"

He grinned against my mouth. "I thought you loved my heroics."

"I hate them. Despise them. I want you alive, and breathing, and in my arms. I demand it."

He kissed me slowly; his voice turned soft. "Agreed. I will never argue such a bargain."

CHAPTER THIRTY-TWO
NIGHT PRINCE

TIME BECAME IRRELEVANT. All that mattered was holding Elise in my arms, knowing she was alive.

Damn prophecies.

Runa and Calder put too much faith in a roll of parchment than they had the strength of Elise Ferus. The second queen stood, she lived, and through her the kingdom would rise stronger.

Because a second *Kvinna* trusted a mindless beast, Etta was healed.

True enough, I could've held her in my arms forever. But my strength had other plans. When my arms threatened to snap off, reluctantly, I let Elise's body slide down mine. I trapped her face between my palms and kissed her once more.

"Hail the Night Prince." A rough voice rang out, drawing us both to remember a great army stood stalwart at our backs. "Hail our Lady Elise."

"Not king?" Elise whispered.

With battle silenced the truth of it sunk into my heart once more. I tugged on her hand. "I am not king."

The warriors bent the knee, their fists pounded over their hearts as we approached. But there were those who remained standing.

Niklas and Junius. The Nightrender, Tova, and a few folk who stood close to them. I didn't care if Alvers bowed here. I didn't care if anyone bowed right now, my attention remained on the faces of my family.

Herja dropped her bow and ran to us; her arms encircled our necks.

"It is over," she said, voice rife in emotion.

Sol approached. His face was coated in blood, but his smile was endless. He gripped my shoulder. I met his eye, hardly believing we'd made it.

"You are keen to listen to me, Elise," Sol said. "You delivered my message, made certain this fool listened, and you made sure to be the last queen on this battlefield. I think you might be my favorite sister."

Herja shoved his shoulder, laughing. Elise chuckled weakly when my brother wrapped her in his arms, a soft, thank you from his lips was enough to break the last of the tension in my chest. Over their heads, my mother and father waited.

I cleared my throat and laced my fingers with Elise. "I want you to meet . . . the king and queen of Etta."

Elise's eyes widened. Her hand pressed against her chest as if her heart might pound straight through. "Valen." She pulled back. "How . . . I don't . . . how is it possible?"

I pressed a kiss to her knuckles. "We have time for answers."

My parents stood shoulder to shoulder. My father towered over my mother in almost a humorous way. We'd often teased my mother over her size, but what she lacked in height she'd many a time made up for in strength.

"Mother. Father." I started slowly, pulling Elise to my side. "This is—"

Words dried up. Before I finished my mother pulled Elise into a tight embrace. "Born of Timoran, with a heart of Etta."

Truth be told, I'd always seen my mother as Ettan. But side by side with Elise, her similar hair, her pearly complexion buried under the blood, she was utterly Timoran.

Lilianna Ferus cupped Elise's cheeks. "The heirs of both lands will heal this kingdom. From the blood of House Eli, from the blood of House Ferus, Etta is restored."

My chest tightened. Hadn't my mother spoken of a prophecy at my birth? The heirs of both lands. Where I interpreted it as a battle between the heirs, it meant the unification of them. Both sides were needed to heal a broken land.

Elise choked on a sob. "I've spent turns reading of you, and now . . . you're here. Both of you."

"We look forward to many turns to know you now." My mother embraced her again. "Thank you for loving him, for saving them all."

The battle had ended, but the pain of it had only begun. We set to work traipsing through the dead, looking for loved ones, for faces we would not see again until we entered the great hall.

Elise clutched my hand, silent tears on her cheeks as we readied our lost for their pyres. Behind us Ari, Siv, and Mattis followed. We took the center of the field, Tor and Sol took one side, while Herja and Gunnar took another.

A cry of agony drew a gasp from Elise's throat.

Ten paces away, Halvar kneeled with Kari, stroking her hair. My eyes closed. Brant lay still, already his sword on his chest, his arms crossed over the hilt.

"He knew," Kari cried against Halvar's chest. "He said those things because he knew."

A premonition? It wrenched against my insides to think he knew he'd fall in this battle, and still he stepped forward without hesitation.

Elise wiped at her tears and went to them both. She hugged Kari and whispered in her ear.

"Valen." Stieg trudged up the hillside, a blade in his hands, bloodied and weary. His face was despondent.

"Stieg," I said in a long breath. I hadn't seen him on the battlefield, but from what Ari explained he'd taken the rivers with Casper and— "Where is Casper?"

Stieg's jaw pulsed and he handed me the blade. One I'd seen in Casper's hands more than once. "He fought valiantly. Saved us in the rivers. Drowned half the bleeding Ravens before getting lost himself. He always said his damn fury grew too strong too fast." Stieg chuckled but there was little humor in it. "Bleeding stupid fool."

I lowered my head, holding his sword to my chest for a few breaths before stabbing the point in the damp soil. "*Vi träffas vän.*" Until we meet again.

When Elise returned to my side, we stayed until she could mark the ground in runes for glory in the Otherworld in Casper's name.

We went on, helping place weapons on the chests of the fallen of Etta.

Elise paused at the mangled body of Jarl. She closed her eyes in a grimace when I tore my ax from his skull. Her face was unreadable. I touched the edge of her jaw, gently. "He will never touch you again."

"I'm glad it was you," she whispered. "Out of anyone you deserved to end him."

Frey and Axel lived and helped gather wood for the pyres. A few paces away, Niklas and Junius stood close together, somber, heads lowered over a row of unmoving folk. The Nightrender and his guild stood beside them, not speaking.

How thankless was I? They came to fight for us, and I left them to mourn their losses—losses for a kingdom not their own—without a word.

"Niklas. Junius." I touched her shoulder.

Her eyes were wet with tears. "Have you lost many, Valen?"

I nodded. "Casper . . . Brant."

Her face wrinkled and a silent tear trailed her face. She pointed to a man on the grass. Young in the face, but he'd died with a smile. Niklas hadn't looked away. "His name was Söt. Like a younger brother to Niklas."

I knew well enough no words took this kind of pain away. "He will be remembered always. Give us the names of all your fallen and they will be written here in honor."

Niklas lifted his eyes to me at that and held out his arm. We clasped forearms with a firm nod of understanding to each other. They fought for us. Should they ever need us, we would fight for them.

I faced the Nightrender. At our short acquaintance on the battlefield, he'd been dark, soaked in shadows. Now he looked like an ordinary man. Bright eyes like a setting sun, dusty hair, no shadows. No magic.

"Did you lose any of your number?"

"No," he said. "Only what the Falkyns lost. We mourn with them."

"I'm sure you know what we were told about you."

"I am. And I still do not give it much thought. Prophecies tend to put wicked targets on the backs of the innocent."

It sounded a great deal like his words had an underlying meaning, but now wasn't the time to ask. If ever. A man was entitled to his reasons and his secrets.

"I hope you will stay for a time. All of you. We wish to honor you here. I would not have survived without you, nor would Elise as I'm told. Please."

The Nightrender glanced at his weary guild. "We shall vote on it and let you know."

"I give my vote to stay," Tova shouted. "I'm exhausted, and I saw more than one disgustingly fine room in that castle. I very much plan to sleep in one of those beds before I'm shoved into a tiny ship with you smelly men."

For the first time—likely in his life—the Nightrender smiled. "Well, there you have it. Tova has spoken for us all."

THE FUNERAL PYRES filled the courtyards and forests around Ravenspire with thick smoke that burned until well after dawn. Some people remained for their fallen, honoring them into the Otherworld. Others remained to meet the dawn in silence.

It was a sight.

Kjell had his hand on Tor's shoulder. I knew the feeling. To touch the one you thought was dead made it real and tangible.

The same reason, no doubt, that Tor's hand had not left Sol's.

Halvar and Kari were surrounded by three of his brothers, who'd been knights in the court before the raids. Dagar looked over what was left of his family with a gleam of pride and reverence. The absence was in Halvar's mother and youngest brother.

Not everyone could survive, not everyone could be saved. It ached, fiercely, but we honored those of old, those who fell in the first battles for this kingdom.

"And I thought it was unsettling to learn you were alive," Ari muttered at my side, adjusting a sword on his hip.

He'd be leaving soon for the township of Lyx alongside those with enough strength to hold a blade. There could be no time wasted in gathering the people of Timoran and embracing them in our courts or killing those who would not stand with us in this new kingdom.

Ari nodded at my parents across the smallest courtyard of Ravenspire. They spoke with Gunnar, Herja, and Elise, faces bright with grins and interest, as they learned more of the two newest members of their family.

I crossed my arms over my chest. "You were surprised? I thought we'd find a bleeding spell or curse. Not them."

Ari clapped me on the back, and—like the bastard he was—laughed when I winced against the ache in my muscles.

"For what it is worth," he said, "I thought you were a magnificent king while it lasted."

"I am nothing compared to the king my father is." I met his eye, my voice softened. "I intend to give him your name, Ari. You have served Etta more than anyone. You never lost faith in what it could be, and you began this fight. I hope, if he asks, you'll consider serving in his court."

Ari pinched his lips, hands on his hips. He cleared his throat. All hells, if emotions did not stop, I would be taunted by Sol for being soft until my last breath.

When his voice steadied, Ari nodded. "It would be an honor."

He left before we did anything to embarrass ourselves further.

The Alvers found place around a large log table. With Stieg, Frey, Axel, with Niklas and Junius they sang their lost friends into the Otherworld. Even the Nightrender, a man who seemed burdened in shadows and secrets, drank, and held up a horn to honor those lives lost.

All of it struck me like a blow to the head. At long last, we'd found peace. Lasting peace.

CHAPTER THIRTY-THREE
ROGUE PRINCESS

At the noon sun, I staggered into the halls of Ravenspire. My eyes grew heavy from fatigue, my insides churned for food, but I could not find the energy to even imagine chewing.

The funeral pyres had faded, and the knights of King Arvad's court had gone with a few folk to Lyx and other townships across the kingdom.

More of my cousins were hidden away in their fine villas and manors. King Zyben's consorts lived among them. I'd not seen them in turns, not even when Calder rose to his short-lived power.

Calder's mother had little love for my dead uncle. As a girl, I'd had no qualms with the third consort of Zyben. But what would become of her, the mother of the false king? Did what was left of Zyben's line even know what happened here?

I had few doubts the Lysander households would be the first to be visited and informed they were no longer the royal bloodline of this land.

Some were good; they didn't provoke violence like Zyben or

Calder. I hoped they'd join us here, hoped they'd find a new, healthier, more vibrant land for their families.

But it would be their choice.

Word would be spread of the fall of New Timoran. It would be known that Etta rose again, and Night Folk were free in this land. Ettans were equal with Timorans. Our people would be united the way Lilianna and Arvad had yearned for all those turns ago.

Those who refused, well, I would leave it to the king and queen to decide their fates.

I covered a yawn with the back of my hand. Somewhere in the commotion and stun I'd lost Valen. Try as I might, I wasn't sure I could keep upright much longer and abandoned celebrations to find a place to wash and sleep.

"Elise." Herja quickened her step to catch up to me. She'd cleaned herself and wore a long fur cloak. Her eyes were bright, her hair long down her back. "Where are you going?"

"To the rivers to wash." I gestured at my bloody clothes. No doubt my face was terrifying with the gore still splattered across it. "Where are you going?"

"Back to Ruskig for Laila and the other young ones. I'll be with Tor and Sol and some of the Alver Folk. I'd hoped the Nightrender might join us, but he seems hells-bent on avoiding me. I think he knows Hagen, Elise."

I shared her suspicions, but I'd learned a few things about our sly friend the Nightrender; he would not give up answers easily. I took hold of her hand. "Now that the fighting is over, we'll search for him, Herja. It will be safe for him here. You can be a family now."

Her chin trembled through a smile. "I'll hold to that hope. By the way, don't bathe in the rivers. You and Valen shall be in his old chambers. Did you not realize Castle Ravenspire is once again ours?"

She directed me toward the right corridors, and I discovered Valen Ferus once occupied the same rooms as a few of my younger cousins before they were fully grown.

"Thank you." I embraced her before she left. "If you see your younger brother, tell him his wife is looking for him. No, tell him she is hunting him."

Herja dipped her chin, snickering. "I am surprised you managed to escape his sights at all."

I smiled and waved as she joined Gunnar, her brother, Tor, and Junius at the front gates of the castle.

The quiet was welcome when I pushed through the door. A library, a study, a washing room, and a round bed chamber made up the space. Comfortable, warm with its own stove and open flame in the study.

Only when the door clicked at my back did I let my shoulders slump. The one thing missing from the comfort would be a delightfully handsome fae prince.

I wanted to tangle myself in his arms more than I wanted sleep. The craving for Valen Ferus without the looming burden of war was that potent. My steps grew heavier as I forced myself toward the washroom.

But when the door swung open, my body shocked itself awake.

Valen glanced over his shoulder, bare-chested, washing away the blood from his skin. "Ah, I wondered if you'd find your way here eventually."

"Eventually?" I narrowed my eyes. "I've been looking for you."

"I've been looking for *you*."

I snorted. "Is this our meeting point then, a washroom?"

"Our washroom, yes." He moved toward me. I tried not to look at the welts and open wounds across his body. I didn't want to think of how close we both might've come to the Otherworld. Not tonight. Perhaps not ever. His arms encircled my waist. "Because, my love, in the washroom it usually means clothing is minimal, and at the moment that sounds perfect."

I sank against him, my arms going around his neck. I kissed him as he peeled the rancid tunic over my head, as he gently washed around the wounds across my skin, leaving kisses there. I washed flecks of blood from the points of his ears, his hair, beneath his fingernails. He slid the trousers off my lower half.

"These will be burned," he said, laughing as I unbuckled the thick leather belt from his waist.

Together we slumped into the large basin with heated stones at the bottom. The warmth of the water chased the pain of battle from my limbs. My husband's tender touch chased the fear of losing him from my heart.

We lasted only until the last of the gore was wiped from our bodies.

With a heated gleam in his eyes, Valen scooped me up and took me to the bed chamber. He pulled me into his arms and never looked away from my gaze as our bodies tangled together. His mouth covered the soft curve of my neck. Valen's fingertips trailed over the scrapes and gashes across my body. He took great care to kiss the bruises across my breasts, sucking and licking the pain away until I could hardly recall my name.

Then, all at once he pulled away from me.

"What do you think you're doing?" I said in a gasp.

"Patience, my love."

I thought I might kill him after all until his tongue ran over my breastbone. I had nothing to say; I froze and let the king do with me whatever he pleased.

"I am a piss poor king," he said, voice rough as he left a line of kisses down my belly.

I adored this new plan of his, this new direction he was taking with his mouth.

"Wh-Why?" I arched my spine, desperate to feel his mouth in the drenched center of my thighs.

He paused, then grinned with a touch of darkness when his gaze locked with mine. "I fought a battle not for a kingdom. I doubt I ever will. I fought for you, Elise. I would destroy everything to see you safe and breathing. I suppose that makes me rather selfish, perhaps wicked, but no less the truth. For you, I would destroy the world."

I laughed and let my head fall back onto the furs as he hooked my legs over his shoulders and proved his words with that wicked tongue.

He licked over my center with the right pressure, the right suction. I lost my words in a garbled cry as his mouth devoured all of me.

When the rush of release took me, when I screamed his name for all of our armies to hear, I rolled onto my belly.

My husband drew his mouth along the shell of my ear and whispered, "On your knees, *Kvinna*."

Limbs trembling, I leveraged onto my hands and knees.

"Gods, Elise." Valen ran a palm down my spine, giving attention to every divot. "Look at you." Two fingers dragged along my core from behind. He hummed in satisfaction. "So wet and ready for me, Wife."

"Valen." His name came out in a rough breath. My body trembled, forcing me to lower to my elbows.

I moaned when Valen aligned his body behind me. With slow strokes, he teased my core with the tip of his length, nudging the crown in and out until I was practically sobbing for all of him.

"This moment," he whispered, tangling my damp hair around

one hand and tugging my head back, "is our prize for victory, Elise. You, me, our life together, it was worth it all. I would fight all over again, fall into bloodlust and curses as many times as the cruel Norns demanded, if it meant I got to live out my days with you."

Tears dripped from my lashes, my chin trembled. All of it broke off in a sharp gasp when Valen gripped my hips and slammed into me.

Blood scorched in my veins.

My name on his lips was soft as he tipped my chin back and pulled my mouth against his. He met my movements with desperate thrusts until I let out a sob of pleasure.

Valen grew frenzied. After a moment, I fell forward again, spreading my knees more, cries muffled in the furs of the bed. With deft fingers, he reached around and rubbed the sensitive apex of my core until I shattered.

He tugged my hips back, shifting us to a new angle, a new depth. Valen's heavy breaths heated the bare skin of my back with vows of hundreds of turns, of a peaceful life, of forever until his length thickened and burst hot streams of his release inside me.

Once we caught our breaths, Valen pulled out of me, rolling onto his shoulder, and pressed a kiss to my forehead.

We were exhausted, energized, broken, and whole.

I could not remember a time when his touch, his kiss, his body had loved as deeply as this moment.

VALEN SLEPT SOUNDLY at my side. I rubbed my thumb over the furrow of worry between his brows, then slowly unraveled myself from his arm slung across my waist.

The wardrobes were filled with gowns and tunics and cloaks,

no doubt for Calder's consorts. I hurried and dressed in a woolen dress a size too big, tying the waist with an intricate scarf stitched in silver thread. Washed, sated, and warm, I could not ignore the sinking hunger any longer. No doubt when Valen woke, he'd be ravenous too.

I knew the halls of the castle, yet still felt like a stranger here.

It would take some adjustment.

On the way to the kitchens, I passed a few Ettans dressed like serfs. They laughed and stood blithely against the walls. Some drank ale straight from curved horns.

At the sight of me, most stiffened as if I might demand they take up their old chores, but when I tilted my head in a simple greeting, they returned it.

One woman came to my side and said, "We will always be indebted to you, Lady Elise."

"No." A knot formed in my throat. "It was a fight won by many."

Her eyes darkened. "This might be strange, but it does not escape me that you lost all your blood family in this war. Your heart must ache."

I smiled. "I did not lose my family. I gained one."

The halls connected to the kitchen were dim, only a few tallow candles perched on sconces. I softened my steps through the door, careful not to wake anyone who might be sleeping nearby, and slipped into the heated kitchen.

"Could not sleep either?"

I jolted back, my spine slammed against the door. "Oh, you startled me."

Lilianna sat at one of the chopping blocks, sipping a steaming drink from a clay cup. "Apologies. I had to get up and move about. Sleeping for centuries, I'm afraid, has caused me to be quite restless." She signaled to a wooden stool beside her. "Join me? Do you have a taste for cloves in your tea?"

"I was raised with it."

A true Timoran drink. Sharp spices and tastes always found their way into a kettle.

Lilianna poured a cup for me and patted the stool top. How was it after all the countless words I'd read of this woman, that I now could sit and speak with her face to face? In some ways I felt as if I'd known her most of my life, in others she was a stranger to me.

"Elise." Lilianna said my name as if she were taking a bite and rolling it over in her mouth. "I am told your namesake is Eli.'"

My cheeks heated. "Yes. He is my great-grandfather."

Where I thought she might look at me with a touch of disdain, Lilianna smiled over the rim of her cup. "It is such a relief to know something lovely came from him." She set her cup down, staring at the tea inside. "I see it in your eyes, but you should not be ashamed of your namesake. Eli was lost, jealous, and greedy. But he once was kind, brave, funny even. He once was a good friend. You have taken from those good parts of the man who lost his way. You have saved my family."

I shook my head. "No. Valen and Sol and Herja, they are the ones who have been resilient."

She grinned. Lilianna had a youthful face, with only a few lines near her eyes hinted she often smiled and laughed. Her hair was long like mine with more fire than ice, but we shared similarly blue eyes.

"When Valen was born, I met my dear friend Greta. She sailed all the way from the Western Kingdoms to deliver a gift to us. At first, I did not think it so much a gift as a curse. She spoke of suffering, warned us that Etta would not remain free. When Eli infiltrated our courts and our own folk turned against us, her warnings would not leave me.

"We fought, do not mistake me. We fought to keep the raiders away. We lost so many, but when Arvad and my sons were captured, I could not deny her predictions any longer. My family would suffer until the blood of the heirs healed the divide of lands. The heirs of both lands."

Lilianna snorted a laugh into her cup. "Not the sort of thing I wished to hear at the time, of course. Anything to do with Eli's heirs made me rather violent."

I scoffed and stared at my hands. Her hand fell to mine, stopping my breath short.

"But it was you," she said. "Greta saw you. I believe even Valen saw you. As a boy he often dreamed of a blue-eyed girl."

"Truly?"

"Oh yes," Lilianna snickered. "He was quite captivated as a dewy eyed young fae." With a sigh she studied her tea. "My children have been resilient, true. They have suffered greater than anyone, but do not diminish the crucial role you played in the war. I know what you did, Elise. I know the choice, the bravery, the love required of you to break through Greta's curses. Valen would not be the man he has become without you. And Sol and Herja would still be lost."

I adjusted on the stool to face her. "Did you know what their curses would be?"

"No." Her smile faded. "I was forced to trust Greta and pray she would be extremely careful with her words since Eli would be the one to select how each of my children were cursed. But she insisted it was necessary, part of some larger plan across the world."

Four queens of fate. I swallowed a scratch in my throat. "Something to do with queens?"

Lilianna stared at me, brow lifted. "Yes. Greta often spoke in riddles and lore, but I do recall a mention of how the Norns were angered by the treatment of their magic in the realms of mortals. She insisted sovereigns of their gifts would rise to take back their power."

Lilianna paused. "I thought she said it to encourage me, as queen, but when our situation worsened, Greta insisted it was necessary to write a new fated path to fit the twisted mind of whatever pain Eli planned to give my family, but also in a way that the will of the Fates would be done. It was one of the most difficult times of my life, knowingly putting my children at the mercy of pain and suffering. Strange to hear you bring it up. I'd nearly forgotten her odd folk tales."

I took a sip of my tea. "I do not think Greta was the only one who believed such a tale."

Thoughts of the Eastern Kingdom, of the dark fete the Nightrender described filled my head. Their people turned the torture and enslavement of magic into a game, and I could not help but think it might have something to do with the man's battle Calista promised.

But I had no answers, I had no knowledge if these four queens were metaphorical or real. I forced a smile and peeled the worry from my voice.

"How did Arvad survive?" I asked. "Valen had been so sure he'd witnessed his father's death. He'd been so sure you all were dead."

Lilianna nodded. "Kjell. The burden of convincing all the Ravens and King Eli that our family had fallen landed on the shoulders of Kjell. He is the most skilled illusionist I've ever known. Arvad was tortured, but somewhere through it all, Kjell locked the guards in an illusion. They believed Arvad was dead. They took what they thought was the body of my husband to show his sons. But it was another fallen warrior with the face of Arvad. In the distraction, Kjell took my husband away from the fury quarries. Through a few more tricks, Eli was able to witness Arvad's body, but he was in the fury sleep. Still, it was enough to convince the false king."

"And you?"

"I went into the fury sleep, yes. Eli believed I took my life. Rumors spread across the kingdom that Herja and I were killed for refusing to be his consorts, but the princess was already far from Ravenspire towers by then.

"Dagar and Kjell and our warriors agreed to being cursed, to defend where we slept. It was more to keep the guards of Eli hesitant to come close. If too many Timorans guarded the Black Tomb, it would prove even more difficult for the heirs to open it, you see."

"They agreed to be cursed?" I said the words in a breathless whisper.

"I've never known braver men and women than our warriors. They knew Etta would die as Old Timoran if we did not do something to end the war."

"How would it die? I know it has something to do with fury."

"It is more to do with those who are chosen by the land to rule here. Etta chose Arvad, it chose me, and our children. Until it chooses another, we will serve the fury of this land and lead its people.

"To kill us would kill the fury of Etta if it was not passed onto another chosen line. Eli did not want to believe it, but I am grateful that Greta was persuasive. She convinced the king the heirs of the Ferus line needed to live since fury had not officially selected which heir would take up the throne of their father. All three would be needed to keep fury dormant but living. But, of course, to Eli they could not be a threat to his crown. So, they were cursed and scattered. It was then that Greta delivered her final prophecy."

I fiddled with the sleeve of the dress. Greta was the first storyteller. Valen's enchantress. A woman he viewed as tricky and wicked had been a trusted ally to his mother. Every word, every action had been part of a grand strategy, and my head still spun at the idea of it all.

"Her last prophecy was given to Eli," Lilianna went on. "She assured him his kingdom would rise through a queen. Eli did not care for queens. I'm afraid after a queen denied him, he had no desire to let women have much of a voice in his kingdom. Greta lost her life after it was all over. She knew she would and fought for us anyway."

I winced. "Eli still hunted her folk, though. They've used fate witches across the turns."

"Ah, he must've determined he rather liked having a speaker of fate after he'd killed one."

"The last storyteller was only a girl. But she was the one who added upon the first curse; she knew of me, and wrote me into the story, if you will."

Lilianna grinned. "It was all part of an intricate web, Elise. One that has unraveled to bring us to this moment, to the queen who would fall, and let Etta rise."

"I did not fall."

"Ah, but you did. You fell from the thrones of Timoran, and rose to the thrones of Etta. And I could not be prouder to know you."

She patted my hand again and together we stayed, late into the night, talking of happier things. Futures we, at last, could dream up.

CHAPTER THIRTY-FOUR
ROGUE PRINCESS

For over a week our people worked clearing the kingdom of lingering threats. Most Timorans put up little resistance. Others did not view the idea of losing their serfs and Night Folk trade kindly. They were brought to the cells in the pits of Ravenspire where they would await Arvad and Lilianna's official re-ascension to the throne for their punishment.

If they opted to raise blades, they were promptly shown the strength of our warriors.

Valen spent time with Dagar, Halvar, and other warriors, the same as he once did. Kari, a former Raven, was the first Timoran to become an Ettan knight. Halvar had been rife with inappropriate promises on ways he'd prove how proud he was later that night.

Arvad and Lilianna had not doled out positions in their court. I guessed they planned to wait until their crowns were officially replaced upon their heads.

I helped Tova and Niklas as they aided our healers with the wounded. The Alver Folk were entertaining. Thieves, perhaps a little villainous, but good at heart. I did not want them to leave. Not even the Nightrender, who'd unintentionally shown a different side at times.

When the young ones returned, the one Ash and Hanna raced to had been the Nightrender. Hanna did not speak, but waved her fingers in smooth gestures, and I caught the Nightrender's smile as he responded, wordlessly moving his hands.

He cared for his guild.

And I agreed with Herja. He avoided her.

I did not believe it was because he didn't want to discuss Hagen, almost like he feared it, or was still considering the right words to use.

"I don't know anything," Tova said when I asked after a week. The Nightrender had dodged Gunnar's questions, Herja's, but when Laila asked if he knew her daj, the man practically fled from the hall. Tova added a few cloth wraps to a healing wound on a warrior's shoulder. "He does act strangely at the name, I'll say that. But I do not know much of his deep past, to be honest."

"I thought your guild was family?"

"Well, my family can keep their bleeding noses out of certain parts of my life." Tova snorted and locked me in her strange eyes. "I've known the Nightrender since childhood, but before that, he seems keen to keep his youngest turns to himself. I don't press. I don't need to know everything to know I trust him with my life."

His guild would never give up his secrets, but I could agree with Tova on one thing. Perhaps he was a crooked kind of man, one who made deals, and robbed, but I, too, trusted the Nightrender and the Alvers of the east.

At nights we spent time in the great hall of Ravenspire dining, laughing, reminiscing. Arvad and Lilianna wanted every detail of the lives of their children, of mine. They were fascinated by the intricacies of Valen's curse, pained, too, but Sol and Herja teased their younger brother endlessly to learn he'd once donned the fine clothes of a Timoran trader.

"In truth, he was not half bad at the trade," Tor said. Perhaps Torsten Bror was the most changed. By the gods, I'd never seen his eyes as bright as they were, nor witnessed so many smiles on his face.

"Thank you." Valen tipped his drinking horn at his friend, the other hand possessively on my leg beneath the table. "I earned my position as negotiator for the stunning *Kvinna* on merit alone."

"True. A curse and fate witch had little to do with it," Halvar said.

"Merit. Cunning. Pure skill, my friend."

Arvad grinned. "I care more that you were able to work together to bring us all here."

Halvar chuckled again. "I think Elise might have a different thought about Valen's ability to work with her, and anyone for that matter."

Valen kicked him under the table.

I traced the edge of Valen's ear. "You were insufferable for a time."

"My brother? No, it can't be true," Herja said.

We laughed, stirring Laila from her sleep against her mother's chest. Her children had hardly left her side, as if these were the moments they'd used to make up for the turns kept distanced. Gunnar's arms were healing in pink scars, but he never allowed any Alver or healer to fade them completely. The boy had found a kinship with some of the folk from the east, and they, in turn, were teaching him of his magic.

"Insufferable? Or a stunning hero?" Valen kissed the side of my head. "Trying to protect you by keeping a distance is a thing a hero would do."

"Forgive me," Halvar said. "I wholly disagree, My Prince. You were simply stubborn and locked in a piss of a mood."

"Agreed." Tor lifted his own drinking horn. "He was like a violent child the more he tried to stay away."

"Torsten," I said, tilting my head. "Let us speak of moods, my friend. The first time I saw you smile, I'm almost certain, was yesterday."

That drew more laughter. Tor rolled his eyes, cheeks red, as Sol draped an arm around his shoulders, pulling him closer.

Arvad rose, holding his hand out for Lilianna. He smiled at the faces at the table. "There is nothing greater than seeing you all at this table once more. But tomorrow is an important day. I suggest you all rest."

"To the rise of Our King." Dagar lifted his drinking horn to Arvad. The rest of us followed suit. Arvad offered a small nod and left with Lilianna to their chamber. We all broke away. Alone in our bed, I curled against Valen's body, holding him close.

With each day that passed, the fear that this would all be torn away started to fade.

"You are perfect as you are." Valen curled his arms around my waist, pressing slow kisses up the curve of my neck. "No amount of fiddling will make you any more perfect."

I scoffed, but dropped my fingers from my braid, studying my reflection in the mirror once more. "I don't know what one wears to a re-coronation of a long-dead king and queen when I am supposed to hand a crown over to said queen."

"This," he said, his hand sliding seductively down the curve of my spine. He regarded the pale blue of the dress. "This is exactly what one wears. Though, you could wear nothing—in fact it is my favorite thing you wear—and you would still look perfect. Now, come. We're needed in the throne room, then we are free to bear half as much responsibility and be feckless lovers until we take our final breath."

I slipped my fingers through his, grinning. "Your arguments are quite compelling, Night Prince. How can I stand against such a plan?"

"You can't. Because it is a brilliant plan." He tugged on my hand and led me out of our rooms toward the hall.

Already the outer courtyard was packed wall-to-wall with our people, Alvers, and those Timorans who'd accepted the fall of their king with grace. I had more than one cousin in the crowd. Calder's oldest brother, his children, and their mothers. A few of Calder's sisters, and all of what was left of Zyben's consorts. Truth be told most of them looked a great deal at ease and had helped assist with some of the surly noble folk who did not want change.

The weak gardens were blooming in new life. Moonvane gleamed in the sunlight, but the grass was brighter, the trees fuller. This was the Etta I'd read about. A vibrant, rich land filled with fury and power.

In front of the dais, I stood in a line with all three of the Ferus heirs. Herja was stunning in a flowing gown, every bit a princess of Etta. Sol was healthier than I'd ever seen him. His eyes were like gemstones, blue and bright. But Valen still looked a great deal like a king to me. Dressed in their finest clothes, they stood shoulder to shoulder, ready to see their parents once more on the throne.

I squeezed his hand, drawing him to smile down at me. The thrill of this day tightened in my chest. The final step to restoring this kingdom—crowning its rightful king and queen.

Elder Klok was invited to oversee the ceremony yet again. He was one of few who hardly ruffled at the faces of Arvad and

Lilianna, then again, he was an odd man who seemed unbothered by even the strangest fury.

Most still gaped at the king and queen like they might disappear should they blink.

Klok held up his hands. "One king and one queen abdicate the crown of Etta, and others rise." Klok came to me and Valen. We tipped our heads and allowed him to remove the narrow circlets we were asked to wear. Like Timorans, Ettans were keen on their symbolism in ceremony.

Klok carried the circlets to where Arvad and Lilianna kneeled on the dais. He placed them atop their heads. Klok invited them to rise as king and queen. Folk cheered as Arvad and Lilianna faced the crowd, grinning.

Until the king removed the circlet. "It was my honor to serve as your king."

What was happening?

Lilianna removed her circlet. "It was my honor to serve as your queen."

"We abdicate our crown." A collective gasp rippled through the crowd as Arvad stepped off the dais. "To our son and heir, Sol Ferus, the Sun Prince of Etta."

I watched with wide eyes as Sol smiled at his father and kneeled as Arvad placed the crown on his head.

Valen lifted a brow and glanced at me with a shrug. He seemed pleased. I was pleased. Sol was a skilled fighter, he'd saved us near Ruskig, and he kept a level head. Perhaps Arvad and Lilianna believed it was time.

Did it matter who ruled? She'd told me the land chose them all, once, so I supposed not.

Sol rose to another wave of cheers. Tor went to his side, the official prince consort. Folk were taken back, but they accepted him with their cries. With lifted hands, he silenced them. "It was an honor to serve as your king."

"Sol." Valen's hand tightened in mine.

The Sun Prince lifted the circlet off his head. "But it is for the benefit of Etta that the next in line take the throne. I abdicate to my sister and heir, Herja Ferus."

A groove formed between my brows as Herja lowered to one knee, allowing her brother to place the crown on her head. Valen's lips pinched together. He looked ahead, and I didn't understand his disquiet.

With a cautious wave of cheers, riddled in the same confusion I carried, the people accepted Herja as she rose off her knees.

She smiled, arms raised. "It has been an honor to serve as your queen."

"Dammit, Herja," Valen hissed before she could finish. "Stop."

Now I understood.

My heart raced deep in my chest as Herja faced her younger brother and lifted the circlet off her head.

"But," she said softly, "the true king and queen of Etta stand before us."

"No," Valen said. "I was not born for this."

I blinked through the stun to Lilianna who returned it with a smile. I had a strong inclination this scheme was planned without including the Night Prince or his wife.

Herja rested her hand on Valen's arm. "You were born for this, Brother. Proven on the battlefield, this land chose you and Elise." She faced the people again. "I abdicate to my brother and sister, my heirs, the Night Prince of Etta, and Lady Elise."

Klok handed her the second circlet.

Valen locked eyes with me. If I refused, he would step away. He would leave the throne to Gunnar, no mistake.

I pressed a kiss to his knuckles, smiling through my nerves. "What do you say, My King?"

His shoulders relaxed slightly. "I will be whatever you ask."

I gave him a gentle nod. Did I wish for the throne? Not particularly, but I could not deny the burn in my veins. As if some unseen thing whispered to my soul that this is where the path of fate led us. To this ultimate end.

We knelt and allowed Klok and Herja to rest the circlets, once again, atop our heads. A few gasps echoed over the courtyard when the ground shuddered. Valen shook his head, letting me know he'd not used fury.

When we rose off our knees, the people had lowered to theirs. Valen and I raised our linked hands to cheers.

The gardens burst with more life. As if I'd stepped into an impossible world, the kingdom of Etta welcomed its king and queen.

CHAPTER THIRTY-FIVE
NIGHT PRINCE

To rule in times of peace was vastly preferable to ruling in a hovel of a refuge in the center of a bloody war.

To have my family at my side was even more appreciated. In the first days as king and queen we dealt with naming our court and our advisors. Tor and Halvar were the clear choices for the positions they'd held in Ruskig. The Crown's top advisor and the First Knight.

But revered positions belonged to others. Those who'd stood with us from the beginning.

"Mattis Virke," Elise said at the edge of the dais in the great hall. "For your service to the crown of Etta, we invite you to serve as a counselor to the king and queen on the royal council."

Mattis bowed his head, hand over his heart.

She turned to Siv. "Siverie Tjänare, for your service to the crown of Etta, we invite you to serve as a counselor to the king and queen on the royal council."

Siv grinned and mimicked Mattis as she lowered to one knee, hand over her heart.

Stieg accepted a position beside Halvar as a strategist with our knights. Frey and Axel would be regents in the townships. They'd oversee the integration of Night Folk once again. Perhaps their most difficult task would be dealing with spoiled Timoran folk who had difficulties adjusting to the new way of things.

Sol smirked at me when he and Herja stood before the throne.

I grinned. "It must be bothersome to see me placed above you, Brother."

"Not at all. I will always be taller."

I laughed and went to them. "We need you both beside us. You will not let my head get too big, and you will always be loyal to Elise."

Sol accepted a role as the head of court politics and the inner workings of the kingdom, while Herja would be the sounding voice with Halvar over battle and our border defenses. Our parents watched it all with quiet guidance. They would be honored but wanted nothing more than to serve as voices of reason, or confidence. More than once my father assured me he had full faith I would not destroy the kingdom.

When it was Ari's turn, he looked much like he did when he wore the crown. Strong, unbending, with a touch of slyness.

"Ari Sekundär. For your service to the crown of Etta, for your leadership, I hope you will accept the position of our ambassador." I stepped closer to him, unblinking. "Ari, we need to reach out to neighboring kingdoms. There is still war against those with Fate's magic. We have seen it with our Alver friends, with the storyteller girl. But magic has power now, we can help change their fates, like we've changed ours."

Ari's jaw pulsed. "Where would you have me go first, My King?"

A smile curved over my mouth. "To the homeland of the fae. As we once spoke of, to the South. See how it is ruled, learn what troubles they have, and make us more allies. I've no doubt your endless need to talk will find a way to convince them to let you in."

He slammed his fist over his chest with a grin that suggested he would very much like to shove me as he had sometimes in Ruskig.

But everyone was watching.

"Consider it done, My King."

I gave him a nod and looked to the back where a table with ale and food was set. "Have it be known, our friendship and loyalty extends to the Alvers of the East. Your sacrifices here will not be forgotten."

Niklas jolted his head up from a plate of sweet breads, mouth full. He held up a drinking horn with muffled sound. The Nightrender kept to the corner, but he hadn't donned his dark hood since the battle ended, nor had his shadows returned. He did not speak to many people, but I would always be grateful to them. The Nightrender in particular had taken to Gunnar, he'd been working with my nephew on his magic, helping him tame the sick that came from too much use.

For that, we would all be grateful.

Next came those Ravens in our prisons. A captain was brought before us two weeks after taking the throne. He stood in ragged clothes, dirty, gaunt, and in chains.

Elise lifted her chin. The way the man winced. I suspected he knew her.

I sat in the high-backed throne and gestured for her to go on. These were once her people, she ought to have the final say.

"For serving the false king," she began, "tell your men they will not be put to death." A rumble of voices rippled through the hall, silenced when I held up a hand. Elise cleared her throat. "Not yet. As a queen of Etta with Timoran blood, it is my duty to see our kingdom united. But the pain and torture you inflicted upon my family cannot go unpunished or untried."

"What would that punishment be?"

"Address my wife properly," I said through a sneer. "Majesty, My Queen, Goddess—whatever you wish, but you will address her as she deserves, Raven."

I thought he might argue, might be snide. Hells, I almost hoped for it. A desire to slaughter them all lived deep inside. But Elise was right, we needed to heal the divide. Beginning with our enemies.

Instead, the captain lowered his gaze, and said, "What is the punishment, Your Majesty?"

"For one turn you and your men will endure what the Night Prince, what the Sun Prince, what the Ferus court endured at the hands of Timoran. You will be caged, sent to labor in the quarries. You will feel hunger, cold, pain. You will know what they suffered. But unlike Timoran, we will offer mercy. At the end of a turn, you will return before us where you will be welcomed into Etta, or if you are deemed disloyal, you will be executed."

He lifted a brow. "It will be hard to know who lies, Your Majesty."

"No. Not when we have friends who can taste them."

I lifted my eyes to Junius. She stood beside Elise, grinning a vicious sort. Niklas stared at his wife with lust and desire. He'd made it clear they'd return for the Raven trials the moment Elise asked.

The captain was led away, and Elise returned to her place by my side. I took hold of her hand, smiling. The court was arranged. Our new rule could begin.

Weeks after the battle, we stood at the shore of Ruskig. Walls were destroyed, and the open fjord expanded out to the ocean dividing us away from the distant kingdoms.

At the far edge of the water, the Falkyns loaded their ships with gifts from a king and queen, new weapons, new trade. They were self-proclaimed smugglers, and the look on Niklas's face when he saw the haul caused me to want to dig out more simply to see him grin with a bit of wickedness, as if schemes ran wild in his head.

I walked with Elise next to the edge of the water where the darkest of the ships bobbed in the gentle tide.

The Nightrender stood between us, staring at the Guild of Kryv as they prepared for the journey home.

I held out my hand. He hesitated for a moment before clasping my forearm.

"You're welcome here, Nightrender," I told him. "You have an ally with a crown should you ever need it."

"Good," he said. "You have a guild of thieves should you ever need it."

"Nightrender!" Gunnar shoved through the crowds of folk bidding the Alvers farewell. My nephew had a pack strung over one shoulder, a bow and quiver across the other. "I'm coming with you."

The Nightrender lifted a brow. "You should stay here. Your family is restored."

"It is not," Gunnar snapped. "Not until my daj is found. You know him. You pretend you do not hear me when I speak of him, but you know him. Help me find him. Please."

Herja caught up, Laila clutching her hand behind her. My sister's breaths were heavy, tears in her eyes. "He insists, Valen. Tell me I'm a terrible mother because . . . it feels as if this is needed. How can a mother send her son to face such a burden?"

"Maj," Gunnar answered instead. "It is needed. I can find him. My blood is from the East. My magic folk are there." He faced the Nightrender again. "You are feared there, Niklas told

335

me. Your name is whispered like a terror. You can help me find him."

"You don't know what you're asking, boy." The Nightrender's voice was a warning.

"I do. I've thought of nothing else. Take me with your guild. I'll be loyal to you."

"My guild is family for reasons you don't know."

"Lynx told me you all were once in captivity for your magic." Gunnar pointed to the thick, meaty Kryv ten paces away. Funny enough, the gargantuan man shrunk under the Nightrender's glare. "I was born in captivity. I am an Alver, you've taught me, helped me. I will do anything you ask, but help me once more until I find my father."

"You are practically a prince," said the Nightrender. "You would leave that life for a life underground with rats and Alvers who hunt Alvers?"

Gunnar swallowed with effort. "Yes. I was taught by my mother, and now my uncles, we do not stop fighting for our family."

A swell of pride filled my chest for the boy. Herja wiped at her eyes. Her reluctance was potent, but like her, I wondered if this was exactly what needed to be done to find Hagen Strom.

"We'll pay you," Elise said, breaking the silence. "You work for coin, so as his family, we will compensate you to find Hagen."

The Nightrender's eyes danced between us. He shook his head. "I won't take it, the coin. Not for Hagen." He stepped next to Gunnar, their chests nearly butting. "You're right. I know your father. I've known him since I could barely take a step. You want to know if he is a truly honorable man? Or did he put on a grand show when he was here?"

Herja's jaw tightened, but Gunnar scoffed. "I don't need to wonder. I know he is honorable."

The Nightrender narrowed his gaze for several breaths. With a heavy sigh he shook his head. "Hagen Strom protected me as a boy."

Herja covered her mouth. It was all I needed to know of my sister's lover to agree with Elise. Whatever it took, we would not stop until he was found again.

"He was like a wise, older brother. One who looked out for us stupid littles who knew nothing of the risks facing unique Alvers like me and . . ." He didn't finish the thought, simply shook his head and altered course. "My mesmer is valued, hunted. Hagen made sure no one knew I had a drop until . . . fate had different plans."

Oh, the secrets this man kept. He gave up little, and I had few doubts he did it to protect himself . . . or others.

"Did he ever speak of us?" Herja asked.

The Nightrender rubbed the side of his face. "I never heard of his family, but it would be dangerous to bring attention to any of you. The east exploits folk with power such as you, princess. No doubt, though, the game he was forced to play was due to his unauthorized protection of Alvers like me. What I'm telling you is I do not need to find House Strom. I know exactly where they are. If Hagen is not there, then he finally crossed too many lines against those in power. Are you willing to risk an outcome you don't want?"

Gunnar's fists clenched at his sides. "I'm willing to risk anything for him. He risked everything for us."

"You will be a Kryv. You do not go against us, or I swear to you, I will kill you with your deepest fears."

"If I betrayed you, I would welcome death, Nightrender," Gunnar said.

Silence hung between us for endless moments. At long last,

the Nightrender faced me. "He is your nephew, King. Does he sail with us?"

I chuckled. "I am king, but I am not brave enough to command or forbid my sister's child anything. Have you seen how she handles a knife?"

The Nightrender smiled. A real, true smile. It was almost unnerving. He glanced at Herja. "Well, does he go with us?"

Herja clutched Gunnar's hand.

"Please, Maj," he whispered. "I can do this."

My sister rested a hand against the side of his face before looking back to the Nightrender. "You will care for him? Keep him safe?"

"I will teach him to be an Alver. You have my word on that. But he will also learn to be a thief, a criminal, and likely a killer. Only if you wish him to survive, that is."

Herja winced but took Gunnar's hand. "If this is where you feel fate is leading you, I will not stand in your way. But I will tear the world apart if you find yourself in trouble."

He chuckled and hugged her tightly. "I will do the same if Uncle Valen and Elise ruin this place over the next months, and you find yourself trapped again."

I shoved the boy, laughing, then wrapped him in my arms. Elise went next, begging him to teach the Nightrender to smile more than once a month.

I had hope they'd find Hagen. We'd conquered the impossible here. They would conquer another impossible task. Still, I could not help but wonder if my nephew had placed himself in a coming storm perhaps the Nightrender did not even realize was building.

I wanted to press, wanted to know why Calista believed a battle would begin for this man once ours ended. What did he know that we didn't?

When Herja and Laila left us to walk Gunnar to the Kryv's ship, the Nightrender turned back to me and Elise. "Since I will play nursemaid to your nephew, and you already know it anyway, I suppose you both may call me Kase."

Elise's mouth parted, then she narrowed her gaze at me. "He told you his given name? When?"

"Blame Niklas, Queen." Kase glanced over to the Falkyns. "He has a remarkably big mouth."

She huffed. "Was that so hard?"

His smile faded. "My name should not be known. Especially not in the east."

"Why?"

Kase stared at the distant glow of sunlight over setting behind the cliffs. "You told me when I first came here that I didn't understand what it is to love another as you love your king. I do. I know what it means to care for another in such a way. I loved enough to let it go."

Elise's brow furrowed. "You are not able to be with your lover?"

"No. Truth told, we were never even lovers." Kase smirked. "She does not even know I'm alive."

"You ought to tell her." Elise took my hand. "Life can end quickly, Kase. Better to live it beside those we love."

He stared back to the horizon. "If we go searching for Hagen Strom, no doubt she will cross my path again. Unfortunately for her." He took a few steps toward the water, a signal that the conversation was over. "It has been educational, and lucrative, fighting with you."

He took a step toward the shore, but paused, a wicked smirk on his lips. "Queen, don't you find it interesting how much choice played a part in you taking the throne? You chose him." He gestured at me. "The land chose you. Choice—a gift all people should have, wouldn't you say?"

Elise's lips parted, but she had no time to speak before his eyes returned to the glossy black and the Nightrender topped his head with his hood. "Enjoy your crown. Until we meet again."

"What was that about?" I asked when he'd boarded his longship.

Elise shook her head. "I think I need to tell you a tale of four queens. Hells, that man is not what I expected."

I laughed and curled an arm around her shoulders. "A man with secrets. I have a feeling if his fight is coming, he will need to learn how to release some of those secrets."

"Yes. Look what lies and deception brought you."

I pressed a kiss to her forehead. "A perfect wife and a throne?"

She pinched my waist. "War is what I was going for, but yes, when you put it that way, the lies of Legion Grey changed my life."

"I'd never take them back."

We waved until the Alver ships were distant spots on the sea. Night came quickly, but Elise and I remained at the shore. I held her close. Kissed her lips. To think back on the moments when I planned to seduce and deceive the Timoran *Kvinna*, only to discover she stole my heart at nearly her first word brought a smile to my lips.

I would die for her, no mistake.

But I planned to live for her now. Every day, every breath, I would not forget for whom my heart beat.

She rested her head on my shoulder. We stayed at the shore until the moon rose high, breathing in the clean air. No smoke. No blood.

Nothing but light faced us at dawn.

EPILOGUE
THE NIGHTRENDER

Sea mist cooled the heat of my face as the currents shifted to the rough tides of the eastern sea. The rocky shorelines of Klockglas, my home—if one could call it a home—darkened the mists in the distance.

Several clock tolls ago, Niklas and his guild had left us to sail toward their region of Skítkast, and I had half a mind to turn about and follow them.

Nothing but trouble, likely a fair bit of pain, awaited us in Klockglas.

At my back, my guild switched positions at the oars. Two days into the journey and Gunnar was finding his place. Lynx stuck close to him, introducing him to the others. The truth? The boy was impressive. He'd fought in a battle, slaughtered many, but he was too gentle. To be a Kryv, to survive in the eastern regions, he'd need to sharpen a few edges.

More so since his journey was leading him—us—to House Strom.

What the hells was I doing? Why was I doing it? I gave up the past long ago to be like Hagen. To keep her free.

All these turns later, and I could not escape the name Strom.

I propped one foot on a lip of the stempost and leaned over my bent knee. From inside my tunic, I pulled out the thin twine and rubbed the wooden rose charm between my fingers. I closed my eyes, and unbidden wretched thoughts filled my head.

A time when littles laughed, a time of first loves.

I hated them. Every memory was a weakness, a threat to my guild, and now I was leading them straight into the fire.

"Kase." Raum came to my side, his silver eyes always smiling. "There is a unit of skydguard on the west shores. We ought to take the south channels."

I nodded. Raum was a good Alver to have close with those eyes. After battling the North's Raven guards, I had little desire to meet our skydguard. They were sods who loved to spill blood for the fun of it.

"Are you going to tell us what troubles you?" Tova slipped around Raum, stretching her arms, and splitting a seed roll in two. She glanced at the wooden rose but didn't ask. She never did.

"No trouble," I said.

Raum accepted half Tova's roll. "It is the princeling's father, isn't it?"

"Don't call him princeling. He is Kryv now and shouldn't be thought of as anything else. Not on our shores. He'd be plucked like a blade of grass should the Lord Magnate learn of him."

"True." Raum flicked his hands for no reason, then again, he rarely stopped moving. "Why does this Hagen Strom distress you?"

"I'm not distressed."

"Bleeding hells." Tova rolled her eyes and pointed at the rose. "It is in your hands, and I've known you long enough to know when you are bothered the bleeding rose is rubbed until your thumbs blister."

I hated them and loved them in the same breath.

"If Gunnar is right and Hagen has brought attention to himself . . . it will not only be his life put on the line." I frowned. These were pieces I'd always vowed to keep silent and hidden in my own past. "There could be another—an Alver—put at great risk of the Lord Magnate and the masquerade."

At the mention of the Masque av Aska, Tova shuddered. We didn't mention the festival, didn't even think of it. Until now. No doubt we'd have no choice.

Raum stared out at the black tides. "What then? Do we not look for the father?"

"No." I tucked the rose back under my tunic. "Hagen is a good man. But he has a connection, and exploiting it, hells, even drawing attention to it could begin a fight more dangerous than a missing Alver."

Raum and Tova shared a look.

Tova popped the last of her roll into her mouth and shrugged. "We would not be the Kryv if we did not revel in tricky schemes. We just fought a bleeding war for a different kingdom and won a crown. Why stop there?"

Raum snorted a laugh but nodded. "We plan, we draw some blood, we live to see another day. This will be no different."

They had no idea how different it could be. How those who'd kept power would fight to the deadly end if they discovered what the Guild of Kryv was about to expose.

"Tell us where we start, Kase," Raum pressed.

I hesitated and looked out to the soft waves.

The prophecy about my fate from the north unnerved me. The truth I'd learned of how Elise had chosen her king despite lies and blood unnerved me. In the north, everything was about choice. It fit too well, too close to old, dangerous tales for comfort.

Now, a secret I'd fought to keep all this time was unraveling bit by bit.

In truth, I'd always had the power to begin battles. But I vowed never to expose it. For her sake.

Hells, I despised the fates. They'd never been kind and it felt a great deal like I was walking into their bleeding trap whether I wanted to or not.

"Kase," Raum said. "What is the first step?"

"I need information."

"Who is the mark?"

My past was about to become my present. "An Alver. A woman who steals memories."

Tova lifted a brow, almost surprised at the Talent. Hard to do being that we'd all known our share of unique Alvers. "Do you have a name?"

Like a fire to my bones, I knew if I opened this never-healing wound, she would be caught in the bloody maelstrom of our life and our survival. I'd be wise to keep quiet.

But I was clever. I never pretended to be wise.

"Malin Strom." I pressed a hand over the hidden rose on instinct. "Her name is Malin Strom."

SNEAK PEEK
THE NIGHTRENDER

Enjoy a sneak peek at NIGHT OF MASKS AND KNIVES

The Guild of Kryv wasn't large, but despite our few numbers, we knew how to kill with gory magnificence. Each Kryv wore blades sharper than anything, and at the front gate little Hanna and her brother, Ash, pounded rawhide drums painted in the oak tree of the gods. Both were dressed in black with rough lines of battle green and dark kohl streaked over their eyes.

Ash lifted his moonlight pale face, finding me as I stepped into the gardens.

"Terrify them!" he shouted.

I responded with a fist pound to my heart. Ash wanted to join the fight, but at only thirteen it was better to keep him back. The only way to convince the boy was to assign him the task of keeping his young sister safe.

Ash would pick Hanna every time.

Shrieks and cries of the dying guards faded beneath the hypnotic beat and delight of Kryv movements.

Raum and Tova were lost to me, caught in the mess of swords carving bodies, likely leading *her* through the fight.

I didn't need to search her out, didn't need to oversee her removal. The Kryv were capable and would be better suited. I had already succumbed to distraction once. There would be no room for more.

I lost count of how many guards bloodied the grass before the air changed. Colder, a little harsher. From the gates to the gardens, darkness spread. Heady, tangible.

On my tongue the bittersweet tang of magic burrowed deep. Each breath drew in the chill of shadows.

There was nothing kind or beautiful about the mesmer of fear. It preyed upon folks' weakest moments. In those moments when the heart stilled, when adrenaline flooded the blood, I took those fears and twisted them.

Enough terror lived on Strom lands tonight to feed my power until dawn.

I envisioned the skydguard in my mind, then directed the shadows to coil around them. Fear of death would give me the power to break bodies, but one slip, and I could strike the wrong side.

That was the trouble with fear. It was everywhere.

In the Kryv, the servants, the guards. Wading through whose was whose took more energy than the use of mesmer.

An ache bloomed up the back of my skull by the time I'd homed the shadows only around the skydguard.

In the next heartbeat, guards seized their own throats with a sort of pathetic desperation as I draped my cruel magic around them. To the naked eye there was nothing around their necks, nothing strangled them, only the night and blood. Inside, fear gripped them, and I transformed it into a weapon.

"By the gods." A voice drew my focus to the edge of the gardens.

By one of the stone walls running the edge of the garden, she gaped at me, hand over her mouth. That fiery hair was damp across her forehead, those sharp, green-sea eyes wide and terrified.

Your hair looks like the sunset, Mallie.
Yours looks like dirt. But the good kind of dirt.
What the hells is the good kind of dirt?
You'd know it if you saw it, Kase. But there is. There just is.

Dammit. I blinked through the memory. A prompt reminder this entire scheme was a wretchedly foolish idea.

From where she stood, a potent mix of fear and intrigue confused my focus, enough some of the gasping skydguard slumped in relief as my mesmer retreated.

She hugged her middle and turned away from me as if my darkness might devour her. It would, should she get too close. I wouldn't let it happen. For her sake or mine, I didn't know, but this conflict of wanting her and resisting her grew tiresome.

I lowered my head, ensuring my hood hid my features. With a raised hand, once more skydguard gasped and clawed at their faces.

I made a tight fist.

The snapping of necks was grisly.

Malin leaned over and retched when a guard five paces from her went still, his body twisted and broken. The darkness recoiled, like serpents in the grass, and left a thin trail of blood spilling from the corner of the dead guard's mouth.

Tova hooked a hand under her arm. "Are you injured?"

"No." Malin's breaths came in sharp, little gasps, eyes on me in horror. "The Nightrender."

Blood pounded in my head. She feared me, and I should want it. But I could not deny there was a dull pain at the thought.

The doors of the longhouse clanged against the sides as Jens Strom rushed out, haggard, half-dressed. The way his eyes took in the bloody scene, the darkness, the Kryv, clearly, he'd been kept from intervening, only to break free to his land upended.

"Lynx." The largest member of the guild hurried to my side. "Handle the woman. We're leaving."

Lynx wasn't one to talk a great deal. Truth be told, beneath all his meat was a man who spent a great deal of time lost in books and thoughts of the stars and how they formed, how the world turned, how the seas shifted currents.

He was a puzzler, a poetic. But brutal in the same breath.

"Stop!" Jens shouted.

Malin whipped her head toward the sound of his voice, but Lynx was already on her.

One of his thick palms coated her entire face. In two breaths she went limp in his arms. His ability to calm the body to the point of sleep was useful, and if I had to guess, could be used for sinister things with enough strength.

With a simple whistle, Ash and Hanna's drums played a new tune, signaling our time here was over.

With the last of my energy, I pulled shadows from the branches of the trees, the corners of the gardens, the forest, tightening them around every Kryv until they were concealed.

"No!" Jens shouted again as Lynx faded into the blackness with his stepdaughter. I was the last to leave, always remaining behind to see the Guild of Kryv safely removed from any fight. Jens had a wild look in his eyes when they locked on mine. I doubted he could see much of me, but he knew who looked back at him. His shoulders curved forward in a bit of defeat. "Bring her back and I will hide her away."

"You had your chance and failed."

"Why do you do this?"

A wicked grin spread over my lips. "Because I always keep my promises."

House Strom was blanketed in night. Not even a single flicker of a candle flame could be seen as I disappeared with my guild. The past at my back and . . . at my front.

KEEP READING

Scan the QR code and continue with NIGHT OF MASKS AND KNIVES

(Elise and Valen will be regular faces in

the remaining books of the series)

Not ready to say goodbye to Elise and Valen? Scan the QR to get a bonus scene with a peek into their happily ever after.

ACKNOWLEDGMENTS

Thank you to all those who have stood by as I've written this world. Clara Stone at Authortree, thank you for your epic design and formatting skills. Along with Merry Book Round for your beautiful covers. I'm so grateful to Jennifer Murgia for your help with smoothing out the edges, I feel like you've been in this world as long as I have. Thank you to Eric for your skill with the new maps and chapter art!

    I'm so grateful to my family for your patience as I devoured caffeine somedays to stay awake after typing away late into the night and early morning. My kids, you are everything and the inspiration for a better world I hope we can create. I love you. Thank you to Derek for brainstorming this fantasy world with me for at least a billion hours. You inspired so much. I love you.

    Thank you to all my beautiful readers for devouring this story and this series. I look forward to bringing more sexy heroes and fierce heroines to life together in the future!

    May we all be the good,

    LJ

Milton Keynes UK
Ingram Content Group UK Ltd.
UKHW031312160924
1675UKWH00041B/210/J